PRAISE FOR FOZ M

"An Accident of Stars' *interwoven, beautifully* ... are filled with rich details, complex family bonds of all kinds, and deeply layered politics. To enter Kena and the surrounding lands is to be irrevocably and powerfully changed. Foz Meadows has created an epic adventure unlike any I've read before."
Fran Wilde, Nebula- and Norton-nominated author of *Updraft and Cloudbound*

"*A portal fantasy for grownups, with grit and realism, and characters I loved from the first page.*"
Trudi Canavan, author of the *Black Magician* trilogy

"*Reminiscent of Ursula K LeGuin,* An Accident of Stars *will take you to a lush, magical new world.*"
Laura Lam

"*I very much enjoyed this. The main character falls out of our world into a life-changing adventure, with compelling characters and a fascinating world. I can't wait to read the next book.*"
Martha Wells, author of the *Books of Raksura*

"*Richly imaginative world building with delightfully complex and diverse characters; a joy to read!*"
Ann Lemay, video game writer

"An Accident of Stars *is anchored in dozens of complex women, driven by the rooted, deep relationships they have with each other. It's a wonderful, rich, feminist book, and I loved it.*"
B R Sanders, author of *Ariah*

Foz Meadows

AN ACCIDENT OF STARS

BOOK 1 OF THE MANIFOLD WORLDS

ANGRY
ROBOT

ANGRY ROBOT
An imprint of Watkins Media Ltd

Unit 11, Shepperton House
89 Shepperton Road
London N1 3DF
UK

angryrobotbooks.com
twitter.com/angryrobotbooks
Out of these worlds

An Angry Robot paperback original, 2016

Cover by Kieryn Tyler
Maps by Stephanie McAlea
Set in Meridien

ISBN 978 0 85766 995 7
Ebook ISBN 978 0 85766 586 7

Printed and bound in the United Kingdom by TJ Books Ltd.

9 8 7 6 5 4 3 2 1

FSC
www.fsc.org

MIX
Paper from
responsible sources
FSC® C013056

For Alis and Kit,
in thanks for the strength
their stories bring;
and for Smott of Swords,
the original worldwalker.

PART 1
The Universe Next Door

1
Look & Leap

Sarcasm is armour, Saffron thought, and imagined she was donning a suit of it, plate by gleaming, snark-laden plate. "Nice undies," leered Jared Blake, lifting her skirt with a ruler. No, not a ruler – it was a metal file, one of the heavy ones they were meant to be using on their metalworking projects. He grinned at her, unrepentant, and poked the file upwards. The cold iron rasped against her thigh. "Are you shaved?"

"Fuck off, Jared," Saffron shot back. "I'd rather have sex with an octopus."

He *ooh*ed at her, a ridiculous noise meant to ridicule. Giving her hem a final upwards flick, he retracted the file and pulled a face for the benefit of his laughing friends, then loudly yelled to the teacher, "Sir! Mr Yarris! Saffron said *fuck*, sir!"

Mr Yarris turned with the lumbering, angry slowness of a provoked bear. He was a big man, block-solid and bald – a stereotypical metalwork teacher, except for the fact that he mostly taught art, and was only filling in for Mrs Kirkland. He pointed a fat, calloused finger at Jared, then jerked his thumb at the doorway. "Out."

Jared mimed comic disbelief as his friends kept laughing. "But sir! I didn't do *anything*, sir! It was Saffron!"

Mr Yarris didn't take the bait. "Out," he said again, folding his arms.

Jared dramatically flung down the file. "This is bullshit!" he said. "I didn't–"

"OUT!" roared Mr Yarris, loud enough that even Jared flinched, but the effect was spoiled when, seconds later, the bell rang for lunch. As Jared leapt from his stool, Saffron pointedly kicked her bag into his path. His sneakers tangled in the straps, and down he went with a crash.

"Oops," said Saffron – loud and flat, so the whole class knew that she'd done it on purpose. "My mistake." And before Mr Yarris could parse what had happened, she reached down, yanked the bag back from Jared and stormed out of class.

She was furious, shaking all over as she sped away from the metalwork rooms. *How dare he. How* dare *he!* And yet he *did* dare, publicly and often, to whichever girl was nearest. Nobody stopped it; nobody even came close. He'd been suspended last year for groping a Year Seven girl in the canteen lines, but once he returned, he was just as bad as ever, snapping bras, making sick comments and bullying Maddie Shen so badly – he stole her bag, opened her sanitary pads and stuck them over her books and folders, all while calling her names – that Saffron had later found her having a panic attack in the bathroom. He was awful, and got up to even worse at parties, but as appalling as Jared's behaviour was, Lawson High apparently considered unrelenting sexual harassment to be insufficient grounds for expulsion. "Boys will be boys," the deputy head had said, the one time Saffron had screwed up the nerve to approach him about it. "Or should I expel them all, just to be on the safe side?" And then he'd *laughed*, like the fact that the problem was so widespread was *funny*.

Saffron came to a halt. She was outside the music rooms, and the air was filled with the yells and shrieks and laughter and profanity of lunchtime. She leaned her head on the rough red bricks and fought back tears. *I can't keep doing this anymore. I can't.*

But she had to. What other choice was there?

* * *

As Gwen saw it, the first rule of interacting with teenagers was simple: *show no fear.* Given its general applicability, it was also her personal motto, and one that had served her well in the decades since she'd first stumbled into the multiverse and out of what she'd grown up thinking was normal. Human adolescents, she reminded herself, were not more terrifying than magical politics and walking between worlds. *You can do this. You have to.*

She took a deep breath, and stepped into Lawson High.

In Kena, where magic was ubiquitous, you could open a portal damn near anywhere. On Earth, however, things were somewhat trickier. The way Trishka explained it – which was, in fairness to Gwen's comprehension, vaguely – some places were simply less accessible than others, resisting the touch of the *jahudemet,* the portal magic, like a knot that won't pull loose. But even once you found a receptive location, you could only use it so many times in succession: the more you ripped a particular patch of reality's fabric in any world, the higher the risk it would start to unravel, and Gwen had no desire to cause an international incident. With her previous portal point thus ruled out, Trishka had gone in search of a suitable substitute, and come up with a patch of bush alongside the local high school. If they'd had more time, Gwen would have protested – the last thing she wanted to risk was an accidental audience – but they didn't, and she hadn't, and now she was here, striding across the playground at what was evidently lunchtime and trying not to look as conspicuous as she felt.

She had a cover story, of course: if anyone asked, she was looking the campus over before applying for a job in the understaffed English faculty. The fact that Gwen had, once upon a time, actually qualified as a teacher meant she could probably bluff her way through an adult conversation should the need arise; the greater risk, as ever, was the curiosity of children. As a flock of shrieking tweens dashed haphazardly past, Gwen suppressed a smile and fought the urge to light up a cigarette, which was bound to attract the wrong sort of attention. *Just get across campus, find the place, and wait,* she told herself.

And then she saw the girl.

She was white, about sixteen. Long-boned and lanky, though her hunched shoulders said she was self-conscious about it. (Gwen, who was tall and had grown up hating it, could sympathise.) Her eyes were green, made prominent by the near-black circles beneath them, while her blonde hair – a natural shade, Gwen judged – hung messily to her shoulders. She was standing by a wall with a bag at her feet, her expression so nakedly lost, it was clear she didn't know she had an audience. Gwen twisted a little to see it, but if not for what happened next, she might still have kept walking.

A rangy white boy came storming up from around the corner, yelling at the girl. He was all raw angles and sharp bones, like he was trying to grow into his body faster than it would let him, and the hooked smile on his face had no friendliness in it.

"What the fuck is your problem?" he shouted, pushing her. "You stupid bitch–"

"Get *off* me!" the girl snarled, shoving him away – or trying to, at least; the boy hung onto her arm with hard, thin fingers, and before she could stop herself, Gwen closed the distance between them. Smiling furiously, she grabbed the boy's wrist, pinching just so to make him give up his grip on the girl, and twisted his arm up behind his back. He yelped, first in shock and then in pain, swearing as he struggled.

"What the *fuck*, lady?"

Gwen tightened her grip. "Say uncle," she said, and looked straight at the girl, who was staring at her with a mixture of hope and hunger, as if the world had just completely rearranged itself.

Flailing, the boy tried to pull free. Gwen responded by tugging his arm up higher, harder. "Say uncle, boy."

"Uncle! Uncle! Fuck!" Gwen counted to three, then shoved him roughly away. He staggered, turned and stared at her, incredulous in his anger. "The fuck is wrong with you?"

And before she could answer, he darted away like a rat from a trap, leaving Gwen alone with the unknown girl, who licked her lips and said softly, "Thanks."

"Does he bother you often?"

The girl snorted. "He bothers everything in a skirt. Are you new here, miss? I haven't seen you before."

"I'm maybe applying for a job," Gwen said. "Though I doubt I'll get it."

"I hope you do." The girl's jaw ticked. "No one else ever stops him."

Anger washed through Gwen. She'd already stayed too long, made too much of an impression, but she couldn't bring herself to leave just yet. "Well, they should," she said, and winced at the inadequacy of the words. "What's your name, girl?"

"Saffron," she said, clearly surprised by the question. "Saffron Coulter."

"Well, Saffron Coulter, let me give you some unsolicited advice," said Gwen, because having already come this far, she might as well go that little bit further – then faltered at the realisation that there wasn't much she *could* say. She didn't know what else was going on in Saffron's life, and the boy's harassment of her wasn't going to stop just because Gwen had literally twisted his arm. What could she possibly say that might make a difference?

"Yeah?" said Saffron, expectantly. "What?"

Gwen sighed. "Life is hard. Some days we get our asses kicked, but apathy breeds more evils than defeat. So, you know. Keep fighting."

It was, Gwen thought, a shitty speech – Pix would

probably laugh until she cried – but the girl, Saffron, lit up as though she'd never heard anything better.

"Thank you," she said again – quieter than before, but also stronger. For the first time, she stood at her full height. "I'll try."

"Good," said Gwen, and with a parting clap to Saffron's shoulder, she strode away in search of a magic door.

Apathy breeds more evils than defeat. Keep fighting.

Saffron couldn't get the words, or the encounter, out of her head. Which made no sense; it wasn't as if she'd never had to deal with Jared grabbing her before – not like she'd even needed the help to get rid of him, however satisfying its delivery had been. And it wasn't like she didn't know the world was a messed-up place, either – you only had to look at the news to see that much. But she'd never had an adult acknowledge the fact to her face, let alone so bluntly, and especially not when it came to the predations of Jared Blake. Whoever the teacher was, she'd done more to make Saffron feel capable, safe and validated in the space of one conversation than either her parents or her teachers had since the start of term, and all at once, she didn't know whether she wanted to laugh or cry.

When the bell rang for the end of lunch, she felt like she'd been jolted out of a stupor; she hadn't touched her food. Suddenly, the prospect of going straight to class was intolerable. Shouldering her bag, Saffron cut across campus and headed straight for the second floor entrance to the library, which was built on a slope against the old English block. Once inside, she hid behind the new arrivals shelf until she was sure that none of the librarians were watching, then moved quietly over to the emergency door. It was meant to be alarmed, but as she'd learned after accidentally falling against it a few months back, it wasn't. For obvious reasons, it wasn't locked either – not during the day, anyway – and Saffron slipped through with unobtrusive ease.

On the other side was a small, square landing stuck between two flights of stairs: one going down to the ground level exit, and one that led up to the roof. Saffron took the latter option, leaping up two steps at a time. The roof door was unlocked by virtue of being broken: the lock and handle had both been hacked clean out of the wood, and now it only stayed shut because the cleaning staff kept a heavy chock wedged under the frame. Saffron opened the door, used the wedge to pin it up against the wall so it didn't bang in the breeze, and headed out into the sunlight.

The accessible section of roof was hemispherical, bordered by a brick wall just high enough to hide her from casual scrutiny. To one side was a fat, square vent, and on the other, protected by a broad awning, was a locked metal cupboard at whose mysterious contents Saffron could only guess. Beside it were two plastic chairs, set facing each other under the overhang, and as had become her custom, she sat down in one and propped her feet on the other, head tipped back against the sunwarmed metal.

The first time she'd skipped class to come to the roof, she'd been equal parts angry and terrified – angry, because the deputy head had just given her the *boys will be boys* speech, and she could no more have sat through Maths after that than flown to the moon, and terrified, because up until that moment, she'd never cut class in her life. She'd been shaking, so certain that someone was going to shout out or stop her that when she made it up without incident, she spent a full five minutes staring at the open door, convinced that someone was following. But nobody came, and when she showed up to her next lesson, it was like she'd never been gone: friends or faculty, if anyone had missed her, they didn't mention it. It was like a revelation, as though she'd spent years preemptively flinching from someone who, it turned out, either couldn't or wouldn't hit her.

Since then, she'd grown incrementally bolder, coming up

more frequently and for longer. She had a half dozen excuses worked out to explain her absence from class in the event that anyone ever asked where she'd been, but so far, she hadn't had to use any of them. Now, she shut her eyes and exhaled deeply, savouring the luxury of privacy and silence as, over and over again, she replayed what had happened.

Apathy breeds more evils than defeat. Keep fighting.

Saffron stayed on the roof for two full periods, only going to her last class of the day for the sake of appearances. As she walked, she found herself surreptitiously glancing around in hopes of spying her rescuer again. She wasn't exactly inconspicuous: where Lawson High's teaching staff was almost uniformly white, the unknown woman was not. Her brown skin was warm and weathered, and when she spoke her rich, smoke-gravel voice was coloured by a faint English accent, marking her as doubly incongruous to Saffron's suburban Australian sensibilities. She'd been tall, too, almost six feet, with kinky, iron-grey hair cut to jaw-length, and when she'd held Jared still, the muscles in her arms had stood out like cords. Such a woman, were she still on campus, should have attracted attention. But though Saffron looked, she didn't see her, and though she listened to her classmates talk, she didn't overhear anything that pointed to her presence.

The portal point turned out to be a nature strip. Technically, it was part of the school grounds, but happily for Gwen, it was right at the outskirts, and – better still – deserted. True, there were some classrooms nearby, but most of their windows were on the other side of the building, leaving the strip in a convenient blind spot.

Now all she had to do was wait.

Gwen hated waiting.

Irritable with unspent energy, she sat down on a tree stump and tried to remind herself why it was she'd left Kena in the first place. With Tevet dead and the rebellion with her, Gwen and her allies had lost their best shot at removing Leoden from power. They'd needed to lie low, regroup, and after a solid year away from Earth, Gwen had taken the opportunity to accomplish both tasks while proving to her parents, who'd retired to Australia years ago, that she was, in fact, still alive. Such reunions were always bittersweet, complex; none of her relatives or remaining friends had any idea how she lived her life, which made the act of lying to them more chore than holiday. And yet she was glad to have visited, if only because it left her that much happier to return to her (dangerous, wonderful) reality. She'd kept in contact with Trishka through the dreamscape, however patchily – and now, at last, she was going back to help fix the mess she'd made. Those were the facts, but just at that moment, they didn't stop her from feeling as if she'd slunk off with her tail between her legs.

Guilt, after all, was the rightful province of people who'd had a hand in ruining whole countries, whether they'd meant it or not. Rationality didn't enter into it. Her lips quirked in private irony: her son, were he privy to her thoughts, would doubtless see things differently. But then Louis had chosen a life stranger even than Gwen's, and though she loved him dearly, she didn't always understand him. Which was doubtless true of most parents, for all that she'd raised him in somewhat exceptional circumstances, even by the standards of the Many – or had she? Certainly Louis himself had seen nothing unusual in it, and if he harboured any resentment on that point, he'd never brought it up. Not for the first time, Gwen wondered if children, even when grown, weren't inherently more complex than the multiverse, and decided, now as always, that some questions were better left unanswered.

Like water flowing downstream, her thoughts turned from Louis towards the white girl – Saffron – and that parting look of gratitude on her face. Helping her in the moment had been easy, but as with so much else, Gwen hadn't really changed anything. That awful boy would likely continue to bother her, and the school's apparent indifference to the problem would persist.

I was still right to help.

It was a small comfort, but against the looming weight of Leoden's coup and Kena's complexities, Gwen would take what victories she could find.

Sighing, Saffron put her head on her desk and stared sideways at the clock. Her last class of the day was Personal Development, Health and Physical Education, also known as PDHPE, also known as a complete and utter waste of time, partly because she'd be dropping it next year, but mostly because the kind of sex education deemed suitable for state school students was vastly less accurate, detailed or relevant than anything she could find on one of a half-dozen sex positive YouTube channels run by people who, unlike Mr Marinakis, could say *penis* without twitching.

I need to find her, Saffron thought. *I need to say* – well, not *thank you,* because she'd already said that, but... something. She wanted to explain herself, or ask the woman's advice, or maybe just spend five minutes in the company of an adult who might actually take her seriously. It was irrational and pointless and she couldn't stop thinking about it, and when the last bell finally rang, she ended up walking towards the bus lines in a virtual fugue state.

"Saff! Hey, wait up!"

Saffron stopped and turned, smiling as her little sister, Ruby, came running over.

"Didn't you hear me?" Ruby asked, glaring. "I had to call you, like, five times!"

"Well, I'm hearing you now. What's up?"

They started walking together, Ruby launching straight

into a lengthy description of her day. But as much as Saffron usually enjoyed her sister's acid observations about high school life, she couldn't quite focus; she was only half-listening, still scanning the school for the mystery teacher.

"...so I told her, look, this isn't a Monty Python sketch, there aren't any strange women lurking in the nature strip, and she said–"

"What?" said Saffron, suddenly jerking back to the moment. She stopped, a hand on Ruby's arm. "What about strange women?"

Ruby rolled her eyes. "God, you really don't listen, do you? I literally *just said*, Cora was *convinced* there was some random lady hanging out in the nature strip behind the chem labs all afternoon, and I just... Hey! Where are you going?"

"Forgot something!" Saffron said, already moving off. Remembering that she'd left her phone charging in her bedroom, she turned and added, "Tell mum and dad I'll be home later, OK?"

"Tell them yourself!" Ruby called, but Saffron didn't answer.

Heart pounding, she made her way across campus, trying and failing to explain to herself why on Earth this felt so important – or why, more to the point, she felt so damn certain that the woman Cora claimed to have seen was her mystery teacher. *What the hell are you hoping to accomplish here?* she asked herself. *School's over, dumbass – even if she was there earlier, she'll be long gone by now.* And yet she kept walking, ignoring the awkward tug in her chest that said she should just go back to the bus lines. She passed the science block, turned the corner, and stopped.

There, standing in the middle of the nature strip, was the mystery teacher. She was side-on to Saffron, but unaware of her presence, head cocked as though listening for something. Saffron licked her lips and stepped closer, too concerned with trying to think of what to say to question why the woman was there at all.

And then it happened.

Scarcely three metres from where the teacher stood, a crack appeared in the world: a gaping, pink-tinged tear in reality's flank, scything through the naked air like some sort of impossible *portal*. It almost hurt to look at, and as Saffron gulped and thought, *It's real, I'm seeing this and it's really real*, her whole body went weak with shock, the way it had done last year when a clumsy driver knocked her off her bike. Her blood was alive with panic, fear, excitement – what should she do? What should *they* do? And only then did she see that the teacher was smiling, striding towards the gap as though its presence was the most natural thing on Earth.

In the split second before the teacher crossed the portal's threshold, Saffron made a decision. All she could think of was that she'd wanted to talk to her, and now she was escaping, moving through a hole in the world that had no business existing *anywhere*, let alone in a nature strip behind the chem labs. And so, in her shock, she did what she had to.

Saffron ran forwards and followed her through the gap.

2

Down, Through, Over

Black light blinded her. A frightened cry died in Saffron's throat, and then she was stumbling, falling into a small, square room. The walls were made of pale stone, the only light coming from cracks in a wooden door. The transition was so sudden as to be unreal, but when she turned, the rip – the portal, whatever it was – had vanished. All she saw was another stone wall and the mystery teacher, staring at her in shock.

"Oh, no. No, no, *no–*"

"I followed you," said Saffron, stunned. "I wanted to talk, and then I just–"

"You *just*? You senseless, impulsive…" She broke off, visibly willing herself to calm, and into the silence, Saffron asked, "Where are we?"

"Somewhere you shouldn't be," came the snapped response. "Down the rabbit hole. Through the wardrobe. Over the bloody rainbow."

"You're not a teacher," Saffron said. The realisation left her fighting inappropriate laughter. "Who the hell are you, anyway?"

The woman sighed. "My name's Gwen Vere."

"Guinevere? Like the queen?"

"Like my father fancied himself a comedian. Gwen-space-

Vere. First name and last." She said it with the tired cadence of someone used to explaining their name to strangers. "Just call me Gwen."

"All right. Are we, um...?" She nodded her head at the door. "Are we going outside?"

"Eventually, yes. Not yet."

"OK," said Saffron, strangely relieved to hear it. Swallowing, she put down her bag and wondered what to say. "So, ah. You come here often?"

Gwen raised an eyebrow, lips quirking in reluctant humour. Saffron mentally replayed the question, recognised its resemblance to a bad pick-up line, and blushed to the roots of her hair. "I didn't mean it like that!"

"I'm flattered, really."

"That's not what..." She broke off, feeling strangely lightheaded, and looked at the room again. The floor was made from the same stone as the walls, the uneven surface covered in dirt, dust, straw. There were some empty sacks in a corner, a broken crate in another. It was all so achingly mundane, it made no sense at all that she'd come here by magic. Maybe she'd been drugged instead, knocked out and put in a van and driven away, and the hole in the world was just some hallucinatory way of dealing with a traumatic situation.

"Go on," Gwen said, suddenly. "Get it out of your system. Tell me what you're trying to convince yourself actually happened, and see if you can still put faith in it once you've said it out loud."

"I'm not trying–"

"Of course you aren't." Her mouth was hard, but her eyes were soft. "Oh, child. You don't know what you've done."

"It's just a room," said Saffron, mouth dry. *A shining rip in the world.* "We could be anywhere. We could've... I could be hallucinating the rest."

"Could you?"

Saffron didn't answer. She scuffed her shoe on the ordinary dirt of the ordinary floor, feeling the exact same mix of fear and exhilaration as when she'd first cut class to hide on the library roof, as though her understanding of rules and limits had quietly rearranged itself.

A tramp of footsteps, coming from outside. Gwen froze, and Saffron inexplicably froze with her.

Someone banged on the door.

It wasn't knocking; more like a solid thump. The handle gave an abortive turn. The door rattled in its frame, unyielding, and whoever was trying to get in – a man, by the sound of it – called out in an unfamiliar language. Faintly, Saffron heard two more people respond, another man and a woman. The door shook again, harder than before, as though someone was kicking it. A woman's laughter followed, more words were exchanged, and then they retreated, the unintelligible conversation growing faint with distance.

Saffron let out a breath she didn't remember holding. There were plenty of languages she'd never heard before, and whose phonetics she was therefore unlikely to recognise. For all she knew, they might be in the Ukraine, or Scandinavia, or Timbuktu. But just at that moment, with the sight of a pink-tinged portal seared into her memory, she doubted it.

"*Arakoi*, most likely," Gwen said, jolting her back to the present. Her voice was even, but the tightness of her shoulders said the abortive visit had rattled her. "Vex Leoden's private forces. They've taken to patrolling outside the city walls since he came to power. Rumour has it, he's started actively looking for temple castoffs and runaways to train as soldiers – anyone happy to use magic without conscience."

"Prove it," Saffron said.

"Prove that magic exists?"

"Prove that we're really in a, a–" god, it sounded so *stupid*, "–another *world*, and not some random cupboard."

"Open the door, you mean? Let us out?"

"Just so."

"I can't."

"Why not?"

"Because it's locked from the outside."

"How *convenient*."

"Yes, as a matter of fact." Gwen's tone turned serious. "If it hadn't been, the arakoi would've found us. Luck only knows what they'd have made of you, but if they'd recognised me, I doubt things would've gone well."

"Recognise you? Why on Earth would they recognise *you*?"

Gwen sighed. "We're not on *Earth*, girl – we're in Kena, on the outskirts of the capital city of Karavos. And that, I'm afraid, is very much the point."

Saffron felt as though she were spiralling inwards, teetering on a precipice she couldn't truly see. *Sarcasm is armour,* she told herself, but for once she couldn't think of a comeback. Her mental blank was interrupted by a soft, sudden knock on the door, followed instantly by the scrape of a key in the lock. Saffron watched as the door swung open, heart right back in her mouth. The light was bright enough that she raised a hand to her eyes, watching through a crack in her fingers as Gwen strode out. Her body blocked the sun as she crossed the threshold, and in that fleeting moment of darkness, Saffron was more afraid of abandonment than of whatever lay outside.

She grabbed her bag and followed.

A white sun many times the size it ought to have been sat low on an unfamiliar horizon. Forested hills and rocky soil stretched out in all directions, blanketed here and there with long, thin grass the colour of gum leaves. Even the sky was the wrong shade of blue. Saffron started shaking. If not for that impossible sun, she could've believed she was just in another country on Earth, but now–

"Shut your mouth, girl. The flies here are enormous."

Saffron shut her mouth. Gwen placed a gentle hand on her shoulder.

"And stay close to me, hmm? You really don't want to get lost."

There was a cough, and only then did Saffron remember that someone had let them out. Turning, she came face to face with a slim, gold-skinned woman with wide-set eyes and four black braids looped back around the rest of her unbound hair. She wore a long, red skirt that was slit at the sides; her belt was tight, made of large, overlapping bronze discs, and her creamy blouse was stiff at the neck and collar with red embroidery. She looked to be in her late twenties, and her lips were twisted in an expression of obvious surprise. Raising an eyebrow, she turned to Gwen and spoke in a language that Saffron didn't understand.

"Gwen?" she asked, hesitantly.

"It's all right. She's a friend." Gwen made a wry noise. "Well, sort of. It's a long story."

"Who's the girl?" asked Pix, by way of greeting. In her court accent, the clipped Kenan words sounded oddly fluid, an affectation that Gwen had always found strangely delightful. "Don't tell me you've found an acolyte. Really," she added, forestalling Gwen's protests with a raised hand, "*don't* tell me. Not yet, anyway. We need to get moving. The arakoi are still nearby." And yet she hesitated, looking Saffron over with a mix of puzzled disdain and shock.

Despite every danger of the situation, Gwen was not above taking a moment to appreciate the effect that the girl was having on Pix's cultural sensibilities. Kena being what it was, the only white-skinned locals were Vekshi expatriates, whose women were known for and distinguished by their shaved heads, loose trousers and long tunics. Saffron, with her dishevelled hair and school skirt, must have looked like a complete inversion of stereotype. Though she usually enjoyed poking holes in Pix's worldview, Gwen knew that they didn't have time for it now. *More's the pity.*

"There were complications," she said instead.

"Aren't there always?" Pix muttered, moving at last. "You're just lucky I brought three *roa* – they needed the exercise."

"Only three?" Gwen blinked, surprised. "Where's Matu?"

Pix's face turned grim. "I'll tell you when we reach the compound."

As Saffron stared uncomprehendingly between them, Gwen sighed and switched to English. "We need to get going," she explained. "And–"

The enormity of the problem Saffron represented hit her like a slap. Language at least was an easy fix, provided they could get her to the compound – but *could* they get there? Curling her right hand into a fist, Gwen gave a small shake of her head and forced herself to confront each hurdle in turn.

"We have to ride somewhere," she said. The thin grass crunched beneath her boots. "Have you ever been on a horse?"

"A few times, at riding camps and excursions and things like that." Saffron shouldered her bag, glancing around the landscape as though fearing attack. "Are there horses here?"

"Yes," said Gwen. "But they're less common in cities than… other alternatives." She didn't attempt to describe the roa; the main thing was that Saffron had riding experience. That problem dealt with, she turned back to Pix and switched to Kenan. "You brought me a *taal* to wear?"

Pix wrinkled her nose. "Don't I always?"

"Good; Saffron can have it." Her own skirt, blouse and

steel-toed boots were odd by Kenan standards, but Gwen looked Uyun, not Kenan, and Saffron's need was manifestly greater. "We should hurry. Being exposed like this puts eyes on my neck."

"Better eyes on the neck than knives in the heart," Pix said, completing the proverb.

As Pix sped up, Gwen turned and hooked her arm through Saffron's. It was less a gesture of comfort than it was an attempt to keep her close, but either way, the girl didn't object.

"What happens now?" Saffron asked, meekly.

Gwen glanced around them. The building they'd exited was one of several empty storage barns, clustered starkly on the hilltop like teeth in a codger's gum. Trishka had brought her through to this distant place for the same reason Gwen had been forced to enter from the high school: they'd used the compound too often and too recently, and each new portal there was an unnecessary risk. They'd hoped to avoid the arakoi patrols by keeping their distance from the city, but evidently they still hadn't travelled far enough.

Leoden's getting paranoid, she thought; it was hardly surprising, after Tevet's rebellion. And yet she couldn't quite shake the suspicion that the increase in patrols was more personal than that, as though Leoden was specifically looking for *her*. It was sheer narcissism, of course – Gwen had erred badly in helping Leoden claim the throne, but the error had been in his favour, and even though she'd opposed him since, she was still only one person. He'd wanted her dead in the aftermath of his ascension, but now that he'd consolidated his power – now that her knowledge of his treachery was no immediate threat – what could he possibly want with her? It was a question with many frightening answers, and she felt momentarily furious that now, of all times, she'd managed to find herself saddled with a clueless initiate. But as Saffron looked to her for an explanation,

Gwen remembered her own first foray into the Many, as she'd come to term the myriad, magically accessible worlds, and wondered, *Was I any better, or less naïve?*

As they passed into the shadow of nearby trees she heard the low, distinctive crooning of the roa, and smiled.

"Now," she said, "we see if you really can ride."

Weird day, Saffron thought, indulging in the sort of understatement that tends to accompany severe shock. She'd locked down on her desire to run screaming, and was now in an alternate mental state characterised by selective ignorance and a vague sense of building panic. *Rapidly getting weirder.*

Their guide, Pixeva, led them away from their arrival building and down the curve of a hill. Though the surrounding countryside was hardly exceptional – Saffron could see nothing other than trees, grass, and yet more hills – small details kept on leaping out at her, like the shade and shape of the leaves and the brightness of some unfamiliar red flowers. But as they entered a copse of strange, twisting trees, she found herself confronted with much more startling proof that this was an alien place.

Saddled, bridled and hitched to a tree were three utterly foreign creatures, snuffling in what Saffron could only hope was a friendly greeting. She couldn't help herself: she let out a yelp, then clapped an embarrassed hand to her mouth.

"They're called roa," Gwen said, lips twitching. "Intelligent, sociable beasties, though they stink like wet dogs."

Beastie. The single word coiled in her chest. Ruby's kitten at home was called Beastie, and that sudden, unexpected reminder of his white-sock paws and deep purr almost brought her to the brink of tears. Yet it wasn't sadness that moved her so, but poignancy: some weird and beautiful emotion all wrapped up in the instant at which she'd drawn a link between the world she'd left and this new place she'd come to. *Kena*, Gwen had called it. All at once, the roa were nothing compared to the fact that she'd watched magic tear a hole in the world – in the *worlds*, she corrected herself, feeling a thrill of excitement at the plural – and been brave enough to cross over.

She approached the roa, made bold by the fearlessness with which their guide was rummaging through the panniers attached to one of their saddles. They looked a bit like cuddly velociraptors – that is, assuming your definition of *velociraptor* included a camel-like head, "hands" with fingers like a tree-frog's toes, and a long-haired coat that resembled nothing so much as a shag pile carpet. Each one was at least Saffron's height at the shoulder, their colouration ranging from a dirty white-and-tan mix to a sort of gunmetal blue. Their ears swivelled attentively at each little sound, while their long, plumed tails swept slowly back and forth, though whether the motion denoted happiness, boredom or anger, Saffron couldn't tell.

"They're, uh…" She was still searching for words when Pixeva thrust a large billow of red-and-yellow-striped cloth into her hands, muttering something incomprehensible as she did so.

"You wrap yourself in it," Gwen said, pantomiming with her hands. "It's called a taal."

Saffron hefted the cloth – the taal – as though it were a bedsheet in need of folding. Setting down her schoolbag, she tried to tie it on like a sarong, but without much luck: the material was too thick to knot in the ways she was used to, and her hands were shaking so badly that she kept dropping it. Seeing this, Pixeva rolled her eyes and began to wind Saffron into the thing as though she were a mummy. Gwen watched the process with evident amusement, the wrinkles at her eyes and mouth deepening. When the guide finally stepped back, Saffron's uniform had disappeared from view completely. Somehow, the taal conspired to cover not only her legs, but her arms and head too, as though she were wearing a wraparound, hooded poncho.

Gwen surveyed her critically, then turned to the guide, speaking again in the other language while motioning at her hair. In response, the guide scrunched a fist at the back of her head, a questioning expression on her face. After a moment, Gwen nodded assent.

"Do you have a hair tie?" she asked, switching back to English. The question caught Saffron off guard.

"You want me to tie it back?"

"Please."

"Oh. I think so. Hang on."

Careful not to unseat the taal – it sat awkwardly over her uniform, and the weight of the extra cloth was already making her sweat – she crouched down and fished around in her bag, eventually pulling out a rubber band. It would sting when the time came to take it out, but it was all she had; in the morning rush, she'd forgotten to pick one up. Gingerly pushing back the hood, she pulled her hair into a ponytail and covered it again. Both women nodded their approval, and for the first time since her arrival, the guide smiled as she spoke.

Gwen snorted and relayed the comment. "Pix says you look like a merchant's daughter, but she apologises if you get too hot – she only bought that taal because it was cheap."

Saffron had no idea what to make of this. "Um... thanks, I guess?"

Gwen laughed. For the first time, it occurred to Saffron to wonder just how old she really was. Though Gwen's hair was uniformly grey and her face lined, her arms were ropey with muscle, her hands long-fingered and strong, and her posture straight as a soldier's.

"Christ, I'd kill for a cigarette. I don't suppose you're one of those delinquent teens I've heard so much about?"

Saffron shook her head, not trusting herself to answer. Almost, she giggled.

Gwen sighed. "Pity. The smoke-herbs here taste like desiccated toejam. I'll take that," she added, grabbing Saffron's bag and tying it alongside one of the panniers. "We need to mount up."

For all she'd been willing to think of them as cuddly a moment ago, Saffron suddenly found herself eyeing the roa with trepidation.

"Are they safe?" she blurted.

Gwen stared at her levelly. "Well," she said, pulling Saffron forwards, "that all depends on whether you're planning to fall off. *Are* you planning to fall off?"

"No!" Saffron squeaked, and in a rash effort to prove her competence, tried and failed to put her foot in the stirrup without completely entangling her taal. Gwen watched her flounder for a moment, then unceremoniously boosted her onto the roa's back.

Saffron reached for the reins, but found none: they were still tied to the tree. Instead, she rested her hands between the roa's shoulder blades – what she guessed would be called the withers on a horse – and tried to get her balance. Though she'd been thinking in terms of a regular riding saddle (or at least, regular by Earth standards), this one was flatter than she was used to, canted forwards so that she had to grip with her knees. There wasn't much support at the back, either.

Swallowing, she nudged her heels to the roa's flanks and rode forward.

3
Learn the World

In the three weeks since Gwen had left Karavos – which is to say, twenty-seven days; Kenan weeks were nine days long, a day for every major god – everything had changed, and yet nothing had. Or so Pix said, and Gwen was inclined to trust her (in this, at least). The two of them rode side by side, Gwen leading Saffron's roa on a lead rope. For obvious reasons, Pix spoke no English, but though it rubbed Gwen against the grain to exclude Saffron so thoroughly from the conversation, the girl was far more preoccupied with keeping her seat. Remembering her own first time aboard a roa, Gwen could sympathise: assuming they made it safely to the compound, her legs and back would be aching by nightfall.

Beside her, Pix swished her braids, oblivious to this inner monologue – which, given the circumstances, was hardly unreasonable. "Leoden might be Vex," she was saying, "but he's not a god. Or if he is, he's only from the third tier." She snorted at her own joke.

Gwen, however, didn't think it funny. "He's a man," she snapped. "An oathbreaker and an empire-builder, and in case you'd forgotten, Pixeva ore Pixeva, it was our profound lack of judgement that put him on the throne. Find me the godly purpose in all of that, and I just might manage conversion to your wretched pantheon."

Pix ignored the rebuke, as calm as any cat, and carried on as though Gwen had never spoken. "The temples are furious at how he's recruiting their castoffs to the arakoi. He's not just after *kemeta*, either – he wants students the temples have rejected, mages willing to break their oaths for whatever reason, whether out of cruelty or curiosity."

Gwen winced; she'd said as much to Saffron, but it was still ill-omened. "Is there any word on what he's training them for?"

"Only whispers, but those are terrible enough. Three nights ago, a man suspected of treason was found wandering the streets, completely out of his mind, speaking only in shrieks and growls. He didn't know his name; he couldn't even speak Kenan, Yasha's informants said. Now, I've heard of beatings bad enough to steal memories, but language itself? It's like someone used the *ahunemet* to make him forget he was human."

"Or the *zuymet*, perhaps," said Gwen, not liking either prospect. She'd had decades in which to acclimatise to the idea of magic as mundane, yet hearing of its misuse still chilled her. Zuymet was word-magic, the ability to learn and bestow language with supernatural ease – it was how she'd first learned Kenan, and if they made it to the compound in one piece, she had plans for Saffron to do likewise. A supremely useful gift, and tricky to abuse in any practical sense. The ahunemet, though, was a different story: whether you termed it thought-theft or telepathy, it was all too easy to imagine how it might be turned to unsavory purposes.

Gwen shook her head, troubled. "Has that been all?"

"It's not enough?" Pix countered, then waved a hand, as though she'd thought better of it. "My apologies. The prospect of such dark experimentation disturbs me. Vexa Yavin went down this path before, in the Years of Shadow; it's why the temples instituted their oaths, why kemeta are subject to so much scrutiny even now. That Leoden would turn to it so flagrantly so soon into his reign–" She broke off, clearly disgusted. "We truly were fools to believe in him."

"Truly," Gwen echoed.

As the woodland began to thin, the broad dust of Cevet's Road became visible, running parallel to the tree line. A subtle reminder of their destination, perhaps, yet one Gwen felt minded to heed.

Sighing, she let her roa drop back from Pix's, reining in alongside Saffron. She studied the girl, who was gawking shamelessly at everything, and felt a pang at how little she could explain about their situation – yet – without spooking her. If Saffron had considered going home at all, she doubtless assumed it would be an easy transition: just open another portal and pop back after an afternoon's adventure. But Gwen, who was more aware of Trishka's strengths and limitations than anyone save Trishka herself, knew it wasn't that simple. She didn't imagine Saffron would respond positively to being told she was stuck in a foreign world, however temporarily: if she panicked and ran off, there was no telling what might happen. And yet her ignorance was a danger, too: Gwen couldn't simply leave her in the dark.

"It's beautiful," Saffron said. Her flicked gaze indicated the sky, the hills, the oversized sun, before finally lighting on Gwen. "Are you... I mean, you're from Earth, right? Not here?"

Gwen let out a breath. It was a good opening, all things considered. Personal – she didn't often talk about her history – but perhaps, in this instance, necessarily so.

"I'm from Earth," she said. "From England, originally. Born and raised in London, though my parents retired near Sydney a few years back. I first wound up here in my twenties." She saw the (politely) unasked question flit across Saffron's face and added, "I'm fifty-four."

"So you've been, ah–"

"Worldwalking," Gwen supplied.

"–worldwalking, right, for, um… thirty years?"

"Thirty-three, if we're being particular. But yes." She sighed – a little wry, a little wistful. "More than half my life. My whole life, really."

Saffron opened her mouth, then seemed to think better of whatever she'd been about to say. She bit her lip. "Did you choose it?"

"No," said Gwen. "And yes. Well. It depends what you mean by choice." She tucked a stray grey lock behind her ear. "The first time was an accident. The magic that makes portals – they call it the jahudemet, in Kenan – is, well… *demanding,* let's say. It's a born gift, one with varying strengths and applications. Most who have it can only glimpse other times and places, but can't necessarily open a door; for those who can, it's rarer still to be able to rip between worlds. Either way, the stronger the gift, the harder it is to ignore. The magic builds up like a static charge – don't ask why, because I don't rightly understand it myself – and sooner or later, it has to be used. And Trishka, who makes our portals, her magic is *very* strong, but her body isn't, and once upon a time, she had the idea that suppressing the jahudemet, refusing to use it, might let her be healthier. So she held it back, and back, and back – and when it finally broke loose, it tore a portal to Earth." She raised a meaningful eyebrow.

Saffron's eyes widened. "And you came through?"

"Fell through, really. I was on my way home from college, and it opened up so close to me, I couldn't have stopped if I'd wanted to. I went straight from a dingy backstreet to the middle of Karavos – no idea what was happening, no guide, nothing. It was two days before Trishka found me, and after that–" She broke off, shying away from harder truths that cut too close to Saffron's own situation, and chose her next words carefully. "Well. Let's just say I was gone long enough that going home raised questions. Oh, I tried to go back to the way things were – I finished my degree, qualified as a teacher, all that stuff – but I'd made friends here, and I wanted..." She trailed off, uncertain if an honest explanation would be met with understanding, disbelief or derision.

"Wanted what?" Saffron prompted, after a moment's silence.

Gwen sighed. "How much do you know about Margaret Thatcher?"

"Not much," the girl admitted. "I mean, my parents talk about her sometimes, and I've seen movies and stuff, you know, about when she was Prime Minister – I know there were strikes and protests – but we haven't exactly covered it in school."

"What about the Brixton Riots?" *Or Section 28*, she almost added, suppressing a shudder.

"Oh! I know a little about them, I think. It came up in some articles I read about the England Riots back in 2011. I didn't understand it all, but we did a class project on it."

I was at Brixton, Gwen thought, with a sudden, distant ache. She'd been nineteen at the time, only a little older than Saffron was now, though still two years away from her first trip to Kena, angry and sad and terrified all at once. She almost said so, until she remembered to do the maths on Saffron's age. Five years ago, she would've been eleven. Whatever she'd learned about it then would likely be too garbled and simplistic to help now, and Gwen had no desire to unburden such an old, sharp part of herself to someone who wouldn't understand what it meant.

She thought for a moment, then said, "All right. So if I told you that I wanted to feel safe, and that I felt safer here, in an alien world, than in Thatcher's Britain, what would you think I meant?"

Saffron opened her mouth. Closed it. She looked from Gwen to Pix, who still rode silently ahead, and back again. "I'd think," she said, very carefully, "that you were talking about racism. And sexism, and violence. Police violence. Things like that."

"You'd be right," said Gwen, relieved. *Perhaps she did learn something, after all.* "I'm not saying Kena doesn't have its problems too, but they're different problems, you understand? I was still an outsider here, but not in the same way."

She didn't say, *the police wouldn't look for me when I vanished, because they didn't think a missing black woman mattered.* She didn't say, *my parents convinced themselves I'd run off with a boy I was too ashamed to bring home, and when I came back, the second thing they asked me was if I'd had an abortion.* She didn't say, *I grew in Kena, and when I wouldn't shrink again, people thought there was something wrong with me.* She didn't say, *you're already changed forever, too. You just don't know it yet.*

Instead, Gwen said, "So now I go back and forth. I visit Earth, but I mostly live here." *I married here, too,* she almost added, the silent thoughts rearing up again. *I married an Uyun woman and a Kenan man in a tiny town by a warm, southern sea, and raised our son a world away from everything I'd grown to fear might kill him.*

Pix didn't know about that, of course, which was why Gwen kept quiet, even though they were speaking in English: the greater marvel was that she'd considered telling Saffron at all. Trishka knew about Naku and Jhesa and Louis, of course, but she was one of a trusted few. Gwen wasn't ashamed of her husband and wife, who'd always understood her restless need for movement; she just preferred to have some part of her life that wasn't subject to external scrutiny, but which existed, beautiful and inviolate, beyond the reach of worldwalking and politics. She loved Naku and Jhesa deeply, platonically, a counterbalance to their mutual romanticism. Gwen had never felt romantic love, and once upon a time, before Trishka assured her otherwise, she'd wondered if that meant there was something wrong with her. Such worries had died out years ago; nonetheless, the fact that her marriage-mates extended their romance to Gwen while accepting her feelings never ceased to be warming.

I should go home again soon, she thought, a little wistfully. *Once things have settled down.* It was good to have seen her parents, but if not for the very real risk of being tailed by Leoden's agents, she would have gone to her partners instead in a heartbeat.

Oblivious to this internal monologue, Saffron said, "I can't imagine what that's like. I keep wanting to take pictures, but my phone's on a different planet." She blinked. "Assuming it would even work over here, I mean."

"It would," said Gwen. "Or the camera would, anyway."

Saffron grinned, and it struck Gwen that she looked less tired than she had on Earth. A cynical part of her wondered how long it would last.

Gwen's roa snorted, forcing her to consider more practical matters. "Once we reach Karavos," she said, "you're going to stand out. White skin is uncommon here. Not unknown, mind you, but as far as this world and this city are concerned, you look Vekshi."

"Vekshi," said Saffron, trying out the word. And then, with more perspicacity than Gwen had expected of her, "Is that a nationality or an ethnic group, or both?"

"A nationality," said Gwen. "Veksh is just north of Kena, but it's very different." An understatement of somewhat epic proportions, though she wasn't about to start listing all the reasons why. "They speak a different language there though, so it won't be so odd that you don't speak Kenan."

Saffron nodded. "And the Vekshi wear, uh, taals like this?"

Not if they've got any choice in the matter, Gwen wanted to say, but even though Pix wouldn't comprehend the slight to her taste, she kept the remark to herself. There was no point making Saffron any more self-conscious than she must already be.

"Some do, if they're naturalised. Taals are Kenan, but even then, not everybody wears them." She gestured to Pix as a case in point. "Most Vekshi women wear loose trousers with wraparound tunics. They also shave their heads. Don't worry, though. A Vekshi girl in a taal is unusual in Karavos, but not odd. Keep your head down, leave the talking to us, and we'll be fine. Just try to be unobtrusive."

Indicating her taal with a downwards tilt of her eyes, Saffron pulled a face. "Unobtrusive? In this? Seriously?"

Gwen suppressed a chuckle. "I'm sure you'll manage."

"I'll do my best," said Saffron. She tilted her head, her expression turning thoughtful. "If Veksh is north of Kena, does that mean they share a border?"

"They do."

"And there's not, like, a big mountain range or a wall in the way or anything? You can just cross over?"

"No, there's nothing like that," said Gwen. She frowned, not sure where the line of questioning was headed. "It's mostly forest and farms, a few noble estates on the Kenan side and a smattering of border garrisons. There's always a little tension around the Bharajin Forest – it used to be Vekshi, and now it's ours – but otherwise, it's open."

"All right. So if anyone asks, why don't we just say I'm from near the border?"

Gwen blinked at her. "What? Why?"

"Because I'm wearing a taal," said Saffron. "You know, like a cultural bleed. We talked about borders in history, and it always seems like that's where clothes and food and languages mix. So I thought, if it's odd in Karavos, maybe it's not odd somewhere else, and we can just pretend that's where I'm from."

"Not with Veksh," said Gwen. "With other countries, yes – like Uyu and Kamne – but not Veksh. It was a good thought, though."

"Oh," said Saffron, sounding deflated. "Right." And then, with guileless curiosity, "Why not?"

Gwen found herself doing a very good impression of a pufferfish. "I don't know," she said, after several seconds of unflattering, open-mouthed silence. "I... huh. I work with Vekshi, but I've never been that far north. There's probably some historical reason for it, if you asked the right person." Gwen made a mental note to do just that. It was the kind of puzzle Matu loved; if he didn't already know the answer, he'd likely want to help uncover it.

"Fair enough," said Saffron. "So how come you were at my school? Is the nature strip, like, a magical hotspot or something?"

Gwen rolled her eyes and started to explain about making portals.

For what felt like the better part of an hour, they'd been riding through woods so unfamiliar that Saffron half expected a fairytale creature to leap at her from the bushes. The trees, in addition to being crooked, had creamy trunks and branches – like paperbarks, she thought – and leaves that were rust red flecked with brown, almost the colour of blood. This explained why the distant hills she'd seen from the building had looked so dark, but it made the woods eerie, the way she imagined a proper European autumn might feel.

Beneath her, the roa rocked like a ship, its two-legged gait both jarring and slippery. Her lower back was tense from the effort of keeping upright, and despite the double protection of taal and uniform, her thighs were chafing against the saddle leather. Excluded from the current conversation – Gwen had returned to Pix's side about twenty minutes ago, citing a need to confer with her about entering Karavos – Saffron began to feel anxious about the passage of time. She had a certain amount of leeway before her parents and Ruby started to wonder where she was, but she didn't want to be sent back prematurely either. Getting in trouble for coming home a few hours late would be more than worth it for this.

They were lower down in the hills now, their view unobstructed as the road took new twists and turns. Where before the only signs of human habitation had been empty barns, like the one into which they'd initially portalled, now Saffron could see settled farmland, tilled fields and small steadings that stretched away into the distance. But next to Karavos, which had just come into proper view, none of that mattered. It was massive, its shadow darkening the valley floor like a winestain on a tablecloth. From a height, the city appeared to be all on one level, but as they grew closer, she saw that the central spires and towers were physically built on higher ground, like the raised hub of a very wonky wheel.

Though protected by walls of reddish-orange stone, the perimeter was far from even, jagging in and out again at random. The walls weren't of a uniform height either, and as their descent changed to afford a closer view of the city's flank, it became clear that some wall sections had been toppled, smashed to rubble as though by an unseen hand. In these places, Saffron could just make out the sight of workers going about repairs, flanked by lines of non-builders. It took her a moment to puzzle this out, and then she realised: soldiers.

For all that Gwen had told her, she still knew next to nothing about this world, and the depths of her ignorance chilled her. Were the guards meant to protect the builders, or to bully them? Was Karavos safe? Back on the hilltop, she hadn't really processed all that talk about arakoi and Vex Leoden, but as she caught the faint glint of light on distant spear tips, it felt rather more urgent. Belatedly, she noticed that many of the surrounding farmsteads were wrecked and abandoned. For every field planted with healthy-looking crops, two others were dead, their plants either burned or rotten. What had happened here?

Without warning, Saffron's roa lurched forwards. She clutched the reins, fearful of falling, then realised that Gwen had tugged on the lead rope, pulling her alongside again.

"We're close now," she said. Saffron blinked in surprise: while she'd been introspecting, they'd entered the valley proper. Now that they were on a level, the city's walls and towers looked truly massive – imposingly so. Which made no sense at all; she was used to looking up at skyscrapers, and those were modern buildings, surely taller than anything that could be built without the use of steel and cranes.

"Magic," Gwen said, following Saffron's gaze. "Karavos is an ancient city, but a strong one." Her smile faded. "Or, at least, it was."

"The broken walls, you mean?"

"And the war that broke them. Well." She laughed, but her eyes were devoid of humour. "I call it a war. More a squabble, really. A tiff."

"What happened?"

"In a way, I did. I backed the wrong man for the throne, and he did that."

Saffron took a moment to digest this information, putting it together with the (very little) she knew already. "Vex Leoden, you mean?"

"That's him. Vex is a title, in case you were wondering. It's not quite the same as a king, but they're comparable terms."

"And you…" Saffron struggled to word the question, not knowing how to make it sound less ridiculous. "You… supported him?"

"Something like that." Gwen sighed. "It's a longer story than we have time for now, as close as we are. Just remember: when we reach the city, keep still and silent. And if we have to run–" she lifted the lead rope slightly, "– then just hang on."

Saffron gulped. "What if I get lost, or we get separated somehow?"

Gwen's reply was forestalled by a comment from Pix, to which she replied in Kenan. Pix spoke again, her expression calculating. Gwen *hmph*ed, but the sound could've meant anything.

"Pix asked what you said. I told her."

"And?"

"And she says to tell you: don't get lost."

Though still sweating beneath her taal, Saffron shivered.

They reached Karavos just as the sun was slipping below the hills. Gwen fidgeted in her saddle, displeased by the sight of a joint contingent of city guards and arakoi stopping travellers at the gate. Though they'd encountered little traffic on the road – an odd thing in itself, and certainly a troubling sign – they nonetheless had to wait in line while two other convoys were questioned, searched, and then finally admitted into the city. Talking in low voices on their final approach, Gwen and Pix had agreed on a story to explain Saffron's presence. Though Vekshi women could come and go as they pleased, it was nonetheless noteworthy that one should be entering the city in the company of a young, native Kenan and an older, Uyun-looking woman. Throw in Saffron's uncut hair (if they noticed it), her lack of a staff (significant, but not critical) and her complete ignorance of either customs or language, and they were potentially in for a very tough time of it.

Getting out of Karavos was easy these days; getting in again was the real problem. For neither the first nor the last time, Gwen cursed herself for ever having been taken in by Leoden's facade. Initially, he'd appeared to be everything a good Vex should be: courteous, quick-witted, compromising at times and rigid at others. But his subsequent actions had proven him to be egomaniacal, manipulative and cold, his plans for Kena so grandiose and twisted that even Yasha struggled to make sense of them. More than once, Gwen had had cause to reflect on the irony of what the Kenan word for a male ruler – *king* being a misleading translation – meant in English. *Vex*, she thought, suppressing a sigh. *Leoden certainly does, at that.*

"You three – step up!"

It was the guard captain. Gwen stilled her face into unthreatening neutrality, even slouching to emphasise her age. "Good afternoon, honoured swords."

The eight guards – all men, though some among the arakoi were female – showed the proper deference to her age and sex, first cupping their extended hands, then closing the palms together. That, at least, was encouraging, though it boded ill that none among the arakoi followed suit.

"Ladies." The captain stepped forwards, the butt of his long spear resting in the dirt. "May I ask your business in Karavos?"

This time it was Pix who answered. "Honoured sword, I rode out this morning to collect this friend of my mother's–" she nodded at Gwen, "–and her travelling companion. My mother is sick, and wished them to help tend her."

The guard nodded. "I understand. Even so, there are questions I must ask. Do you carry any weapons?"

"No, honoured sword," said Pix.

"Does anyone in your party possess any talent for magic?"

"None, honoured sword."

"And do you consent to a search of your possessions?"

Pix hesitated for less than a heartbeat. "Of course, honoured sword."

The guard frowned. "Very well." He waved the arakoi forward. "Do what you will."

Gwen didn't hold her breath; she had too much self-control. Instead, she sat immobile while two arakoi – one male, one female – circled their trio of roa, lifting pannier flaps and peering disdainfully at their contents. But what could they possibly find? Not even Pix was foolish enough to tempt fate by bringing something likely to attract the wrong sort of attention. Perhaps this could be easy, after all. Perhaps–

"That's an odd pannier," the female arakoi said, tilting her spear to indicate the right flank of Gwen's mount. The remark startled her, until she realised she meant Saffron's schoolbag. Internally, she cursed herself for a sentimental fool. Though Pix had seen enough of the materials of Gwen's world not to remark on the bag, of course a normal Kenan would. Though battered and dirty, the bag's purple colouring, plastic buckles and synthetic fibre were nonetheless distinctive. She should have made Saffron leave it behind, but she intimately remembered what it was like to be stranded on a strange world with nothing from home, and knew she could never have brought herself to enforce the decision.

Thinking fast, she shrugged in an offhand way, thankful for the first time that Saffron spoke no Kenan.

"You've a good eye," she said. "I bought it from a trader as a curiosity, along with all the contents. I've no idea what they are, and nor did he – the man who'd sold it to him was a sailor. I'd hoped a scholar here might recognise the make, perhaps even give me a good price for it." She patted the bag and laughed. "At my age, it pays to think about a nest egg."

The arakoi's mouth twitched in what was almost a smile. "Too true, mother," she said, and to Gwen's infinite relief, both she and her companion stepped back. "You can pass. Good travels."

Then she turned to Saffron and – to Gwen's utter horror – repeated her words in Vekshi.

Time slowed. Saffron's heart was hammering so loudly, it felt as though everyone must be able to hear it. What should she do? The woman was looking at her, clearly expecting an answer, but she had no idea what she'd said. Praying it was the right response, she nodded, and almost wept with relief when Gwen tugged firmly on the lead rope, urging her roa onwards.

But as they passed the guards, she couldn't help noticing that their leader kept her eyes on them, as though puzzled by something. Ahead, the city gates stood open, revealing a bustling marketplace. Karavos was loud, busy, crowded – and pungent. Food, sweat, livestock, spices, excrement, heat, garbage, vegetables; the overall odour was hot and sour and somewhat unwashed, strong enough that she desperately wanted to cover her mouth and nose. Only fear that the mannerism might be taken incorrectly kept her from doing so.

They were halfway between the guards and the gate when the leader called out to them again. Saffron kept quiet, waiting for either Pix or Gwen to respond. When neither did, her stomach twisted. What if the guard's question – and it surely had to be a question – was directed at *her*? She froze, panic surging through her like an electrical current, and before she could properly grasp what was happening, her roa lurched forwards, the lead rope stretched taut as Gwen shouted at her to hold on.

And then they were running – or rather, the roa were, stretching out their legs and necks like ostriches racing across a plain. This wasn't like before, when merely clutching the reins had been enough; now, every stride threatened to send Saffron flying. Behind them, the guards shouted and gave chase, but in an open space the roa had the advantage, surging ahead of their unmounted pursuers.

Once they were through the gates, however, the crush of the market quickly forced them to change tactics. Though the roa didn't slow, there was simply no room for three of them to ride abreast, and all of a sudden Pix was riding away from them, whipping her reins from side to side and shouting as she plunged through the crowds. Gwen was forced to ride at an angle, the hand that held the lead rope stretched behind her while the other tried to steer. As the roa sped and dodged – missing a laden wagon here, turning a corner there, baulking sharply at a brightly coloured wall, then racing on again – Saffron's cowl slipped back, revealing her unshaven head to the world. Worse still, her feet were coming loose from the stirrups. With each zig and zag, she felt like a champagne cork being steadily forced from its bottle.

"Gwen!" she shrieked.

The worldwalker risked a glance over her shoulder and cursed. "Hang on!"

Saffron felt a sob rising in her throat. She could barely stick the saddle now, her balance completely shot, and though she tried to wrap her fingers in the roa's long coat, all she succeeded in doing was dropping the reins. Completely unanchored, she felt the next turn almost before she saw it – a sharp alley corner, a stone wall – and rose up with exquisite slowness, aware of the exact moment when both feet slipped the stirrups completely.

She fell.

4
Severed

Saffron hit the wall shoulder first, a solid smack that knocked the air from her lungs, and crumpled to the ground. Most of her weight landed on her left arm, but she twisted enough that her back wrenched too. Pain punched through her. Everything was black. Her head rang; she'd clipped her skull on the wall, hard enough that she felt like she might throw up. But then came the adrenaline, a rush of furious fear that drowned out everything else, telling her to *move get up run hide move move now!* Eyes and muscles burning, Saffron forced herself upright. People were staring at her, strangers with startled faces and bright taals, alternately shouting in consternation or extending their hands, all speaking in a language that she didn't understand. There was no sign of either Gwen or the roa, and over the tumult, a different commotion was drawing close.

The guards! Unable to turn or follow Gwen, Saffron took the only available course of action and darted into the crowds, sobbing as she stumbled. She didn't know how to move in the taal, and whatever knots secured it had weakened; the cloth was slipping, threatening to tangle her even further. Both shoulders felt vilely bruised, her wrenched back aching with every step, while a low, pulsing headache and nausea were the legacy of her bumped skull. Swamped by sudden dizziness, she forced herself to slow down. Black spots swam in her vision; breathing burned her throat. She couldn't run any further, and besides which, it was only making her more noticeable. Allowing herself to walk, she gulped in air and tried to figure out where she was.

So far, she'd only noticed Karavos as a blur. Now, with the threat of pursuit fading and a pressing need to calm herself, she focused on her surroundings. Shadows lay everywhere, cast by the taller central spires she'd noticed from the hills, occasional lines of dying sunlight giving the city a tiger-striped appearance. Though many of the larger structures were made of the same pale stone as the hilltop barns, others used wood or bricks. All, however, were painted; colour was everywhere, taals and murals and food stalls alike. These latter mostly sold what Saffron took to be fruit and vegetables, though on no stronger basis than shape and colour – for all she knew, they were something else entirely. The variety was as dizzying as the scope of her ignorance was terrifying, and she found herself choking back panic. She remembered passing a market on the way in, which meant that either she was completely turned around, or else that there was more than one within the walls. Most likely, it was the latter; Karavos was a big place. Fearing discovery, she sped up again, knowing rationally it wouldn't help but compelled by some buried prey instinct to move. People stared as she passed them, and as each new pair of eyes latched onto her, she tensed.

"Calm down," she told herself, the words spilling out in a whispery rush. "Calm down, calm down, calm *down*."

Strangely, this worked. Her pulse and pace slowed in parallel, until she came to a halt. Looking around, Saffron found herself in an open square dominated by a three-tiered fountain whose waters poured from the hands of various figures. Foot traffic from at least four other streets constantly bustled in and out, while various stallholders proffered their wares at the crowd. At the sight of water, her thirst returned with a vengeance, and though she'd managed to cease her tears, she almost wept all over again when she realised she didn't know if drinking from the fountain was allowed, or even safe. *Why did I have to come here?* she berated herself. *What kind of person just jumps through a hole in reality?* But though the recriminations stung, they were also unhelpful. Standing against what looked like an unobtrusive stretch of wall, Saffron forced herself to think rationally, rubbing dried tears from her cheeks.

I can't run anymore. There's no point. I don't know where I am or how to find Gwen, and anyway, I'm hurt. By that logic, waiting in one place – particularly an open place like this, where a girl alone wasn't so conspicuous – was a sensible thing to do. Saffron's only hope was that Gwen or Pix would come looking for her. Both women knew the city; they must have some idea of where she'd fallen off and how far she might reasonably have run. Until they found her, Saffron would have to be patient. To pass the time (and to keep herself calm), she decided to keep watch on the fountain. If any of the locals drank from it, she'd take that as a sign that she was allowed to do so too. If not, she'd stay where she was.

Nobody's missing me yet. She took a deep breath and repeated the thought, clinging to it even though it wasn't quite true. As best she could reckon it, less than three hours had passed since her arrival: assuming she'd still been on Earth, she would have well and truly missed the last bus home. But that wasn't necessarily cause for her family to worry. She might just have chosen to walk instead, or been caught up in whatever it was they thought she was doing. Saffron's parents respected her independence, and though she tried to be considerate of this, she wasn't perfect. Surely thinking the worst about what might have happened to a daughter would be their last resort? If only she could get home somehow, even if it was as late as tomorrow afternoon, she could make some excuse for her absence – a secret boyfriend, perhaps, or an impromptu bushwalk. Whatever the punishment was, she'd take it gladly – grounding, no internet, no phone, no TV, everything – if it meant she could stop their worrying.

But though she fought against it, the tears returned, a thin trickle of silent salt that seeped down her cheeks and into the stripes of her taal.

Gwen pulled up in the compound's courtyard, jerking so hard on the bridle that her roa tossed back its head and *kree*'d in protest. Leaping down, she dropped both her reins and the lead rope of Saffron's mount. The beasts stood free, their long coats matted with sweat.

"Pix!" she shouted, striding towards the group of women emerging from the main building. "Is Pix back yet?"

"Why isn't she with you?" snapped Yasha, thumping her staff on the earth. Despite her age, the Vekshi matriarch remained a formidable woman. "What happened?"

Though normally tolerant of Yasha, Gwen had no time for her now, and felt strongly enough that without thinking, she reverted to English. "Fuck! Exactly when did the arakoi start speaking Vekshi?" At Yasha's raised brow, she swore again and switched languages. "A white girl came through with me – don't ask why, I'm still not sure myself – and she's out there now, alone. I need to find her."

Yasha's gaze narrowed. "Not you, Gwen. Send a Vekshi to find a Vekshi. It attracts less notice."

"She doesn't belong to your people, Yasha," Gwen growled. "That's the problem! She doesn't know even a word of Kenan, and right now–"

Yasha raised her staff and jabbed it into Gwen's solar plexus, hard. Coughing, Gwen staggered back, glaring daggers at the matriarch. *Stubborn old hag!*

"Zechalia!" Yasha called imperiously, ignoring Gwen's resentment. A scrawny, androgynous girl of eleven darted forwards, waiting patiently for instructions. Her skin was weirdly mottled – a calico mix that always made Gwen think of vitiligo in reverse, a light base turning dark. "You will find Gwen's stranger and bring her here. Use your magic if you must, but *don't* overstretch yourself. Even the supplest reed will snap if bent too far." She turned to Gwen. "Zech is fast. She knows the city. Tell her what to find, and she'll find it."

Gwen pinched the bridge of her nose, fighting irritation. It made sense not to go herself – she was tired, her legs stiff after riding a roa for the first time in months – and even at her full strength, Zech would still be faster. Nonetheless, it rankled. Saffron was her responsibility, and she was loath to entrust her safety to anyone else, let alone a child. But Yasha was stubborn as a stableful of mules, and Gwen was woman enough to admit that she had no choice, whatever the cost to her pride.

"Her name is Saffron," she said, finally. "She's sixteen, wearing a red and yellow striped taal over foreign clothes – and if you can see them, you'll know them as such. She fell after the Third Wall, but before the Blue Gate, along the market stretch. Pale skin, green eyes." She took a breath, not liking what would come next. "Blonde hair, worn long. We made her tie it back, but still, she doesn't understand–"

"Go." Yasha spoke softly, but her command was unmistakable. Zech shot off like a stone from a sling, her bare feet kicking up dust. Gwen watched the girl until she was out of sight.

"Trishka has been asking for you," Yasha said, offhandedly. "Unless you plan to stand here like a lump until Zech returns, I'd suggest you come and pay your respects."

"Pix isn't back yet," Gwen pointed out. "Something could have happened to her."

Yasha snorted. "Pix has a wife, two husbands and a strong knife-arm. She can take care of herself. Now, come!" She emphasised this last remark by thwacking her staff against Gwen's thighs.

Stifling her protests, Gwen began to follow the old woman inside. *That's the problem with life,* she reflected sourly. *No matter how old you get, there's always someone older in charge.*

After fifteen minutes of being stared at by curious strangers and wondering what she was doing wrong, Saffron finally twigged to the obvious: her hair was visible. Swearing under her breath, she reached up, feeling for the hood of her taal, only to provoke an unwelcome slithering sensation as the whole thing started to slip. Her fall and subsequent dash through the city had loosened the wrap, and now she was in serious danger of accidentally disrobing. Gingerly, she lowered her hands, and was rewarded when the garment stayed put. As carefully as possible, she started to run her fingers over the taal's folds, trying to understand how Pix had wrapped it in the first place. If she could just figure out where the main creases were meant to be, then she might be able to tighten it up. Once her body was secured, she could try for the hood again.

She'd been doing this for scarcely a minute when someone at the opposite end of the square started shouting. Immediately fearful that the guards had found her, Saffron whipped her head up; she'd run if she had to, despite feeling like she'd been shoved through a blender. But instead of the gate guards, with their Roman-style kilts and breastplates, she found herself watching quite a different panoply approach. Surrounded by a phalanx of attendants all clad in identical blue and gold was a beautiful woman riding not a roa, but a handsome, blood-bay horse. Yet it was the woman herself who caught Saffron's attention. Not only was she the first white person she'd seen on this side of the portal, but her blonde hair was uncovered, bound in the same sort of complex braids that Pix had worn. The only difference was that where Pix had four braids long enough to touch her back, this woman had an uneven three – one on the right side, two on the left – that were so short they barely reached past her jaw.

Saffron raised a hand to her head, momentarily heedless of the danger to her taal. Had Gwen lied to her? This woman's hair was neither shaved nor covered, and she was clearly someone important. Perhaps the Vekshi had changed, and Gwen had been mistaken.

As the woman and her escort came closer, the rest of the crowd pulled back to a respectful distance, silent after their initial shouts. Gracefully, the woman dismounted, handed the reins of her bay to the nearest blue-robed man, and approached the fountain on foot. Like so many people here, she wore a taal, but where theirs were cheerful and casual, hers was opulent. The material of it shone like silk, coloured a deep red that rippled gold in the fading sunlight, and it was so long that it trailed along the ground like a bride's gown. Cinched at the waist, it was carefully belted with a ring of overlapping metal discs not dissimilar to the one Pix wore, but golden rather than bronze, and studded with red stones. The woman's feet were bare, and when she reached the fountain, she knelt.

The entire square fell silent. Saffron was transfixed as any local, unable to look away. From somewhere within the folds of her taal, the woman pulled out a knife. She began to speak, her voice melodious and strong, though the words themselves remained utterly foreign. Hefting the knife, she began to cut a tiny lock of hair from each of her braids, murmuring what sounded like a benediction as she dropped the golden threads into the water. Having done this, she held up her arms as if in prayer, and Saffron instantly understood two things: firstly, that the woman meant to cut herself as part of whatever ritual she was undertaking; and secondly, that she was missing the two smallest fingers on her left hand.

Entranced, Saffron watched as the woman moved the knife closer to her arm, feeling intensely relieved that she hadn't drunk from the fountain after all.

But just as she touched the blade to her skin, the woman looked out across the square and stopped mid-chant, her eyes widening at some sight or other. Slowly, she pulled the blade away and stood, walking around the fountain to get a better look. Behind her, the men of her escort began to glance and murmur amongst themselves, evidently puzzled by their mistress's behaviour. Saffron looked left and right, curiously trying to catch a glimpse of whatever oddity had caught the woman's attention.

It wasn't until the crowd fell back that she realised it was her.

Zech ran through the city, her sharp eyes peeled for a foreign girl foolish enough to wear her hair like a priestess of Ashasa. Several times, she paused to ask if anyone had seen a Vekshi girl run by, and was finally rewarded when a middle-aged stallholder answered in the affirmative. Her elation died, however, when he pointed her towards the Square of Gods. Thanking him, she ran off at top speed, all while panting the foulest words she knew – and as she'd learned at Yasha's knee, that made them foul indeed.

Don't let it be today, she pleaded, her inner thoughts contrasting with her spoken oaths. *Ashasa and Sahu, don't let it be today!*

But the gods evidently had other plans. Not only *was* the ceremony happening today, but Zech was too late to stop the foreigner getting caught in the middle of it. Squirming her way through the crowd, she was just in time to see no less a woman than the Vex'Mara Kadeja hauling a civilian girl into the open.

"Thorns and godshit!" she whispered, Gwen's description

in no way having prepared her for the full reality of the situation. Saffron was barely dressed, her taal in such disarray it was a miracle it hadn't fallen off completely. She looked utterly terrified, though doubtless she had no idea how appropriate her reaction really was. At least ignorance bestowed on her the good sense not to struggle; though clearly straining against the Vex'Mara's hold, she neither screamed nor twisted, which was the only mercy on offer in such a hideous situation.

"The Mother Sun is speaking, truly!" Kadeja announced, a sharp smile playing at her lips. "Who are you to walk without penitence in Ashasa's sight? Speak!"

At Saffron's silence, the Vex'Mara pursed her lips and repeated her command in Vekshi – unaware, as Zech was not, that the hapless girl couldn't speak a word of either tongue. When Saffron shook her head, her mouth firmly shut, Kadeja grew furious, slapping her first across one cheek, then the other.

"*Speak!*"

Zech felt frantic. Her job was to bring the foreigner back to the compound, but how could she stand up to the Vex'Mara? Not even the temples were that brave! But Yasha had boasted of her skills to Gwen; they were counting on her to bring the girl, and there was no time to run back home and ask for help. As Kadeja shook and slapped her captive before the mute crowd, Zech summoned all her courage and stepped forward. Shaking in every limb, she made the proper obeisance due a woman of the Vex'Mara's rank and knelt, her outstretched hands turned palm-up and crossed at the wrist. "Most noble and exalted Vex'Mara Kadeja, I beg you to show mercy to my cousin."

Kadeja paused, her free hand raised for another blow. Coolly, she dropped her arm and looked at Zech, though if anything, her grip on Saffron had tightened. Her eyes widened as she took in Zech's appearance – not even the Vex'Mara was immune to the novelty of her calico colouring – then narrowed again as she spoke, her Vekshi accent turning the Kenan syllables harsh. "She will not speak. She disrespects her betters and our Mother Sun. Why should I show her mercy?"

Zech licked her lips, desperately trying to concoct a lie. "My cousin is… is moonstruck, Vex'Mara, and newly arrived in Karavos. Her aunts and mother let her run wild – she doesn't understand any proper tongue, nor why her hair should be cut, and when we raised a blade to shear it, she ran. She is… very stupid," she finished lamely, her usual eloquence subsumed by fear.

And yet – and yet! – the Vex'Mara's grip on Saffron's arm was loosening. "I see," she said softly, and Zech felt weak with relief. She'd done it; she'd talked Kadeja down! "But moonstruck or not, it behooves us all to honour the goddess. Your cousin ran from your mother's blade; she will not run from mine."

Zech's veins turned to ice. Saffron was staring at her desperately, hopefully, unable to know what was being said yet understanding, at least, that Zech had stopped her from being beaten.

"Come with me," Kadeja said, and if her words meant nothing to Saffron, the gentleness with which she tugged her arm was a form of translation. Still uncertain, the foreigner obeyed, kneeling by the fountain like a penitent. Her strange green eyes were expectant and wary.

"I have been given a sign," the Vex'Mara announced, loud enough for the whole square to hear. "I came here today to pray for unity in our realm, but Ashasa tells me we are already united, that I need not shed my own blood for her sake. Instead, she has sent me this child. A gift from the Mother Sun should never be refused."

Reaching inside her taal, she pulled out a ritual knife – the same one she must have carried before the temple disowned her. Zech marvelled that they'd let her take it; but then the stories said Kadeja had always been a hard woman to cross, even before she bound herself to Vex Leoden in the *mahu'kedet,* the many-partnered marriage of Kena.

Letting go of Saffron's arm, the Vex'Mara used that hand to bend her head forwards. Visibly trembling, the foreigner obeyed, submitting as Kadeja gripped the tail of her hair and cut it off, dropping the whole lock into the water. Though Saffron's body stiffened, she relaxed a moment later, signaling that she understood this, at least: that Kadeja would not let her keep her hair. *And even if the Vex'Mara didn't take it, Yasha certainly would have.* The silence of the crowd was eerie and unbelievable, a hundred or more people watching as Kadeja shaved the girl's head down to a fine gold stubble. She was oddly tender in her work, even wetting the blade in the fountain to lessen Saffron's pain, though Zech put this down more to her temple-taught habits than any innate kindness. The whole process took only a few minutes, and when every scrap of hair had been gathered up and dropped in the fountain, Kadeja cupped Saffron's chin in her hand and kissed the girl lightly between the eyes, the way a priestess would.

"Our light is Ashasa's light," she said, straightening. Saffron moved to step away, but Kadeja set her free hand on her shoulder, pressing down until the girl knelt obediently before the fountain. The Vex'Mara knelt in turn on Saffron's left, then reached out and rearranged the foreigner's hands, so that they rested palm down on the fountain's edge.

Throughout this performance, Zech had been tense – but it wasn't until Kadeja pinned Saffron's left wrist firmly in place that she realised the enormity of what was happening. She opened her mouth to shout, but the sound froze in her throat. As a priestess, the Vex'Mara had learned to wield her knife in many ways, and despite her choices, no one could ever claim she'd lacked talent.

"Balance my sins with hers," Kadeja murmured, softly enough that only Zech could have heard it.

And then, so fast it was like watching a snake strike, the Vex'Mara severed the two smallest fingers of Saffron's left hand.

5

Walking Wounded

Pain filled her, it defined her, there was nothing but pain so savage it was like having the very roots of her ripped free. Saffron screamed and screamed, wrenching her hand back, but it was too late. The woman who'd been holding her pulled away, leaving her to clutch at the wrist of her bloody hand, screaming even harder as she understood the extent of the mutilation. She stared, gaping, as the woman dropped her severed fingers – *her fingers!* – into the fountain, with no more expression on her face than if it were only hair. Bile beat out the air in her throat, and Saffron had just enough time to lurch sideways before vomiting violently onto the ground.

How could anything hurt so much? Her stomach wrung itself in knots. She gagged and retched, coughing up every last scrap of food she'd eaten since breakfast – food from another world, a safe world, a world that no longer existed, all of it drowned out by this terrible throbbing pain that threatened to break her in pieces. Unable to brace on her hands, she fell backwards against the fountain edge, panting and crying, the acid still hot in her mouth. The woman and her entourage were leaving, she distantly noticed. The crowd was starting to stir again, going about its business as night fell. The air was cool, the last light silver against the blue, so that her dripping blood gleamed purple-black.

Someone crouched down beside her. Saffron shrieked and pushed herself away, unable to feel the hurt in her back and shoulders over the agonising throb of her missing fingers. It was the kid, a part of her thought distantly, the skinny – boy? – who'd said… something. She didn't know what. At the time, she'd thought it was in her favour, but given what had happened next, it no longer felt so likely. But there was sympathy in the child's pale eyes, and when he reached out and rested a palm on Saffron's cheek, the contact was gentle and soothing.

And then, just as quickly, it turned electric; not an unpleasant jolt, but a fizzing, tickling sensation, as though she were standing near a current without actually touching it. Pulling back, the kid indicated himself and spoke.

"Zech." The same hand pointed at Saffron. "Sa'ferryn." And then, to her absolute astonishment, a third intelligible word: "*Follow.*"

Comprehension was a tiny miracle, and yet it was significant enough that despite everything – her lost fingers, her shaved head and every other disorientation the day had brought – she laughed. The sound came out shallow and twisted, but it was laughter nonetheless, and when Zech stood up, somehow Saffron found the strength to copy.

Darkness was coming fast now, and falling had dizzied her even before she'd had to contend with slaps and blood loss. She swayed on her feet, staring numbly into the fountain. Her severed fingers lay on the bottom like a pair of weird fish, still leaking thin ribbons of blood into the water. The thought of reaching in to claim them was repulsive. Only then did she notice she was still holding her wrist out in front of her, as though offering her mutilated hand to whoever would take it. She turned to Zech, but despite his youth, the boy didn't flinch.

"Follow," he repeated. The word sounded funny, and suddenly Saffron knew why.

He wasn't speaking English. And yet, she'd understood.

Saffron stared. Was this magic, then – a fleeting touch

that somehow made languages bleed together? She couldn't move, paralysed as much by this fact as her throbbing hand.

Zech sighed, approached her cautiously, then slipped a skinny arm around her waist. It was pathetically comforting.

"I can't do this," Saffron said. Her voice cracked like an old woman's. "Mum. I want my mum. I want to go home. I can't do this."

"Walk," said Zech. It wasn't quite a plea. For the first time, Saffron looked down and saw there were tears on the kid's cheeks. "We walk. Just walk. Be... *OK*."

The last word was in English. Presumably, whatever magic allowed them to understand one another went both ways. And so, because there was nothing else she could do, Saffron walked.

Gwen glared at Yasha, for all the good it did. Having brought her to Trishka's rooms, the matriarch now stood guard on the door, refusing to let her leave. So far, only two people had been allowed in: a young child, running to tell them that Pix had returned, and then, a few minutes later, Pix herself, dishevelled yet triumphant. Her smile had vanished, however, on hearing what had happened to Saffron – and not just because the girl had fallen. Only then did Yasha reveal what everyone else in the compound already knew: that every morning for the past week, Vex'Mara Kadeja, fallen priestess of the Vekshi goddess Ashasa and now the foremost consort of Vex Leoden, had read the omens, seeking the proper day to make a dusk offering to Ashasa in the Square of Gods. That she'd declared her intentions openly beforehand was an act of breathtaking heresy, almost equal in kind to her choice of venue. Though situated in the Warren, the holy fountain in the Square of Gods was no less sacred to the Kenan pantheon than if it had been part of the palace temple.

Of course, none of them had any way of knowing if today

had been that day – not until Zech returned, at any rate – but as soon as Yasha spoke, Gwen knew in her bones that it was, of *course* it was, because the Many as she understood it was incapable of working any other way. Kadeja's decision to worship Ashasa in the Square of Gods was roughly equivalent to the Queen of England holding a full Christian mass in the Dome of the Rock. What else would happen, but that her charge be caught up in events she couldn't possibly understand?

"Why didn't you *tell* me?" Gwen asked Pix, her voice low and dangerous.

Pix flushed. "Would it have changed anything if I had? It was out of our hands. You didn't need another reason to worry about the girl."

"Yes," said Gwen, through gritted teeth, "but if you'd told me Kadeja was planning a jaunt to the Square of Gods, I might have ridden a different route to avoid it!"

"Enough!" snapped Yasha, thumping her staff on the floor. "We'll know soon enough what's happened."

Gwen bit back a retort, knowing the old woman was correct, but not liking it. She glanced at the bed, where an exhausted Trishka slept in a swaddle of blankets. Though she'd woken briefly to greet Gwen, she'd subsequently lapsed back into sleep. The power needed to open portals between worlds was considerable even before you factored in Trishka's physical frailties, and while Yasha made periodic attempts to dissuade her daughter from overexertion, it was only a formality. Trishka's magic demanded use, and after her one disastrous attempt at suppression all those years ago, there was no question of her repeating it.

A wild thumping on the door disrupted Gwen's reverie. Yasha responded at once, revealing the same messenger boy who'd previously announced Pix.

"They're back!" he said, but there was a gulp to his words. "They're... Zech said I should run for one of Teket's Kin."

"Do it," Yasha said. Nodding fearfully, the boy vanished,

leaving Gwen's imagination to conjure up all the very worst reasons why Saffron might need a healer.

Without another word, Gwen, Pix and Yasha left the room, hurrying down the hall and out into the courtyard. They were just in time to see the gates pulled close behind a haggard-looking Zech, who was barely managing to keep Saffron upright.

"Lights!" Yasha roared, and several onlookers scrambled to obey, their features obscured in the evening blue. But Gwen's eyes were sharp as ever, and despite the darkness, she saw what the matriarch could not: that Vex'Mara Kadeja had found her precious omen in Saffron Coulter.

"Gods be good," she whispered, and ran to them. Saffron was dead on her feet, clutching her left arm sideways across her body. Her taal hung awkwardly from her hips, forcing her to stumble over its hem. Her head was shaved, and her hand was bloody.

"Got her," Zech croaked, staggering back as Gwen put an arm around Saffron's waist and lifted her up. The girl was deadweight, but not yet unconscious; she whimpered at the contact, still clutching her maimed hand. Despite the urgency of the situation, Gwen nonetheless made a point of catching Zech's gaze.

"Thank you," she said. The child sagged with relief. "You've done well. I won't forget it, and nor will anyone else."

Zech nodded, rubbing her eyes with the back of a hand. "Can I sit with her?" she asked. "I used the zuymet. We understand each other a little."

Gwen managed a weak smile. "Come. I'll be glad of the company."

Belatedly, the lights came on: a series of round globes situated at intervals along the compound wall, made luminous by magic. Gwen turned, Saffron heavy in her arms, and saw the expressions on Yasha and Pix's faces as they realised what had happened.

"Use the room next to mine," said Pix, her face ashen. "It has the best light."

"I plan to." Gwen strode past, Zechalia trotting at her heels, and felt a flash of bitter satisfaction that Yasha, for once, was rendered speechless. Climbing the steps to the veranda was a challenge. Saffron's weight put an extra strain on her hips and knees, but she managed it all the same.

"You go ahead and open the doors," she grunted to Zech, and despite her obvious exhaustion, the girl was quick to obey.

Once in the room, she deposited Saffron gently on the bed. Zech hovered in the doorway, her eyes darting from Gwen to the single chair and back again. Gwen gave a bark of laughter.

"Take it, girl. I've things to do."

As Zech sank onto the chair with sheepish gratitude, Gwen knelt carefully by Saffron's side and proceeded, with as much tenderness as she could muster, to remove the bedraggled taal. It was tricky work – Pix had done a good job securing it, which was the only reason it hadn't fallen off entirely. She'd just managed to wrestle the last corner out from under Saffron's prone body when Yasha and Pix arrived, the latter bearing a bowl of warm water and a washcloth, the former only a scowl. On seeing the matriarch, Zech instantly leapt to her feet and proffered the chair, but Yasha declined with a wave of her hand. Folding the taal into a neat, bloody square, Gwen passed it to Pix in exchange for the water.

"I boiled it with alcohol," Pix said. "It's clean."

Gwen nodded absently. "If you can hear me," she murmured to Saffron, moistening the cloth, "I'm going to clean your hand now. All right, girl? This will sting, but there's no helping it."

Saffron stirred a little, though her eyes remained closed. Her creamy school blouse was stained with red. Gently, Gwen lifted the injured hand and began to dab away the blood, first from the surrounding skin and then, finally, from the stumps themselves. Saffron shuddered, but didn't scream – presumably, she'd already exhausted that response. It was an ugly sight, though at least Kadeja had made a clean job of it. Nothing remained but ragged flesh and the gleam of knuckle, the proximal phalanges completely severed from the metacarpals.

"How long before the priest arrives?" she asked.

"He'll be quick enough," Yasha answered. "Teket's Kin know us here."

Old pain tinged her voice, and Gwen couldn't help but share it. None of them were sure whether Trishka's weakness was caused or simply exacerbated by her magic, but whatever the case, the *sevikmet* couldn't heal it, and though Gwen had done some research on Earth, she was yet to uncover anything to work as either mitigation or cure. Fibromyalgia was the closest thing she'd found to a comparable condition, and it was still so poorly understood that, even without the added complication of Trishka's magic, they were both leery of using it as a starting point.

Now, as she set her cloth aside, she found herself hoping that Saffron and Trishka might have occasion to talk, once they'd both recovered; and once Saffron had learned to speak Kenan through the zuymet, of course. Teket's Kin could no more regrow Saffron's missing fingers than Earth's leading scientists could render Trishka pain-free and healthy. Accepting what she'd lost would be hard for Saffron, Gwen knew – not just because of the circumstances under which it had happened, but because of what it would mean for her eventual return home.

But all that was a way off yet, and beyond her power to control. Until then she knelt at Saffron's bedside, and waited for the priest.

Zech was weary in her bones. Though possessed of a strong stomach, she'd nonetheless been shaken by the sight of Saffron's ruined hand. Using the zuymet and then carrying the older girl home had tired her too; every muscle ached as though she'd spent the whole day at staff practice. Sleep would come easily, if she let it. And yet she stubbornly stayed awake, curled up on her chair and watching as the purple-robed priest used his magic to close Saffron's wound. Gwen stood beside her, concern evident in the way her hand would suddenly grip Zech's shoulder, but she needn't have worried. Though he looked more like a warrior, the priest was nonetheless a gentle, practiced healer. Thanks to her own small talents, Zech could feel his magic, the sevikmet, as a vibration in the air; could even see it a little, as though a blue mist were seeping into Saffron from his hands.

Finally, after what felt like an hour but was probably much less, the priest straightened.

"It's done," he said, his dark skin glistening with sweat. "The wound is closed and free of infection. She had some other hurts too – I've eased them as best I can. When she wakes, tell her the stumps will be tender for a week or so, but that it shouldn't prevent her from using the hand, particularly not once the new skin starts to toughen. In the long term, only her grip will be truly affected by the loss – she won't be able to fight like she used to."

Zech was so worn out, it took her a moment to grasp that he thought Saffron was Vekshi too, raised to wield a staff as all their women were. *If she were one of us*, Zech thought, *she'd either have to switch to a heretic staff, or else wield a child's staff one-handed. Her whole fighting style would have to change.*

All of a sudden, Zech was gripped by horrible, crippling guilt. What if she'd told a different lie to Kadeja, one that hadn't made Saffron out to be Vekshi? Would the Vex'Mara still have taken her fingers?

Gwen, who had been in the middle of thanking the priest for his services, broke off mid-sentence and looked at her.

"Zech? What is it?"

"My fault." She could barely force the words out, tears

slipping down her cheeks. "I told the Vex'Mara that Saffron was Vekshi. I called her cousin. If I hadn't done that, she wouldn't have held her to Ashasa's law. It's my fault!"

"She's not Vekshi?" the priest asked, but that only made Zech cry harder. *I should have waited until he was gone!*

Gwen didn't answer him. Instead, she crouched down in front of Zech and pulled the girl into a hug.

"Hush," she murmured, stroking her hair. "None of this was your fault. Kadeja is what she is, we both know that. Nothing would have changed if you'd told her the truth, except that she might have questioned you about where Saffron came from. And who would that have helped, hmm?"

As quickly as they'd come, Zech felt her tears dry up. Nodding into Gwen's shoulder, she took one last shaky breath and calmed herself.

"Apologies," she said, though the guilt still rattled inside her. "I was overset."

"We're all overset tonight," Gwen said, straightening once more. Even the priest smiled, and of course Saffron's secret was safe with him. Didn't Teket's Kin take vows to keep the confidence of those they healed?

Cupping his hands respectfully to Gwen – and then repeating the gesture for Zech's benefit, such a cheeky deference that she giggled despite herself – the priest signalled his intent to leave.

"Send for me if anything else happens," he said, "but Teket willing, it shouldn't be necessary."

"Gods watch over us," Gwen answered graciously.

But no sooner had he left the room than Gwen sagged, as though her strength had suddenly run out, and when Zech offered her the chair, she took it wordlessly. When she spoke, her eyes never left Saffron.

"Tomorrow, you'll need to tell us all what happened in the Square of Gods. Everything you can remember. Try not to talk about it until then – the more often you tell a story

like that, the more likely you are to exaggerate the details."
She paused. "It would be best if you slept tonight in your
own room. I'll need to speak to Saffron when she wakes.
Alone."

"Of course," said Zech, though in truth she felt a little
deflated.

"Good girl. Don't worry, though. I'm sure you'll have
time enough to meet her when she's recovered." Finally,
she looked up. "Tell Pix and Yasha I'm sleeping here, would
you? And if either one wants to hash this out now, you keep
quiet and send them straight to me."

Zech was torn. She wanted to stay with Saffron – it was
one of the consequences of using the zuymet – but when
Gwen yawned, she forced herself to nod and exit, shutting
the door behind her.

6
Catching Up

Saffron squirmed through a sea of uncomfortable dreams, each one more disquieting than the last. Long-haired velociraptors chased her down a series of unfamiliar hallways, getting closer and closer until she tumbled into a fountain. Gasping, she swam through a portal at the bottom of the sea, but when she hauled herself out on the other side, her mother was there, saying that she'd ruined her academic career and needed to be declawed. Saffron tried to explain that there'd been a mistake – it was Beastie the kitten they wanted to declaw, she didn't even *have* claws, but her mother just smiled and took her into the garage. The rest of her family was lined up and waiting for her, their faces solemn. Saffron began to beg and plead. She tried to run away, but then her father grabbed her, pinning her hand to the hood of the car, murmuring to *be a good girl, Saff, hold still,* and all while her mother advanced on them with a pair of pliers. The cold metal clamped down on the two smallest fingers of her left hand. Her mother started to pull – "They've got to come out!" – and even though Saffron tried to scream, instead she was choking, unable to say a word. With a sickening wrench, her fingers popped free like deciduous lizard tails, twitching and writhing on the car bonnet. Still gagging, Saffron turned around to confront her parents, only to find that both had vanished; instead, there was only Gwen, watching her with sad, apologetic eyes.

She'd woken up. Gwen really was present, sitting opposite Saffron in a cushioned wicker chair. Still foggy, she didn't immediately understand what had happened or where she was. She was in an unfamiliar room, the walls and floor both painted stucco white, though the latter was covered by a faded red carpet patterned with geometric designs. A low, square window covered with wooden shutters let in glimmers of daylight. Seeing that, Saffron felt a lurch of panic. How long had she been asleep? Had a whole night passed? In a wash of fear and pain, her memory came flooding back, bringing with it a new, strange tingling in her left hand.

"No," she whispered, not wanting to look, knowing she had to. Sitting upright, she pulled her hands out from underneath the rough blanket and laid them in front of her, unwilling to believe the evidence of her eyes. The two smallest fingers on her left hand were gone, the skin healed over as pink and seamless as if they'd never existed. And yet she could still feel them there, a phantom twitching so strong that when she closed her eyes, it was as though nothing had changed. But it had; she'd seen her fingers sink in the fountain, remembered the blinding agony as the smiling woman had severed them with her knife, a series of quick cuts to the joint, efficient as a butcher. Then she raised her right hand to her head, and felt what else she'd lost: her hair, reduced now to nothing more than stubble. That, too, was bizarre, though in a different way. Her whole head felt naked, each turn of her neck too quick and light without the familiar weight. She kept on reaching up to reflexively brush the strands away, startling when her fingers hit flesh instead.

Her uniform was covered with blood. She was sore – though surprisingly not too sore – and covered with yesterday's sweat.

Only her shoes had been removed, the black Clarks eerily normal where they'd been placed by the bedside. A strangled noise that was neither a sob nor laughter lodged in her throat. Saffron stared at her hands, at her missing fingers, and remembered dimly the feeling of magic flowing through her: a foreign, fizzing sensation, not quite unpleasant, yet certainly not comfortable, that had knitted her skin together. She found herself wondering how long a wound like hers would take to heal on Earth, in the care of doctors. *Weeks at the very least–*

The implications hit her like rough surf.

Saffron turned and looked at Gwen, not trusting herself to speak. The older woman's face was lined with exhaustion, her hair in disarray.

"How long…" She gulped back the question, shying away from the hardest question. "How long have I been asleep?"

"Just one night," said Gwen, unable to disguise the heaviness in her voice. "Do you remember Zech bringing you back here?"

Saffron thought of a skinny boy with gentle eyes and strong arms. "Yes. I remember him."

Almost, Gwen managed a smile. "Not him. Her. Zechalia's a girl."

"Oh." For some reason, this simple fact made her want to laugh. Instead, she found herself saying, "My parents will be worried. I told my sister I'd catch her up, but that was hours ago. They'll think that something's happened to me."

"Hasn't it?" Gwen asked, softly.

Saffron felt her throat constrict. *Don't cry,* she told herself, but it was easier said than done. She knew what was coming. She stared at her hands, wanting to knot them together for comfort's sake, but was too repulsed by the sight of her missing fingers. Sooner or later, she'd find the courage to touch the stumps, the impossibly well-healed skin, but not now. Not yet.

"I can't go home, can I."

It wasn't a question. Across the room, Gwen sighed.

"No," she said, after a moment. "Not for a while yet, anyway. There'd be too many questions about how your hand had managed to heal so fast, let alone how it even happened."

"Couldn't the magic just grow my fingers back?" She hated the desperation in her voice. "I mean, it's *magic*, right? Why only heal the stumps?"

"Healing magic – sevikmet – is miraculous in many ways, but it still has its limits. Most of the time, it does nothing more than what your body would do on its own, only faster – and bodies don't regrow fingers."

"Most of the time?"

"There are some few exceptions," Gwen admitted, "but they don't apply to you. And even if you could somehow convince the temple to try, you don't get something like that for nothing, and not without risk. When the priest healed you, he used your strength, your physical reserves, to speed a process your body would've undertaken on its own – he didn't try to undo what was done."

Saffron frowned, confused. "The magic came from me?"

"No, no. The magic was his. Think of it…" Gwen paused, chewing her lip. "Think of it like this: if the priest was a woodworker, his magic would be the blade he used, and your body the wood he carved. No matter how sharp the knife, he can only use it to cut what's there, not make more of it. The wood is finite. The crafter must work with what he has." She paused. "Most of the time, anyway. It's a tricky business. The point being, unless you sacrifice something else – and unless we could find a temple willing to heal what would, in their eyes, be a minor hurt – your fingers aren't coming back."

"Oh," she said again. Silence fell, and in the space between heartbeats, Saffron realised she was crying.

"Forgive me," Gwen said, softly. "This is my fault. I was…

At your school, I intervened. Incautiously so. I should have just left you alone."

"It's not your fault," said Saffron, rubbing her eyes with her good hand. "You didn't bring me here. I'm the one who came after you, who jumped through a random portal." But what did it matter? Her fingers were *gone*, they weren't coming back even by magic, and her parents must be worried and there were multiple worlds and she didn't know what to feel anymore, and so she just cried and sat there while Gwen rested a hand on her shoulder and said, "It's all right, girl. It's all right."

"Would it have made a difference?" Saffron asked, when the tears had finally stopped. "If that woman hadn't... if I hadn't lost the fingers, I mean, if I never fell, and we'd come straight here instead, could I have just gone back home?"

"Not right away," said Gwen. "I told you before that Trishka, who makes the portals, isn't physically strong. Opening one drains her for days, sometimes weeks afterwards, and even if it didn't, we'd have to find a new portal point, somewhere outside the city walls."

Oddly, Saffron wasn't upset to hear it. But then, she supposed, it would have been a thousand times worse if the only reason she'd lost her fingers and couldn't go home was because she didn't know how to ride an alien animal. That thought really did make her laugh, the sound bubbling out beyond her ability to control it. Her family would be worried sick. Mum, dad, Ruby – they'd all be terrified that something horrific had happened to her, and the very worst thing was, it had.

But so had something wonderful: she was in a different world. And even now, with her phantom fingers aching against the blanket, she couldn't quite make herself believe that the horror of it outweighed the marvels.

"There's nothing I can do." She'd spoken aloud without meaning to, and yet the words had a calming effect. She turned to Gwen. "There really isn't, is there?"

The older woman relaxed a little. "No, there's not." She paused. "So. Do you want to know what it is I'm doing here?"

Saffron straightened. "Tell me."

Gwen folded her hands in her lap, resisting the urge to fidget. "For the sake of clarity," she said, meaning, *I don't know how to tell this story, so one beginning's as good as another,* "you ought to know, this isn't the only other world besides Earth. It's a multiverse out there. I call it the Many, from manifold, and over the years, I've seen a little of it–" Saffron's eyes widened pleasingly at that, "–but Kena is where I came first, and Kena is where I live. It's flawed, like I told you yesterday, but I love it here.

"Now, maybe there's a world out there with no magic at all, and that magic can't touch, though if there is, I've never seen it. So far as I can tell, all worlds have at least a little magic, even if it's a secret thing, diminished or misunderstood."

"Like Earth, you mean?"

"Exactly so. But big or little, magic is different everywhere, and here... I told you that I'm a worldwalker?" She made it a question, only continuing when Saffron nodded. "Well, that's an English translation. In Kenan, I'm a *vekenai-asahuda*, which more literally means all-worlds pilgrim. We show up in stories and history, and that gives us a sort of cachet, a novelty, when we appear in real life. Assuming, of course, that whoever you're talking to believes you."

Saffron smiled at that, which was the desired effect. Heartened, Gwen went on. "I mention this, not just because it's something you ought to know – you're a worldwalker now, after all – but because it's a shorthand way of explaining how an outsider came to have any influence at Kena's court. Pix is a noblewoman, a courtier, and once we met, she introduced me around. Not everyone knew where I was from, or believed it if they were told, but enough did that my knowing her gave Pix status, which gave me power in turn. Not much, at first, but after four years moving in those sorts of circles, it accrued."

"How did you meet Pix?" Saffron asked.

"It was Zechalia, actually – the girl who found you last night. She's Vekshi – most of the women in this compound are, though you'll hear more about the why of that later – and when her magic came in... Ah!" Gwen made a frustrated noise and muttered, "I should write you a bloody pamphlet. I'm bound to miss out something important, the rate we're going." And then, in a normal voice, "Right. Well. The Vekshi, among other things, are monotheists. They've got one goddess to Kena's pantheon, but in both cultures, those with magic usually learn from their priests and priestesses, a sort of religious devotion. The thing is, there aren't any Vekshi temples in Karavos, and Yasha – she's our resident matriarch, who runs this place – she didn't want Zech to learn from a Kenan temple, because it would've been heresy. Not," she added, irony shading her tone, "that she's above hypocrisy or even occasional pragmatism in such matters; mostly, she just likes to get her way."

Saffron snorted. "I have an aunt like that."

"So do I," said Gwen. They grinned at each other, sharing a moment of unity, until Gwen waved a hand, determined to get things back on track. "Anyway. There are trained mages outside the temples – kemeta, they're called – though being freelance, they're usually considered a bit disreputable. So Yasha, who wanted the best for Zech, hunted around for one with a bit of a pedigree, and finally stumbled on Matu, who's Pix's brother. Pix decided to vet us on his behalf – because we're not exactly reputable, either – and, well. There you go. Following?"

"Just about," Saffron said, wryly.

Gwen snorted. "Fair enough. At any rate, that's how I came to be at court. How Pix and I ended up involved in the succession debate, though... Well. Partly, it was just proximity. Mostly, I suspect, it's because the whole thing was a nightmare, and we were both, for various reasons, seen as objective parties. We weren't the only ones to throw our hats in the ring, but we're the ones who fucked it all up, so here we are." She paused again, considering what to say next, and steeled herself for the inevitable segue. "Changing the topic not as wildly as you might think, what do you know about polyamory?"

"Um," said Saffron, with a deer-in-headlights look. "That it, um... exists?" And then, frowning slightly, "Wait, do you mean polygamy, or is that something different?"

"Polygamy means one man, many women, and that's not what we're talking about. Polyamory is when multiple people are all in a relationship together, regardless of gender. And Kenan marriage, the mahu'kedet, is fundamentally polyamorous. Usually, you start with a core couple or trio, and then other partners are brought in later, though it works in a lot of different ways. Maybe everyone sleeps together, and maybe only some people do, but any children are raised communally, and every household takes its name from the most prominent member."

"Most prominent?"

"Most powerful or accomplished, and don't think nobody ever argues about it, because they do. If you want more details–" and here she teetered again, on the precipice of admitting her own marriage, "–Pix is the best person to ask. She has two husbands, Araden and Pelos, and a wife, Mayenet. But right now, we're talking about the royal family, and for them, the mahu'kedet has different rules. By design, it's a hierarchy – it's meant to mirror the marriages of the gods, lots of specific affiliations between roles and tiers and deities, but you don't need to know all of that now. What matters is, the children born to the royal mahu'kedet don't necessarily have royal blood, and while most noble families prefer to pick their heirs based on competence, not birthright, it's different for the throne."

"But how do they know whose children are whose?"

asked Saffron, blushing slightly. "I mean, are there rules about, um, about having sex, or–"

"Magic," said Gwen. "It's called *maramet*, the blood-spark. Among other things, it's used to determine paternity, though it's commonly part of healing. A specialisation, rather than a discipline in its own right – but I'm getting off track again." She took a breath. "The point is, the ruler before Vex Leoden – Vex Ralan, his name was – died without either siring an heir or naming one. Killed in his sleep by an aneurysm, no sign of foul play, though you can be sure there was plenty of speculation and panic before Teket's Kin gave their verdict. So: a sudden death, the court in flux, and everyone scrambling to see who'd get the crown. You still with me?"

"I'm with you."

"Good. There were three main contenders: Tevet and Amenet, sisters related to the royal line through their mother, and Leoden, who was Ralan's nephew and born to the mahu'kedet besides. Which made things tricky – Ralan had always favoured Tevet, but Amenet was the elder, and neither sister was likely to step aside for the other without a fight. Which left Leoden, who was younger than both, but had the closer blood claim. Not an ideal situation, to say the least. Factions started forming almost before Ralan was cold, and the way things were headed, the worry was that we'd end up in a civil war. We wanted, Pix and I, to make sure it didn't come to that. The best laid plans of mice and men." She laughed bitterly.

"I won't bore you with the politics of how and why and who helped, but in the end, we came up with a possible solution: if Tevet and Amenet would support Leoden, he'd bring them both into his mahu'kedet as Cuivexa and Vex'Mara – that is, his most powerful marriage-mates. It was Leoden's idea, of course, though he made us think it was ours. There was plenty of negotiating on all sides, but in the end, only Amenet agreed to Leoden's terms. Tevet didn't."

Abruptly, Gwen fell silent, the grief of it lodged in her throat. Saffron watched her, silent and still, and though her lips parted, she didn't ask.

Softly, Gwen said, "When Leoden met with Amenet, he ambushed her. Killed her, and all her faction leaders. Tevet was furious; we offered to stall with negotiations, give her more time for her levies to arrive, but rivals or not, she'd loved her sister. Wanted to avenge her. She tried–" she broke off, laughter jagged at the painful absurdity of it, "–gods, she tried to siege Karavos. It was her forces that broke the walls, but once she was here, she had to try and fight her way through the city. You've seen the streets. It's a maze, uphill, and even if she'd had all her forces, it would've been nigh impossible with Leoden entrenched on the high ground. He picked off her troops on approach, and by the time she reached the palace, all he had to do was circle around and cut off the remainder. It was a massacre. He hung Tevet's body from the walls afterwards." *My fault. My fault.*

She bowed her head, and breathed until she could speak again. "He didn't want the competition, you see? Didn't want to share power. If Leoden had really married Amenet, she was independently loved enough that his rule would have been a constant negotiation. Instead of Tevet, his Cuivexa is a young noble girl from one of his faction's families, and instead of Amenet his Vex'Mara is a former Vekshi priestess, one whose people exiled her for the same heresy she's now determined to spread throughout Kena." Gently, she reached over and tapped the back of Saffron's maimed hand. "You met her yesterday, in the Square of Gods. The Vex'Mara Kadeja. She's the one who took your fingers."

For a long, silent moment, Saffron couldn't breathe. She'd been taking care to follow Gwen's story, trying to get a sense of the situation, but at the mention of Kadeja, everything went blank. She stared at Gwen, dimly aware that she was still talking – something about gods and omens, Vekshi laws and blasphemy – but unable to process any of it. "She cut my fingers," she said, numbly. "She cut my fucking *fingers*!"

She wanted to laugh, or scream, or maybe both. A queen... An *almost*-queen – the Vex'Mara – had cut off her fingers and dropped them in a fountain. How the fuck was anyone meant to process a thing like that?

She was saved from trying to answer by a fortuitous knock at the door. Without looking up, Gwen called out in Kenan, and in came Zech, the skinny girl who'd rescued her. Seen in daylight, her skin looked calico, like a cat's fur: mostly pale, but splotched with varying darker shades in streaks and patches. Her eyes were grey, her face pleasantly androgynous, and her hair – which, weirdly, was also grey – hung raggedly at jaw level. She was small and wiry, dressed in wide-legged pants and a square-necked tunic top, both made of washed blue cloth embroidered around the hems with white vines and flowers. Her feet were bare, and in her hands was a tray of breakfast: strange foods whose thick aroma of yeast and sharp herbs caused Saffron's mouth to water.

She was the perfect distraction. Saffron almost cried with gratitude.

"Good morning," Zech said – in Kenan, Saffron was startled to note, and yet the words were intelligible. Her gaze whipped to Gwen, who smiled and stood up, snagging a strip of flat, pale bread from the tray.

"Zuymet," she said, by way of explanation. Biting into the bread-thing, she chewed and swallowed meditatively, then said, as gently as before, "You're in good hands, and I need to speak with the others. Let Zech teach you some Kenan, and then you can both join us. Until then, stay. Eat. Get cleaned up. I won't be far away."

Almost, Saffron begged her to stay. But then she caught Gwen's gaze, and knew she was being given the chance to digest their conversation in private – or, better still, to pretend it away entirely, at least for a while.

"OK," she said, and forced herself to smile.

Zech waited until Gwen was gone from the room before setting the tray down and dragging the chair over to Saffron's side. Saffron watched her with sharp resignation, as though nothing Zech could do or say would surprise her. Impishly hoping to disprove this attitude, Zech resettled the tray on her own knees, gestured to its contents and said firmly, in the language her magic told her was called English, "Eat."

Much to her satisfaction, Saffron's eyebrows shot up. She started speaking eagerly in the same tongue, but much too quickly for Zech to comprehend. Raising a hand to stop the tirade, she reached out and took the older girl by the hand, letting her magic seep between them.

"Zuymet," she said, and this time, she could tell Saffron understood. Closing her eyes, she concentrated on strengthening last night's connection: a tentative mind-link, poorly built, that had nonetheless fostered trust between them. Matu would be proud of her, she thought, which was the highest praise she could imagine. Though kemeta, he'd once been offered a coveted place with Sahu's Kin – but then, one had only to look at Matu to realise he would've been poorly suited to a life of worship, study and service.

At that thought, Zech's concentration wavered. Nearly a month had passed since Matu had left the compound on some unknown errand for Yasha: his departure had come bare days after Gwen's, and in all that time, Zech had had no word from him. Biting her lip, she steadied her connection with Saffron, then broke it off cleanly.

"That's enough," she said in Kenan. "Do you understand?"

Saffron blinked, then slowly answered in the same language, "Yes, I do. I... wow. I'm really making sense?"

Zech beamed at her. "Yes! That's it. I speak, you speak, the magic moves, and we both understand. It's tricky, though."

"How does it work? What are the, ah, *limitations*?" This last word in English: evidently, Saffron hadn't yet received the Kenan equivalent from Zech's vocabulary.

Zech frowned, trying to remember how Matu had originally explained it to her. "Learning from other people is harder, though still faster than regular learning. But talking to me is different. The more you talk to me, the quicker you learn. Even without the magic, we're linked now. Zechalia and Saffron."

Saffron gave a small shake of her head, but offset it by smiling. "*Saff*-ron," she corrected. "Not Sa-*ferrin*."

Zech tried to copy her, but the syllables sat strangely on her tongue. She called up some of the English words she'd acquired, trying to find others with a similar cadence. *Battle. Lecture. Copycat.* When she tried again, her attempt was closer, but still not right. She pulled a face.

"Safi?" she offered – a compromise. *Saffron* was too long for everyday use, anyway, no matter how you pronounced it.

The older girl laughed. "Safi," she agreed.

Zech grinned. "You say mine now," she instructed. "See if it sounds right."

Safi considered. "Zech," she said at last. "Zechalia."

Gleefully, Zech corrected her. "Soft at the end, not hard."

Safi tried again and again. Even knowing that the zuymet extended only to vocabulary, not accent, there was still something delightful in seeing it proven true.

After her eighth failed attempt, Safi laughed. "Fine! You win." Shyly, she gestured to the breakfast tray and asked in English, "What is all this stuff, anyway?"

With growing happiness, Zech began to tell her.

"She's awake, then?" Yasha asked.

Gwen nodded. "And coping surprisingly well, too –

certainly better than I did the first time. Zech's with her now. As soon as she's all cleaned up, we can hear about Kadeja's latest heresy."

"And won't that be exciting?" Pix said sarcastically.

The three of them were seated around a table in Yasha's wing of the compound, sipping warm cups of *mege*, a Vekshi tea brewed from sweet, caffeinated leaves and soup stock. It was a great favourite among traders and travellers alike, but though Gwen was far from being a convert, she'd gone long enough without a cigarette to appreciate its restorative properties. Beside her, Pix fidgeted in her seat like a miscreant schoolchild. The ex-courtier, for all her airs, felt partially responsible for Saffron's fate, and as Gwen considered this to be a right and proper state of affairs, she was in no hurry to alleviate her guilt. Besides, she had bigger things to worry about. Though the same priest who'd healed Saffron had declared Trishka to be on the mend, she was still confined to bed, her usual chair disquietingly empty.

As, indeed, was Matu's. Though discussion of Kadeja's crimes could certainly wait until after they'd heard Zech's testimony, no such restriction applied to Matu's mysterious absence.

Turning to Pix, Gwen assumed a blank expression. "Speaking of excitement, it's not like your brother to miss any. Where is he?"

Pix made a noise that was half disgust, half anger. "Who knows? I certainly don't. If Yasha deigns to tell me now, it'll only be for your sake, never mind that I've been out of my skin with worry!"

"Enough!" In lieu of thumping her staff, which was propped up against the far wall, Yasha settled for banging her mege cup emphatically on the table, though without, of course, spilling so much as a single drop. "Am I allowed no peace in my own house?" She rolled her eyes, invoking her goddess as witness. "As though Ashasa didn't make men to go wandering! It's unnatural, the way you Kenan women cling to them. No wonder your palace is in such disarray!"

Mercifully, Pix didn't rise to the bait, being long since accustomed to Yasha's outbursts on the subject. Like Gwen, she merely waited for the matriarch to take another sip of mege, smack her lips and then, finally, continue.

"As it so happens, he's running an errand on my behalf." Pix snorted in triumph. Yasha ignored her. "Just after you left, Gwen, one of my little friends–" this being a favourite euphemism for the matriarch's spies, "–suggested I take a closer interest in the goings-on at Kena's northern border. Well, it was vague enough advice that I paid it no mind, even with all that scandal over Kadeja's expulsion. Still, it hardly seemed useful. Such obvious advice!" She waved a hand. "But once that died down, the friend came back to me. He said that someone on the border wanted to speak with Pixeva ore Pixeva, and was willing to try to reach her through me. So of course, I sent Matu instead. That was a month ago."

Pix looked murderous. "Someone on the border wanted to speak with me, and you said nothing? You sent my *brother*?"

"And what if it was a trap?" Yasha asked archly. "You're good with a knife, girl, but Matu is better with many weapons, both sharp and blunt, and unlike you, he has no dependents."

"No legal ones, anyway," Pix muttered. "Honestly, I swear that boy should've been born Vekshi. He's bad as a tomcat."

"High praise indeed!" chortled Yasha.

Pix flushed. "I didn't mean it as a compliment!"

"How sad for you, then, that I take it as one."

"This friend," said Gwen, interjecting before Pix could embarrass herself. "Can I meet them?"

Yasha turned abruptly sombre. "Not unless you can wake the dead. His throat was slit two weeks ago. Whether for what he told me or some other pettiness, I can't say, but dead is dead, and Ashasa alone shall judge him. But Matu should return any day now – it's why we sent for you when we did."

"Is it?" asked Pix, acidly. "Well! I'm glad to know that someone, at least, is worthy of your confidence." With that, she pushed back her chair and stood. "If nothing else, surely I can be trusted to see that our guest is given fresh clothing? If Zech's ever seen the linen cupboard before, I'll cut my braids."

Gwen watched in silence as Pix stormed out. As much as she found Yasha wearying at times, the ex-courtier was no better, always so quick to take offence and quicker still to act, as though she were incapable of remembering that her status had been lost when Leoden took power. But then, Gwen supposed, that was as much her fault as anyone's, which ought to make her more tolerant. It didn't, of course – Pix had been just as exhausting as a courtier, if not more so – but at least then she'd gotten her way often enough to be tolerable.

"Tell me," she said, when Pix's footsteps were no longer audible, "did you really send Matu just because he's a better fighter?"

Yasha snorted with laughter. "Goddess, no! I needed him out from underfoot, and fast. It's one thing him bedding down with Vekshi girls, but Kenan women have no idea how to raise a child without twining themselves round its father and half his friends, and one of the town ladies had started claiming the babe she carried was his. It wasn't, of course – and who is she, to try and spite the maramet so? – but word got about, and several other persons who'd been hoping to snare him in mahu'kedet began to get a bit, shall we say, tempestuous. All a load of nonsense, of course; Pix might not think it, but Matu's sensible enough to have Teket's Kin seal off his fertility until he's ready to use his cock the way Ashasa intended. He's all too lamentably Kenan that way. Honestly! It's enough to drive a sensible woman mad. I'd forgive him, if only he'd give Sashi or Yena a child."

"And I suppose it didn't hurt this plan that Pix was left in the dark?"

"Oh, Gwen. You do me a disservice." Yasha dimpled her cheeks like the sweet old grandmother she sometimes pretended to be, and occasionally even was. "Of course I have every faith in her. But sometimes going without does a body good, as well you know. I was only acting in her own best interests."

Gwen raised an eyebrow. "Intellectual deprivation as a form of self-betterment? You're in danger of turning philosopher on us all."

"I'll thank you not to sully my ears with such talk," said Yasha, taking a dignified sip of mege. "I'm a respectably settled matron."

"Not the words I'd have chosen," said Gwen, "unless, in my absence, *respectably, settled* and *matron* have suddenly become synonymous with *smuggler, spy* and *politically devious expatriate.*"

Yasha *hmph*ed, a disapproving sound entirely at odds with her smug expression. "Young people nowadays," she muttered grandly. "Always prone to exaggeration."

Gwen choked on her drink.

A week ago, if anyone had told Saffron she'd one day be elated at the prospect of bathing in a tin tub full of cold water, she would have assumed they were either drunk or speculating about life after the inevitable zombie apocalypse. Or both, the two states being far from self-contradictory, but either way, she wouldn't have considered it a likely outcome. Now, however, just getting clean felt blissful. Her school clothes were disgusting, streaked with sweat, blood, vomit, dirt and assorted other substances; removing them had felt more like peeling away a full body scab than undressing.

"Are you all right?" asked Zech, her silhouette hovering on the other side of the modesty screen.

"Fine!" Saffron dipped a toe, then lowered herself in so quickly that water slopped over the side. It was a tight fit – she had to sit with her knees sticking up like mountains – but even though the water was cold, it was also bracing. Using a cloth and a piece of pleasantly scented soap, she began to tidy herself up, maintaining the conversation with Zech as she did so. Though still uncertain about how the zuymet really worked, it was undeniable that her Kenan vocabulary was rapidly increasing.

"So," she asked, "what do you do here, anyway?"

"You mean, in the compound?"

"No, I mean generally. Do you, um, go to–" she didn't know the Kenan word, and so substituted the English, "–*school*?"

"School?" Zech echoed. There was a soft thump as she sat down. "Huh. That's odd."

"What is?"

"The word. *School.*" She rolled it on her tongue. "There's nothing quite like that here, but the concept's still in my head." A pause. "You mean, where you're from, everyone spends years in a... a sort of temple thing, only with no magic, and learn lots of things they might not need to know, all so they can go on to *university*–" another English word, "–and do it all again?"

"That's one way of putting it," Saffron said, scrubbing the dirt from her neck. "So what *do* you do, then?"

"Well, I learn how to use my staff. Yasha says all self-respecting Vekshi women need to know that much. Observation, memorisation, tactics – spying skills, you know. And I learn the zuymet and writing from Matu – or at least, I did when he was here. You'll like Matu," she added, almost as an afterthought. "Everyone else does, though Sashi and Yena sulk sometimes that he won't give them babies."

Saffron, who'd been in the middle of washing her face, actually spluttered. "They *what*?"

"*Babies*," Zech said in English, misunderstanding the

problem. "They want his *babies*. Or at least Sashi does; Yena just likes teasing him." Then she paused, as though belatedly assessing Saffron's tone. "Are babies had differently where you're from? Do girls not want them? Am I missing something?"

She sounded so scholarly, Saffron had to fight the urge to laugh. Instead she said, "No, no, we want babies. I mean, we want them *eventually* – or some of us do, anyway. How old are Sashi and Yena?"

"How old are you?" came the pert reply.

"Sixteen."

"They're older, but not by much. Sashi is nineteen, Yena is seventeen."

"And they both want babies," Saffron repeated, just to be sure. "They both want Matu's babies. What is he, a rock star?"

"A *what*?" came the confused reply. "That doesn't make any sense, Safi. Stars are made of fire, not earth."

At that, Saffron really did laugh. "Never mind," she said. Some concepts, apparently, were beyond translation. "I mean, wouldn't they want to marry him first? Or... something?"

"Oh, *that*!" The sound of Zech pulling a face was almost audible, and for an instant Saffron was so reminded of Ruby, who couldn't be more than a year or two older, that her chest constricted with loss. *Don't*, she told herself sharply. *Don't even think about it. Just listen.*

"Vekshi women don't bind themselves," Zech, oblivious, was saying. "Ashasa has no husband, Yasha says, and nor should we. Do your people join in mahu'kedet, then?"

"Not quite. For us, it's just one person at a time – I mean, not everyone actually *does* that, but lots of people still think you should, and that it should only ever be boys with girls, never boy-boy or girl-girl. Lots of people don't agree with that last bit, though, but it's still illegal in lots of places." It felt like a ridiculously infantile way of explaining it, but then she was talking to a grinning tween in a foreign language facilitated by magic, which probably counted as extenuating circumstances.

"You marry like the *Kamne*?" Zech sounded aghast. "But that's barbaric!"

"I guess it is," said Saffron, not wanting to argue, but just as equally disquieted by the possibility that maybe Zech had a point. Lifting herself onto her knees, she took a deep breath and plunged her head underwater, ridding her stubbled head of soap.

"Ah!" she said, coming back up again. "That's better. I'm all done here." She looked ruefully at her filthy clothes. "Is there anything clean I can change into?"

"Oh! I didn't think of that. There's a towel there, anyway – I'll see what I can find!"

"Thanks," said Saffron, but before Zech had even crossed the room, the door opened.

"I see I'm just in time," a woman said. It took Saffron several startled moments to recognise Pix, and that she was speaking Kenan. As her footsteps came closer, Saffron was suddenly overwhelmed by self-consciousness. Almost tripping over the tub in her haste, she hurried to stand and wrap herself in the towel, barely achieving modesty before the other woman poked her head around the edge of the screen.

"Can you understand?" Pix asked, taking care to speak slowly.

"Yes," Saffron gulped, feeling abruptly chilly. Pix was beautiful: somehow, she hadn't quite noticed yesterday. The observation brought a blush to her cheeks and speeded her pulse, but if the other woman noticed, she refrained from comment, instead placing a folded set of clothes by the edge of the screen.

"They should fit," she said. "And there's a..." Her next words were indecipherable. At Saffron's blank expression, she sighed and repeated the phrase to Zech, who translated it into English.

"A bra and underpants," she said, stepping into view. "I might need to help with the bra. Pix says that Gwen says it's not like the ones you're used to. We can wash your old things, though, so it doesn't have to be forever."

"Oh!" If anything, Saffron's blush deepened. "Thank you." She directed this last to Pix, who smiled, bowed, gave a final, incomprehensible instruction to Zech, and then walked out again, shutting the door behind her.

It was strange, Saffron thought, how much she understood while talking to Zech compared to the gaps she'd experienced with Pix. Even so, the rapidity of her comprehension was terrifying. "What else did she say?"

"That after you're dressed, I should bring you to Yasha's quarters," Zech said. "And also to say that if you have your bleeding while you're here, you should go to her for some bloodmoss."

Utter embarrassment warred with pragmatism. After a moment, pragmatism won, though it was a near thing not helped by a morbid curiosity as to what bloodmoss actually *was*.

"I'll do that," she said, awkwardly.

But for all she was disconcerted by Pix's unexpected frankness, she couldn't fault her consideration. The "bra," such as it was, turned out to be little more than a piece of fabric sized to wrap around her breasts, more like a binder than anything else, and without Zech's help, it doubtless would have gone the way of yesterday's taal. The other clothes, however, fit surprisingly well, and with not too much fuss. The loose trousers, called *kettha*, turned out to fasten much like a pair of fisherman's pants, while the tunic-top, called a *dou*, was fitted and slit at the sides from thigh to hip. Unlike Zech's outfit, however, Saffron's had no embroidery: the kettha were a plain dark green, the dou lighter.

"How do I look?" she asked, when she was finished.

Zech grinned. "Like a Vekshi woman. It suits you."

Does it? Saffron wondered. The room had no mirror, and given what she'd seen of the open windows – none of them had glass – she doubted whether asking for one would help. But then she remembered the tub, which, despite the water's distortions, could still show a reflection. Taking a deep, anticipatory breath, she looked down.

A shaven-haired girl with high cheeks and a narrow, stubborn chin stared up at her. Though her clothes were unfamiliar, and her left hand, when she held it out, was undeniably maimed, Saffron was startled by how much the strange reflection looked like her. The shaved head sharpened her features in a way that was almost flattering. The thought was dizzying, and for a moment, she couldn't see anything at all.

"Come on," Zech said, holding out a hand. Saffron took it automatically, her vision returning, and felt a shudder of indescribable relief when the younger girl showed no revulsion at her missing fingers. "We need to go. Yasha's waiting."

"All right," she said.

She didn't look back.

7
Hurt, Not Broken

Yasha, the Vekshi matriarch, wasn't what Saffron had been expecting. From Gwen and Zech's descriptions, she'd been picturing some cackling, bent-backed crone going bald with age, like a stereotypical cartoon witch. Instead, and despite the disconcerting incongruity of a woman in her eighties having a shaved head, she reminded Saffron more of Judi Dench: powerful, self-assured, and sharp enough to skewer with a glance. Though her papery skin was frog-spotted in places and slack with age, the scrape of grey stubble across her skull lent a military sharpness to her features, while her eyes were such a distinctive shade of brown as to be almost topaz. They made her look tigerish, and every time they fixed on her, Saffron gulped.

Thankfully, this wasn't often: like everyone else in the room, Yasha was far more concerned with what had happened the previous evening than with the strange girl in their midst.

Throughout Zech's recitation, Saffron kept in contact with her, feeling her Kenan vocabulary expand at a dizzying pace. It felt as if a balloon of knowledge were being inflated inside her skull: the magic was blizzarding her, not just with words, but with images and feelings too, the combination so overwhelming that she struggled to parse the actual narrative.

Even so, it was impossible to miss either Yasha's near-continuous interjections or the effect they had on Gwen, who was visibly gritting her teeth. If the matriarch noticed this disapprobation, however, she didn't show it, continuing to probe Zech on the makeup of the crowd, the presence of the arakoi, the reactions of nearby stallholders. Mercifully, Yasha remained silent as Zech narrated the loss of her fingers – Saffron shuddered to hear it, fighting off a sudden attack of nausea – and once the tale was told, the room fell silent.

Saffron squeezed Zech's hand, and was relieved to feel her squeeze back: Yasha's scrutiny had left them both trembling. For her part, the matriarch sat back in her chair and scowled.

"I don't like it," she muttered. "All Karavos has been buzzing since yesterday. Whatever my little friends have to say, I'd wager it won't be good."

Gwen nodded agreement. "I don't like that talk of unity in the realm, either – not when Kadeja's the one saying it. Who knows what she means?" She turned to Zech. "You said she was wearing a taal?"

Zech's brow furrowed. "If you could even call it that. It was belted with metal, made of silk–"

"–half lady, half penitent," Pix concluded, not without disgust. "Very nice. Next thing you know, she'll shave half her head and laugh as the courtiers call it fashion."

Saffron looked hesitantly at Gwen. "I don't understand," she said. "Why do her clothes matter? Why shave half her head?"

Gwen answered in Kenan, speaking slowly. "The taal is a commoner's garment. There are lots of different kinds, and if you know how to look for it, they tell you who the wearer is. How they're wrapped, the material they're made of – everything points to class, wealth, status. It's not something a noble would wear unless they wanted to show humility. It means Kadeja went to the Square of Gods as a penitent, trying to show deference to Ashasa. But it was richly made, designed to show her beauty at the same time. The Vex'Mara is vain, girl. She claims still to be a priestess – it's why her hair is uncut – but if she meant true deference..."

Squashing down her fury at the woman, Saffron scoured her own memories. "Before Zech came, she did cut some of her hair and drop it in the fountain. She was going to cut her arm, too, but then she noticed me." *And all while you stood there wondering what she was looking at.*

Pix frowned. "A small penance, but even so–"

A sudden commotion from outside cut her off. Yasha stood instantly, her staff in hand before Saffron could so much as blink. The noise grew louder: voices shouting, the stamp of feet, and the unmistakable whinny of horses. This last surprised her, as the only horse she'd thus far seen belonged to the Vex'Mara – and at that thought, her blood turned icy. *What if she's found me? What if she tracked us here?*

"Everyone with me. Now." Yasha's tone brooked no disobedience.

Saffron walked between Zech and Gwen. The latter flashed her a grim smile.

"This won't concern you," she said in English, "but whatever it turns out to be, you keep with me, just to be on the safe side. All right?"

Saffron nodded, not trusting herself to speak in either language.

Though she'd caught glimpses of people other than Zech, Yasha, Gwen and Pix around the compound, it hadn't prepared her for the reality of how many women – and they were overwhelmingly women – were filing through the hallways and out to the courtyard. Blinking in the daylight, Saffron felt a clench of trepidation. The gates were open, though several children rushed hurriedly to close them, and a pair of snorting, lathered horses pranced awkwardly around a third whose rider had fallen from the saddle, one long leg comically raised where his boot was caught in the stirrup. In the middle of all this, a skinny boy with golden skin and hair like black feathers was struggling and failing to grab hold of the trailing reins, trying not to step on the man in the process.

It was like something out of a pantomime. Yasha made a disgusted noise and clicked her fingers at Zech.

"Go and help that useless master of yours, will you? And Jeiden, too, if his pride will allow it."

Grinning, Zech rushed to obey. She was, Saffron had to admit, quite effective; whereas the boy's quick movements had startled the horses into dancing away from him, Zech approached calmly, grabbed their reins, handed them to the boy – who favoured her with a truly mutinous stare – and then began to free the man's boot from the stirrup.

"Zechalia!" the man called out, lifting his head slightly from the dust. Even to Saffron's unpracticed ear, his words were decidedly slurred. "Good t'see you! Ugh!" As Zech freed his boot, his leg fell down with a thump that further startled his mount.

"Matuhasa idi Naha!" Yasha called angrily. "Get up this instant or I won't be responsible for your sister's actions!"

Perhaps it was a side effect of the zuymet, or maybe she was imagining things, but just at that moment, Saffron would've sworn that Zech's whole body went tense. Too quietly for anyone else to hear, she saw the man say something to his student; then Zech relaxed again, and began the laborious process of trying to haul him upright by his armpits.

Saffron couldn't say later why she chose that moment to walk forwards and help, despite the strangeness of the situation and the fact that Gwen had specifically told her to stay put. But move she did, earning herself a scowl from the boy and a grateful smile from Zech, who quickly made room for her.

"You take his left arm; I'll take his right. On three?"

"On three," Saffron affirmed.

"You're new!" said Matuhasa, squinting up at her. He tried for what was probably meant to be a roguish smile; it looked more like a grimace. "Be gentle with me, will you? I've had a hard ride."

"One," said Zech, favouring him with a stern look.

"You know, I can prob'ly manage on my own, if you'll just let–"

"Two," said Saffron.

"Or not," said Matuhasa. "Remember, be–"

"Three!" said Zech and Saffron, hauling together.

With a drunken half-roar, Matuhasa braced against the ground, pushed backwards, and somehow managed to stagger to his feet. He was so tall that halfway through his straightening up, both Zech and Saffron had to step backwards. Matuhasa staggered, bracing himself against the neck of the nearest horse, which snorted and rolled an eye at this ungainly treatment.

"–gentle. Or not," he muttered, reaching out and ruffling Jeiden's hair. "Good lad. You'll see to the horses?"

"Right away," said Jeiden, his voice stiff with humiliation.

"Good lad," Matuhasa said again, swaying upright and clumsily brushing his hands down his clothes. "Well, then. Let's go, hmm?"

Saffron stared at him, trying to work out if Matuhasa – Matu – was the tallest man she'd ever seen. Either way, he towered at a height of well over six feet, positively dwarfing Zech and Jeiden. For all his loftiness and long arms, however, he had no bulk; Saffron's mother would have called him a tall streak of pump-water. Like Pix, his skin was golden brown, his hair the same glossy black as hers, but where his sister's was worn neatly in braids, Matu's was left to cascade freely down his back and shoulders, long enough to swing above the middle of his back. His face was scruffy and his brown eyes bloodshot, but even so, he was undeniably handsome, sharp-featured and straight-jawed enough for a magazine cover. Besides the boots that had apparently been his downfall, he wore fitted brown pants beneath a short-sleeved black tunic that was both like and unlike the ones worn by Vekshi women.

Kenans might not know what a rock star is, Saffron thought, dazedly, *but that doesn't mean they don't have any*.

As Jeiden sulkily led the horses away, Matu made a faltering gesture of obedience to Yasha, first cupping his outstretched hands, then closing them together.

"You're drunk," said Pix, into the silence that followed.

"Very," Matu replied, still swaying on his feet. His bloodshot gaze slid to Yasha. "But then, I s'pose that's less surprising to some than others."

Now, that's interesting, Gwen thought.

There was a split-second pause before Yasha elected to reassert her authority. "All right! Everyone, back to your chores. What is this, a temple day? Matu's back, and he's drunk, and that's it. Move!"

She emphasised the final word with a habitual thump of her staff. When Matu had the temerity to grin at this, she promptly whacked him about the legs with it, just as she'd done to Gwen the day before. "And you!" Her glower could have melted an iceberg. "Inside now, before you bring further disgrace to that shambling boarding house you Kenans call a family! No offence," she added, presumably for Pix's benefit, but for once the ex-courtier appeared more concerned with her brother's antics than anything the matriarch had to say.

Gwen glanced back at Zech and Saffron, and cursed under her breath to see that both were flushed. Though the younger girl's exhilaration undeniably came from having bested Jeiden in front of the whole compound, Saffron's reddened cheeks were another matter. To say that Gwen was immune to the pleasures of the flesh was inaccurate – her aromanticism by no means precluded her enjoyment of sex, on those (now lamentably rare) occasions when the opportunity of having some presented itself. Nonetheless, she'd grown old enough to appreciate Matu's beauty in a strictly ornamental sense, the way she might similarly admire a well-made sword or a Ming vase. Or so she told herself, anyway; it made things easier. She'd therefore failed to anticipate the effect he might have on Saffron Coulter, even if her first impression of him was as an unshaven wreck who'd fallen off his own horse. *Which isn't like him at all,* she thought, frowning. *So far as I know, he hasn't drunk since–*

Her head jerked up of its own accord. Matu, Pix and Yasha were already heading back inside, but just for an instant, Gwen felt sure she'd seen a flash of triumph in the old woman's eyes. *Surely not,* she thought, but her heart was racing anyway, and as she waved Zech and Saffron over, she forgot to be angry.

"Come with me," she said. Exchanging a glance, the two girls obeyed, flanking her as they headed back inside.

"Gwen?" Zech asked, catching her mood. "What's happening?"

"I don't know yet, but I'm starting to have my suspicions."

One thing was certain: Matu wasn't feigning drunkenness, nor had he been exaggerating its effects. He could barely walk in a straight line, continually trailing a hand on the wall for balance. His black hair swung like a horse's tail – which, if Yasha's assessment of his private life could be believed, wasn't far wrong, assuming the horse in question was a stallion. *Ming vase,* Gwen thought sternly.

When they reached the matriarch's quarters, Matu barged ahead to his usual chair and sat down heavily, resting his head in his hands. He was muttering to himself, and once Pix closed the door behind them, he looked up, and Gwen was startled – and, guiltily, thrilled – to see that he was weeping.

"You vindictive old crow," he said, staring at Yasha. "You knew, didn't you? Why else would you send me?"

Yasha's eyes glittered. "It's true, then? She's alive?"

"She's alive," Matu whispered. "I saw her. Gods forgive me, but I saw her, and I wept, and I've scarce stopped since."

Pix sucked in breath, gripping the edge of the table. Her whole body tensed from hip to shoulder, as though she were made of wood. "Matu, if I'd known–"

"–you'd have sent me anyway. Don't try to pretend otherwise." He swiped a hand fiercely across his face, as though such a gesture were all it took to turn off his grief. "Yasha did you a favour. Now I need only hate her, not you."

"Who's alive?" asked Zech, cutting to the quick of it. Saffron looked equally bemused. All the adults froze, as though even saying the name out loud would bring the wrath of Leoden down upon them. Then:

"Amenet," Matu said softly. Coming from him, it sounded like a prayer, and even though she'd already guessed as much, hearing it confirmed set Gwen's head to spinning.

Saffron blinked. "But isn't she dead?"

"She was," said Matu. "We thought she was, I mean. Everyone did. When she met with Leoden to accept his terms, he poisoned her, killed her guard, then came for her supporters. But whatever she drank didn't kill her. Instead, she woke up three days later outside the city, protected by men and women she'd never seen before. None of them knew who'd saved her – or if they did, they weren't telling. Guards don't have the imagination for long term lies, I've found. One of them said they thought a Shavaktiin had got her out, but that can't have been right."

The mention of the Shavaktiin made Gwen think of Louis; it always did, ever since he'd joined that peculiar order of storytellers and mystics. Not, of course, that anyone in the compound besides Trishka knew of it, or of Louis himself, for that matter. Suppressing a maternal pang, Gwen turned a close eye on Matu, wondering how much she ought to revise her previous assessment of his drunkenness. Maybe anger had sobered him, she thought – or maybe he really was that good an actor. Either way, he didn't slur his words when he spoke of Amenet.

"She's been hiding on the border," he went on, when no one interrupted. "Far enough away from Karavos that no one's looking for her, close enough to hear the news. And from Veksh, too. All the news from Veksh." He lolled his head on his palm and stared at Yasha from a drunkard's angle. "She's heard a lot about Kadeja, you know. Like how the Kenan Vekshi never spoke out against her joining the mahu'kedet."

At that, Yasha at least had the grace to blush. Contrition, however, had never been one of her strong suits. "And what was I to do – endanger everyone under my care for the sake of a dead woman's pride? What exactly has Amenet been doing all this time?"

"Healing," said Matu. "She didn't die from the poison, but it still weakened her. It's taken her almost this long to be able to walk again." He glanced at his sister. "She looked for you, she said, because it's in the nature of snakes to survive the venom of their own species."

"It takes poison to know poison," Pix muttered, but without any real rancour. Gwen rolled her eyes. Back when she'd been resident at old Vex Ralan's court, Pix had been famed for her lack of tact as much as for her beauty – but for all that, her loyalties had always equalled her grudges in strength and number. Amenet was a different creature entirely: political to the bone, yet forgiving; graceful in speech and manner, yet sharp as a sword edge when roused. If only Leoden had possessed a lick of sense, he'd have married her instead of trying to dispose of her; but of course, that would have meant a life of constant scheming against a beloved Vex'Mara, one whose family and allies were strong enough to match him when it came to running the realm. Better to kill her straight up, then marry a woman whose instabilities aligned more closely with his own, and who came unburdened with anything so infuriating as independently-minded allies or blood-kin.

"Sister," Matu said wearily, "please desist from apportioning blame. You know full well Yasha will hit me again if I leave anything out."

"You deserve it either way."

"Probably. Oh, gods." Matu slumped onto his elbows. "It hurt less when I thought she was dead."

"Only in your case, which hardly matters," said Yasha, with typical mercilessness. Somewhat unexpectedly, her gaze then flicked to Gwen. "Well, worldwalker? You're the expert. Tell us what comes next."

Several decades had passed since Gwen was last a student, and yet the matriarch effortlessly made her feel like one. "The obvious option is, replace Leoden with Amenet. He has no heirs yet, legal or otherwise; word is, he hasn't touched that child Cuivexa of his, and Kadeja is his only other consort. But we'd need an army to do that, and thanks to Tevet, there isn't one. Or rather," she said slowly, "not in Kena."

"Go on," said Yasha, as though encouraging a bright pupil who was taking an unexpectedly long time to reach an obvious conclusion.

Gwen stared at her with flat eyes. "You want Amenet to claim the Kenan throne with the help of a Vekshi army?"

"What else is there to do?" Yasha shrugged. "So long as Kadeja is Vex'Mara, the Council of Queens would be fools to sleep easy. Whatever omen she sought yesterday, I guarantee it doesn't augur well for them."

"Omen?" Matu frowned. "What omen?"

Of course he had no idea who Saffron was, what had happened to her, or why she was even here. Doubtless, he'd just thought her another Vekshi expatriate newly come to the compound.

"It's a long story," Gwen said, getting in ahead of Pix. "One you can hear about later."

"Quite." Yasha favoured her with a rare, approving nod. "Until then, we should make plans for our departure."

"What departure?" Saffron looked at Gwen. "I don't understand. Did I miss something?"

Gwen sighed angrily, running a hand over her head. Once Yasha made up her mind, there was no changing it, and yet she mistrusted this turn of events. "We're going to Veksh, girl. First to the border and Amenet, and then to the Council of Queens."

"To raise an army," said Yasha. "And then to orchestrate a coup."

"A coup?" The bitter laugh broke free before Gwen could stop it. "Oh, you'd just love that, wouldn't you? A chance for Veksh to choose who rules her neighbour."

Yasha's glare was cold and hard. "And that would be less hypocritical, I suppose, than you choosing who rules in a world that isn't yours?"

The rebuke stung, but only because there was some truth to it. "I don't pretend to speak for my world," said Gwen, with as much dignity as she could muster, "nor for any country in it."

"And I do?" Yasha's yellow eyes gleamed dangerously. "I live in exile, Gwen Vere. My words have no more sway with the Council of Queens than yours would; less, perhaps, since I have enemies there, and you do not. Kena is my punishment. But perhaps you're right; perhaps I do have aspirations beyond mere penitence. Is that so wrong?" She pushed herself to her feet. "You, at least, may run home when danger threatens. I cannot."

It was a low blow, and Yasha knew it, especially as she'd been the one to suggest Gwen's most recent departure.

That did not, however, keep her from talking into Gwen's stunned silence.

"Leoden will kill this realm. You know it. I know it. The Vex dreams of a new empire, while his Vex'Mara dreams of hybrid gods and heresy with which to rule it. They are scheming, they are traitorous, and they are in power because neither of *you*–" and here she whipped her head to glare momentarily at Pix, "–had sense enough to see through them. Well, as you say, it's a mess that needs fixing. It's a mess you helped to make. But the fixing will be dirty; it will be underhand and bloody, not like those oh-so-glorious days at court when all you did was talk and smile and maybe, if you could spare a moment, think.

"You, worldwalker, you only pretend to live here. With your mouth you say, *Karavos is the city of my heart*, but in your head, you remain an alien creature; you wish to love our world, but only on your terms. Hah! Ashasa forbid you should feel the blood on your hands, or suffer the weight of knowing it won't scrub off. And do you know what? I don't care thorns or godshit for your problems, the big ugly *why* that drives you. But at my table, in my house, if you wish to join our treason, then you will have the simple godslapped courtesy to call it by its name. If I call for a coup, Gwen Vere–" and here Yasha raised her staff, prodding it into the soft flesh of Gwen's throat, "–*you do not contradict me.*"

The whole room held its breath – all except Gwen, who let hers out, slow and steady.

"Kena is your punishment," she said, meeting Yasha's tawny stare. She held her ground, throat pointedly bumping the staff before she pushed it away. "Your words, Yasha. Not mine. You say this isn't my world, that I only pretend to live here – but what are you doing? What is this compound, this piece of Veksh-yet-not that you've built, but a refusal to adapt? The difference between us isn't that I love this place on my terms, where you do not; it's that I *choose* to stay." *I married here. I raised a son, and kept him from your sight.* "But you, Yasha – we both know you'd fly to Veksh in a heartbeat if your exile lifted. You didn't choose this, now or then; you're *relegated*. You want me to call this a coup, then fine. I'll call it a *fucking* coup." She dropped the English swearword with relish, drawing strength from Yasha's scowl. "But don't you point that staff at me like your meddling belongs on a pedestal; as though you share no ownership of this–" she waved an angry hand, unable to find a suitable Kenan invective, and reverted to English again, "–*clusterfuck* and its consequences. Are we agreed?"

A muscle worked in Yasha's jaw. Her answer, when it came, was bitten off.

"Agreed."

Gwen smiled, sharp as flint. "A coup it is, then."

"Come on, Safi. Let's leave them to it."

Nodding queasily, Saffron let Zech lead her out of the kitchen. She'd missed some of Gwen and Yasha's argument, her fledgling comprehension struggling to keep pace with their ire, but what she did understand had rattled her badly. The leashed violence of the exchange had been just as upsetting as the content; with or without the addition of weapons, she wasn't used to shouting adults getting in each other's faces. Her missing fingers throbbed, a phantom ache that left her nauseous.

"Wait."

Saffron froze, though Zech did not. The deep, rough voice belonged to Matu, who'd evidently chosen to leave then as well. He looked dead on his feet, but forestalled Zech's clear desire to help with a weary shake of his head. "No, no. I can manage."

He shadowed them through the hall, a looming, long-haired presence. Saffron tried not to look at him; it would've felt rude, somehow, though she wasn't sure why.

As they turned a corner, Matu overtook them, moving ahead to an unknown door. "Zech," he said, not looking at her, "would you do me a favour?"

"Of course."

"Find Jeiden and make up, will you? No doubt Yasha will insist that you both come north, and it would be easier all round if you make peace before then."

Zech made an exasperated sound. "Is it my fault I'm a better student than he is?"

"No, but you rile him up on purpose, and that I can and will blame you for."

Zech flushed at the rebuke. "Yes, Matu."

"Good. Now leave me be. I need rest."

And with that, he slipped through the door and left them.

Zech sighed, tugging again on Saffron's hand. "Come on, then. You can be my witness."

Saffron made it three more steps before stopping dead. She yanked her hand away from Zech's, her pulse so suddenly thunderous, it was almost audible. Zech stared at her, shocked and worried.

"Safi? What is it?"

Saffron didn't answer. She was shaking, not with fear, but anger. She stared at her mutilated hand and fought an irrational urge to smash it against the wall.

"Fuck everything," she said, almost conversationally. She looked at Zech, who was staring at her, and said it again. "Fuck absolutely everything."

And then she turned and strode away, ignoring Zech's calls to come back. Her bare feet thumped against the floor, propelling her through halls and rooms until, with a sudden flash of light, she broke out into the courtyard.

The sun was warm on her skin, and Saffron was angry. She had so much to be angry about, she couldn't even articulate it, and now it had taken her over. At home, she spent an inordinate amount of time and energy pretending she was fine, crying quietly if she was upset because she'd get in trouble if she yelled, not exploding at Jared Blake so she didn't get detention, tamping down her distress and rage until they festered like ulcers, and now it had all broken open, because there was magic and war and other worlds and *she'd lost her fucking fingers*, and no amount of soothing words was going to make it better.

Saffron clenched her fists and screamed, a loud, raw noise that ripped itself out of her throat like a rupture, startling a flock of strange birds from the wall. Except for when her fingers were cut, she hadn't screamed since she was a kid, and the volume of her newly-healed voice was shocking. She fell silent, feeling the vibrations fade in her throat, trembling all over. She screamed again. It wasn't as loud the second time, and it hurt more, enough that tears pricked her eyes. Dimly, she was aware of Zech watching worriedly from the doorway, but just at that moment, she didn't care.

Jaw set, she headed for the double gates that led out into Karavos. They were massive and metal-banded, made of weathered wood, held shut by a solid crossbar that was almost as tall as Saffron. Opening them would take time and strength, or – more plausibly – the help of another person. Saffron had none of those things, and so she did the best she could, setting her shoulder and palms to the underside of the bar and trying to shove it upwards. It budged only slightly. She swore and tried harder, pain spiking through her neck and sides. The bar raised three full centimetres before her strength gave out; she let go, and it dropped back with a soft, disappointing thud. She hadn't really expected success – and even if she'd managed it, she didn't have anywhere else to go – but it was still frustrating enough that she stepped back and whacked her fist on the wall.

"Let me *out*!" she yelled. Her voice was hoarse with unshed tears. "I have to go! I have to get home! I have to get back to… to…"

Back to what? a snide voice whispered. *Back to Jared Blake and the dozen other boys who aren't quite as bad, but who still think it's OK to snap your bra and text you dick pics and call you a frigid slut if you don't laugh? Back to Mrs Rutherford's lesson plans and condescending vice principals and sleeping three hours a night because the strain of trying to act like there's nothing wrong is giving you insomnia? Back to taking twenty minutes for the class to read aloud something you could've read yourself in three, and knowing your grades will ultimately matter more than whatever you had to memorise to get them?*

She dropped her hand and shut her eyes. *Back to mum and dad and Ruby. Back to my friends, to the people who love me.*

Back to everyone who hasn't seen I'm screaming.

"Safi?"

She turned. Zech stood a few metres away, her features tight with concern.

Saffron bowed her head, the anger gone as quickly as it had come. *I don't have a choice. Not there, not here. No good choices, anyway.*

"It's all right," she said softly. "I just… needed some air, that's all."

Courteously, Zech pretended this to be true. "That's understandable. It gets pretty stuffy inside." She licked her lips, not quite meeting Saffron's gaze. "Actually, I was just thinking – I know Matu said I should talk to Jeiden, but it's not like he's going anywhere, and you haven't met Trishka yet. And I thought it might be a good idea. But if you want to do it, we should go there now, before she goes to sleep."

"Right," said Saffron. "Right."

Shyly, Zech held out a hand. Saffron took it, exhaling as Zech led her back inside. Trishka, she recalled, was Gwen's friend, the woman who made the portals – which meant she was indirectly responsible for Saffron being in Kena. She shied away from the thought, not liking the implications. Seeking distraction, she glanced at Zech and blurted out the first question that came to mind.

"Why isn't your head shaved?"

"What? Oh!" Zech gave a relieved laugh, running a hand through her short grey hair. "Only grown women cut their hair to honour Ashasa, and I haven't had my first bleeding or turned sixteen yet. Whichever one happens first, that's when you start."

"Oh," said Saffron. "That makes sense, I guess." She opened her mouth to ask the other obvious question, but paused, uncertain if it was something she ought to mention at all, or how to do so politely if it was. Zech, however, was clearly well-versed in that particular brand of awkwardness, and took pity on her.

"My skin isn't common, if that's what you're wondering." She shrugged, indicating her calico markings – here white, here black, there brown, there gold – with an unconcerned flick of her fingers. "My hair went grey when I was about three, I think. It was brown before. Who knows? Maybe it'll change back one day. But I was born mottled."

Saffron digested this. "So neither of your parents look like you?"

Zech shrugged. "It's possible, I suppose, though not very likely. I don't know who my father is – which isn't uncommon, in Veksh – but my mother gave me away as a baby, which is."

Saffron blinked in surprise. "She gave you away?"

For the first time, Zech looked discomfited. "In Veksh, to have my skin, it's called being *shasuyakesani* – 'one on whom the sun smiles and frowns.' It means I could be good luck or bad luck, depending on whether Ashasa has marked me as servant or traitor, but not even the temples can agree on which it is, so instead they say it varies from person to person. Either way, it's still meant to make me special, but my mother must've thought I was bad luck, after all."

"Oh," said Saffron. Her cheeks burned with mortified sympathy. "Zech, I'm sorry, I didn't realise–"

"Why would you?" She shrugged. "Don't feel too sorry for me. I like my life. That doesn't mean I can't wonder how it might've turned out otherwise."

A brief silence fell. They turned a corner, entering a part of the compound Saffron didn't recognise.

"Matu isn't usually like that," Zech said, suddenly. She came to a halt, though slowly enough to suggest that it wasn't a conscious decision.

Saffron blinked, stopping beside her. "Like what?"

"Drunk. Sad. Falling off his horse." She looked at Saffron sidelong. "It's because Amenet is still alive. He loved her, you see, back before all this happened, but he could never join with her in the mahu'kedet – Pix was a brilliant courtier, but Matu was useless at it, and even though Amenet loved him too, she was practical enough to see it wouldn't work, even if they belonged to the same rank, which they didn't. Don't." She tilted her head thoughtfully. "If she were Vexa, though, she could just make him her Vexa'Halat, and then it wouldn't matter."

As English lacked an equivalent concept, Saffron ventured her own translation, switching languages in the process. "The, um... vitality husband?"

Zech giggled. "*Vitality husband?* No! It makes him the pretty one, that's all. I mean, it's *meant* to be strength, you know, liveliness, someone who's good breeding stock, but really it just means beautiful. Nobody expects a halat partner to do anything but look nice, so they can be as tactless and dull or lowborn and wild as they please, and nobody cares. Or maybe they *do* care a bit, but they don't expect better."

"Like arm candy?"

"I have no idea what that means." Zech looked at her suspiciously. "Is this like those *rock stars* you were talking about before?"

Despite herself, Saffron managed a smile. "Sort of."

Zech snorted. "Your language is ridiculous."

"I could say the same to you." And then, in Kenan, because she was curious and lacking an answer, "So, how does the royal mahu'kedet actually work? Gwen said it was a hierarchy with different roles, but she didn't say what they were."

"Oh! Well, all right." Zech looked oddly pleased by the question. "The Vex, or the Vexa, rules absolutely. Their primary consort is the Cuivexa or the Cuivex, and while they're fairly powerful, they can still be overruled. Usually, it's a practical match: someone with good connections, but who'll make a good administrator. Does that make sense?"

"So far, yes."

"Good. So, say we've got a Vex and Cuivexa, just like we do now. They're the main pair of the mahu'kedet, and each of them is expected to pick another three partners, bound to them in particular. But it's not like a regular Kenan marriage, where everyone has to agree to it and everyone does what they're best at – it's more like special government posts that decide who you get to sleep with. And each partner, on each side, is meant to represent one of three qualities: mara–" *blood*, "–sehet–" *soul*, or perhaps *wisdom*; the zuymet translation was suggestive of both, "–and halat, like we just talked about." *Vitality*, or *beauty*. "And then you put cui or vex in front, to say which partner is whose. And because the Vex is more powerful, his partners are more powerful – or at least, that's the theory. It's stupidly complicated in practice, but Kenans are like that." She grinned, shrugging as if to say, *what can you do?*

Saffron thought this through, repressing a shiver at the thought of Kadeja. "So the, uh, the Vex'Mara... that's meant to be an alliance match?"

Zech nodded gravely. "It's meant to be *the* alliance match, even more important than who you choose as Cuivex or Cuivexa. There's a sort of unwritten rule, Pix says, that the Cui'Mara is for foreign alliances, Vex'Mara for Kenan. But

Leoden broke it, and the only reason more people aren't still angry about it is that he killed the ones who were." And then, as if realising for the first time that they'd stopped walking, "Come on. It's not far now."

Sure enough, another two turnings brought them to an unremarkable door. Zech raised a hand to knock, then hesitated. "Trishka's not very strong," she said. "I mean, *she's* strong enough, in her mind and magic – her body just has a hard time keeping up. The priest said she'd be better today, but if she gets sleepy or starts twitching too much, we have to go. All right?"

"All right," said Saffron, though the disclaimer brought on a tingle of apprehension as to how she should behave. Zech knocked, and after a moment, someone called out, "Come in!"

The room was dominated by a massive bed, occupied by a middle-aged woman whose smile, though genuine, was also tired. Her grey-streaked hair was otherwise black, her eyes a beautiful dark amber. Her brown skin was neither as dark as Gwen's nor as golden as Matu's, but somewhere between their shades. Saffron was surprised to find that her face was familiar, until she realised with a jolt that Trishka's features – her chin, her nose, the shape of her cheeks – were all reminiscent of Yasha.

"I'm her daughter," Trishka said.

Saffron jumped. The older woman chuckled, patting the edge of the bed. "It's all right. Come sit down. Everyone who meets her first gets that look on their face when they see me."

Obediently, Saffron came and perched on the edge of the bed. Zech followed, keeping one small hand close about Saffron's wrist but otherwise standing quietly by; a translator, nothing more, though she and Trishka nonetheless exchanged a brief, warm smile.

Up close, Saffron could see that there were dark circles

under Trishka's eyes, and that her hands, where they rested on top of the blankets, trembled slightly.

"Well, now," she said. "You have, I think, good reason to resent me for bringing you here."

The word choice wasn't an accident. Saffron swallowed, staring. Trishka was offering herself as a scapegoat for Saffron being stranded, and to her shame, there was a moment where she felt genuinely tempted to accept it. How much easier would everything be if she were guiltless – if her decision to jump through the portal was really Trishka's fault for putting it there in the first place? But the choice had been hers alone, and as ugly as the consequences were, she couldn't shift the blame.

"You didn't bring me here." Saffron didn't look away. "I chose to come."

Trishka's smile deepened, her exhaustion ebbing away. "And so you did. It's a brave thing to admit, Saffron. That's your name, isn't it?"

"Yes."

"Does it mean something in your language?" Trishka sounded genuinely curious. "Or is it just a sound?"

"It's an expensive spice, made from a type of flower. It's very yellow, like–" she raised a hand to indicate her hair, realising only belatedly that it, too, was gone, "–like the sun," she finished, gulping. "Well, like the sun I'm used to. Yours is much whiter."

"I see." Turning slightly, Trishka looked fondly at Zech. "Thank you for bringing her here. I think we might keep each other company for a little while – she speaks well enough now to talk alone, I think. Is there something you can be getting on with, my girl?"

"Matu told me I have to find Jeiden and be nice to him." Zech scowled theatrically. "I *suppose* that counts."

"I'm sure it does," said Trishka.

Zech swung her shoulders and slipped out the door. The

latch clicked shut behind her. Trishka gave a maternal sigh. "Honestly, those two – they're like oil and water now, but give it a couple of years, and they'll be inseparable."

A not-quite-comfortable silence settled between them. Saffron felt oddly disquieted, as though she were being studied, while Trishka emanated a gentle calm. At last, the older woman spoke.

"I saw what happened to you, in the Square of Gods. My magic is good for more than making portals. It shows me things, too – different people, different places – and when you came through with Gwen, I watched. I've even seen into your world at times."

Saffron felt her heart begin to pound. Somehow, she already understood what Trishka was going to say next. "My family," she whispered. "Are they all right?"

Trishka shuddered. Her eyes didn't close, but they rolled backwards, lids flickering as she gazed through worlds. "Two men in blue are at your house. Your mother sits listening, as your father paces. Your sister refuses to come downstairs. She's in her room, weeping. They think you've been stolen away."

Saffron felt like she'd been punched. Tears wormed their way down her cheeks, as hot as acid. "Why would you tell me that?"

"Because you needed to know. It's what you feared, isn't it? That your absence hurts them. That it hurts you, too. Worlds away, and worrying for each other. That's what family is."

And suddenly Saffron was crying in earnest – not the furious, grief-maddened bafflement of the morning, when she'd refused Gwen's offer of comfort, but a sodden wrenching of tears, the way she used to cry in childhood. Nose running, body heaving, she threw her arms around Trishka and sobbed on her shoulder like a toddler with a skinned knee, feeling only relief and comfort when the Vekshi woman hugged her in return, rocking her, murmuring, "Shh now, shh, it's all right, it's all right."

"I left them," Saffron whispered. Her face was wet, but the tears were slowly drying up, receding like a tide. "I left them there, and I don't know how to get back."

"It's all right," Trishka repeated. "Let it out. That's a girl."

Slowly, Saffron recovered. Leaning back, she disentangled herself from Trishka and sheepishly wiped her face on her sleeve. "Is it wrong to say I needed that?"

"Not at all. If anything, it's the opposite." Gently, Trishka brushed the stumps of Saffron's fingers. Electricity shot down her arm, but though it fizzed and tingled, it didn't hurt. "In Veksh," said Trishka, "our mothers teach us that there's a type of story called *zejhasa*, the braided path: a new tale that starts before the old tale has ended, and which could not exist alone. Every life is zejhasa. Before we are born, our mothers live their own stories, and when we are young, our existence is twined with theirs – small threads in a wider pattern. But as we grow, these threads begin to separate, forming new strands, new lives, new purposes. Our mothers' stories go on, enriched; but ours will always begin before theirs have ended. You are not Vekshi, but some truths are bigger than kinship. Letting go hurts. Growing up hurts. Sooner or later, we all leave home. By choice and magic, you've wrenched yourself out of everything you know, and all those many worlds away, your mother grieves your loss. But you are *not lost*, child; you never were. Your story has begun; you're on the braided path. What we do here, the things we fight for… perhaps you'll come to share those goals. Perhaps not. Only remember: you will go home in the end, and see your mother again."

"I won't be able to tell her the truth, though," Saffron whispered. "About all of this. I'll have to make up some horrible lie about being kidnapped and having my fingers cut off. How can I do that to her? To any of them?"

"Are you whole?" Trishka asked, suddenly.

"What? You mean my hand? You know it's not."

"Not your hand." Trishka shook her head. "Your *heart*, child. That's what matters. That's what your family will see, no matter what lies you tell them. Are you whole inside?"

"I..." Saffron stared, surprising herself the answer. "I am. At least, I think I am." She licked her lips, and knew it to be true. "I'm whole."

Trishka smiled. "Then hold to that, and hope."

PART 2
The Braided Path

8
The Cuivexa & the Shavaktiin

Iviyat ore Leoden ki Hawy, Cuivexa of Kena, was running away.

Not literally running, of course, which would have attracted too much attention, but walking as quickly as she dared, head bowed with pride and fear. Battling nervous energy, she smoothed her hands down her skirt. Though she'd dressed in clothes that gave no hint as to her true station – a dark riding skirt and boots, green scarves at head and waist, a stained cream blouse and a knotted silk vest – they would still have stood out if she'd taken the servants' stairs. Instead, she walked in the open, trusting to the preoccupation of any passersby to shield her from notice. So far it was working, but the wing of the palace in which she lived was, with the exception of those servants and guards set to care for her, uninhabited. Under Vex Ralan, it had been where the royal children slept, and as those boys and girls were now either dead, fled or grown, she had the place to herself.

She clenched her teeth, shivering with adrenaline and anger. For neither the first nor last time since her wedding day, she cursed Hawy's stubborn blindness, her blank refusal to see the danger in Leoden that had split their clan in two. Only now, with her bloodmother's promises shown to be empty as cicada shells, did Viya truly understand why

Leoden had chosen her: not to flatter Hawy, but to threaten Rixevet. *Your daughter is my hostage. Stay your tongue.* Leoden would never bend to Viya as a husband should, not even if she were beautiful as thirdmother Sava and older to boot; not when his heart was so tightly coiled in Kadeja's fist that the blood of it stained her fingers.

Reaching the junction that separated her wing from the palace proper, she hesitated. The doors to the next hallway were closed, which was usual, but what if they were locked too? With her guards elsewhere, it would have been a simple thing for Leoden or Kadeja to imprison her here; a more expedient means of keeping her out from underfoot than trusting to Viya's usual spoiled disinterest. Heart in mouth, she tried the handle and crowed to feel it turn, peering through the crack into the next hall. Distant footsteps echoed, accompanied by a ringing shout that could only have come from Javet, the majordomo. But of actual bodies, the hall remained mercifully clear, and so Viya slipped through, being careful to close the doors again behind her.

She'd slept late that morning on purpose, not knowing when she'd next have a chance to rest. No servants had rushed to attend her: in preparation for her planned escape, she'd feigned a tantrum the previous evening, banishing them all on the pretext of some imagined slight and declaring that none were to return save at her express command. The lie had been believed, Viya's temper being as well-known to the servants as it was to the Vex and Vex'Mara. Ordinarily, such a dramatic fit would have earned her a royal reprimand, but as she'd hoped, both Leoden and Kadeja had been too busy to bother, instead content to let her stew in self-imposed isolation. Now, as she navigated the twists and turns of the central palace – hiding behind columns or in doorways when she heard someone coming, slowing her pace and dropping her gaze when a servant went by – she found herself touching the bag of jewels she wore around her neck like she would a favoured talisman. When the habit proved distracting, she forced herself to stop. As though the meagre wealth might somehow bring her luck!

Viya tossed her head. She didn't need luck – not when she was driven by the will of Ke and Na, the Heavenly Parents.

The further she went, the more Viya became aware of the size of the palace. How scantly she'd explored! Much of it was still unknown territory, and with every sudden detour necessitated by the approach of boots or the skirl of voices, she became increasingly fearful of getting lost. This ignorance, too, could be laid at Leoden's door – even the lowest servants were granted more freedom of movement than Viya, and at least *they* weren't constantly shadowed by guards.

As she rounded a corner, two servant girls with their heads together hurried past. It took all her willpower not to react when one of them looked directly at her and smiled. Instead, she just kept walking, her breath kept tight in her throat until they were out of earshot. *Rixevet could do this,* she told herself firmly, *and so can I. Would you shame your secondmother, Iviyat? No? Then keep walking.*

Chin held high, she reached a broad flight of stone steps and rested her hand on the banister. Now came the hardest part of all: leaving the domestic levels and descending to where Leoden and Kadeja would soon be feasting their most important guests and allies in the Hall of High Moons. Not, of course, that Viya had any plans to pass the Hall itself – both it and the smaller Gold Room, where the council was taking place, were at the opposite end of the floor from where she needed to go – but there would be guards, more servants and possibly even guests she'd have to dodge.

All at once, she wanted to give up. *Treason. I'm committing treason.* She let the word fill her like poison smoke, expanding through her heart and lungs until her whole body clenched around the threat of death. *He wouldn't kill me,* part of her pleaded, but a colder voice, the one that sounded like

Rixevet, said, *Yes, he would. In a heartbeat, if he truly thought you threatened him.*

Viya gripped the banister, her fingers hard against the stone. *It's all the same choice, no matter what I do.* The realisation was oddly freeing. Licking her lips, Viya placed one foot on the stairs, and then another, and slowly began to descend.

Predictably, Jeiden was still in the stables, tending to Matu's horses – the last expensive legacy of Pix's former status. Zech watched him for almost a minute before making her presence known. When she knocked on the open door, Jeiden turned and glared at her, his expression changing instantly from attentiveness to rancour.

"You again?" he grumbled.

"Me again," Zech agreed. "How are the horses?"

"Fine. They don't like being near the roa, though. There were hardly any up north." Putting down a currycomb he'd only just picked up, Jeiden crossed his arms. "What do you want, anyway? Come to gloat about how you're better at helping Matu than I am?"

Yes, thought Zech, but remembering her promise, said, "No. I just… well, Matu said I should come and apologise, seeing as how we'll be going north together, and that we should try and be friends, because it would make things easier for everyone."

Jeiden made a face. "Did he really say that?"

"Would I be talking to you if he hadn't?"

"Good point." Jeiden scuffed a foot on the stable floor. "I guess we could have a truce then. If Matu says so."

In a spontaneous show of good faith, he put his right hand over his heart and kissed the back of his left, a gesture which Zech, awkwardly and with some surprise, copied. Their usual hostilities thus suspended, they stared at each other, each one visibly uncertain as to what happened next.

Jeiden even blushed. He was, Zech thought resentfully, a very beautiful boy. It was understandable, of course, given that he was Pix and Matu's blood-cousin, and yet also frustrating, because in Kena girls were meant to be the beautiful ones, and by the standards of her adoptive nation, Zech wasn't. Certainly, no one except Matu had ever told her otherwise, and as he said the same thing to all women, most men and his beloved horses, it clearly didn't count. If she was honest, Jeiden's prettiness was a significant factor in her mistrust of him – but then, she was equally certain that her greater skill with animals, staff proficiency and possession of the zuymet were part of why he disliked her in turn. Thinking about it, she supposed that of the two of them, he had the greater cause for complaint, because while he would have traded his beauty for competence in a heartbeat, Zech would never have swapped her talents for prettiness, no matter how she envied his.

"Who was that girl today?" Jeiden asked suddenly. "The one who helped you pull Matu up? I don't remember her."

"Oh, that's Safi," said Zech, feeling pathetically grateful for the change in topic. "She's a worldwalker, like Gwen, only she came through by accident and got lost in the Square of Gods, but her hair was still long then, and Vex'Mara Kadeja cut off her fingers and threw them in the fountain."

Jeiden blinked, impressed. "Really?"

"Really," said Zech – and then, much to her astonishment, she found herself telling an enthralled Jeiden the whole story in detail, beginning with Gwen's arrival at the compound and ending with the events of that morning. By the time she'd finished, her mouth was dry and Jeiden, for the first time in his life, was looking at her with an expression that approached respect.

"You know," he said, glancing around as though they were suddenly in danger of being overheard, "I'll bet everyone in Karavos is gossiping about yesterday. If we went out, we could find out what people are saying about the Vex'Mara, then come back and tell it to Yasha. Just like her little friends do."

Zech felt a sudden tingle of excitement. Technically, neither of them was allowed out into the city unaccompanied, but that had never stopped her before, and nor, apparently, had it stopped Jeiden. But then she remembered Kadeja's face as she cut off Safi's fingers, and the sharp, hot anger of Gwen and Pix and Yasha. She wanted to go, but maybe it was a bad idea; maybe the adults had plans of their own afoot, and she and Jeiden would mess them up without even knowing it.

When she hesitated, Jeiden flashed her a mocking grin. "Too scared, are you?"

"I never was!" Zech shot back. But then, because she could all too well imagine Yasha's fury if something went wrong, "Only, what if we make things worse?"

Jeiden snorted. "Worse? You slugwit, what could we possibly do? We don't know anything." And then, more bitterly, "Nobody ever tells us what's going on."

Zech bit her lip at that, because whether he knew it or not, she *did* get told more than Jeiden. It wasn't his fault he'd been born a boy, and if Pix and Matu had only left him with the rest of their Kenan kin, it wouldn't have mattered. But in the compound, Yasha's word was law, and her law was always that of Veksh and Ashasa – and neither that nation nor goddess had much use for boys. Men, at least, were useful: they could sire daughters and fight and be put to trades, travel as messengers and even provide companionship (though Yasha tended to be dismissive of this last, to the point where Zech had grown doubtful of it too). But boys were useless – little more than stripling men, without even the grace of a blood-day or the budding of breasts to mark the point at which Ashasa deemed them adult. *No wonder he wants to spy things out,* Zech thought.

It was this realisation as much as the sting of Jeiden's challenge that swayed her.

"All right," she said. "But we have to go now, before anyone sees us."

"Really?" Jeiden made a belated attempt to look nonchalant, but his tone betrayed him. "Which way should we take?"

Zech didn't hesitate. "Over the rear wall behind the little kitchen. There's no windows on that part of the house, and you can use the wood-box for a boost."

"You've done this before." He glared at her, but the expression was more impressed than accusing.

Zech only grinned. "I won't tell if you won't. Come on – race you!"

And then they were off together, sprinting from the stables.

The stairs had a twist in them, turning onto a landing midway up. If you stood at the bottom of the first long flight, as Viya did now, you were invisible to anyone coming up from the level below. She dithered, hidden and hovering for no real reason she could name, suddenly afraid to move. It must have been the guidance of gods: the sound of someone ascending came seconds later, and when they spoke, she felt the words like a slap.

It was Leoden.

Viya shoved back from the banister, barely daring to breathe. He was with someone else – another man, by the sound of it – but she couldn't tell who.

"...deal with the worldwalker," Leoden was saying. "She's meddled enough, her and the Vekshi crone both."

The unknown man spoke carefully. "And how will the Vex'Mara feel, should you take such action against her kinswomen?"

Leoden gave a hard laugh. "She has no kin. Not anymore."

Viya's pulse leapt urgently in her throat, and not just

because the voices were so close. *Leoden knows a worldwalker?* It was impossible, of course – or at least, it should have been. Worldwalkers existed in moon-tales, not the real world.

Didn't they?

The footsteps had stopped. She squeezed her eyes shut, picturing the scene: Leoden and his companion standing little more than a horse's length from where she hid. Once they climbed the last few steps, they'd see her, shoulder blades pressed hard to the wall, as if she could burrow through backwards.

"As you say," the stranger said. "At whose feet will the deaths be laid?"

Viya could almost hear Leoden's smile. "Why, mine, of course."

The other man sounded startled. "Truly?"

"Well, what other choice do I have? Even as we speak, a Vekshi spy is creeping her way through the halls of this palace, slipping poison into the Uyun ambassador's favourite wine. Doubtless, he'll call for a jug of it at the feast, though for the sake of his table-neighbours, I only hope he won't offer to share. Though tragically too late to save the ambassador, the spy will, of course, be caught and killed – but not before divulging the name and location of her mistress and fellow co-conspirators."

"And justice will be swift," the other man murmured. "I'll admit I'm surprised that you'd take no care to capture the woman who actually wields the jahudemet. Surely she'd be an asset?"

Dismissively, Leoden said, "I have no need of other worlds. Kena is our holy place, the founding of our future. You'd do well to remember it, Shavaktiin."

The Shavaktiin! So that was who he was speaking to! Viya shivered to think of him, remembering their encounter at her wedding. Luy, he called himself, which was no proper name at all. After that first time, they'd never spoken again, though she'd seen him about the palace. His facelessness unnerved her almost as much as his strange religion did.

"My apologies, Vex," Luy murmured. "I forget myself."

"Indeed you do." A short pause. "I should get back. We'll see you at the feast?"

"I wouldn't miss it."

"Good. Be quick, then. We've much more to discuss."

And then – Viya could scarcely credit it – there came the sound of receding footsteps. Leoden was walking away! In that moment, her relief was so great that she forgot the significance of Luy not going with him, that the Shavaktiin would soon resume his progress. She could have retreated back from the landing, made it look as though she was only just coming down, but she didn't move in time. When Luy ascended the second flight, he saw the Cuivexa for what she was: a frightened, guilty eavesdropper.

"Well!" he said, looking her up and down. Or at least, that's what Viya assumed he was doing. Like all his kind, the Shavaktiin wore a long veil over his head and face, with only a mesh to see through. His flowing robes likewise left his body shapeless and concealed, so that all you could ever see of him were his hands. And yet she could feel him staring at her, invisible eyes watching from behind a one-way screen.

Viya's throat was dry with terror. All Luy had to do was grab her or shout, and then she was ruined, her gamble lost before she'd even made it downstairs.

"Cuivexa Iviyat," he said, slowly. "What an unexpected pleasure." When Viya didn't answer, he cocked his head, his blue veil fluttering silkily. "How long have you been here?"

"Long enough." The words rasped out of their own accord. She was terrified, but part of her thought, *Rixevet would show no fear*, and so she forced herself to step free of the wall and stand before him, shoulders straight. "I'm leaving the palace," she said, startled at her bravery in saying so. "Are you going to stop me?"

"Stop you?" Luy shook his head. "Why would I do that? Don't answer," he added, quickly. "It was a rhetorical question." He crossed his arms. The motion revealed a flash of his bare hands, and Viya was startled to see how dark they were – just like the Uyun ambassador's. But then, she supposed, the Shavaktiin came from everywhere, and Luy was a foreign-sounding name, so why shouldn't he be from Uyu? And yet–

"You're going to let Leoden kill the ambassador," she blurted out, "but he's your kinsman, isn't he? But you asked if Kadeja would care that he planned to kill Vekshi, so it must bother you. Mustn't it?" And then, because even terror couldn't quite quell her temper, "Answer me!"

The Shavaktiin chuckled. "The Uyun ambassador is neither friend nor kin to me. But you, Cuivexa Iviyat ore Leoden ki Hawy–" and here his tone turned mocking as he delivered her full set of titles, "–your predicament is the opposite. You have too many ties, too many obligations – all of them conflicting, and all of them family. And so you run, to make the problem simpler."

"I run," said Viya, stiffly, "to be safe."

Luy bowed and stretched out a hand. "Then I will help you."

Viya stared. "Are you going to betray me? Why are you doing this?"

"I will not betray you. Only and ever, my reasons belong to the story, and the will of the one who scribes it. Today, that makes me a traitor to many people, but you are not among them. Come." He curled his fingers at her, impatient. "We don't have much time. I can help you to the stables, but after that, you're on your own."

"I don't trust you," Viya said, accepting his hand, "but I don't have a choice, do I?"

"Everyone has a choice," Luy murmured. "Some are just more precarious than others. Now forgive me for this, but we need to stay close."

Looping an arm across her shoulders, he hurried them down the stairs. It was unnerving being so close to someone and yet unable to see their face. His fingers dug into her shoulder – not painfully, but tight enough to prevent her escape.

They reached the lower floor, where servants laden with platters of food were already en route to the Hall of High Moons. Viya kept her eyes on the floor. The Shavaktiin moved quickly, navigating their way down a series of corridors, past several high-ranking guests – none of them spared Viya a second glance, though she glimpsed them from the corner of her eye and recognised their faces – and then out into a long, glass-fronted walkway that faced onto the south gardens.

"We're going the wrong way!" Viya clicked her teeth. "Slugwit, the horses are in the *north* stable!"

"I'd advise against it," Luy answered, voice low. "Horses are for nobles or soldiers, and you are fleeing in disguise. A horse would stand out. You're better off taking a roa."

"A *roa*?" Viya couldn't hide her distaste. "One of those shaggy, smelly beasts? Haven't you seen their *hands*?" She shuddered.

"It's the better choice, Cuivexa."

"I thought you said that everyone had a choice."

"They do, but that doesn't mean all choices are equally sensible. Are you acting like a Cuivexa in this, or a spoiled child?"

Viya wrenched away and slapped him. It was an odd feeling. Her palm connected with the cloth of his veil, muting a blow whose strength had been scant enough to start with. "I am *not* a child," she hissed. "Do not presume to insult me, Luy Shavaktiin."

If the slap had bothered him at all, it didn't show in his tone. "I'll take it back," he said, "if you'll take the roa."

Viya grit her teeth. "Done."

"My apologies, then."

"Thank you."

They glared at each other. It wasn't truly a staring match, as the Shavaktiin's eyes were hidden. Nonetheless, he looked away first.

"Now," he said, as though nothing had happened, "we'll have to pass the guards up ahead. You keep your eyes down, and if I squeeze your arm, you giggle. Understand?"

Viya made a disgusted sound. "You'd have me pretend to be your servant lover? That's original."

She'd thought to make him angry, disliking the opacity of his emotions, but in this, as in so much else, she failed. "Some tales thrive for a reason," he said, mildly. "Now, come."

And so they resumed their previous posture: Viya tucked firmly against Luy's side, his arm curled around her shoulder. They kept on down the walkway, turned the final corner – and there, sure enough, were a pair of honoured swords, guarding the outside exit. When Luy halted before them, Viya began to tremble.

"You may pass, Shavaktiin," said one, "but who's this little miss?"

"Some chuckle from the silks, no doubt," said the other. "Slipped away, has she?"

"Slipped and been caught by willing hands," Luy said, smoothly. Both men laughed. "Come now! Surely you won't deny my fun? Just because I wear these robes doesn't mean there's nothing under them." And he gave Viya's shoulder a squeeze.

Like a bellows, she forced out a wheezy giggle. The first guard leaned in close, peering at her. Viya's heart beat fast as a tambour. She flashed up her gaze coquettishly, then down again, which evidently satisfied the guard; he laughed and leaned back.

"Tell me, Shavaktiin," he drawled, "when you ride, do you keep that face-smock on? Or do you let them as mounts you peer beneath?"

"Why, honoured sword!" Luy's tone turned smoky. "Was that an invitation?"

"It might have been." The guard leaned in again, his voice low. "I've a powerful curiosity for hidden things. When you're done with her, you find me after the feast tonight, and I'll show you tricks your stories never have."

"I just well might," Luy purred.

The other guard rolled his eyes. "You're incorrigible," he told his friend.

"Better that than a self-gelded mule." He winked and stood aside. "Go on, then. If you decide to find me later, ask for Rican."

"I will," said Luy, but kept his arm around Viya. Through the gate they went, and out to the gardens, following the goldstone path to the roa stables.

Once they were out of earshot, Luy chuckled under his breath. "He wasn't bad looking, truly. I might well take him up on it."

Viya bit back a rude reply and pressed her lips together, sending a silent prayer of thanks to Ke and Na, who understood all things, and to Sahu, who governed wisdom. *Gods grant me safety and knowledge.*

In sight of the stables, Luy left her crouching by a flowerbed and went on alone in case there were any grooms about. The minutes of his absence crawled by for Viya like insects over bare flesh; she yearned to leap up and follow him, skin prickling with the threat of exposure, and yet she didn't dare move. Had Luy abandoned her? The possibility made her sweat, until she remembered she'd never asked for his help. She'd taken it because she had no choice, but if he truly had gone, then she was still capable of setting herself free. That realisation soothed her, and when Luy finally did return with a white-and-grey roa, she was able to thank him calmly.

"Take the Green Gate," he advised, "and tell the guards

there you're riding a message for me. They'll let you through."

"How could they know that already?"

"Because I do plan to send a message today, which I told them at sunup. When my rider finally does go through – I'll make it late tonight, for your sake – they'll realise something's gone wrong, and come looking. I'd advise you to be well on your way by then."

Viya mounted while he spoke. The roa snorted uneasily beneath her, as though able to sense her dislike of it. It was Rixevet who'd insisted she learn to ride roas as well as horses, making it one of the few things Viya had resented her for. Now, though, she was forced to concede the wisdom of her secondmother's choices.

"My thanks to you," she said formally. And then, more out of curiosity than concern, "Will Leoden blame you for this, do you think?"

Luy laughed. "Your husband is not the only one skilled in laying the blame for his actions on other people. The difference between us is that I don't scapegoat innocents. Ride on, Cuivexa. And if..." he hesitated, voice changing slightly, "...if you should happen to meet my people in your travels, tell them... tell them the story will speak for itself."

"I will," said Viya, though privately she wished never to meet a Shavaktiin again. Luy had helped her, true, and she was grateful for that, but except for the shape of his hands and the sound of his speech, she had no conception of who he was, and disliked the disadvantage that put her at.

"Go on, go!" he repeated, and with that, Viya clicked to the roa, riding out of the palace and into treason.

9
Hide & Seek

A day ago, the idea of being present while another person washed, let alone assisting in the process, would have freaked Saffron out completely. It still did, if she was honest, but there was something about being in Karavos, or else the fact that Trishka had seen her cry, that suspended normal conventions. So when the older woman sat up a little straighter and declared that she was feeling much better for having rested, and asked if Saffron could help make her presentable? Her response had been, "Of course."

Following Trishka's instructions, she left the room and went in search of the same tub she'd washed in earlier. It was just where she'd left it, along with the bucket used to fill it from the pump in the courtyard. For a moment, she contemplated just filling the tub and then carrying it inside, but it would be too heavy to lift when full. Irritation stung her. She'd have to go back and forth, back and forth, until Trishka had enough water to wash in. Couldn't someone else do it? But then she felt guilty, realising that this was how everyone in the compound washed – she was just resentful of how long it took because she was used to indoor plumbing.

Trying not to sigh, Saffron carried the tub back to Trishka, and then began the arduous process of walking out to the pump, hauling down on the arm, then heaving the full bucket all the way back to Trishka's rooms. The whole process took nearly twenty minutes, and even though she knew that someone must have done the same for her earlier, she still resented the way her arms ached by the end of it.

With the final bucket emptied into the tub, Saffron set up a modesty screen, standing aside as Trishka came gingerly to her feet. She was short and stocky, dressed in a long-sleeved robe like a dressing gown that belted at the waist. She was shaky on her feet, but managed to walk to the tub unassisted. Even so, she needed Saffron's help to pull her arms free of the robe, and then further assistance to lower herself steadily into the bath. Not sure what else was expected of her, Saffron perched on the end of the bed, waiting.

"I'm not normally this weak," Trishka said. "But the jahudemet is always draining, the more so the further I have to reach."

Saffron rolled the Kenan word, jahudemet, around in her head. It meant something like *the spark that moves through air*, though that was a deeply imperfect translation. Her knowledge of Kenan was instinctive and incomplete, and every time she ran up against such an alien term, a little shudder went through her at the strangeness of it.

"That must be frustrating," she said instead.

A sloshing noise came from behind the screen, which Saffron took to indicate a shrug.

"I'd like to say I'm used to it, but if I could wish away the side effects, I would." A pause; the sound of scrubbing. "You'll need to learn Vekshi, too," she said suddenly.

Saffron blinked. "What?"

"I was watching earlier, when Yasha and Gwen were talking. You're heading north. Gwen doesn't speak much Vekshi – there was never a need – but if you're going to act the part, you'll need to speak the language." A languid splash. "You're already joined in zuymet with Zech, which is good, but she's still new to her gifts, and I'm not sure she'd be best suited to teaching you two tongues at once. Matu ought to do it."

Saffron chose her words carefully. "Is he very, ah... stable?"

Trishka laughed. "Oh, he's wild enough at times, but we like him that way, and he knows it. Even Yasha approves of him, and there's not many men of whom that's true, though she'd never admit it. At any rate, he's Zechalia's master in the zuymet, and a skilled practitioner. You can trust him with that."

Saffron raised an eyebrow, remembering what else she'd heard about Matu. "And can I trust him with me, too?"

"Now *that*," said Trishka, "depends entirely on what you want to do with him. If it's children you're after, don't bother, but for anything else, it's your own affair. Only don't go chasing his heart, child, or you'll get yours burned. However he might pass his nights, he's only and all for Amenet."

A mortified blush crept up Saffron's cheeks. "That's not what I meant! I wouldn't want any of that – I'm way too young for kids and anyway, I prefer women to men. I mean, I do sometimes like men, but I usually like women more." The latter admission slipped from her by accident. She'd never outed herself as bisexual to an adult before, and was a little scared by how easy it was. "I mean, am I *safe* with him? If he's so... free with himself."

She thought that was the right way to phrase it; she'd meant to say *promiscuous*, but none of the equivalent Kenan terms had quite the same inference as in English. As best as Saffron could figure it, saying Matu was free with himself simply meant that he was an untethered, unmarried, uncommitted person who nonetheless enjoyed sex.

"Safe?" The question took Trishka aback, though to

Saffron's relief, she was utterly unfazed by her orientation. "Why wouldn't you... oh. This is an Earth thing, isn't it? You worry he might try without your consent?"

"Not *worry*, exactly." Saffron twisted her hands, embarrassed, and tried not to think about Jared Blake. "I just want to know where I stand."

Trishka sighed. "I won't pretend this world is perfect. Men and women force others here, the same as they do in your realm. But it is not tolerated, not excused, and especially not in Veksh or Kena. Whatever you want from Matu, or don't want, he'll respect it."

"Good to know," said Saffron, awkwardly.

Trishka only chuckled. "I'm not offended you asked, child. But if you feel the need for penance, come over here and help me out. This water's so cold, I'm like to freeze my nipples off. Oh! And there's a towel on that chair in the corner, if you please."

For neither the first nor last time, Viya cursed Luy for making her take a roa. Surely she'd have been just as well off with a horse? Better, even, because she could ride them more competently, and because common crowds knew to step aside when they saw one coming. Instead, she was forced to endure being jostled about by low-ranking ignorants who didn't know any better. The beast itself – she'd named it Mara, for spite – was hard-mouthed and stubborn, responding so slowly to Viya's commands that by the time they'd moved, whatever gap she'd spied in the crush had closed. Part of her wanted to scream, *don't you know who I am?* But of course, she was in disguise; it was good that they looked away, and anyway, shouting about rank was ugly and undignified.

If real life were like the moon-tales Rixevet had told her as a child, Viya thought, some stalwart or other would recognise her anyway. They'd creep up, lay a hand on

Mara's bridle and in low, passionate tones, declare their undying loyalty to the Cuivexa and her cause. Then she'd be led down secret paths, away from the crowds and into the protection of her secondmother's agents, who would long since have set out to reclaim her.

But of course this didn't happen, and instead Viya was forced to sweat and push and wait and dodge her way through the chaos of roa riders, carts, foot traffic, stalls, corners, dead ends and shouting that made up the Lower Circle. When she finally spied the massive gates that led to the Warren, she hissed with impatience, dug her heels into Mara's sides and made for it so quickly that the roa clipped a man in passing.

"Hoy!" he shouted after her. A ripple of murmurs spread through the crowd.

Viya didn't turn. The man didn't matter. She was almost at the gates–

An irate stranger in the opulent taal of a wealthy merchant laid a hand on Mara's bridle, jerking them both to a halt.

Viya was furious. "Let *go*!" she shouted, trying to tug the rein from his grasp. But the man refused to obey her. Mara tossed his head back, *kree*ing as their tug-of-war put pressure on his mouth.

"Insolent chit!" the man bellowed. "I don't know what hovel you rode in from, but above that gate–" he gestured to Viya's destination, "–we act and ride with decorum. Apologise for hitting me!"

"*Hovel?*" Viya hissed, goaded by the term. It was too much, all of it! Oh, if only he knew who she was! "You dare, you filthy thumbcoin?"

Now it was the merchant's turn to look furious. He flushed above his beard, but his voice, when he spoke, was dangerously low. "You would be well-placed, girl, to reconsider that insult." He tightened his grip on Mara, winding the rein about his hand, so that the poor beast's head was pulled backwards at an angle. Viya felt him shift under her, and tasted metallic fear in her mouth. Even so, it hurt her pride to back down.

"I will apologise for hitting you," she said, stiffly, "if you will apologise for insulting my home."

The man's eyes glittered dangerously. "And what of your second insult?"

"I will retract it," Viya said, "the instant you take your hand off my mount."

A moment of tension hung between them. Then, in voice that was chiselled ice, the merchant said, "My apologies for the slight to your house."

Viya's smile was a slice of spite. Even so, she condescended to incline her head. "My apologies for the affront to your person. It was unintentional."

"And the other?"

"Your hand first."

"Of course," said the merchant – and wrenched on the bridle, just as he slapped Mara hard on the flank and shouted, "Ha!"

Pained and startled, the roa bolted, and Viya, who hadn't been prepared for it, very nearly lost her seat. Only a frantic grab at Mara's coat saved her, but she dropped the reins in the process, and it was all she could do to gather them back up again without pitching head-first from the saddle. By the time she had them in hand, they'd passed through the gate and were well into the Warren, where Viya had seldom ridden before, and never once alone.

Panicked that she didn't recognise her surroundings, she hauled on the reins, praying Mara would come to a halt. Instead, the roa lowered his head and twisted in a strange sideways jerk, as though attempting to buck her off. One bystander yelped at the sight, the sound sharp enough to startle Mara anew; and then they were off again, running downhill through the twisting residential streets. The city was a blur of walls. Viya tugged on the bridle, but though she pulled and pleaded, nothing she did made any difference at all.

And then, of his own volition, Mara slowed to a halt. His flanks were heaving, head and tail drooped low. Somewhere inside, Viya was furious at his disobedience, but in that moment she was so relieved they'd stopped that instead of scolding the beast, she patted him weakly on the neck. Her hands shook violently; she could barely stretch her palms out flat.

They were in the middle of a narrow alley, its cobbled surface cracked and uneven. On either side towered high, square houses, their walls vividly painted with murals and further brightened by the colourful washing strung on lines between each opposite pair of windows. Ahead, the alley twisted down a slope and out of sight, while the way they'd come was hidden behind a blind corner. The city was more pungent here. Viya could smell cooking and refuse mixed together, a hot, sour scent that lingered in her throat. She could hear children shrieking in play too, mixed in with the muffled clatter of families in their homes and even the discordant jangle of music. It was alien to her, strange and commonplace and terrifying.

"Wretched beast," she whispered. "Where have you brought me?"

Yasha was talking, and Gwen was trying – and failing – to listen. Unlike Matu, she'd had no pretext for retiring to bed, and so was forced to endure the resulting diatribe. Silence was the path of least resistance, and besides which, for all Yasha's intent to orchestrate a coup with Vekshi aid, she lacked the power to make it so. Only the Council of Queens could do that, and whatever sway she held in her homeland, not even Yasha was so well-connected that she could take their cooperation for granted. Not that Gwen had never been to Veksh, though she'd travelled to other nations in this world besides Kena; even so, she knew enough of the culture to appreciate just how difficult things could get on the other side of the border.

"Am I boring you, Gwen?" Yasha asked sharply. She'd been talking about possible routes north for at least the second time.

"Yes," said Gwen, too tired to lie. "Matu had the right idea. I need a rest."

Pix stared at her. Yasha only laughed.

Ignoring both of them, Gwen stalked out of the kitchen and walked clear to the other end of the house, where she stopped, resting her head against the wall. The plastered stone was cool on her temple.

What are you doing? she asked herself. *Do you even know anymore?*

She closed her eyes as though waiting for an answer. When none was forthcoming, she sighed, straightened and headed back the way she'd come, to Matu's room.

She didn't bother to knock, and Matu, in turn, ignored her entry. The room was dark, the only light seeping in around the curtain pulled across the window. Matu was sitting upright in bed with his back to the wall, still fully dressed, his elbows crooked on his knees. His hair hung like sheets of black water around his face.

"I might be too, in your position," she said, leaning back against the door.

"Might be what?"

"Staring into space. Angry. Drunk." She paused, assessing him. "Reevaluating my friendships?"

"Three out of four's not bad." He didn't say which three, though. "I could kill Yasha."

Gwen snorted. "So could we all. Often, and with great imagination."

"You? Kill Yasha? You wouldn't know what to do with

yourself without a wall to bash your stubborn head against."

She'd braced for Matu's bitterness, but the blow hit hard and she couldn't disguise the impact. "I suppose I deserve that."

"No more than the rest of us. My apologies." His gaze flashed up. "At least you can escape her. No wonder the Council spat her out." This last was muttered, but Gwen still caught it.

"Yasha sat the Council of Queens?"

"You didn't know?" Matu grinned blearily up at her. "Huh. That probably means I shouldn't have told you. I'm not lying," he added, tipping his head back. "I swear by my braidless head. She's got the scars to prove it."

Gwen frowned. "Scars?"

"Now I really have said too much. Ashasa will have to forgive me the insolence, assuming that she does forgive men. I've never been clear on that point." He reached into his tunic and withdrew a small leather wallet. "This, though, does breed clarity. I picked it up on the border." He opened the wallet, revealing a quantity of dried, blue-green leaf. "It's imported from Kamne, I think, or maybe some Shavaktiin brought it through the worlds – the rumours don't agree. Either way, it's like inhaling the dark edge of a star." He held up a square of bark paper. "It's called *cahlu*. Care to join me?"

"Give me that!" Gwen sat herself on the bed and took away both wallet and papers. Grinning quietly, Matu acquiesced. "Trying to roll up in your condition. It's a wonder you didn't spill the whole lot – your hands are shaking well enough." She rolled two cigarettes as she spoke, her fingers deft and assured. "You're a bad influence, you know that?"

She proffered the finished tube. Matu leaned forward and took it, waiting. Gwen rolled her eyes, then fished in her own skirt pocket for the lighter she carried everywhere. It was bronze and heavy, made in the shape of a Chinese dragon. The fire came out of its mouth (of course), and with a soft *chnk*, she lit them both up.

The smoke was hot and dark, imbued with a fierce citric bitterness that made it a little like smoking lemon rind mixed with coffee. Gwen savoured the taste, then exhaled. She could feel Matu watching her.

"Well?" he asked.

"It's adequate," she said, tapping ash onto his foot.

"Adequate? Don't give me adequate. You've just got the palate of a fire-swallower."

"I'll take that as a compliment."

They both fell silent, filling the room with blue-grey smoke. It wreathed between them like mist. When the cahlu was done, Gwen stubbed it out on the tip of Matu's boot.

"Say the Council of Queens agrees to all this," she said, "and Veksh sends her soldiers to pull Kadeja home. What makes them stop there? What makes an invading army hallowed by Ashasa and sanctioned by its leaders turn away from the empty throne of a rich and disorganised state? You say the Council threw Yasha out, but even a despised exile could be welcomed home again if they came offering a whole country."

Matu took a long, last drag, then dropped his cigarette to the floor. "You really think she'd go that far?"

"I think she'd try."

"She's not that foolish. The Kenans would rise up against it. Their gods are in their name, in their soil. You can't get rid of Ke and Na by claiming they were only and ever false echoes of Ashasa. The Council couldn't dismantle the temples. It wouldn't work. It couldn't."

"There's more than one way to claim a throne. She has Pix. She has you. If this all works, she'll have Amenet, too – and that's just for starters. Whatever role Yasha plays, if we succeed, it'll be to her advantage. You'll embed her right in the heart of Karavos. Is that really what you want?"

"You make it sound like it's my decision."

"I only meant–"

"I know exactly what you meant." He sighed. "I can already feel her eyes on my neck."

"Better eyes on the neck than knives in the heart," Gwen murmured. The proverb was too applicable lately for its own damn good, let alone her comfort.

"What do you want me to say? Everything's a risk. Yasha is difficult, but I'd rather have her than Leoden and Kadeja. Will Veksh invade? I doubt it, but you never know. Take the chance, Gwen. You've no more choice than I do, but we might as well go willing to the consequences of our own shortsightedness."

"Our own?" She raised an eyebrow. "And what have you done lately that's so shortsighted?"

"Stayed single," said Matu, "in the deluded belief that it would keep me out of politics."

Gwen chuckled. "Deluded indeed."

Matu rubbed his head. "And don't I know it."

All at once, Gwen recalled what Saffron had said about borders on the road to Karavos, and frowned. "Speaking of Veksh," she said, "I have a puzzle for you."

"A distracting puzzle?" Matu asked, in hopeful tones.

"Possibly, yes. Why is the Kenan-Vekshi border so barren?"

"Barren?"

"You know what I mean." She waved a hand. "The land there is flat, no rivers or mountains, but nobody mingles. Shit, nobody even fights, except for the odd skirmish in the Bharajin, and that hardly counts. It's weird."

"How long has this been bothering you?"

"Since Saffron asked me about it, and I didn't have an answer." She glanced at him. "Any thoughts?"

Matu mulled the problem. "Huh. I'd always thought it was Vekshi isolationism, but you're right. It's an open border.

There should still be more... history there, or something. More exchange."

"So you don't know?"

"Not offhand, but then a lot of knowledge was lost in the Years of Shadow. Back in my temple days–" by which he meant his magical apprenticeship with Sahu's Kin, "–we used to joke that if an obvious historical question lacked an obvious historical answer, it was probably Vexa Yavin's fault. Four hundred years, and we've barely recovered any of what she destroyed." He looked thoughtful. "Still, though. The Vekshi must have their own records. Maybe if this alliance goes to plan, we can ask to see them?"

Gwen snorted. "Sure. Good luck with that."

They grinned at each other.

A knock on the door interrupted their conversation. "Yes?" Matu called.

Speak of the devil, Gwen thought; it was Saffron, a worried look on her face.

"Trishka sent me," she said – in decently-accented Kenan, Gwen noted with pride. "I'd finished helping her and she said I should look for Zech, but I couldn't find her, so Trishka said she'd use her magic to see, but when she did–"

"Where is she?" Matu asked sharply.

"In the city. With Jeiden." Saffron inhaled. "They're in the Square of Gods. And something's happening."

Viya rode on down the narrow street, reasoning that it was better to go forwards than back. This instinct was proven sound when the strains of music she'd heard grew louder. The sounds of a crowd were audible too; she was headed for an open space, some market or square or gathering spot, and even with what little she knew about the Warren, such a place would surely help her get her bearings. As a last resort, she could always ask for directions, but that would be a bitter shame to her pride and gender both. Men could get lost with impunity, but women were gifted by Sahu with the knowledge of orientation – admitting failure in that respect would open her up to mockery.

The closer they came to the noise, the more Mara began to fidget against the bridle, tossing his head from side to side and *kree*ing. As much as this irritated her, Viya still couldn't bring herself to castigate the beast, partly through fear that he'd bolt again, but mostly because she, too, felt unsettled. The music was sharp and urgent, the crowd sounds tense rather than jubilant, and when she glimpsed the source of both, she instantly understood why.

Somehow, she'd managed to find her way to the Square of Gods, which was, if not packed, then certainly full of passersby who'd long since paused in passing. There was the fountain where Kadeja had sought her omen last afternoon; only now it was ringed by Shavaktiin players, their face-veils replaced with dramatic masks. Three were robed all in pinkish red, their masks showing weird white faces with twisted red grins. These were the musicians, armed with reed pipes, a zither and metal twindrums. The sound they produced was high and haunting, eerily discordant. It wasn't Kenan music they played, nor of any style that Viya understood, and the strangeness of it set her teeth on edge. Mara didn't like it, either; his ears were laid flat to the sides of his head, and his urgent *kree*s had grown louder.

But more disconcerting still were the players – or rather, their play. Viya had seen Shavaktiin performers once or twice as a child and found them amusing, if strange. Nothing in those memories compared with what she was seeing now. The blasphemy of it caused her chest to constrict. There were nine players, each one robed and masked to suggest a different deity of the First and Second Tier. There were Ke and Na, unmistakable in white and black, their masks marked with stars and the black lines of heaven. Beside them were Hime and Lomo, Yemaya and Nihun, Sahu and Teket: lilac robe and green, red and blue, yellow and purple, all ringing the fountain like children. And there, worst of all, was Kara, the sexless Heavenly Child in silver robes and a trickster's mask, kneeling in supplication as Ke and Na crowned them with Ashasa's wreath of fire. As Kara-Ashasa rose again, the other gods fell to their knees, crying out in pairs.

"Trickster ascendant!"

"Fire and malice!"

"Sunchild Vexa!"

By this point, the crowd's agitation was evident. Angry murmurs pervaded; the air was thick with fear and confusion, yet no one moved to intervene. *Kadeja did this,* Viya realised. *She tied Ashasa to the true gods, and now no one knows if the Shavaktiin are allowed to do the same.* But either way, the import was clear: the play declared that a female mischief reigned in Ashasa's name, usurping Kara's place in the celestial hierarchy and legitimised as ruler by Ke and Na.

And then, one by one, the other gods began to strip away their masks, behind which – the crowd roared in outrage – their faces were painted with the orange-gold-red of Ashasa's flames. The whole pantheon writhed, devoured from within by the Vekshi goddess's fire while Kara-Ashasa looked on and laughed.

Laughing chaos claimed them all; the Square of Gods became a churning mob as people surged forwards, shouting and throwing things at the players. The music faltered and ceased altogether, replaced by yelps as the Shavaktiin belatedly tried to flee. But the mob was everywhere, pinning them against the fountain. A stone hit Hime in the temple; she staggered, blood dripping down her painted face, and had to be caught by Na.

Fear went through Viya like lightning. She had to get out, get away – she was meant to be leaving Karavos! But the play had transfixed her, leaving her blind to the danger. Somehow she and Mara had managed to get boxed into a corner of the square, and her skittish beast was refusing to approach the mob. Fists clenched in frustration, Viya kicked hard at the roa's ribs, shouting for him to *move, move on!* but to no avail. The Square of Gods was the Trickster's domain – a woman started screaming ahead, and then another; she could hear a child crying, young men shouting and old men roaring, and from her vantage point on Mara's back, she saw a squadron of honoured swords enter the fray alongside the Shavaktiin.

Had Kadeja ordered this, after all? Viya didn't know. Maybe the guards really had come to help the players; or maybe they'd simply arrived through the entrance closest to the fountain, forcing them into confrontation with the crowd. Either way, the mob drew the same conclusion she first had: that the soldiers were there to protect the blaspheming Shavaktiin, and that all sense of rightness and piety was therefore lost. The crowd surged anew – Mara tossed his head back, snorting with fear – and the outraged guards drew their weapons.

Again, Viya cursed Luy's refusal to let her take a horse. Horses were bulky; they had square, solid chests and hard, sharp hooves that could plough through a crowd with ease. But roas were lighter, their balance less ideally suited to the task. Unlike their equine cousins, they lacked the sheer muscle and propulsion to shoulder their way through a mob, and their two legs were much more vulnerable to being knocked from beneath them than a horse's four. Ordinarily, their nimbleness was an asset within the cramped space of a city, but against a mob, they were worse than useless. Viya glanced desperately around the square, throat clenching at her predicament. She needed the crowd to let her through–

Her gaze lit on a pair of children. They stood on a barrel against the opposite wall of the square, and so, like Viya, were lifted above the crowd. One of them, an absurdly beautiful boy, noticed Viya's scrutiny and elbowed his companion, a skinny girl dressed in Vekshi clothes whose skin was a patchwork of calico shades. Her pale eyes narrowed as she sized Viya up, then widened as though in realisation. Urgently, she turned and began whispering to the boy, though of course the distance between them was such that Viya had no idea what was being said. Beneath her, Mara fidgeted in earnest, crow-hopping from one foot to the other like an anxious bird. More screams cut the crowd, whose members were moving now in a whirlpool motion; those at the back were struggling to get forwards, while all of a sudden, those at the front were desperate to get back.

Only Viya and the children, with their superior vantages, could see why: the honoured swords had started attacking the crowd, and alongside them now were a furious trio of arakoi. At least one of these latter possessed the *kashakumet* and was using it like a whip. As Viya watched, terrified, the arakoi's magic lifted a man and sent him flying. He crashed into a stall front, his limbs contorted brokenly, and lay still. A moment of stunned silence followed, and then the screaming began in earnest. The churning bodies pressed back into Mara, elbows and arms digging into the roa's sides and bruising Viya's legs. A hoarse cry of outrage slipped from her throat, but there was nowhere left to go – and then, as though the gods had winked at her, a gap opened up before them.

"*Go!*" she shouted, and for a miracle Mara obeyed, lunging awkwardly away from the wall and into the press of the mob.

But now they were like a tree branch caught in a river current. Bodies crashed into them, shoved and buffeted by the mob's agitations. Mara *kree*d loudly in panic. Turning in the saddle, Viya saw with dismay that his tail was caught in the crush; people were grabbing hold of it in their struggle to keep upright, but their weight was wrecking his balance. Truly frightened now, she jerked on the bridle, trying to steer them forwards, but met only the resistance of unmoving flesh.

And then a tiny, calico hand reached up and gripped her wrist.

10

The Road (Not) Taken

Zech looked up at the girl on the roa, teeth gritted with the effort of keeping steady. The mob around them thrashed like cats in a bag. Beside her, Jeiden hissed jerkily, "Hurry up, or we'll all be trampled!"

Zech ignored him. "We can lead you out," she said to the girl. "All right? You can come with us!"

"But he won't *move!*" the girl wailed, and as if to demonstrate her point, the roa jerked backwards as yet more strangers grabbed his tail.

"He will for me!" Zech said, and before the girl could protest, she grabbed the reins, looped them over the roa's head and began to forge through the mob.

It was tough going. Alone, she and Jeiden had been able to take advantage of their smaller size, slipping through gaps that adults couldn't fit. Now, though, every step was treacherous: neither Zech nor the roa had any weight to throw around. At least the beast was moving. Tugged forwards by her pressure on his mouth and pushed at the back by Jeiden, who'd thrown an arm over his rump, the roa had little choice but to obey, responding to their guidance as he hadn't to his rider's panic. As a flailing elbow caught her a sharp blow to the cheek, Zech bit back a profanity and wondered if she'd made the right choice. They needn't have helped the girl – as frightened as she was, she was still better off mounted than the rest of them were on foot – but having made the choice, they were stuck with it.

She'd deal with her injury later. Right now, there was still the crowd to face, and worse still, the Square of Gods was in danger of being closed off. At the far end, honoured swords and arakoi were blocking the main routes in and out, while behind them, the narrow side-streets leading into the bustling market district had formed a natural bottleneck. Still, it would be easier to squeeze out through the back way than to brave the guards, and so Zech pressed onwards, the roa's breath hot and slobbery on her shoulder. The pace was a strange mix of fast and slow: the mob wanted to run, but lacked the space for it, and so settled for a sort of angry, frenetic jostling that accomplished little while causing much pain.

Unbidden, a word from Safi's language popped into her head to describe the sensation. *A moshpit*, she thought, savouring the alien concept. *Like being in a moshpit.*

The weird word gave her strength. Though her body was numb from the sustained buffeting of the crowd, her shoulders sore from dragging the reluctant roa, Zech continued to force them forwards. Once or twice, Jeiden shouted something, but she couldn't hear him above the crowd, and didn't dare look to read his lips lest she lose her footing and fall. She was dimly aware that the honoured swords and arakoi had slacked their assault, evidently not wanting to force a massacre in the crowded square. Yet still people shrieked and struggled to get away; still she could smell blood and sense the sharp sting of the kashakumet on the air like lightning before a storm.

And then – Ashasa be blessed! – they were through the turmoil and out into the regular, freeform chaos of the market streets, stumbling like drunkards flung from an unfriendly door. Only now with the mob's roar muted could Zech make sense of Jeiden's shouts. With a spike of irritation, she realized that he hadn't been talking to her at all, but to the nameless girl on the roa. And who was *she*, anyway? Something about her niggled at Zech like a tongue tip probing a loosened milk-tooth.

"You have my gratitude," the girl said shakily to Jeiden. Zech startled: their mystery friend spoke Kenan with Pix's court accent, which meant she must either be noble or rich and mannered. But Zech had never met any nobly-born Kenans aside from Pix and Matu – how then could the girl be familiar?

No. Surely not. If Zech's heart hadn't already been hammering, she felt it might have chosen that moment to drum itself free of her chest. The girl hadn't recognised Zech, and with her skin the way it was, she was seldom forgotten by anyone, and if the suspicion building in her heart was right, then nobody at the compound – least of all Jeiden himself – would ever forgive her for letting this be an end to it.

"You should come with us," she called over her shoulder, as casually as she could. "Your roa is spooked. We can eat while he calms down a bit, and then you can be on your way."

Zech could feel the beast trembling through the reins, with soft little *kree*s of distress still punctuating his breath. Left to his own devices, it was clear he wanted to bolt. Evidently, the strange girl shared this assessment. Her knuckles were pale where she gripped the saddle horn, and her dark eyes were huge with barely-conquered fright.

"That would be most appreciated," she replied, inhaling sharply. "My name... I am Rixevet ore... idi Naha." The correction was quick, but there was no mistaking it. This time, Zech really did feel her pulse quicken. Idi Naha – *belonging to oneself.* It was the same title Matu used, indicating not only that he was unmarried, but that he chose to remain unconnected with his birth-clan. It was a name of anonymity and individualism, and Zech would have eaten a whole, live frog if "Rixevet" had ever used it before.

"I'm Zech," she said instead, turning to smile at the girl, "and this is Jeiden."

"I already told her that," said Jeiden, shooting her a look that clearly asked, *why are we keeping her with us? Not that I mind.* To which Zech sent an answering glower: *trust me, I know what I'm doing.* Or so she hoped. If it turned out she was wrong–

A faint scream echoed after them from the Square of Gods. Rixevet shuddered, but Zech only pushed her shoulders back and kept walking. She'd start to hurt if she stopped – her cheek still throbbed where an elbow had struck her, as did a dozen other places on arm and chest and leg – and anyway, there was nothing more they could do.

Something flickered in her peripheral vision – a streak of silver, there and gone like pale fire. Zech blinked, not sure at first what she'd seen. Her pace slowed slightly, but neither Jeiden nor Rixevet noticed, too busy talking in quiet voices. What had she seen? They were still surrounded by market stalls and market goers. Movement and colour were everywhere; there was no good reason why one such thing should catch Zech's eye when none of its fellows had. She scanned the streets with the edge of her vision, loathe to appear to be staring. Were they being followed? The idea was absurd. No one could possibly be after Zech or Jeiden, and as for Rixevet, anyone with reason to want her certainly wouldn't flinch at reclaiming her from children. And yet – there! She caught the flash again, a wisp of silver robe disappearing around an adjacent corner.

Zech remembered the Shavaktiin players, and specifically the silver-robed Kara, who'd been so blasphemously crowned as Ashasa. All the performers had run when the crowd turned sour, but after the honoured swords had

arrived, she'd paid no attention to who had gone where.
Yasha would want to know about the play, but why did a
Shavaktiin shadow them now? Because they *were* being
shadowed, however clumsily; of that much, Zech was
certain. Predictably Jeiden hadn't noticed, and promise to
Matu or not, Zech had every intention of chaffing him about
it later. Part of her wanted to dismiss it as simple foreign
behaviour, the sort of strange, inscrutable fancy for which
the Shavaktiin were known. But that was lazy thinking,
the sort of thing that would easily fetch her a cuff on the
ear from Pix or a smack from Yasha's staff. If their shadow
weren't a Shavaktiin, Zech would consider it meaningful –
why, then, should those weird robes make a difference?

Maybe they know who Rixevet is, she thought. That made a
certain sort of sense – the Shavaktiin were a religious order
of travellers, tale-tellers and mystics whose puzzling creed,
insofar as it could be made comprehensible to outsiders,
held the discovery and encouragement of story patterns in
true events to be a sacred duty. Zech wasn't sure what that
meant, exactly, and nor was anyone she'd ever met. Lacking
any more sensible explanation, though, she supposed that
anyone who found significance in stories might naturally
be interested in the actions of a calico girl, especially if
they knew what her condition meant in Veksh. Even so,
that wouldn't preclude trouble on the Shavaktiin's part.
Zech decided to stay vigilant, and for the remainder of the
interminable walk back to the compound – Jeiden and
Rixevet talking all the while – she kept one eye peeled for
that telltale flash of silver, gleaming like a knifeblade in the
sun.

When Trishka first revealed where Zech and Jeiden had gone,
Saffron had assumed that Yasha would be furious, with Gwen
and Matu amused. Instead, the exact opposite happened:

Yasha only rolled her eyes, stating that if Zech could steal Saffron away from Kadeja, she could certainly see herself and Jeiden safe through a mob; but Gwen had been angry, while Matu looked near to murderous. Pix had said nothing, though whether out of shock or boredom, Saffron couldn't say.

"Those two!" Matu bellowed – then winced, evidently having re-awoken his own hangover. More quietly, he said, "The Trickster is mocking me. I only told them not to fight, and now they're conspiring together."

"Youthful conspiracies," Gwen muttered – sourly, in English – "are the very worst conspiracies." Given how cross she looked, Saffron fervently hoped the linguistic lapse was an accident and not, as it otherwise had to be, a warning directed solely at her. "Where are they now?"

"Still walking," Trishka said calmly. They were seated in the kitchen – or rather, Yasha and Trishka were seated, and everyone else was hovering in the vicinity, Matu and Pix both leaning against a wall while Gwen braced her palms on a chair back. Saffron wanted to sit herself, but given the mood, it probably wasn't a good idea. She was also starting to feel faintly bored. Like everyone else, she'd been surprised to hear that Zech and Jeiden had picked up a roa-riding companion, but after that and the revelation that all three had escaped the crush unscathed, there was really nothing else to do but wait for them to return.

Just then, two unfamiliar girls – Saffron jumped at this sudden reminder that the compound had other occupants – poked their heads into the kitchen. Both looked Kenan, with brown skin and brown-black eyes, though one was significantly taller than the other, easily approaching six feet.

"What's happened?" asked the shorter girl. She had a dimpled, devious smile, a vulpine chin, and glossy corkscrew curls cut at jaw-level. "Someone said Zech and Jeiden were missing."

"Clearly they are," said the taller one, shooting her companion an annoyed look. Her features were broader: high cheeks and a wide, full-lipped mouth, the elegant shape of her skull accentuated by a close-cropped pixie cut. "The question is, what are they doing *now*?"

"Bringing a stranger home," said Trishka, flashing her gaze their way. A certain fond exasperation suffused her features as she turned to Saffron. "My daughters, Sashi and Yena. Girls, this is Safi. She came through the worlds with Gwen. Why don't you take her–" she glanced at Gwen, who was muttering under her breath, "–outside, and she can fill you in?"

"Works for me," said the shorter girl, now revealed to be Yena. Sashi, the elder, glared at her again, but there was no heat in it.

"Come on then," she said to Saffron. "Dealing with these four is strain enough to crack stone."

"I heard that!" Yasha grumbled, but with what appeared to be a genetic aplomb, both granddaughters ignored her. Instead, they each stepped forward, hooked arms with Saffron and proceeded to march her out of the kitchen and down the hall.

"So, worldwalker–" Yena began.

"–tell us–" Sashi continued.

"–what's been happening?" they finished together.

As unsettling as their synchronicity would have been under normal circumstances, it was considerably multiplied by the stereo effect of having one speaker on either side of her head. Fighting nervousness, Saffron began to explain what Trishka had seen: the square, the mob, the rescue of the girl. It didn't take long: neither Sashi nor Yena asked any questions, and soon enough the three of them were out in the sunshine, seated on the steps that led down from the house.

"Interesting," said Sashi, when Saffron was done. She'd unhooked her arm, though Yena was yet to follow suit.

Which might have bothered Saffron more, if Yena wasn't quite so beautiful. "Has anyone said who the stranger is? I mean," she added quickly, as Yena opened her mouth, "does anyone recognise her? Any theories?"

"No, sorry," said Saffron. All at once a question burst out of her. "Why isn't Yasha angry at them? I don't know much about this place, but it doesn't seem like unexpected visitors are welcome."

"Really?" Yena raised an eyebrow, and Saffron blushed at the belated realisation that *she* was an unexpected visitor too. "What makes you say that?"

"Don't tease, Ye," said Sashi, bracing her arms on her knees as she met Saffron's gaze. "She's not angry, because there's no real risk. If Zechalia brings home an ally or someone useful, then Yasha will profit. But if she's bringing danger, then Yasha won't hesitate."

"Hesitate?" Saffron asked, confused. "To what?"

By way of answer, Yena mimed stabbing her fingers into her throat. "To kill," she said simply.

Saffron was dumbstruck. "But what if they're just a nobody? Not bad, not useful, just..." she wanted to say *random*, but found the Kenan word had a different inference to the English one, "...dull?"

Sashi smiled. "If they were dull, Zechalia wouldn't bring them."

"She knows we've got dullness enough already here," Yena muttered.

Saffron blinked at her, thrown by the sudden change in topic. "What?"

"We're between things here. We're *nekveksanayun*." The strange term wasn't Kenan, and its oddness caught Saffron off guard, until she realised it must be Vekshi.

"It means," supplied Sashi, catching her confusion, "that we aren't truly Vekshi, but not Kenan either. We are *neither the right thing nor its opposite*."

Saffron felt completely out of her depth, and floundered appropriately. "Why?"

Sashi snorted. "A number of things," she said, raising an eyebrow to demonstrate the breadth of the problem and Saffron's ignorance of it both. When Saffron quailed, she softened her glance with a shrug. "We don't shave our heads, for one. Yasha hates it as an affront to Ashasa, but she's practical too – it means we look Kenan enough to spy for her without actually *being* Kenan. Not that there aren't any dark-skinned Vekshi – our mother, for one – but it's nobody's first thought about us here, even if our hair is still too short for braids." She ran a demonstrative hand over her own cropped locks. "Yasha says that being darker wouldn't matter in Veksh, but we have to take her word for it, even though she won't tell us why she had to leave in the first place. Instead we live here, which is properly Kena, but not so Kenan at all within these walls." She waved a hand at the compound, as though disgusted with it.

"We can't keep living with what other people want for us, or don't want for us," Yena said. "We have to live for what *we* want. But everything that's in your head, the things you've been told to believe and do, you can't just throw it all out like bathwater, even when you know it's hurting you. So instead, we wait."

"For what?" asked Saffron.

"For Yasha to either die or change," said Sashi dryly. "Though fire would sooner turn to ice, in either case."

"For a chance to defy her," Yena added. "Something that will prove our worth. She dislikes ordinary defiance, but respects extraordinary rebellion."

"What's the difference?" Saffron asked, fascinated.

"Whether it bores or impresses her, mostly," Sashi said. "But we're working on that."

"Which is why," Yena said, "we're so keen to see what Zechalia drags in. Yasha is content for now; that doesn't mean she'll remain so."

"Ah," said Saffron. "Right."

A not-quite-comfortable silence descended – which is to say, Saffron felt vaguely as if she should say something more, but as the sisters didn't share her affliction, it put her in the minority. She found herself looking for signs of their inbetweenness, trying to parse the differences between her still-fledging expectations of Kenan and Vekshi customs, and coming up short. It wasn't just her ignorance of obvious things, like symbols and clothes and permissions; it was the realisation that all of them together constituted a different language, an automatic series of thoughts and associations that no amount of zuymet-bonding could teach. She knew she could learn – she wanted to learn – but where could she start, when she no longer knew if a question was obvious or complex, harmless or sensitive?

"What's the matter?" Sashi asked. "You look like you've stones in your throat."

"I just realised I don't know anything about anything," Saffron said, put out.

"Oh, well done!" said Yena, hug-and-tugging her still-captured arm. "That means you're on your own road now."

And she brushed her palm against the still-raw stumps where Saffron's fingers had been.

Saffron yelped, jumping as the touch shot through her like ice and wine and lightning all at once, even though there was no pain, not really; just a sort of tingling, and the heart-shaking remembrance of what she'd lost. The hand in her lap was a mutilated starfish, and it was hers now, hers forever. Lungs tight with breath, she steeled herself and touched the stumps. Little more than a tap – two whole fingers dancing down against the flesh, then back again – but this time there was no shock; only an icy certainty that this was real, all of it, a slice of ongoing experience as neatly pared away from her old life as her missing fingers had been from her hand.

"Maybe I am, then," Saffron said softly. "On my own road."

Sashi blinked at her. "Only maybe? Where else would you be?"

Saffron might have answered, but at just that moment, someone behind them let out an angry "Hah!"

She turned, startled. Save for Trishka, everyone who'd been in the kitchen was broaching the steps. It was Gwen who'd shouted, and when Saffron looked back to the courtyard, she saw that Zech and Jeiden were slinking in through the gates. Zech came first, leading a white-and-grey roa ridden by a teenaged girl whose whole body boasted of the same awkward, child-into-woman phase that was currently reshaping Ruby. Even thinking the comparison hurt. Saffron shoved it aside and concentrated on Jeiden, whose eyes were fixed on the rescued girl with an expression wavering midway between contempt and adoration.

"Yasha," Zech began, handing the roa's reins to Jeiden, "I can explain–"

"I'm sure you can," said Yasha, stony-faced as she descended the stairs. Reaching Zech, she raised the hand not gripping her staff and cuffed the girl soundly around the ear. Saffron flinched in shock at the casual violence – while Gwen, behind her, made an outraged sound – but Zech only rubbed the side of her head, grinning a tight, rueful grin that said she'd expected as much. "And you!" said Yasha, pointing her staff at Jeiden, "Matu will deal with *you* later."

"Gods willing I will," Matu muttered. He was standing to Yena's left, and though he hadn't spoken loudly enough for his words to carry, Jeiden nonetheless reacted by hunching in on himself.

Sashi stood first, followed by Saffron and Yena. All of them were watching Yasha, held silent by a strange, sudden tension that had washed up in the wake of Matu's grumbling.

"And who is this?" the matriarch asked, swinging her staff up to point at the girl. Her roa *kree*d his anxiety as the wood hissed past his head, but didn't pull at the bridle.

"I am Rixevet idi Naha," the girl said, straightening her shoulders. Her voice was surprisingly deep, but not warm.

To Saffron's eye, she still retained a certain younger-sibling softness about her, but pride gleamed in the planes of her face, as yet only half-distinct from a child's stubbornness – much, in fact, as her cheeks and jaw were yet to emerge from baby fat. Loose black hair curled free from beneath a backwards-slipping scarf, giving her what Saffron instinctively thought of as a hippyish look.

"Are you indeed?" mused Yasha, rocking back on her heels. "And why–"

"That's not who she is."

It was Pix, taking the stairs two at a time, her gaze locked with that of the girl on the roa. Saffron felt her heart speed up. Even Yasha looked surprised, moving aside as the ex-courtier came and grabbed the beast by the bridle. Jeiden looked startled, but Zech – Saffron did a double-take – actually looked smug, as though she'd been expecting such a reaction. No, not expecting: *hoping for*.

"I know you," said maybe-Rixevet, frowning imperiously at Pix. "Why do I know you? Tell me!"

Pix tilted her chin and grinned like a hungry leopard. "I am Pixeva ore Pixeva ki Tahun, little moon-girl. Once I braided your hair and declared you married to the wind and earth and sky, for you stamped your foot and swore you'd know no other mahu'kedet than that. Yet times have changed, I see. Your lawful braids are come undone, and now you flee the ones who bound them."

"Pix? Who is that?" Matu called, a worrisome note in his voice.

But it was the girl who answered, and this time there was steel in the words. "I am your Cuivexa, Iviyat ore Leoden ki Hawy. And if you are truly Pixeva ore Pixeva, then I command you: give me sanctuary!"

Gwen stared at the girl on the roa, unable to wrap her head around the sudden change in events. The Cuivexa! Even knowing how Zech had found her, she still didn't understand why it had happened. The very idea was incredible, and yet the girl – the queen – was undeniably here, dismounting with a glint in her eye that said she'd noticed Jeiden's slack-jawed reaction to her identity, and was pleased by it. As Pix linked arms with Iviyat, Gwen stepped forward – they needed to talk, this had to be done properly; did they even need Veksh and the Council of Queens, if the Cuivexa joined their camp? – but found herself quite literally rebuffed, Yasha holding her back with the head of her arse-damned staff.

"Not you, Gwen," she muttered, wavering between anger and excitement as she helped Pix shepherd Iviyat up the stairs. "Not yet." And then, to rub salt in the wound, she turned and called over her shoulder for Zech – Zech! – to join their conference instead.

It was unbearable, an insult that left her with both fists clenched and a jaw hard-set as concrete. She whipped around to Matu, hoping he'd share her indignation at their (though mostly her) exclusion. Instead, he only shrugged, his silky hair twitching like cat whiskers. "What can you do?" he asked. "My sister is what she is, and Yasha will do what Yasha will do, and Cuivexas and calico girls alike can fall in line behind them."

"And the rest of us?" Gwen seethed. "What in the name of thorns and godshit do *we* do, Matu?"

His mouth quirked. "Pick up the pieces, perhaps?" Then he sighed, clapping a hand to her shoulder. "Let it go, Gwen. She'll speak to you soon enough. Trickster knows she despises listening to sense, but that doesn't mean she rejects its value entirely."

With that, he dropped his hand and sauntered over to Jeiden, who was still gawking hopelessly after Iviyat, the roa left loose beside him. Gwen watched them for a moment, the way Matu collected the abandoned reins while putting a gentle arm around Jeiden's neck, leading both of them off to the stables. He really was a better man than anyone gave him credit for, and at times like this, when his kindness matched his beauty, it was hard for Gwen to remember that she was older than his mother, and had no business staring after him as though she were Saffron's age.

"Oh, hell," she said quietly, and just like that the anger went out of her. She turned back to Sashi and Yena and Saffron – all so young, so unaware it wouldn't last – and plonked herself down at their feet.

"I give up," she announced, savouring the self-indulgent drama of the proclamation. "I really do."

As if on cue, both Sashi and Yena sat down with her, one on either side. Saffron alone remained standing, fidgeting in her uncertainty.

"Did that really just happen?" Yena asked.

Sashi rolled her eyes. "Stop wasting breath on answered questions," she scolded. Then, after a moment's hesitation, "Gwen? Did it?"

"Something's always happening somewhere," she hedged. But Sashi was still looking at her, stubborn as her mother, and so she said, "Yes, it did. I don't know why, though. Whenever I think I've got a grip on the worlds, they twist out from under me again." She closed her eyes. "Go and see to lunch, you two. I could do with something to settle my stomach."

"It's not our turn!" Sashi protested.

But Yena said, "All right."

Gwen felt the vibrations of their exit through the steps beneath her. Once they were gone, she opened her eyes. There was only Saffron left.

"Is... is there anything I should be doing?" she asked – in English, as the two of them were alone. She looked older with her hair shaved off, Gwen thought; it brought out the shape of her cheekbones, strengthened the line of her neck.

Gwen laughed at the query, a wry, choked sound. "Oh,

my girl," she murmured, shaking her head. "What a mess
you've dropped into here. A right royal mess! No, there's
nothing you can do for the moment. But later – later, when
Zech is free, talk to her. She'll tell you what's going on. And,
if you can, talk to Iviyat."

"Is she really a queen?" Saffron blurted.

"A Cuivexa, not a queen, and yes. She really is," Gwen
said. "But that doesn't mean you can't talk to her."

Saffron looked sceptical. "Won't I have to, I don't know…
bow, or something? Curtsey?"

"Under normal circumstances, yes, but here she's
incognito. She only told us the truth because Pix already
knew her, and because if Pix is with us, then we must be
opposed to Leoden. The rest of the compound, though –
there's more people here than you've met so far. Some are
Vekshi, some are Kenan, but they've all got different ties to
Yasha, and most of them don't keep her confidences. *We* all
know who Iviyat is, but no one else here does, and I doubt
Yasha will want to change that."

"What about Sashi and Yena, though?" Saffron persisted.
"What if they tell?"

"They won't," Gwen said simply. "They know their
grandmother too well. No. Whatever Yasha's planning,
she'll want this secret."

Viya stared at Yasha, wondering why Ke and Na had seen fit
to include the Vekshi crone in their schemes. As soon as she'd
recognised Pixeva ore Pixeva, she'd known the gods had made
Zech their envoy, guiding her through their holy square and
into the hands of allies. Their intervention was self-evident to
anyone with sense – but of course, the Vekshi were all sun-
worshipping heretics like Kadeja, and couldn't be trusted to
understand their proper role in things. Yet Pix, for whatever
reason, was bent on including Yasha in their conversation –

and worse still, deferring to her. No matter how Viya ignored the old woman or hint-dropped to Pix that their conversation was better had in private, Yasha refused to leave her betters in peace.

And then there was Zech, lingering like a child even after she'd already told her version of events: their meeting, the mob, the journey home. To Viya's deep unease, this had also involved mention of a Shavaktiin who'd followed them; she felt furious not to have noticed it herself. Yasha grilled the girl closely on that point, but according to Zech, whoever it was had vanished a good ten minutes before they reached the compound. A small part of Viya wondered if she should mention Luy's role in her escape. Was it possible, she wondered, that he'd had something to do with the Square of Gods? Might *he* have been their shadow?

But in the end, she rejected the notion out of hand. She didn't like Yasha, with her sharp eyes and ugly pale skin and bristle-bald head, and though she might – just *might* – have seen her way to confiding in Pix, the sky would rain fire before she told that wrinkled old woman a single thing more than she had to.

Unable to help herself, she glanced again at Zech, resenting her continuing presence almost as much as Yasha's. Now that the threat of the crowd was gone, she noticed how unsettling the calico girl truly was. Her whole skin was blotchy, white and brown and gold; together with her weird grey hair and pale eyes, she looked like a ragdoll stitched together from scraps. Viya owed her nothing for the rescue: she was Cuivexa, after all, and anyway, it was Ke and Na who'd truly saved her. But asking for her to leave would have implied that Viya considered her presence meaningful, and as such a thing was beneath a Cuivexa's dignity – even a Cuivexa in flight – she was forced to endure her company.

Ever since Zech had stopped talking, Yasha had been enumerating what might be meant by sanctuary, but Viya wasn't listening. Thanks to Luy's interference, she was fed up with lowborn strangers telling her what to do. All she wanted now was for these people to show her the deference she was owed as Cuivexa – give her shelter for the night (*and a horse tomorrow*, she thought savagely, *they ought to at* least *give me a horse!*) and help her on her way, none of which was being achieved by Yasha's prating.

"Enough!" she snapped, cutting the old woman off mid-sentence. "Pixeva, have you had any contact with my secondmother, Rixevet ore Hawy? She went to our holdings at Avekou before Vex Leoden was crowned, along with my fourthfather Kadu and bloodfather Iavan."

Irritatingly, Pix glanced at Yasha before answering. "No," she said slowly. "But if you're travelling north, Cuivexa, we'd be happy to offer escort."

"That won't be necessary," Viya said, inwardly shuddering at the thought of travelling with Yasha. "A horse and supplies will suffice."

Yasha raised an eyebrow. "You'd brave the roads alone?"

"I know the way," Viya said, "and a single rider covers more ground than a convoy. As for bravery, I have already abandoned the palace. Riding alone could hardly require more courage than leaving did." *There*, she thought, *let that remind you of what I've done and who I am!*

"Fairly spoken," said Yasha, but though her tone was mild, there was a hard glint in her eye that Viya mistrusted. "Even so, I hope you'll spend the night within our walls. While I trust the discretion of everyone who learned your identity in the courtyard, I am more discerning when it comes to our other occupants. I would suggest we refrain from the usual deference–" *As though you've shown me any!* Viya thought, "– and continue to call you Rixevet. Or is there another name you'd prefer to be known by?"

"Viya will suffice," she said, firmly. As much as she disliked the idea of being called her intimate name by Yasha, it would have been dishonest to reclaim Rixevet's name among people who already knew it for a lie, particularly as Pix knew her secondmother personally.

"Well then, Viya," Pix said, gesturing to the door, "if you're going to be with us for the night, I'll show you where everything is, shall I?"

"Yes, and my thanks," said Viya. She was only too glad to exit the room, but as she left, she could swear she felt Yasha's gaze burning her neck, like coal-sparks kicked up from a fire.

The compound was quiet at night, and Gwen savoured it.

She sat alone on the front verandah, rolling a cup of warm mege between her palms. A faint breeze stirred the courtyard dust. She clutched the shawl wrapped around her shoulders, the action more reflex than necessity. She didn't yet know what to make of the fugitive Cuivexa; she was young and prickly and powerful, and watching her snub Yasha had filled Gwen in equal parts with schadenfreude and secondhand embarrassment, but as to what she was planning…

Lifting her chin, Gwen contemplated the Kenan stars and wondered, for neither the first nor last time since Leoden's betrayal, exactly what Kadeja had done to be cast from Ashasa's priestesshood; how Leoden had met her; what the two of them saw in each other. She knew now, with the bitter certainty of hindsight, that Kadeja had been working with Leoden long before Gwen and Pix ever knew she existed; and worse, that Leoden had always planned to make her his Vex'Mara. His lengthy "negotiations" about the conditions of his marriage to Tevet and Amenet had been a stall tactic in the first instance, and a means of getting close enough for murder in the second. Nothing more.

Kenans didn't play poker, Gwen thought sourly, but if

they did, Leoden would make bank on it. He'd fooled her
– fooled them – so comprehensively that, even now, even
knowing what he was, a part of her still couldn't separate
out the lies from the truth. Was Leoden Kadeja's pawn,
or vice versa? It was, of course, entirely possible that they
were equal partners in crime, but on the basis of having met
them both – albeit briefly, in Kadeja's case – Gwen somehow
doubted it. Or maybe she only wanted to doubt it, hungry
to believe that the man who'd betrayed her was himself
in danger of betrayal. If Leoden and Kadeja were quietly
working against each other, then they were vulnerable,
which was a comforting thought. But if they were truly
pulling in harness, then what did that mean for Kena?

Gwen sipped at her mege, and remembered.

Kadeja had been there, the day they'd finally persuaded
Leoden to sign the marriage contracts. Her head was shaved
then, and together with her piercing eyes and fine-boned
face, it had given her the look of a bird of prey, for all that
she sat demurely in a plain white gown, her bare arms
banded with heavy gold bracelets.

"And who is this?" Pix had asked, her eyebrows shooting
up. In all the times they'd come to Leoden's residence,
he'd never had company beyond his servants. Which, in
retrospect, made sense: he'd taken care to keep them from
seeing who else he'd been talking to. "An ally?"

"A friend," replied Leoden, smiling in that brisk, warm
way of his, like winter sunlight flashing through glass. He
was more magnetic than handsome, and when he spoke, his
hands could be as eloquent as his words. "Pixeva ore Pixeva,
Gwen Vere, this is Kadeja Etmahsi."

Etmahsi. It was a word, not a name, but for all the time she
had spent with Vekshi women, it still took Gwen a moment
to place the meaning. When she did, her gaze sharpened.
Etmahsi meant *motherless*, and in a culture of matriarchs,
it wasn't a title you earned through anything good. Still,

Gwen didn't like to judge – the Many knew, she found Vekshi customs strange enough at the best of times – and so she said nothing, moving aside as Pix laid out the contracts on Leoden's writing desk.

As the two nobles went through the documents, Kadeja rose and padded over to Gwen.

"You're the worldwalker," she said – a statement, not a question. Gwen nodded, silent beneath Kadeja's appraising stare, and waited for the other woman to speak again. After a moment, she did. "Kenan aristocrats are peculiar creatures, aren't they?"

Gwen hadn't contradicted her, not least because Pix had spent an hour that morning deciding how best to wear her marriage-braids. "They certainly have their moments."

"I was worried, when I first came here, that I wouldn't understand them."

"Oh?" said Gwen, gaze flicking to track the movement of Leoden's fingers over the vellum. "What made you change your mind?"

"Power is power," Kadeja said simply, and Gwen wished then – as she'd wished many times since – that she'd seen her face as she said it. Instead, she turned too late, and any further insight into the remark was lost forever.

"This looks to be in order," Leoden said. His words were for the room at large, but Kadeja smiled as though at a private joke. "Let me get my quill."

"Here," said Kadeja, passing it to him, and if any part of Gwen thought it odd that a Vekshi woman, newly-disgraced – she knew what her missing fingers meant, even without the inauspicious name – would rush to act so submissively around a Kenan nobleman, she must have ignored it. *Or maybe*, she thought, *you were so used to feeling odd yourself that you privately welcomed a little oddness from others*. Regardless of whether strangers truly believed her to be a worldwalker, she was still a foreigner here, and even after so many years, the sting of being thought alien was undiminished.

Then Leoden signed the marriage contracts – the ink was purple, Teket's sacred colour, and ferociously expensive – and that was that.

"I look forward to meeting Amenet in particular," he said, unfailingly polite as they made their parting courtesies, and all the while Kadeja stood back and watched, a slight smile on her face.

Two weeks later, he'd poisoned Amenet, married Kadeja and crowned himself Vex of Kena.

Now, Gwen drained the last of her mege, rubbing her head as she set the cup aside. She wanted to trust in Iviyat, but past experience made her wary. *She's a child, Gwen. Younger than Saffron is, even. Would you force her to prove her innocence before offering aid?*

Yes, said a different inner voice, the one that sounded disconcertingly like Yasha. *A hundred times over, if it saves us the same mistakes.*

But what if mistrust is a different error? the first voice persisted. *What then?*

Gwen sighed and straightened, heading back inside. *Pray that we learn from it quickly enough to matter.*

Saffron lay awake in bed, turning the day's events over in her mind. Even once Pix had presented Iviyat to them properly – they were to call her Viya, with no more to be said about it – an air of unreality clung to the situation. The Cuivexa herself had mostly remained in a haughty silence, occasionally initiating conversation with Pix, Matu and Jeiden, but otherwise dealing curtly with everyone else. Though Zech assured her this was all to do with rank – Pix's family were aristocrats, and had been highly placed at court before Leoden came to power – it still felt brattish and rude to Saffron.

The problem, she reflected, was that it was almost impossible for her to comprehend that plump, imperious

Iviyat was a queen. Partly, this was due to the fact that she reminded her of Ruby; partly because she'd already taken to thinking of Kadeja that way; and partly, too, because the very idea of meeting a Cuivexa, or a queen, or a princess – or whatever she was in whatever language – was not one that came naturally to a girl from New South Wales whose entire family thought it was long past time that Australia became a republic. Mostly, though, it was because they were all pretending she *wasn't* royalty, and without any communal sense of awe or deference to tip the scales, it was hard for Saffron not to think of the whole thing as a sort of abstract joke.

Pix and Matu belonging to the nobility was one thing; she could get away with thinking of them as the Kenan equivalent of private school alums with property in Rose Bay, or, at worst, as politicians. But a queen – *the* Queen – was a smiling old white lady who gave the Christmas speech and had her face minted on coins. It would have required more mental agility than Saffron currently possessed to instantly confer identical status on a fourteen-year-old brown girl shorter than she was. *Not*, she thought hastily, *that race has anything to do with it.* The idea that it might, even a little, left her feeling deeply uncomfortable. But with sleep the only escape from her thoughts and it proving hard to come by, she was forced to confront the possibility that maybe it did. After all, she'd had no trouble believing in Kadeja's queenliness, and that was after the woman had cut off two of her fingers. (She touched her stumps again in the dark. The new skin felt waxy, like candles burned down to their nubs.)

Disquieted, she rolled over on her mattress and stared at the moonlight sifting in through the shutters. "Not seeing Viya as a queen because she's not white is racist," she whispered into the pillow. "I'm being racist. Stop it." She felt bad because it was true, but slightly better for having admitted it. After all, if she didn't admit she was doing something wrong in the first place, how could she possibly fix it?

Saffron closed her eyes and, some minutes later, finally fell asleep.

And dreamed.

She stood in a place she didn't know, beneath a huge, white sun. The earth underfoot was brown and hard – a crossroads, placing her at the nexus of four different paths. Each one was narrow, not even as broad across as her outstretched arms, and all were surrounded by tall, lush grass, a blue-green sea that waved as high as her calves.

"Weird," she murmured, feeling the dream-words sting her lips. "Either I'm in Wonderland, or due to meet the devil."

"Why not both?"

The voice came from behind her. Turning, she found herself face to face with a handsome, dark-skinned man who looked to be about Pix's age. His hair was braided in leftwards-curving cornrows, and there was a quizzical tilt to his head. Like Matu, he wore a tunic and trousers – both deep blue – though his sleeves were short and his feet bare. His brawny arms were folded over his chest, and as he studied Saffron, a crooked smile tugged his lips.

"That's odd," he said. "You really are here."

"Why wouldn't I be?" said Saffron. "It's my dream."

His smile broadened. "Are you sure about that?"

"It's a dream. I don't have to be sure."

He laughed at that. "Good point."

Movement flickered in the corner of her eye, but when she turned to follow it, the whole world somersaulted around her, spinning like a merry-go-round. She fell and kept on falling, rolling over endlessly as though down the world's longest slope. Then something caught in her throat, and suddenly she was on her hands and knees, gagging groggily as she vomited a spool of cloth onto the grass. With one hand, she pulled the last of it free and stared at the pattern: a golden dragon rearing on a scarlet field studded with flowers. The dragon twitched against its stitches, hissing like a punctured hose; the flowers opened, withered, regrew; and all around the crimson fabric rippled like blood–

Hands grasped Saffron's shoulders, pulling her up and away. She lurched to her feet, blinking spots from her vision.

"Well," said the man in blue. "That was interesting, wasn't it?"

"Was it?" Saffron asked. Her tongue felt muzzy and slow, as though she were talking underwater – but then, dreams were often like that.

The man raised his eyes as if in prayer. "Come on. Walk with me."

He held out a hand, and Saffron took it. His palm was calloused and warm. As he led her forwards, the world around them changed again, the long grass turning ruby-red, punctuated here and there with golden flowers. The white sun dipped low and the sky grew darker, a deep, friendly indigo streaked with lilac.

"You're not from Kena, are you?"

"No," admitted Saffron. "I don't really know what I'm doing here."

"That's true of most people, never mind where they've ended up or how it happened. But like I said before, it's odd that you're here, specifically." He gestured at the never-ending fields.

"You said it wasn't a dream," said Saffron. She frowned, her thoughts flowing thick as treacle. "So what is it?"

"A crossroads, of sorts. A way for me to try to find the patterns in the world. Or in this world, anyway," he amended, grinning. "It's not like there's only one."

Abruptly, Saffron stopped walking. She pulled her hand away, vaguely resentful of being told she was trespassing in her own subconscious. "Why am I here, then? What's happening?"

The man cocked his head and looked at her. "I'm not quite sure. Well, that's not true – you must be part of events, or else I couldn't have found you. But that's true of lots of people, and they don't all show up on my patch of the dreamscape. No. It's something else."

Movement flashed in her peripheral vision. Wary of what had happened last time, Saffron tried to refrain from looking, but the motion was insistent. Slowly, she turned her head. Away to her right, the grass was catching fire – no, turning into flames, a spreading carpet of red tongues crackling and dancing.

"Do you see that?" she whispered.

"I do."

"Can it hurt us?"

"I wouldn't think so."

"Good." But still, she felt uneasy. "The ground keeps changing."

He gave her arm a gentle pinch. "Do you still think this is a dream?"

"All dreams change," said Saffron. "That's how you know they're dreams."

"So does reality," he replied. "That's how you know it's real."

The fire was closer now, licking towards them like an incoming tide.

"Tell me your name," he asked, suddenly. "Who are you?"

"I'm Saffron. Saffron Isla Coulter."

"I don't know you in waking then. That's not it." He went silent for a moment, then his eyes lit up with delighted suspicion. "You didn't come alone to Kena. Who brought you here?"

White smoke rose up from the fire-grass, blooming in clouds like mushrooms.

"Gwen Vere," said Saffron, coughing. "A worldwalker. She didn't bring me though. I just sort of... followed her in."

But the man was grinning in triumph. "Hah! Of course you did!" His gaze turned serious. "And don't ever make the mistake of thinking that things you didn't intend or plan don't matter. It's a big, disorganised multiverse out there – an accident of stars. Almost nothing ever works out like we want it to, and when it does, there's guaranteed to be unexpected consequences. Randomness is what separates life from entropy, but it's also what makes it fun."

"Who are you?" Saffron asked. The smoke was boiling everywhere now, wreathing them so thickly that she could no longer see the fire, the grass, or anything but the strange man's face and torso.

He smiled at her sadly. "You'll probably forget this meeting, Saffron Isla Coulter, or else brush it off as just another dream. But if any of this breaks through as real–" and here he kissed the tips of two fingers, touching them to her forehead, "–you tell Gwen Vere that Luy ore Jhesa'yu of the Shavaktiin is helping as best he can. You tell her–"

But then there was only smoke, and white, and silence.

11
Firefight

"Wake up, Gwen. Please. There isn't much time."

Gwen struggled into wakefulness, shrugging off sleep like a borrowed shawl. Her dreams had been flat and unmemorable, and yet her brain was reluctant to let them fade.

"Trishka?" she said, blinking up at her friend. "What is it?"

"Leoden," Trishka said. "He's coming for us. We have to get out now, as quick and quiet as possible."

That brought her up cold. "Devils and gods in an orgy!" she swore. "*Damn* him!"

Muscles protesting the sudden movement, she swung herself out of bed, grabbing for her boots and belt while Trishka spoke, her voice unnervingly calm.

"Some of the Uyun ambassador's men are with his honoured swords. I don't know why, but he's told them where we are. There's about fifty of them. I think..." She hesitated, voice trailing off as her vision went far away. "They have torches," she said at last. "I think they want to burn us out."

Gwen went cold all over. The compound's roof, flooring and outbuildings were wooden, as were the stables and gates. Fire wouldn't destroy the building, but it could certainly drive everyone into the open, trapping them between flame and stone. Though Yasha's Vekshi were proficient staff-fighters, their hardwood weapons strong enough to match all but the sharpest swords, they drilled to fight either in ordered ranks or alone. But in darkness, disordered, with children and animals underfoot and no space to either form up or retreat? It was a recipe for a massacre.

Gwen's thoughts raced ahead of her pulse. "We need two groups," she said. "One to travel north, and the rest to head to safety." Her gaze darted to Trishka, who was perched on the end of her bed, and weighed her next words carefully. "Do you trust Sashi as a leader?"

So briefly that anyone else would have missed it, a shadow of fear passed over Trishka's face. But when she stood, her back was straight and her voice firm. "She's a good choice. Yes."

"And Yena?"

"Should come north." Her response was instantaneous. "It's time they travelled apart from each other."

The braided path, Gwen thought, but even so, the weight of the choice wasn't lost on her. She reached out and squeezed Trishka's shoulder. Their eyes met in silent accord. "Go wake your daughters. Tell Sashi to round up everyone who doesn't know about Viya – they'll be the eastern group – and get Yena to grab as many supplies as she can. I'll have Zech and Jeiden go to the stables: roas and horses both, as many and as quiet as they can manage. Then I'll wake the others and meet you out front."

Trishka grinned savagely. "Yasha last?"

"Yasha last," Gwen echoed, and as though they were still young and miscreant enough for that ancient pact to apply, they pressed their foreheads together in brief affirmation. "How long do we have?"

"Twenty minutes at most, I'd guess."

Gwen swore, borrowing a favourite Vekshi curse of

Yasha's. Literally translated, it meant *arsegullet. We'll never get clear of the compound in that time, let alone free of the city.* But there was nothing to do but try.

They parted – Trishka one way, Gwen the other.

She went to Jeiden first. The boy woke easily, eyes wide in the darkness, and hurried off almost before Gwen had finished explaining the need. Zech, though, famously slept like the dead; rather than wasting time, Gwen simply pinched her nose shut until she came to, gasping indignantly. Still, she sobered quickly enough when told about the troops and went to join Jeiden, slipping down the hall like a dappled shadow. Next came Matu, who swore furiously under his breath, hauled on a tunic and promised to help Yena get her supplies out to the pack animals; and then, finally, Pix, who reacted – typically, yet unnervingly – with her trademark vicious calm.

"What do we do about Viya?" she asked, binding her marriage-braids back in a tail. "Maybe she set this up somehow. Leoden's always loved twisted plots – that pustule has a brain like a rat's maze."

"He couldn't have known that Zech and Jeiden would bring her here." Yet even as she said it, Gwen felt an unpleasant stirring of doubt. The last time she and Pix had underestimated Leoden, thousands of people had died. Better to play it safe, at least until they were out of Karavos. *Assuming we even make it that far.* She shook her head, frustrated. "Even so. There's a jar of moonsleep in Yasha's chambers. Knock her out with that, then have Matu tie her to one of the horses – sitting stance, though, not slung sideways like a carcass." She'd been carried once that way herself, and still had faint scars on her arms and hips to prove it.

Pix eyed her coolly. "And is Yasha awake?"

"Not yet," Gwen admitted. "I was leaving her for last."

"Coward."

"You say that like it's an insult."

"It should be." Pix made a face. "Fine. I'll wake her once our pet Cuivexa's safely trussed and bound. Always best to greet her with good news – that little wretch ground so much salt into her godslapped pride, I'm surprised they both survived it."

Gwen snorted. By now, she gauged, most people were awake: the compound was tense with whispers and muffled movement. *Why now?* she wondered. Leoden had known where Yasha was for years, but had never attacked like this, so satisfied with the presumed impotence of his adversaries that it was easier just to let them be. He'd briefly come after her and Pix in the aftermath of his betrayal, but he'd never bothered the rest of their allies. Maybe Pix was right; maybe it was down to Viya. But then she remembered the arakoi: sniffing around the warehouse, keeping watch at the gates. Was it arrogance to think he was after *her*? *Not arrogance,* she cautioned herself. *Prudence.* But even so, something had changed beyond the mere fact of her return to Kena. Leoden had a plan, and until she knew properly what it was – or better yet, was in a position to stop it – Gwen could assume nothing.

"My thanks," she said to Pix. "I doubt she'd welcome the sight of me right now under any circumstances, good or bad."

"You owe me." Her knife-belt now buckled, Pix pulled on a fingerless pair of fighter's gloves, the padded leather studded with sharp metal.

Gwen raised a brow at her armoury. "Planning ahead?"

Pix's smile was sharp as winter. "Always."

As they parted ways, Gwen experienced the sudden, nagging sensation that she'd forgotten something. The reason struck her a moment later: Saffron. She bit her lip to keep from swearing, abruptly furious at herself for having let the girl slip so thoroughly out of mind. *If I'm not responsible for her, no one is.* Irritation and sympathy flashed through her in equal measure: irritation that Saffron had followed her through the worlds; sympathy because she of all people knew how irrevocable a choice it was, no matter how thoughtlessly made. *Well, at least Pix has Yasha in hand,* Gwen thought wryly, and walked to the white girl's room. Saffron slept curled up, knees to chest with an elbow crooked under her head. Her lips moved soundlessly – she was dream-talking, Gwen assumed – yet when she reached out and touched her shoulder, her eyes snapped open instantly, as though she'd been only dozing. "Smoke and fire," Saffron whispered. "Everything burned. Didn't it?"

Gwen gaped at her, momentarily stunned. Maybe it was a coincidence, but just at that moment, it didn't feel like one. "Not yet," she found herself answering. "But that's why we have to go. Leoden is coming."

Saffron sat up, her mouth an O of surprise. "But I thought – he said to tell you…" She frowned, her words trailing off like the tail-end of clouds. "I don't remember."

"It was only a dream," said Gwen, because there was no space in which to consider otherwise. "Come on. There's not much time."

To her credit, the girl dressed quickly and quietly, pulling on the Vekshi clothes she'd been given the day before. She reached for her school shoes too, but stopped. "I don't have any socks," she said. "They went to the wash."

"Go without?" Gwen suggested, trying not to sound impatient. The imminent threat of danger itched in her skin.

Saffron shook her head. "I'll just go barefoot. Those shoes give me blisters, anyway."

Sighing with suppressed relief, Gwen nodded and motioned Saffron out. The girl obeyed without another word, and together they navigated their way through the compound and out to the dimly lit courtyard, where – thank the Many! – two separate clusters of people and beasts had gathered. One, the largest, was under Sashi's supervision. Comprised mostly of Vekshi expatriates and their children, the group waited nervously by the main gates, mounted on roas and with plenty of staffs in evidence. Between the two groups stood Trishka. Supported by Yena, she swayed within her magic, eyes closed. And then, finally, there was their own small party: Pix, Matu and Yasha, all on horseback; Viya strapped firmly to the same roa she'd ridden in on, its reins tied to Pix's saddle; Zech scuttling about in response to Yasha's whispered commands; and Jeiden standing by, his hands full to brimming with the reins of six more horses and two supply-laden roas.

"What's wrong with Viya?" Saffron asked nervously. "Why's she tied down?"

"Do you trust me enough to believe it's for a good reason?" Gwen asked.

"I guess," said Saffron, though she obviously wasn't happy about it.

"Good." Gwen sighed, smoothing a hand over her flyaway hair. Braiding would have been convenient, but braids had meaning in Kena, and though her marriage entitled her to certain convenient styles (she winged a silent prayer of apology to Jhesa and Naku) their usage would have betrayed her privacy. "I'll explain later. Until then–"

"They're coming," Trishka said, loudly enough to cut through the chatter. Everyone fell silent. "We need to leave. Now."

Gwen hissed in surprise, urging Saffron to go and mount up – "If you need any help, ask Zech!" – before hurrying over to Trishka.

Though strong, Yena was visibly struggling to keep her mother standing. Slinging an arm round her friend's shoulder, Gwen took Trishka's weight onto herself. Yena didn't need to be told anything; she headed straight for the horses, trusting Gwen to see that her mother did likewise.

"You've done enough," Gwen chided, frightened by Trishka's obvious exhaustion. "Come on, we need to get you mounted."

Stumbling, they made their way to the others. Trishka was panting by the time she'd pulled herself into the saddle, but there was a glint in her eye that Gwen didn't like.

"You're planning something," she accused.

Rather than answer, Trishka turned and rode to Sashi's side. Gwen mounted and followed, her sense of foreboding now so strong that the hairs on her arms stood up. Beyond the compound walls, she fancied she could hear the soldiers forming up, then shivered with the realisation that it was no fancy. Leoden's men were here, their presence betrayed by the noise of strange roas, the tramp of feet and the flicker of torchlight under the gates. Were they close enough to know their quarry was awake and ready, preparing to flee? Gwen hoped not, but all too soon, she'd know the answer for sure.

"We'll ride through first, like you told us – half the fighters will engage, while the rest split off and take the children to safety," Sashi said. She looked ageless to Gwen in that moment, both a woman grown and far too young to be facing any sort of battle. By Vekshi reckoning, Sashi and Yena were her nieces, and the thought of either of them being in danger almost overwhelmed her. But then Sashi said, "We'll buy you the time," and all her fearful attention refocused on Trishka.

"You can't!" she hissed. "The compound is worn thin enough as a portal point. The risk–"

"There's no other way." Trishka looked at her steadily. "You know I'm right."

"We could cut through them, head for the city gates–"

"We can't." She was calm, implacable, though already a ragged note had crept into her breathing. "You know we can't, Gwen." She reached out to Sashi, briefly touching her daughter's face. "Zejhasa," she murmured. "Still, you have my heart."

Sashi grabbed her mother's fingers and kissed the tips. "I plan to be worthy of it."

And with that, each of them pulled away. Sashi turned to face her charges, while Trishka wheeled her mare around, leaving Gwen no choice but to follow.

"You can't," she repeated – pleading this time, even though she knew it was pointless. Trishka was right; there was no other way. "At least try t–"

A burning arrow sailed over the wall, streaking through the night like a tiny star. Gwen watched its trajectory with a lump in her throat. It struck the wooden roof. The fire spread with a cackling crackle, flaring along the wood; and then there were more lit arrows, and vials of oil flung in their wake to help feed the blaze. The courtyard was red-lit. Smoke began to pour from the roof, and the whooshing roar of fire filled the air.

"Now!" Sashi yelled, and on her order the gates were flung outwards, revealing a startled pack of soldiers who, by their faces, clearly hadn't expected any resistance. Shouting in unison, the Vekshi women charged forwards, scything their staves down and across from the backs of their roas, knocking the men to the ground. The lead fighters held firm in a wedge, keeping the soldiers occupied while Sashi led the rest of the riders out and away, bulling through the remaining men and into the city night. But the Vekshi fighters didn't follow, instead pulling back to fill the gates: a human blockade between Leoden's men and Gwen's remaining party.

A shout from outside – more arrows began to fall, but unlike the first few, these were unlit and aimed at skewering anyone still in the courtyard. Matu's mount reared and screamed in fright as an arrow grazed its flank.

"We need to go!" he yelled, fighting to keep the beast under control.

And then Trishka began to glow, a pink-tinged halo forming

around her head and upraised arms. She'd dropped her reins, and Gwen, who was closest, swore and grabbed them, pulling them over the unhappy mare's head. Sweat beaded on Trishka's skin; her eyes rolled back in their sockets. The light around her expanded, crackling with lightning, all her strength concentrated on this single use of the jahudemet. As fire ripped through the compound roof and the clash of fighting came from the gates, Trishka cried out – half pleasure, half pain – and ripped a hole in the world.

The gateway tore itself into existence with a whine like the world's largest mosquito: a portal linking, not different realities, but two different parts of Kena. Though initially little larger than a melon, it rapidly grew in size, irising open until it stood tall and broad enough to accommodate a horse or roa and rider. The edges roped and wobbled; Trishka couldn't hold it for long.

"Ride through!" Gwen bellowed, waving at the others – they hesitated, clearly stunned by the sight, and only then did she realise that Trishka had kept this part of her plan a secret from all but her and Sashi. "Through, through, through!"

And for a miracle, they obeyed; even Yasha, whose face was pale and furious in the firelight. Gwen watched them pass the gateway, and noted too the fierce pride in Yena's eyes, the undisguised awe in Saffron's. Only once everyone else was through did she move, still leading her friend's horse. But as the mare surged forward, Trishka gasped and dropped her arms. Her trance was broken, the magic gone. The portal began to telescope shut, shrivelling as they approached. Terror took Gwen. If they didn't make it all the way through; if the gate collapsed while they were still crossing–

They reached the portal. Heart thundering wildly, salt on her cheeks, arrows flying past and the smoke from the compound burning her lungs, Gwen closed her eyes, skin stinging as the collapsing magic burned her flesh, and prayed.

They emerged into darkness, a nothing so deep and featureless that for a dizzying moment, Zech thought the portal had gone horribly wrong, trapping them all in the black between the stars. But then she looked up and saw that the greater moon, Kei, was still full and bright beside its smaller twin, Mei, as they turned through their curious orbits. All around them shone constellations she knew by heart: the Trickster, the Lovers, the Man-and-Mare. They were still in Kena! Only then did the darkness make sense: the fire had left her night-blind.

Around her seethed a chaos of shouting and snorting horses, the softer *krees* of the roas an eerie counterpoint. Her gelding pranced beneath her; Zech reined him back, squinting to make out the crest of his neck, the shape of his ears, and beyond that... what? Everyone was talking at once; there was no point adding to the confusion.

"Light, light!" Yasha demanded. "Someone make light!"

Fire bloomed to Zech's left, momentarily dazzling her – it was Yena, holding a lit torch. Her face beneath it glowed like hot gold, while everyone else was limned in bronze and shadow. They all stood in a disorganised cluster, horses and roas facing every which way as their riders, unable to see where they were and therefore unwilling to risk separation, swivelled in saddles to stare at those around them.

"Quiet!" Yasha bellowed. Her voice cut through the shouting, and the group fell silent. "That's better. Yena, do a headcount – there ought to be ten of us."

A moment of tension while Yena counted; then she called the all-clear. No one was unaccounted for. Everyone had made it.

"Good," said Yasha, and Zech was surprised to hear a note of relief in her usually steady voice. "Now, where's my

fire-blessed fool of a daughter? Trishka! Where in the world
have you brought us?"

But it was Gwen who answered, her tone made sharp
by worry. "She's unconscious, Yasha," she snapped. "I think
the gateway burned her. Bring that light over here!" This
last to Yena, who blanched and hurried to obey.

Fear fluttered in Zech's stomach like a swallowed moth.
Her mother – her bloodmother, Kenans would say – had
given her up at birth to a woman who had in turn given
her to Yasha when she was two years old, so long ago now
that Zech had no memory of it. Yasha had never been
coy about the reason why: it was because of her skin, her
shasuyakesani markings too obviously a bad omen. Her
mother was simply gone, and in her place, despite Yasha's
nominal guardianship, had been Trishka. Zech knew about
Trishka's nameless, strength-draining affliction; how it
punished her use of the jahudemet. And she knew, too, that
under normal circumstances, Trishka ought still to have been
recovering from the portal that summoned Safi and Gwen.
To make another major gateway so soon afterwards must
have taken extraordinary strength of will, to say nothing of
courage – and now she was paying the price.

Clutching her horse's reins, Zech watched as Yena pushed
through to Gwen's side, wincing to see the angry, cauterised
burn that ran from Trishka's right temple down to the underside
of her jaw. Her horse had been burned too, though of course no
one else was concerned about that now; the poor animal was
burnt from behind its right ear to midway down its neck, at
which point the scarring transferred itself to Trishka. The horse
was trembling, its breath a rasping pant; the gate had collapsed
on both of them, but without proper light or access to a healer,
there wasn't much anyone could do to alleviate their pain. At
least Trishka had the benefit of being unconscious, though as
Gwen dismounted and tried ineffectually to wake her friend,
Zech had a hard time seeing it that way.

"Well!" said Yasha. This time, the shake in her voice was unmistakable. "We still need to know where we are. If it's within a night's ride of Karavos, we need to get out of Leoden's reach."

As the others began to murmur in answer, Zech felt a jolt go through her. The year before, one of Yasha's guests at the compound had taught her how to find her way by the stars, but she needed an astrolabe to do so properly. A strange frustration welled in her. She wanted to help – there had to be a way she could help...

"We're on the Envas stretch of the North Road," Jeiden said quietly. Though his voice was soft, every adult stopped speaking and stared at him. "I remember it from when Matu and I passed through. That tree over there–" he pointed at a forked shape Zech could barely make out in the darkness, "– reminded me of a snake's tongue. We had lunch beside it."

"Gods in heaven," Matu murmured. "So we did!"

"We're four days' ride from Karavos," Jeiden went on. "Almost halfway to the border. They'll never catch us now."

"You're sure about this, boy?" Yasha growled.

Jeiden straightened in his saddle. "I am."

The matriarch let out a breath. "Good then." After a pause, she added, "Well remembered."

Before their conversation in the stables, Zech would have felt intensely jealous of Jeiden for this – and if she was honest, she still was, a little. *Of all the luck, landing right by a place he's been before!* But now she could hear how grudgingly Yasha praised him, when the same information from her or Yena would have earned them more and warmer words. Worse, Jeiden knew it; he'd slumped once the matriarch's gaze was elsewhere, and though Matu had reached out a hand to comfort him, she could tell that the slight still hurt.

"We'll rest here for the night then," Yasha declared. "It won't be comfortable, but we'll cope, and in the morning, we can–" her eyes slid to Trishka, "–better assess our position."

With that, it was like a spell had been lifted. Everyone began moving and talking at once, dismounting as they discussed whether to keep a watch, sleep on this side of the road rather than the other, to hobble or merely hitch the horses. Zech glanced at Safi, wondering how she'd cope with a night spent outside. From their conversations together, it likely wasn't something she'd ever done before. For a moment, Zech thought she ought to take her aside and help, but then she realised Yena, having left the torch with Gwen, was already doing just that, and so decided to speak with Jeiden instead.

He was one of the few still mounted, apparently frozen in place. Careful of those on foot, Zech nudged her horse over to his side. His face was dejected, and when she placed a hand on his arm, he startled.

"What?"

"That was… that was really impressive," she said, taking a deep breath. "Yasha should have said so. It's wrong that she didn't. *She's* wrong," she added, and was instantly shocked at her own defiance. "Anyway. I just thought you should know."

Slowly, like the onset of dawn, a smile spread across Jeiden's face. It was shy and sweet and, like the rest of him, beautiful, and Zech felt something in her rejoice at having caused it.

"Thanks," he said. "I–"

But whatever he'd been about to say was lost in a sudden, outraged shriek. Zech jumped in her saddle, fearing they were under attack – then burst out laughing when she realised what had happened.

The Cuivexa was awake.

"Where am I?" she screamed. "Untie me at once! You *peasants*, you lousy, filthy spittle-skinned snakes! You freaks, you worms, you, you–" And then, with her face screwed up in genuine horror, she wailed, "–and *why am I still on a roa?*"

12
The Envas Road

Saffron fidgeted in the saddle, wincing in her futile search for a posture that didn't hurt her back. They'd been riding since dawn, and even though she'd stretched at lunch, the pain was only getting worse. It was last night's rest that had done it. She'd been camping before, of course, but never without a tent, and certainly not without a blow-up mattress or camp bed to sleep on. Though the roadside grass was comfy enough at first, the ground beneath had soon turned hard and uneven. She'd slept shallowly, tossing and turning against the press of cold earth into her shoulders, and had woken that morning with stabbing pains in her neck and lower back. It was small comfort that everyone else had suffered just as much; she'd never had to keep doing something that truly hurt before.

She tried thinking of Trishka, whose awful burns and magic-wracked body inarguably meant she was in more pain than anyone. Dawn had revealed the extent of her injuries more fully than Yena's torch: the skin of her face was taut and shiny red, a smatter of blisters weeping clear fluid down her cheek. Her poor horse, too, was suffering. Gwen had given it something called moonsleep the night before, allowing it to rest peacefully, but with a long road still to travel, the only possible concession to the mare's injuries was to have Zech, who was smallest and lightest, ride her instead. Trishka was now on Zech's old horse, tied in place with the ropes that had previously been used to restrain Viya, after the Cuivexa had agreed, however peevishly, to refrain from running off. Trishka's consciousness was intermittent, but whenever she did wake, they halted immediately so that Gwen, who'd taken charge of her friend, could check on her.

Saffron had never seen burns like Trishka's. Looking at them made her stomach twist. She was frightened of what might happen if they became infected, if they couldn't find a healer in Envas. It ought to have put her own problems in perspective, but no matter how she berated herself for being spoiled and selfish, she couldn't push through her own discomfort. *You lost your fingers and lived!* she told herself fiercely. *This doesn't hurt more than that!* But the reminder that she was maimed forever only made her feel worse, as though she was compounding her moral failings with the sin of vanity. Was she really so shallow that she was worried about how the loss of her fingers made her *look*? Her thoughts began to spiral inwards, down to a place they hadn't been since before she'd come to Karavos; the place where she felt stunted, inadequate, wrong. Tears welled up and she dashed them furiously, hating that she couldn't control herself. *Stop it*, she told herself. *Just cut it out. Stop crying. Stop crying right now!*

"Are you all right?"

It was Yena, looking at Saffron with a mixture of concern and uncertainty. Her curls were covered by a faded red headscarf, accentuating her forehead and cheeks. There were circles under her eyes – attributable both to her mother's condition and a poor night's rest – and a long smudge of dirt on her neck.

"I just..." Saffron gulped, faltering. "I mean, it's nothing. I'm just not used to any of this, and I know that shouldn't matter right now – there's so much more going on – but I still keep getting stuck on it. I'm sorry."

Yena blinked at her. "Why are you sorry for that? Feelings are feelings, no matter when they happen. Our bodies don't stop being ours just because worse things happen to other people. And why should you be used to anything here? This isn't your world." She hesitated. "Gwen's told me a little about *Earth*–" she dropped the English word haltingly into her speech, "–and how different it is. How all your magic is scrunched and hidden, so no one believes in it anymore. How you only have one moon, and a yellow sun, and your kings and queens have no power, but men who look like Vekshi men do." She grinned suddenly, foxish and fey. "To me, it sounds like a challenge. But if you stranded me there by accident, made me ride through strange streets on an animal I'd never even seen before, if I fell into rituals I didn't understand, and a stranger cut off my fingers – if all of that happened, and then I had to run away with people I'd only just met as part of a fight that started before I arrived and was bound to continue after I left – well, then, I would certainly feel at least a *little* lost."

She said it simply, a kindness so matter-of-fact that Saffron almost stopped breathing. Yena smiled, her cheeks dimpling with empathy, mischief – and then she reached out and grazed her knuckles gently along Saffron's cheek. It was an incredibly intimate gesture, and despite the context, it was also the single sexiest thing that Saffron had ever experienced. Her breathlessness intensified for a very different reason.

"It's all right to be lost," Yena said, softly. "How else can we find ourselves?"

And before Saffron could answer, she pulled her hand away, grinning, and cantered back to see how her mother was faring.

Saffron sat still for a moment. "Whew," she breathed, exhaling the word like a promise. "Wow."

She didn't stop feeling terrible, of course. But something

inside her eased that only moments earlier had been close to breaking.

It was a start.

Viya was livid, full to bursting with fury and humiliation she couldn't afford to show. Waking up tied to a roa four days distant from where she'd gone to sleep was the least of the indignities she'd been forced to suffer – far more distressing was the fact that the awful Yasha was genuinely in charge. The reason for this completely escaped Viya. Pix, after all, was a noblewoman: a skilled politician, mother and warrior in the prime of her life, to say nothing of the fact that she was actually Kenan. The idea that such a woman would voluntarily submit to the authority of a dried up, heretical, spittle-skinned crone like Yasha was inconceivable. It angered her as an affront to the gods and the natural order of things; an affront made all the more personal by the fact that only now, too late, did she understand how badly she'd embarrassed herself.

Over and over, bloodfather Iavan had drilled into her the importance of always paying attention to eddies and shifts in power, no matter what else was happening – and despite what she might think of the people involved. Not long before his departure with Rixevet and Kadu, he'd sat her down for what was to be their last such conversation. His handsome, scarred face – half frown, half smile, the legacy of some distant squabble never fully explained to Viya – had turned oddly grave as he dropped a kiss on her forehead, his marriage-braids swinging down to brush her throat.

"Listen carefully, Ivi," he'd murmured. "One day soon you'll be at court. Enemies might charm you. Allies might disgust you. Supplicants might bore you. Elders might condescend to you. And sometimes, you'll be in a position to let them know it. Sometimes – but not always. Not even often. Instead, you show them all a calm, smiling face and hide your truth with innocence, like a pretty knife tucked in a sleeve. You listen to everything they say and everything they don't, and you *remember*, because knowledge is greater than magic. You understand?"

And Viya had nodded and said she had, though Iavan must have known it wasn't true. Three days later, he was gone, and Viya had been left in Hawy's care – Hawy, who had all but sold her to Leoden.

She frowned at her use of the word. *Sold.* As if she was a horse or roa, with no say at all in where or with whom she went. The thought irritated her, hinting at implications she was in no way inclined to entertain; and so she set it aside, more concerned with how she was going to get to Rixevet. She didn't doubt Pix's version of last night's events, though she might have done, had one of the other women, Trishka, not been so clearly injured. *At least,* she thought sourly, *we're heading in the right direction.* But even though her arms and legs were no longer bound – she quivered with anger that it had happened at all – she was still stuck in Yasha's company, and stuck riding Mara, the same wretched, stinking roa Luy had foisted on her back at the palace.

Had she been nicer to the Vekshi woman – had she intuited, as Iavan doubtless would have done, that Yasha was the one in charge – she might have been given supplies and permitted to ride off alone, as they'd originally planned. At the very least, she could have made a case for departing once they'd travelled closer to Rixevet's holdings. Instead, she was under suspicion of having been somehow involved in the compound raid, and therefore bound to the group by Yasha's ominous intimation as to what might happen if she strayed. It was ludicrous – why would Leoden involve the Cuivexa in such a petty escapade?

A memory twitched against Viya's consciousness, trying to make itself recognised. She frowned, unable to place it for several minutes – and then it hit her. The conversation she'd overheard between Luy and Leoden. *She's meddled enough, her and the Vekshi crone both*, her husband had said, and all at once she realised he must have been talking about Yasha; it was too big a coincidence otherwise. That same conversation had also mentioned a worldwalker, which Viya had thought was pure nonsense, dismissing it out of hand. But she'd already been mistaken in one such assumption, and refused to lose any more allies by leaping to another.

So who, then, was the worldwalker?

Viya decided on a process of elimination; Iavan would approve. The thought steadied her, and for the first time that day she felt her frustration settle. *Now, what do I know?*

It wasn't Pixeva, her feather-haired cousin Jeiden or her disreputably unmarried brother, Matuhasa idi Naha; they were all Kenan, their family known to hers. Nor was it Yasha or Trishka: the former was too obviously Vekshi-born, while the latter had the jahudemet, which suggested she was the portal-maker Leoden and Luy had also mentioned. Zech was a real possibility: she certainly looked strange enough to be from another world, and nor did she appear to belong to anyone. True, she was young, but having already mistaken Yasha's role in things on the basis of first appearances, Viya wasn't about to make the same mistake twice. Yena was disqualified on the grounds of being Trishka's daughter – she'd picked up this last by inference after watching how the younger girl kept hovering by the wounded woman's side, as well as noting the similar shape of their faces.

Which left only two other possibilities: the Vekshi girl, Safi; and the Uyun woman, Gwen. Both were equally likely prospects, but as Gwen was completely preoccupied with caring for Trishka, that left Safi as the most logical person for Viya to talk to. Not, of course, that she had any inherent desire to learn about other worlds: however else they disagreed, she shared her husband's conviction that only Kena mattered. But as he'd held both Yasha and the worldwalker in equal disdain, as though they were two separate, albeit related, nuisances, it opened the possibility that the group might, in fact, have another power-broker. There was no chance of redeeming herself in Yasha's eyes, and in any case, the self-abasement required by such a gambit would have crippled Viya's pride. Which meant that her best bet now of being set free was to get the worldwalker onside.

Thus determined, she hauled Mara around – more harshly than was needed, as she was still annoyed at being lumbered with the wretched beast – and rode over to Safi. The Vekshi girl had just finished talking to Yena; her cheeks were slightly flushed, and her hands clutched tightly at the reins.

Her hands.

Viya stared, heart beating faster, as she stared at Safi's left hand. The two smallest fingers were missing, just like Kadeja's were. A mark of disgrace among the Vekshi; yet how many young white girls with such a mark lived in Karavos? Even before she'd opened her mouth to confirm it, Viya knew, bone-deep, what the answer would be: that Safi was the Vex'Mara's heretical omen.

"Hello?" asked Safi, a note of surprise and uncertainty in her voice. Viya had been silent for too long, and winced – not in sympathy, but at the thought of ruining this opportunity too.

"Hello," she replied. "My apologies. I didn't mean to be rude. It's just, your hand... are you the one Kadeja cut?"

Safi's cheeks turned even redder. "Yes," she said softly. "I didn't understand what was happening."

Viya exhaled, exalting in her deductive success, though she was careful to keep her delight from showing on her face. Safi was a worldwalker! Nothing else could explain her ignorance of Vekshi customs. She might look like one of Yasha and Kadeja's people, but underneath she was alien to them.

She turned back to Safi, and found, with some small shock, that she was sympathetic.

"I'm sorry for that," Viya said honestly. "My marriage-mate is… well, I'm not sure what she is."

"Don't be. It wasn't your fault." The ghost of a smile flickered on Safi's face. "And I'm sorry, too, that the others tied you up. I asked Gwen why they'd done it, but she didn't have time to tell me."

The apology took Viya by surprise – so much so that, before she could think to check her response, she exploded with, "How *dare* they suspect me! I *ran* from Leoden – I came to them by accident – and they drugged me, tied me, brought me here and accused me of making it happen!" And then she clapped a hand to her mouth, mortified that, once again, she'd let her tongue get away from her.

But rather than being outraged, Safi just nodded gravely. "Yasha's pretty frightening," she agreed. "I don't think she really likes or trusts anybody – but then, I'm not sure if anyone really likes or trusts her either. Well, except for Trishka, but she's her daughter, so…"

Viya goggled. "Trishka's her *daughter*?" She swivelled in the saddle, craning for a look. "But she's Kenan!"

Safi looked at her oddly. "What makes you say that?"

Viya snorted. "What else do I mean? She has proper skin."

"And is that all it takes to be Kenan?"

Almost, Viya shot back a quick retort, but checked herself in time, noting Safi's perturbation. Viya licked her lips, trying to think how best to get things back on an even footing. "I only meant," she said, after a moment, "that she doesn't look like Yasha, and so I assumed she was Kenan. Besides, I've never met a Vekshi who wasn't white, or heard of their children being fathered by Kenan men. Though I suppose it must happen often enough at the border," she added, thoughtfully.

"Less often than you might think, apparently," Safi said,

distractedly. This annoyed Viya until, with a second glance at
Trishka, she saw what she'd overlooked before: the woman
had no marriage-braids, her hair cut short as Safi's. Irritation
stabbed at her. Why hadn't she noticed? Only last night,
she'd eaten at the same table as Trishka: the incongruity
of a Kenan woman with Vekshi hair ought to have stood
out like a beacon, and yet she'd been just as blind there as
in her meeting with Yasha. Despite all of Iavan's training,
she'd simply unseen everything and everyone who wasn't
Pix, assuming that the woman who most resembled Viya
herself – Kenan, noble, familiar with court – must naturally
be the one who mattered most.

She faltered, unsure how to proceed. Safi raised an
eyebrow. For an instant, Viya was tempted just to ride away
and damn her chances of making an ally, but for the sake of
Iavan and Rixevet, she forced herself to bite back her pride
and speak.

"I hate Kadeja," she said, her voice vibrating with a rage
that, up until now, she'd been forced to suppress. "I *hate*
her! Leoden caught me eavesdropping once – that's what
he called it anyway, as though I had no right to walk freely
in my own palace! – and as punishment, he gave me to the
Vex'Mara. She went to the gardens and cut a rod of star-
nettle – it's flexible and sharp, and the thorns have a sting
in them. She said the Vekshi called it Ashasa's whip, that
priestesses used it to deal out discipline to heretics. She said
that all the world belonged to Ashasa, not just the north,
and that now she was Vex'Mara, that meant Kenans should
be subject to the goddess, too. She said that, under Vekshi
law, my discipline was her responsibility. So she had her
servants hold me down, and then she whipped me raw. Like
a *criminal*."

When she saw the horrified look on Safi's face, she
rejected it fiercely. "Don't you *dare* feel sorry for me! I'm the
Cuivexa of Kena, Iviyat ore Leoden ki Hawy, and I will not

have my strength diminished by pity! I didn't tell you this for the sympathy; I told you this so you understand why, when I look at Yasha, all I see is Kadeja's wrath; why the idea of not being able to tell Vekshi from Kenan unsettles me; why I don't want to travel with you." Almost shouting, she fought to regain control of her voice. "If I must walk in Veksh, I will walk there in my own right, as Cuivexa, and make my own envoy with the Council of Queens. But I will not go there captive as a show of Yasha's strength."

"Now that," said a dry, laconic voice, "was a very impressive speech."

Both Viya and Safi jumped and turned. It was Gwen, her lips curled up at the edges. Viya felt her neck flush with a mix of hope and embarrassment. How long had the Uyun woman been listening? Was she really impressed, or would she run straight to Yasha? Viya stiffened, holding her chin up high. If Gwen was going to punish her, she'd endure it straight-backed.

Much to the cost of her dignity, Gwen chuckled. "Don't fret, girl," she said. "I'm no tattletale."

Viya bristled. "The correct form of address is *my liege* or *your highness*."

"I'm not your subject. And even if I were, it's generally advisable to respect one's elders."

"I will," Viya said, coolly, "if you respect your betters."

"Hah!" Gwen barked merrily. Her brown eyes shone with approval. "That's the spirit, *my liege*. Never let politics get in the way of a good argument!"

Unable to help herself, Viya snorted with laughter. Safi glanced between them, clearly enjoying the show.

"Now," said Gwen, "while I have a moment, will you do me the courtesy of explaining why it is you're so keen to get away from us, and who it is you're wanting to see?"

And so, because it was a respectfully-worded question, and because the older woman had made her laugh, Viya told her everything: Rixevet's defection, Hawy's politics, the circumstances of her marriage, Kadeja's poisonous influence and her decision to head north. Her only omission was how she'd managed to leave the palace, as she neither wanted to credit Luy for his interference nor betray the fact that, in one sense, Yasha was right: she *had* known about the compound raid, even if that knowledge was only apparent in retrospect.

Both Gwen and Safi listened in silence. Once she'd finished, the older woman raked her with an appraising look.

"Well then, Iviyat ore Leoden ki Hawy. My thanks for your tale. As to whether or not I can help you, that's a different matter." She spread her hands, shrugging. "I'll try. We're on the same side in this, but there's more going on than can bend to a single person's desire, no matter how important. You understand?"

"I do," said Viya. Briefly, she hesitated. "And thank you for your consideration. I am – I have been – Cuivexa in name only, and though I want to change that fact, this isn't how I dreamed it would happen. I have a temper, I know, and it... disquiets me, to be working with other Vekshi. But I was raised to believe that the hottest fires temper the strongest steel. It wasn't of my choosing, but perhaps the gods have sent me here for a reason – and if that is so, the very best I can do is to try to learn their purpose."

"Fair-spoken," said Gwen, and looked to say more, but at just that moment, a panicked-looking Jeiden returned to the group at a gallop. Throughout the day, Yasha had been using him as a forward scout, riding down the road ahead to report on any difficulties or dangers. Always before, he'd found nothing, but from the look on his face, things had definitely changed for the worse.

"The Vex's men are coming!" he shouted, loud enough for everyone to hear. "Twenty honoured swords riding this way from Envas, fast – on horses, not roas! They saw me and chased – Leoden must have sent them word! They'll be here any minute!"

Yasha swore and wheeled her mount around, facing the rest of the column, barking out a string of orders. "Everyone form an outward-facing circle, Trishka and the packbeasts in the middle, quickly! Pix, Matu – dismount and see that everyone's armed, then lead out with me. Jeiden, you're in charge of my daughter – don't move from her side, don't let the beasts bolt, and if anyone asks you to pass them something, do it! Gwen, take the van and keep an eye on Safi – she fights too, but it's your job to keep her alive! Yena to the left flank, Zech to the right – you girls remember what I've taught you, and keep your grips firm! Cuivexa Iviyat, up here with me – we open with knives and close with fists, and if you run, Ashasa help me but I'll hunt you through this world and any other you care to name. Now move!"

No one hesitated. Already, the drumming of hooves was audible: as Jeiden had said, the riders were evidently wealthy and well-trained enough to ride horses rather than roas, which boded evilly for their presence on such a remote stretch of road. Viya's heart beat at double-time as Pix, already on foot, stopped by her stirrup and handed up a courtier's knife-belt and a pair of blade-knuckled gloves.

"My second-best set," she said, her grin sharp with battle-frenzy. "Yemaya give you strength!"

"Nihun give you courage," Viya replied. Like all Kenan noblewomen, she'd been trained in the proper use of knives since age six, and though Leoden had taken her blades and denied her practice, still she'd kept up her forms in private. Trotting to Yasha's side, she met the Vekshi matriarch with the calmest stare she could manage.

"I won't run," she said. "Not until after we win this."

Surprisingly, Yasha cackled. "Good enough for me!"

As Pix and Matu reclaimed their saddles, Viya sat side

by side with Yasha, drew her knives, and watched as a whooping, screaming line of riders crested the hill.

Saffron stared at the axe in her hands, unable to comprehend quite how it had got there. The whole world was a roar of white noise; then Gwen was shaking her, swearing and shouting, "Focus, girl! You *focus and listen to me*!"

"I'm listening," Saffron said. Her voice came from far away.

Other people were shouting, too – both men and women, their voices an angry wave.

"You stay beside me," Gwen was saying. "Beside and behind, and if someone gets past, don't aim at them – aim at their horse. You listening, girl?"

"I'm listening." Her breathing was shallow. The axe was short and surprisingly light, with a wedge-shaped, double-headed blade whose edges tapered to thin-honed sharpness. The grip, which she held, was wrapped with leather and cloth – *like a tennis racket*, she thought desperately. Even the length was similar, and she clung to that sense of it as something more comprehensible, more familiar than a weapon. She gripped it tight in her right hand – hefting it slightly, as if it really were meant for tennis – and clutched the reins with her left. The horse beneath her, a steady grey mare, snorted and tossed her head.

"Oh god," Saffron moaned. "I think I'm going to throw up."

But there wasn't time for that. The riders were closing in, and though she didn't want to look, she somehow couldn't stop herself from pivoting in the saddle, turning to stare, open-mouthed, at the scene unfolding before her.

Over the hill came a double line of riders armed with swords and daggers that glinted in the fading light. Almost half were women, and all were Kenan, their hair either bound in marriage-braids or, more rarely, clasped in simple tails. Suddenly, four riders were down, tumbling catastrophically from their saddles as Pix and Viya's knives hit home in their throats. *It's just like a film*, Saffron told herself desperately, *a film, a film* – because even knowing it was a lie, she had to at least try to believe, or else she'd just seen two women she liked take the lives of four total strangers, and that was a truth she couldn't process now.

And then there was Yasha, riding out to meet the line with only her everyday staff in hand. It was agonising – Saffron wanted to scream at her to *come back, come back,* but gasped instead when, contrary to every expectation she had, Yasha swung sideways and down at the horse's delicate forelegs. There was an audible cracking sound; the horse gave a shrieking whinny, stumbled, and ploughed head-first into the ground, catapulting its rider through the air like some twisted mammalian trebuchet. Five down, fifteen to go; the world moved in slow motion, every detail shining and illuminated like lead-lined glass.

Now level with the charging line, Yasha roared like a lioness as her horse reared back on its hindquarters and swung around, pressing herself to its neck as she drew her own knives and, quick as lightning, flung them sideways into the backs of two more riders.

Matu broke ranks and followed her lead, his horse bodily charging side-on into another while he struck out with his sword. And then the line was at Pix and Viya – they drew their last knives, screaming and grappling – flowing around their circle like water, reaching Yena and Zech, the horses adding screams of their own – and then the world was flung back into vicious real-time. Three riders were pressing Gwen; she was armed with a sword, her horse reined sideways in front of Saffron, slashing at whoever came in range. But a fourth – a woman – had bypassed Zech and was coming up on her left, and suddenly, suddenly–

The stranger's horse rammed into Saffron's mount, chest to chest. The rider was right-handed, armed with a knife, and in the moment when she raised it up, Saffron's single, terrified thought, activated by the barely-there part of her brain that thought of the axe as a tennis racket, was *backhand slice*. Her axe-as-racket scythed through the air, connecting meatily with the woman's wrist. It severed her hand with vicious ease, continuing in its downward arc to embed itself in the horse's muscled neck.

Vomit rushed up Saffron's throat. The woman shrieked and flailed, her marriage-braids flying as the horse reared backwards, the axe still stuck in its flesh. The rider, unable to grab the reins, began to slip from the saddle; the horse reared higher and higher, forelegs beating the air in a grotesque pirouette. It staggered away; the woman fell. The horse screamed, and then – Saffron gagged – it collapsed backwards *onto the rider*, crushing her. Landing on the axe. Audibly, something snapped. The *sound* the horse made was terrible, a pain-wet noise like metal being wrenched apart. There was nothing but fear and bile and stench, and darkbright blood on Saffron's hands, the spray from the woman's severed wrist. It was on her face, too, and it hit her then, a raw stunning slap, that she'd just killed someone. *I killed her – I killed it – I killed them –*

She sobbed, and fainted, and fell.

"*Jesus fuck!* You *fucking fuckers*, you *fucks* – come on, *come on!*" Gwen screamed, the words ripped from her throat like scabs from a wound. Years ago, she'd learned that rage was more use in such moments than terror, and though she was no fighter either by nature or tutelage, she'd been forced to learn enough self-defence to (thus far) stay alive. She'd taken down one and Saffron another, but then the girl had fallen and maybe she was dead or wounded and maybe she wasn't, but this next fucker was still pressing her, his blade meeting hers with a strength she couldn't surpass. She was over-matched and tiring fast, they all were, and with no reinforcements to back them up – she thought of Jhesa, Naku, Louis, prayed with a fierceness she seldom felt to find her way back to them again–

A green-fletched arrow sprouted from her opponent's neck. The woman faltered, choked on blood, and slipped sideways off her horse, a look of surprise on her face. Gwen stared at her, panting, unable to comprehend what was going on. Shouts from the surviving riders suddenly turned to gargled screams as more arrows zipped through their midst, each one piercing an honoured sword until none remained alive.

The sudden silence was deafening. Gwen trembled, her breath coming in ragged gasps, and slowly lowered her sword. The anger and fear that had fuelled her fighting ebbed away like a tide, leaving behind a bone-deep ache that penetrated every fibre and sinew of her body. And pain, too: there were cuts on her arms where she hadn't quite been fast enough to block, and one on her cheek that must have come from the upwards flick of a sword.

"Good girl," she murmured, patting her horse on the neck. The animal snorted and flicked her ears back in displeasure, clearly unsettled.

"Allies! Allies!" came a shout – presumably in response to the question of who their deliverers were, though Gwen had no idea who'd asked it. One by one, a group of brightly-clad strangers began to emerge from the woods on the left, each one covered head to toe in flowing robes, so that only their eyes and hands were visible. She laughed out loud, though the sound was more of a rattle.

"Shavaktiin," she muttered, half in wonder. "Saved by the bloody Shavaktiin."

And with that realisation, she knew they were safe. It was over. Only now could she let herself worry about the prospect that not everyone had survived the battle intact. Arms and legs protesting mightily, she forced herself to dismount, grimacing as she stepped between the bodies of dead men and women and that one dead horse to examine Saffron Coulter.

Jeiden had care of the girl, evidently having pulled her out from under the hooves of her blood-spooked mount and backwards into his lap. She was curled on one side, her head on his knees. Tears made grimy tracks on his cheeks as he stared up at Gwen.

"I couldn't help," he said, choking on the words. "She wouldn't let me *help*."

Gwen knew the *she* in question wasn't Saffron, but Yasha. Like a tapped ember, she felt some of her rage rekindle in her chest, letting it muster a flame as she crouched before Jeiden. He looked nothing like Louis, but in that moment, she saw them doubled, the memory of one boy overlaying the other's flesh.

"Is she hurt?" she asked, but even as she spoke, she knew it was the wrong question. Saffron's body was unscathed; it was her mind that mattered. *Yasha, I will burn you for this. You and Leoden both.*

"She's unconscious," said Jeiden, visibly trying to pull himself together. "At least, I think she is. She just sort of… fell."

"I can't say I blame her." Gwen rubbed her eyes and straightened up. She wanted to stay with Jeiden, with Saffron, but thirty or so Shavaktiin had just emerged from the trees, and rather than crowding near, they were waiting respectfully for someone to approach them. Inwardly cursing, she cast about, then pointed her sword at a single, thick-trunked tree growing at the roadside between Gwen's party and the Shavaktiin camp.

"Do you think you can get her over there?" she asked Jeiden softly. "She's not cut, but you'll have to be careful all the same; she might have hurt herself falling off like that."

"I can," said Jeiden. He was calmer now, the prospect of responsibility working on him like medicine.

"Do it then. And after that..." she faltered, restraining what she wanted to say in favour of what he needed to hear, "...wait and see what else needs doing. You're good at so much, I trust you to keep an eye on things."

The praise steadied him further. Nodding, he woke Saffron and got her moving, his small hands deft and gentle. Gwen watched them go, heart aching, then limped stiffly away to see what had become of the others.

Minutes later, she had her answer. Though nowhere near as bad as it could have been, in that none of their party were dead or dying, there were still a fair number of serious injuries. Almost as soon as the line had reached them, Viya's roa had been cut from under her. The Cuivexa had fallen badly, but had redeemed the situation by cutting the hamstrings of the nearest horse. Her action had saved Pix's life, but earned her a truly spectacular gash from the rider's sword: barely missing the bridge of her nose, the blow had sliced up the centre of her forehead, then flicked to the left in such a way that a flap of scalp was left fluttering loose. The only mercy was that her actual skull remained undamaged – nonetheless, she was bleeding fast, and once it had been established that the Shavaktiin included two healers graced with the sevikmet among their number, one had immediately rushed forwards to see to her wound.

Yena and Zech had fared little better. Zech's horse had died taking the brunt of a blow that might otherwise have severed her left leg, but which instead had cut hard into the top of her thigh – almost down to the bone. She was white as a sheet and barely breathing, her injury the most serious of anyone's for having gone so deep. She'd lost a lot of blood, though mercifully the blow had struck well above Zech's femoral artery. Even so, without a healer present to stop the damage, the shock alone might have killed her. Instead, she lay semi-conscious on the grass, tears of pain leaking out of her eyes as the healer knit her up. Yena was lucky by comparison: armed with a staff, she'd raised it to protect her upper body from a sword-strike, only to have the blade cut down on her left hand midway between her wrist and the base of her littlest finger, crushing the bones (though not, fortunately, cutting all the way through to her palm). The wound oozed blue-black blood and was so painful that Gwen was forced to knock her out with moonsleep while she waited for the healers.

She sat with Yena until they arrived, one hand clasped gently around her wrist, the other stroking her hair. Gwen's tears were hot and silent, shed for a child who was, in every way that mattered, her niece. Too many places on Earth were dangerous for girls like Yena, boys like Jeiden, but oh, luck, to have spared them this – to have spared them all–

No world is ever truly safe, Gwen thought, half bitter, half grieved. *Just safe enough, until one day it isn't.*

The adults, by contrast, were virtually undamaged: Pix and Matu, like Gwen, had only minor cuts on their thighs and forearms from weapon-tips that had snuck past their guard, while Yasha – having charged through the line and emerged behind it – was utterly unscathed. And then there was Trishka, still tied to her horse, as burned now as she had been at the start of the attack, and just as stable. The healers would see her last. *But of course,* Gwen thought savagely, *that's how it goes in warfare. The eldest scheme and the youngest suffer.*

Of Leoden's twenty guardsmen, not a single one had survived, despite the fact that the quality of their arms in combination with their horses suggested they were elites, maybe even arakoi. Or – she frowned – perhaps they were simply regular troops who'd been recently resupplied with better mounts and weapons. Either way, seven boasted Shavaktiin arrows through eye or throat, and another six had fallen to the knives thrown two apiece by Viya, Pix and Yasha. Matu's sword had accounted for a further two, while one had broken his neck after Yasha tripped his horse. One to Gwen's sword. One to Zech, who'd cut the throat of the man who'd cut her leg. One to Saffron, a kill of luck. And one to Yena: her staff had crushed his windpipe. Only Jeiden and Trishka had been spared the battle, and even then, Jeiden was still scarred by it – or, more specifically, by his exclusion from it, the fact that Yasha had, in essence, forced him to stand helpless while his friends were hurt.

There were other casualties too. Wandering the battlefield of the Envas road, Gwen counted three dead animals – Zech's horse, Viya's roa and the enemy mount felled by Saffron's axe – and was forced to give final mercy to two more who were beyond salvation: the gelding Viya had hamstrung, and the mare whose legs had been tangled by Yasha's staff. Working with quiet efficiency, the Shavaktiin moved through the chaos, some stripping the dead of arrows, weapons and anything else of value while others rounded up the remaining horses with calm efficiency. At Yasha's instruction, Pix and Matu pitched in to help, though Gwen had no strength left. Wearied by death, she sat on the grass and watched as the soldiers were steadily carried to the opposite side of the road and respectfully laid out: faces cleaned, eyes closed and hands crossed over their chests.

For a moment, Gwen wondered if they shouldn't be burned instead, rather than leaving them at the mercy of the wild – but then, she supposed, their superiors would know when and why the soldiers had ridden out, and would look for them when they didn't return. Then, when the bodies were discovered, they could be returned to their families for proper funeral rites.

Which left them with seventeen horses – a net gain of fifteen mounts, given their loss of a horse and a roa – thirty unexpected Shavaktiin, and five adolescents in varying stages of injury and emotional trauma.

Soon, Gwen knew, she'd have to get up and start asking

questions, like: *Where did the Shavaktiin come from? Why did they help us? Where are we going, if Envas is enemy territory? How did Leoden know where to find us so soon, and how did his troops know, too?* But just for the moment, she was content to sit, and catch her breath, and feel the salt sting of sweat in her cuts, and suffer the weight of the dead.

Until she noticed Yasha daubing blood on the girls' foreheads.

White hot rage electrified Gwen. It was a baptism, a wretched Vekshi ritual of initiation offered when the recipient had taken a life in battle. And maybe there was a universe where the sight of the matriarch daubing red first on Yena's unconscious brow, then Zech's, might have failed to move to her to fury – after all, they were Vekshi-born, and for them, at least, the hideous rite had some cultural application, even if both of them were unconscious and therefore unable to appreciate it. (As, indeed, was Viya, whose ruined head she also touched.) But when she moved over to Saffron and pressed her bloody thumb to the girl's forehead, breaking her out of her catatonic distress in the worst way possible, Gwen lost all control. As Saffron began screaming, Gwen leapt up, strode over to Yasha and bodily hauled the matriarch back by the scruff of her tunic.

"*Enough!*" she roared in English. "You selfish, sadistic, bloody-minded old witch! You stay away from her! This is all your doing!"

Yasha reeled, staring at Gwen in shock. For a moment, she looked unbalanced, undone. Then her gaze narrowed furiously. The message was unmistakable in any language. "I kept us alive!" she hissed. "What would you have had me do, Gwen – surrender?"

"Rather than defend yourself with children? Yes!"

"Those *children* saved all our lives, and ensured we were free to fulfil our purpose! You demean them; you belittle their competence."

"And you put too much faith in it! Look over there and

tell me the price they paid was the same as yours or mine – you tell me this was an equal fight!"

Yasha laughed harshly. "Fighting is never equal – if it was, it wouldn't be necessary. And tell me, Gwen Vere, did those honoured swords look minded to surrender? They would have cut us down like rotten crops!"

"We attacked them first!" Which was true, but the anger in Gwen was burning out. She knew Yasha had a point, however awful, and the matriarch knew it too, eyes glittering as she honed in on Gwen's hesitation.

"Which is why we won," said Yasha. "But if I'd gambled – if I'd let us stand there like lambs for the slaughter and trusted them to accept surrender – then we'd either be captured or dead right now. Instead, we are free and wounded and *alive*."

Gwen rallied. "That may be so, but you didn't need to have Safi fight. She's completely untrained – you could have let her stay with Jeiden, kept them all back–"

"And left them unarmed when their absence saw us overwhelmed?" She raised an eyebrow. "I did what I thought was best. Jeiden played his part, and Safi played hers. That rider slipped through your guard, Gwen Vere; if the girl hadn't stopped her, *you* might be dead, and we wouldn't be having this argument." And then, more quietly, "Enough. This was not a perfect battle, if such a thing truly exists. There's no gain to fighting it over again with words. I regret the choices I was left to make, but not what use I made of them. Leave it at that."

All the strength went out of Gwen. She was still angry, but less at Yasha than at circumstance. She nodded, too tired to argue, and when Yasha held out an arm, Gwen took it, the two of them leaning on each other as they headed back to the healers.

13
Blood Will Out

When Zech awoke, night had fallen. Her wounded leg ached with a bruising pulse, and though she didn't know exactly where she was, she knew from Jeiden's presence that it was where she was meant to be. Wherever that was, it was clearly outdoors: Zech was covered with a patchwork blanket and lying on a well-stuffed bedroll, while Jeiden sat cross-legged at her side, his face illuminated by a nearby torch. Almost absently, as both his gaze and thoughts were clearly elsewhere, his right hand grasped her left, but as soon as she squeezed his fingers, he fixated on her in unabashed relief.

"How are you?" he asked.

Zech smiled weakly. "I've been better." She pulled her hand free, tentatively seeing if she could push herself upright. But even lifting her head off the bedroll dizzied her; the stars blurred and swum like silver fish.

"You need to rest," Jeiden said, worriedly. "Zech, you nearly *died.*"

She remembered the battle then – the bite of steel in her leg, the sound of her horse screaming, and the bright spray of blood as she'd slashed the throat of her attacker. Her pulse quickened, bringing with it an increase of pain. The memories threatened to overwhelm her, but Zech was nothing if not strong-willed, and so she pushed them away.

"The others," she forced herself to ask. She was shivering, though whether from cold or grief, she couldn't say. "Is everyone else all right?"

"Everyone's alive," Jeiden said quickly. "Some wounded, but none worse than you, and all alive."

Zech almost wept with relief. Sensing this, Jeiden put a hand on her shoulder, squeezing gently. Zech covered his hand with hers, and wondered how she'd ever thought him snobbish. "But we were overwhelmed. There were so many riders, I... How did we get here? How did we win?"

At that, Jeiden's eyes lit up, though Zech felt her own glaze over, curiosity fighting a losing battle against pain and exhaustion. She tried to follow Jeiden's explanation, but couldn't quite keep the thread of it: something about the Shavaktiin aiding them – she flashed back to the player who'd shadowed them from the Square of Gods – though why was still anyone's guess. Who knew, when it came to the Shavaktiin? She shook her head, confused, as Jeiden fell silent.

Zech nodded to show she'd heard. Her shivering was getting worse, her leg ached, and her body felt weird and empty, like her bones had been hollowed out. She ought to just lie down, she knew, but some stubborn, ancient part of her didn't want to let Jeiden know that she was struggling. "Where are we now then?" she forced herself to ask.

"The far side of the Dekan River," Jeiden said, as though he expected Zech to know exactly where that was, and promptly launched into another explanation about the Shavaktiin and stolen horses and diversions, and how it was they'd been found and attacked in the first place. She forced herself to listen to this last, gut tightening as Jeiden talked about the arakoi tracking Trishka's magic, messages ahead to Envas, the lot of them branded dangerous traitors – and then, just as her vision began to grey out, Jeiden said, "We're safe," and finally fell silent.

"Good," Zech whispered, hoarsely. "Good. "A feeling of peace spread through her. Dimly, she was aware of Jeiden shouting, but it all seemed so distant, it hardly mattered. She lay down again, or maybe fell, the ground beneath her giving way like a broken branch. The cold in her bones, which had hurt only moments earlier, now felt like the touch of her long-since-absent mother. Almost, she could picture her face, smiling fondly as she stretched out a welcoming hand.

I'll come with you, Zech said – or at least, she thought she said it. Her tongue wouldn't work, but like so much else, it didn't matter. She let herself drift, eyes closing as she tried to follow her mother. *I'll come with you and stay.*

Gwen was just checking on Viya when she heard Jeiden shout. Though exhausted, she forced herself up – she'd given the Cuivexa moonsleep, the better to aid her healing with a deep, dreamless rest – and hurried to Zech's side. Though the Shavaktiin healers, Kada and Dom, had done their best back at the road, even a single serious injury would have been taxing, and instead they'd been forced to deal with three, plus Trishka's burns and innumerable smaller hurts besides. Without their magic, Zech would have been dead hours ago, but that didn't mean she was out of danger.

Gwen's heart skipped, and as she reached Jeiden's side, the feeling only intensified. Zech was shivering violently, convulsing in her blankets, eyes rolled back in her head. Jeiden was ashy and terrified.

"She was fine a minute ago! We were talking, and then she just... She just–"

"Go and get the healers," Gwen said, doing her best to keep her voice steady. "Now."

Jeiden obeyed.

His absence felt like hours, though in reality he was only gone a few minutes. Gwen sat crouched by Zech's side, one hand clamped to the girl's forehead in a futile effort to ease her shaking. When Jeiden finally returned with the Shavaktiin – Kada in pale red robes, Dom in dark yellow – she moved away, watching with a fear that verged on fury as they worked their magic. *Yasha, if this girl dies, I will never forgive you.*

Slowly, Zech's shivering stilled, but her skin was even paler than before, her breathing hoarse and shallow.

"She's lost too much blood," said Kada, standing up. His voice was warm and deep, and the skin of his hands was darker than Gwen's own. Though even his eyes were hidden behind a veil, there was no mistaking the worry in his voice. "She needs a transfusion."

Instantly, Jeiden held out his arm. "Give her some of mine, then. Please!"

"It's not that simple, Jei," said Gwen, squeezing his shoulder. Her eyes remained fixed on the healers. "Blood has a type, and yours might not match. The wrong kind would only hurt her."

"But we can test you," Dom said kindly. Though it was hard to tell with the Shavaktiin, Gwen thought the other healer was female; her voice was lighter than Kada's, at any rate, and her body smaller. "Give me your palm."

Obligingly, Jeiden obeyed, standing straight and stoic as Dom pricked his thumb-pad and placed a finger on the wound. After a moment, she drew away.

"Not a match," she said, apologetically. "The girl's blood is unusual – none among our Shavaktiin shares it, and unless someone in your party does, there's not much we can do."

Gwen's heart sank. Proffering her own hand, she let Dom test her too, but was unsurprised when the healer shook her head.

"Come," she said. "We should test your friends."

While Kada and Jeiden stayed behind to monitor Zech, Gwen accompanied Dom on her quest. From personal experience, Gwen knew that race was sometimes a factor when it came to matching rare blood types, which was why she hadn't been surprised when Dom disqualified her. But Zech, despite her mottled skin, was Vekshi, and from what she'd seen of their Shavaktiin rescuers, none among them shared that nationality. As Pix, Matu and Yena were all rejected, Gwen entertained the brief, satisfying notion that Yasha would be the one to give her blood for the girl; but when the matriarch, too, was ruled unsuitable, she felt her hopes shrivel. That left only Trishka and Viya, both of whom were badly wounded themselves, and Saffron, who had lapsed back into shock.

Remembering what had happened when Yasha had decided to smear the blood of the dead on Saffron's forehead, Gwen quietly suggested that they leave her for last. But when neither Trishka nor Viya proved a match, there was nothing else for it: they had to test her too.

With everything that had happened, Gwen was intensely grateful for Pix's foresight in bringing the moonsleep she'd originally used to drug Viya. A powerful sedative, it had not only helped their treatment of the wounded, but had, in a much smaller dose, calmed Saffron enough after the battle that she'd been able to get back on a horse and ride under her own steam. Arriving at the camp, she'd let herself be led about like a doll, so that for the past two hours, she quite literally hadn't moved, sitting blank-faced and cross-legged near one of the bigger campfires. The Shavaktiin understood her blank state, and didn't try to interfere. Instead, they kept an eye on her, occasionally leaving food or water within easy reach, but otherwise letting her be.

Now, though, such courtesy was no longer an option. As they approached Saffron, Gwen's heart broke afresh at what all four girls had suffered. Saffron's injuries might not have been physical, but that didn't make her any less wounded than Zech or Viya.

As Dom waited respectfully to one side, Gwen knelt in front of Saffron, studying her before speaking. Dried blood still streaked her face and forehead. Her eyes were glassy, fixed on her lap. From time to time, her fingers twitched, but otherwise she remained motionless.

"Saffron," Gwen said. She didn't so much as blink. Gwen sighed, stifling the commingled sense of guilt and impatience that threatened to well up within her. Gently, she reached out and took Saffron's hand in her own. "Saffron Coulter."

Saffron shuddered, gaze jerking fearfully upwards. Her eyes were wide, and there were tear tracks on her cheeks. "I killed her," she whispered in English, her voice raw with despair. "Gwen, I killed that woman."

"It was the fall that killed her," Gwen said softly, in the same language. "She broke her neck when her horse went down." Almost she added, *you only cut off her hand*, but stopped herself in time. Saffron needed fewer reminders of guilt, not more. "And she was trying to kill you. It was self-defence."

"I know." Saffron blinked, lifting a hand to rub new tears out of her eyes. "At least, part of me does. But I just keep seeing it happen, over and over. I keep hearing that horse scream, and the sound of the axe... I killed a *horse*." She made a choked sound. "I *like* horses. And I know that's not worse than killing a person, but it still counts, doesn't it? And she was *married*, Gwen, I saw her braids. I can't stop seeing them. What if she was a mother, too?"

"I know," said Gwen, though she dearly wished otherwise. She didn't want to change the topic, but the immediacy of Zech's need demanded it. "Saffron, you know the others were hurt in the fight?"

"I know." The words were barely audible.

"Well, Zechalia's lost a lot of blood. The healers need to give her a transfusion, but no one else has the right blood type. The only person left to check is you."

She braced, waiting for the fear to return, but strangely, the news had a calming effect on Saffron, just as the moonsleep had done. "I can help?" she asked, straightening a little.

"Maybe," Gwen said, not wanting to get her hopes up. "We need to test your blood first." She turned and motioned to Dom, who came forward, crouched down, and showed Saffron the pin she'd been using to prick people's fingers.

"Like this," she said in Kenan.

"All right." Saffron nodded, and Gwen watched, heart in mouth, as she held out her hand for the needle.

As the blood welled up, the girl winced, but nothing more. Dom placed her finger over the cut, paused – and nodded. Gwen exhaled a breath she didn't remember holding.

"It's a match," Dom said. "Come with me. We need to act quickly."

Slowly, her muscles visibly stiff from being locked into the same posture for hours on end, Saffron stood. Gwen caught her arm when she staggered.

"Sorry," Saffron murmured.

"It's all right."

Saffron limped at first, but soon straightened out as her muscles uncramped. Gwen snuck glances at her from the corner of her eye, not wanting to appear overly concerned. For all she'd responded well so far, there was still something of the dream-state about Saffron's movements, as though she'd only managed to function by convincing herself that nothing around her was real.

Or was that giving her too little credit? Gwen faltered mid-stride, caught off balance by the realisation that she'd slipped into thinking of Saffron as helpless; that because she was blonde and pretty and a foreigner to this place, she wouldn't be able to cope. The other girls had all been taught to fight, but none of them had ever properly done so before today, and training was no guarantee of competence or composure when it came to the real thing. Yena, Viya and Zech's physical injuries didn't mean they weren't also hurt emotionally; and yet somehow, Gwen had managed to trick herself that it did. It made her angry, unspeakably angry, to think that she'd done so, even for a minute–

Or maybe, a more helpful internal voice whispered, *you're just in shock, too. You can't process everything at a time like this, rationally or otherwise – it's too much to take in. They're all children, all hurt. Help them now, and deconstruct yourself later.*

As they came in sight of Zech and Jeiden, the red-robed healer, Kada, stood, motioning with his head for Saffron to step forwards. She did so, taking Jeiden's place at Zechalia's side.

"Will it hurt?" she asked suddenly, looking up at the healer.

"A bit," the Shavaktiin answered. "Does it matter?"

"No," said Saffron, looking at Zech. "Not at all."

For all the urgency preceding it, the transfusion itself was comparatively simple. Using a small knife, Kada made a small incision on each girl's wrist. As both began to bleed, the healers joined their right hands together while keeping their respective left palms clasped around the cuts – Dom with Saffron, Kada with Zech – to form a magical conduit. Despite her lack of supernatural senses, Gwen could nonetheless feel the electricity of the process, a sort of ambient energy as the Shavaktiin steadily guided Saffron's blood into Zech's body. To her surprise, the effect this wrought on both girls was clearly visible, a pink glow suffusing the lighter parts of Zech's skin while Saffron visibly paled. The Shavaktiin balanced the transfusion perfectly: Saffron was left woozy but upright, while Zech, in addition to her regained colour, stopped shivering, her eyes slipping peacefully closed as she relaxed into normal sleep.

Gwen let out a long, sharp sigh of relief. "She'll live?"

Though her veil made it impossible to tell, Gwen felt

that Dom was smiling. "She'll live. Still, we ought to keep camp here tomorrow too, so that the wounded have a better chance at recovery."

"And for us to replenish the sevikmet," Kada added, weariness in his tone. Knitting Saffron's fingers closed had left a single healer sweaty and drained, but the Shavaktiin had been working for hours on far more serious wounds. Without their veils and robes, she would have seen it earlier, and yet the Shavaktiin's garb, so adept at hiding gender and age and origin, had also concealed their exhaustion.

"Is there anything I can do?" Gwen asked.

"Let them heal," Kada said, tiredly.

"You think I wouldn't?"

Dom shook her head. "Not you. Yasha."

"Be their advocate," Kada said, and then repeated, "Let them heal."

For what felt like a long time after the pair departed, but which in reality was only a few minutes, Gwen stood, shocked, and stared into space. After her altercation with Yasha on the Envas road, she'd kept her distance from the matriarch, who in turn had kept her distance from Gwen. Each woman had, in her own way, tended the wounded: Gwen had overseen the injured girls, while Yasha had taken the opportunity to remember that Trishka was her daughter, and had stuck to her side like a burr.

Only now, thinking about it, did she realise that she'd fallen out of touch with Pix and Matu. All she'd seen of them after the battle was that they were whole, and well, and willing to help the Shavaktiin as they cleared away the bodies. But though it had been a long ride to the camp, Gwen hadn't spoken to either of them since the road. Instead, the Shavaktiin had become intermediaries as well as healers, taking charge of their group so naturally and comprehensively that none of them, in the aftershock of the battle, had thought to question it. Even Yasha, who was usually so sensitive to anything that even remotely resembled a challenge to her authority, had acquiesced to the Shavaktiin – and with that realisation, Gwen shivered. Yasha quiescent was Yasha planning, and after today, she wasn't minded to view that benevolently.

Coming back to herself, she glanced down at the trio of children: Saffron, Jeiden and Zech.

"Will you be all right?" she asked, as much of Jeiden as Saffron.

"I will," they said in unison. Their likemindnedness startled them both into smiling: a tiny, unmagical miracle. The fact that they were capable of it at all lifted yet another worry from Gwen's shoulders, freeing her to go and find Pix and Matu. *I need to know what Yasha is up to. And I really ought to see how Trishka's doing.* She'd managed to push her friend's injuries to the back of her mind only because there'd been so much else to preoccupy her, but now her old concern came flooding back.

"Find me if you need me," she said, and when they nodded, she headed off in pursuit of Yasha's plots.

Saffron sat with Jeiden and Zech for a long time. She wasn't reconciled to the death she'd caused by any stretch of the imagination, and deep down, she suspected she never would be. The fact that Gwen was right, that it had been self-defence, didn't mitigate her horror at the willingness with which she'd swung the axe, nor did it erase the terrible, ear-burning memory of the horse's screams. She knew she'd have nightmares – or at least, she couldn't see how to avoid them – and when she looked down at her hands, they were shaking. But even so, somewhere between Gwen talking to her and the Shavaktiin transfusing her blood, she'd slowly come back to herself. She could function now, if she needed to, more or less. Saffron was shaken, hurt and lost, but she wasn't yet broken.

"Thank you," Jeiden said, breaking the silence. "For the blood, I mean."

Saffron looked at him. He was pretty in a way that she'd never before associated with men or boys, and though it didn't attract her – he was far too young, and even if he hadn't been, her preferences ran more to women – it nonetheless soothed her now: a reminder that there was still beauty in the midst of a horrific situation.

Still, she faltered, not knowing how to respond. The regular niceties didn't cover it, and she was too worn out to think up a better response. Instead, she blurted, "Why are they veiled like that? The Shavaktiin?"

It was a question part of her had been wanting to ask ever since the Envas road, but which grief and shock had kept locked away until now. To Saffron's eyes, the Shavaktiin's robes were virtually indistinguishable from colourful burqas, and so she'd been startled to learn that some of the wearers were male.

If Jeiden was perturbed by her sudden change of topic, he didn't show it. "I don't know why, exactly," he said, "but I think it's part of their beliefs. The Shavaktiin are... well, they're the Shavaktiin." He spread his hands, as though this somehow explained everything.

"They're storytellers," said a new voice.

Saffron leapt to her feet, frightened of another attack. Her panic was such that it took her several long, heart-shuddering moments to recognise the speaker as Yena. Clearly startled herself by Saffron's reaction, the other girl took a half-step backwards, hands raised in a show of peace. One, the left, was tightly bandaged with blue cloth, and the sight of it brought Saffron back to the moment.

"Sorry," she gulped. "Sorry, Yena. I didn't hear you come up, that's all." She ran a hand over her stubbled hair, the smallest loss of many.

"It's all right," Yena said quietly. Even in the torchlight, she looked paler than usual. Her headscarf had slipped back, so that several messy curls hung free around her face. "I shouldn't have snuck up on you." She hesitated, glancing down at Zech. "Will she be all right?"

"The healers say so," said Jeiden. "She's just resting."

Yena let out a sigh of relief. "Good. I... Good."

With a feeling like hackles being lowered, Yena sat, a gesture that Saffron soon copied. They were side by side, with Jeiden close between them and Zech. The proximity was comforting.

After a moment, Yena said, "I don't fully understand it, but the Shavaktiin believe that all stories are true, and that all truth is stories. So when they act in the world, they do so as storytellers: to shape events, rather than be the subject of them. For them, it's a holy calling. With their veils, they're anonymous, and that puts them outside of things: stories are about individual characters, not interchangeable servants. If they act unveiled, it means they're taking a personal path in the story, though I've never really understood how they draw the distinction. I mean, even veiled, *they* still know who they are."

Saffron blinked, trying to comprehend the idea. "So they're, what – religious narrators?"

"Something like that." Yena shrugged.

"And they came to help us." She gulped, an odd sense of foreboding settling in her stomach. "So what story do they think we're a part of, then? Or whose?"

To that, neither Yena nor Jeiden had an answer.

After that, the three of them fell silent. Exhaustion covered them all like a thick fur cloak, and one that nobody had the strength or inclination to shrug off. Despite her discomfort of the night before, Saffron felt so heartsick and weary that when her eyes began to close, she had no compunctions about stretching out to sleep on the ground, and when Yena tentatively curled up against her back, her injured left hand wrapped around Saffron's waist, it felt like the most natural thing in the world.

Inexplicably, her final thoughts before falling asleep were of a dusty crossroads, and a field of burning flowers.

14
Stories Within Stories

To her mingled relief and irritation, Gwen found Trishka, Pix and Matu talking quietly around a small fire on the eastern edge of the camp – relief because Trishka's burns had been healed, and irritation because Yasha, too, was in attendance. Not that she'd counted on the matriarch being elsewhere; it just made ignoring her impossible.

Swallowing a sigh, Gwen approached and inclined her head respectfully, though the effort set her teeth on edge.

"Yasha," she said.

A slight pause. Then:

"Gwen," Yasha said, returning the gesture with equal stiffness.

Some tension went out of the air. Trishka flicked her gaze from Gwen to the empty space beside her – a tacit invitation to sit. Gwen accepted it gratefully, joints protesting as she lowered herself to the ground. She favoured Trishka with a long, careful look, eyes raking the place where, up until a few hours ago, the skin of her friend's face had been raw and burnt. Now only faint, clean scars remained: a testament to the strength of the Shavaktiin healers.

"Well," said Pix. Her voice was unusually soft, and despite the warmth of the firelight she looked pinched and drawn, the strain of the day's events clearly etched on her face.

Matu looked little better: his long hair was filthy with sweat, blood and dirt, resisting his efforts to comb it clean with his fingers. Pix leaned her head on his shoulder, prompting him to put an arm around her.

"What a pretty sight we make," he murmured, giving his sister a squeeze. Almost, Gwen smiled; for all that the siblings bickered, their affection was real.

"Pretty indeed," said Yasha, "considering that we mightn't have lived to see it."

"Must you always ruin the moment?" Gwen said, then waved away the remark with a weary hand when Pix and Matu tensed. "Sorry. I don't want to fight."

"Hmph," said Yasha, but she shrugged too, which Gwen took to mean that no offence would be taken. "It doesn't matter in any case. We need to get rid of these heretics and ride for Yevekshasa as soon as the girls can bear it."

"Yevekshasa?" Pix lifted her head. "Shouldn't we go to see Amenet first, at Avekou? Without her support, the Council of Queens–"

Yasha cut her off with a vehement snort of derision. "Don't speak to me of the Council, Pixeva ore Pixeva. Amenet would be unwise to reject the strength of Veksh, but twice and twice again unwise to accept it without bargaining, the process of which takes time that none of us can afford. Present her with the idea of an army, and she can counter with ideas of her own; present her with the army itself, and what can she do but accept or surrender to it? And even if she were rash enough to agree upfront, there's still the queens to contend with – and how would we look if they refused us after we'd already bartered their aid? No. We go first to Yevekshasa, and only then to Avekou." Her empty hand twitched, as though she'd forgotten she no longer held her staff and was therefore unable to thump it down, this being her preferred method of emphasising such proclamations.

"Still, though," said Gwen, glancing at Trishka for backup, "Amenet might stall us even if we arrive with an army. For one thing, she'll have to appease her allies, make them understand that we're there to support her claim, rather than Kadeja's – which, of course," she added smoothly, preempting Yasha's hiss of irritation, "is exactly the sort of prejudicial ignorance one should expect from Kenan nobles. But one way or another, we have to deal with them, and if haste's the plan, then better to have it done with by the time we arrive, rather than waste more time in debate."

"Makes sense to me," said Trishka. Yasha flashed her an irritated look.

"I could go back," said Matu, just quickly enough that Gwen winced on his behalf. Of course he'd want to see Amenet again! But Matu had always been a hopeless courtier and an even worse negotiator, at least when it came to people he actually liked; and in any case, they needed his skills with the zuymet.

"You can't," said Gwen. "If nothing else, you still need to teach Saffron Vekshi – and don't try to palm it off on Zech, you know she's not ready to teach two tongues at once. Your sister, however, has no such commitments."

"*Me*?" Pix looked genuinely startled. "Why in the worlds should *I* go?"

"Why not?" Gwen countered. "It was you Amenet wanted to speak with originally, wasn't it? And you're certainly a better choice than your brother. No offence," she added, prompting Matu to throw up his hands in mock resignation, "but you both know it's true."

Yasha frowned. "I suppose," she said, reluctantly, "there *might* be some merit to your suggestion, Gwen Vere."

Gwen braced herself. "And she should take Viya with her, too."

Instant silence. Yasha's stare was as cold as week-old embers.

"Hear me out," Gwen said. "Leoden has no children, and

nor does Kadeja. If both of them are deposed, then interim control of Kena will pass straight to the Cuivexa – whose family, might I add, are probably in Amenet's camp already. The best hope for stability will be if Viya joins Amenet's mahu'kedet, but that won't happen if you insist on taking her to Veksh."

"And why not?" Yasha growled.

"Because–" Gwen began, but Trishka cut her off, laying a hand on her mother's arm as she spoke.

"It'll be hard enough to convince the queens that saving Kena is worth their while without giving them the option of a royal hostage too. It's been more than a hundred years since any Kenan monarch set foot in Veksh, and you want to take the girl there against her will? What would happen to Amenet's cause if Viya were seen to be killed by the Council? We can't guarantee her safety; not with a party this small. But send her to treat with Amenet, and you legitimise her rebellion by putting a member of the royal mahu'kedet at the forefront of it. And besides, the girl wants to go – this way, you don't have to worry she'll try to escape, and she'll owe you a boon for your kindness into the bargain."

Yasha looked livid, which was how Gwen knew they'd won; only the forced acknowledgement of her own shortcomings could possibly make the matriarch that angry.

"Fine!" she barked, throwing up a hand. "As well to be rid of her anyway, the disrespectful snip. Let Pixeva deal with her nonsense, and whatever else comes will come. And," she added fiercely, glaring at Pix, "you can take the damn Shavaktiin with you!"

"Some of us, anyway," said a new speaker.

Even Yasha jumped, though Gwen herself was so startled that she forgot to find it funny. A figure emerged from the shadows beyond their circle of firelight. It was the Shavaktiin leader, a green-robed woman with light brown hands and a soft, melodic voice. Her name, Gwen recalled after a moment, was Halaya, and though her latticed veil concealed her expression, her head inclined in apology.

"Forgive me. I didn't mean to startle you." Without invitation, she gathered her robes and sat between Trishka and Yasha, completely unfazed by the matriarch's affront. "Nonetheless, I'll be blunt: it was neither by luck nor accident that we found you when we did. One of our sisters in Karavos witnessed the rescue of the Cuivexa by your young ones, and reported it through the dreamscape as a shift in Kena's story. Our dreamseers watched your flight to the Envas road, and as our coterie was closest to hand, it was we who came to find you. Knowing the danger of ambush was great, we hurried; had we done otherwise, all of you would be either dead or captured."

Gwen shuddered. Yasha clamped her jaw shut. Pix, though, looked enlightened.

"Zech said she thought a Shavaktiin was following her," she mused. "And just as well too, it turns out." She smiled at Halaya – the first genuine such expression Gwen had seen on her all day – and though it wasn't clear if the gesture was returned, when Halaya spoke again her voice was noticeably warmer.

"I can understand why you might wish to travel without us. But the matter is out of my hands, and therefore yours. The story moves as it may, and we are bound to follow its threads. Ride from us, and we will be forced to follow. Count us as companions, and we may yet be of assistance."

"And what makes you think," said Yasha, her words dangerously soft, "I'd ever beg assistance from the Shavaktiin, or willingly lend myself to your heretical schemes?"

Halaya sighed, the exhalation gentle with amusement and regret. "Because we know you, Yasha a Yasara. We tell your story. You're the Queen Who Walked."

To Gwen's complete astonishment, Yasha flinched. Her face grew cold and closed.

"Some stories are not yours to tell," she said sharply.

Surprised by this reaction, Halaya raised her hands palm out, to show she'd meant no offence. But as everyone looked to her for an explanation, all Yasha could do was shake her head, some past fury riding the lines of her face. It was easy to forget how old she truly was – early eighties, at Gwen's best guess – when her usual strength and vigour belied even the numerical evidence of her having a full-grown daughter and granddaughters. For the first time, Gwen found herself wondering how much effort it took Yasha to project the image she did, and how much else she successfully kept hidden.

"Mother?" asked Trishka, breaking the silence.

The sound of her daughter's voice brought Yasha back to herself.

"You'll travel with us," she croaked. "Ashasa strike me for all my sins."

And with that, she rose and walked away, retreating into shadow.

For a moment, everyone looked stunned.

"I did not expect that," Halaya said quietly.

Trishka stared at her. "What did you expect then?"

"Pride, maybe?" The Shavaktiin shrugged and sighed. "My apologies. I forget sometimes that others prefer to keep their stories secret."

"The Queen Who Walked," Matu murmured. "I'd almost forgotten that name."

Pix was incredulous. "You know the story?"

"My dear sister, you can accuse me of being many things, but a bad listener isn't one of them."

"I think you're bluffing."

"I think you're jealous."

"I think–"

"*I* think," Trishka said, cutting Pix off, "that the pair of you should show some respect. There's a time and place for every tale, and now isn't right for this one. Whatever else you think of my mother, you can grant her that much at least."

The siblings quieted instantly, as shamefaced as children: Trishka's reprimands were rare enough that in some ways, they were even more fearsome than Yasha's.

Abruptly, Gwen stood. Exhaustion had claimed her, a sleep-winged eagle diving down to latch its claws in her bones. Yasha's departure had left a sour taste in her mouth – not out of sympathy, but because it stood as a reminder of her own ignorance, a quality she had never enjoyed acknowledging.

When the others looked at her, she meant to say *goodnight*, but what came out was, "I'm too tired for this."

Without waiting for a response, she turned and walked heavily away – though where to, she couldn't have said. She had no idea where she was meant to sleep, and despite her weariness, her feet kept moving, propelling her on an aimless, slow trajectory.

"Gwen?"

Halaya's voice. Gwen paused mid stride, just long enough for the Shavaktiin woman to come alongside her.

"What is it?" she asked.

Halaya put a hand on her arm, pulling her to a halt. "There's a bedroll and blanket set up for you, on the other side of the camp. I wasn't sure you'd been told."

"I hadn't been, but my thanks. I'm glad to hear it."

"It was never my intention to cause Yasha distress."

"I wouldn't worry about it. You set her reeling a bit, but she'll recover soon enough. She always does."

Gwen let Halaya lead her back the way she'd come, towards the promised bed. Around them, the sprawling camp alternated between fire and shadow, small campfires sending sparks up into the darkness like tiny wayward stars. Horses and roas stirred sleepily at their perimeter pickets, snuffling in their dreams. Here and there, robed Shavaktiin moved silently between groups of sitting people, some to join the sentries who ringed the camp, the rest on whatever unfathomable business motivated those who believed above all in the will of stories.

As they passed the place where Zechalia lay, Gwen paused, finding strength enough for fondness at the sight of Zech, Jeiden, Yena and Saffron curled together like pups in a basket.

"Like a little mahu'kedet," Halaya said fondly.

"Indeed," said Gwen, her gaze lingering on Zech and Saffron. She'd been so worried for both of them, their respective hurts in the wake of the battle forming an awful, perfect continuum between wounds of the body and wounds of the soul, but at the sight of them sleeping, she felt part of herself relax. *Thank luck for the blood transfusion,* she thought – then stopped, a belated realisation forming in her mind.

"I know little enough about magic," she said, slowly. "Only that it works. And most of the time that's enough for me, however it bends my head. But it strikes me as odd that a gift which can reknit skin and bone would stumble at the manufacture of blood, or be unable to change one type into another at need."

Halaya chuckled. "The truth doesn't always make for a good story. Some lies are useful, not because they trick us into thinking the world is different, but because they show us that it could be. One girl needed purpose; the other needed blood. Had they not been depleted from tending so many injuries, I'm sure that Kada and Dom could have saved Zechalia alone; but as they couldn't, neither they nor I saw any harm in taking the opportunity to give meaning to one who required it."

"You couldn't have known how she'd react."

"Maybe, but I could guess." Halaya sighed. "She was lost, Gwen. Everything was beyond her control, and so we gave her a choice that wasn't – one that allowed her to help. Perhaps that was a risk, but it still paid off."

"And so it did," Gwen murmured.

A brief silence fell between them, broken only by the murmur of the surrounding camp and the sound of their own footsteps.

"I know your son," Halaya said quietly.

Gwen stopped dead.

Halaya stopped with her. They were distant enough from the others not to be overheard, yet even so, Gwen's heart was hammering. Though the possibility had occurred to her in the battle's aftermath, she hadn't let herself hope that her Louis might be among their Shavaktiin rescuers; on top of everything else, such yearning might have undone her. Now, though, the buried hope flared anew. She tamped it down sternly: if Louis were here, he'd surely have sought her out himself, not sent Halaya as messenger. Even so, it was several long seconds before she trusted her voice enough to answer.

"Is he well?"

"He was, when last we spoke."

"He's not here then?"

"No," said Halaya.

Gwen suppressed a wince. "Of course."

"He's a good man," Halaya said softly. "He… Understand, there's only so much I can say about our politics to an outsider, but the path he's chosen – his guidance of the story – though some in our order oppose it, we do not. I do not."

"Is…" oh, it was a bad question to ask, especially today, but she still couldn't stop herself, "…is he safe, do you think?"

Halaya was silent for just long enough that Gwen's heart sank. She'd last seen Louis just before her departure to Earth from Karavos; he'd hinted then that he was already involved in something she wouldn't approve of, and rather than argue, she'd declined to press the issue. She hated to think of Louis putting himself in danger, but given her current occupation, it would've been hypocritical to deny him his own adventures, which made for an uneasy truce between them at the best of times. And yet. *And yet.*

Finally, Halaya said, "He is as safe as he can make himself. Safer than we are now, certainly." And then, some wryness creeping into her tone, "It is, I'm told, safer to run beside a charging horse than to stand in its way."

Gwen snorted. "I'll bet." And then, because she judged herself to be happier without further details, "Come on, then – show me this fabled bedroll. If I stay on my feet much longer, they're like to mutiny."

Saffron walked through the field of burning flowers, her nostrils filled with the sickly-sharp smell of hot sap. White smoke was everywhere, and yet she remained as calm as if it were nothing but fog. *I don't fear this*, she thought, and as though her will had the power to shape the space around her – which, this being a dream, she supposed it did – the smoke began to thin, the fire blown out like birthday candles. As the air cleared, Saffron found she wasn't alone: a thin, short figure stood up ahead, staring in obvious mystification at their surroundings.

"Zech?" she asked.

The girl turned, surprised. "Safi? Is this real?"

"I'm not sure. I think it all depends on what you mean by reality."

"Oh. All right, then." She blinked. "Have you been here before?"

"Once. I'm still not sure why, though, or what it means."

"Hmm." Zech bent down and picked a flower, twirling the stem between her fingers. "I don't know why, but I feel like there's something I'm meant to find here. Will you help me look?"

"Of course," said Saffron. "But should you be walking already? You were so cold before. I don't want you to get worse again."

"Maybe not," said Zech, rubbing her injured leg. She peered over Saffron's shoulder and smiled. "We can ride, though."

Turning, Saffron laughed to find a pair of roas, saddled and waiting, woolly ears flickering back and forth. A brightly striped cloak covered each saddle, and as Zech moved to choose a mount, Saffron said, "Did these come from you or me, do you think?"

"Maybe they came from themselves," said Zech, shrugging into the cloak. It was blue and purple, red and gold – a flowing, gorgeous thing. *A technicolor dreamcoat*, Saffron thought, and fought the urge to giggle as she donned her own. "Who knows? Maybe roas dream too."

"I've heard of stranger things," said Saffron, and swung herself into the saddle.

Together, they began to ride, the roas snorting softly. Ahead of them, the field of flowers started sloping upwards, rising like the flank of some sleeping beast. The higher they climbed, the more it felt like riding up the spine of a towering wave, and when they reached the summit, the view rendered both of them speechless.

"Oh," said Zech.

Before them stretched Karavos – the same vista Saffron had seen on arriving with Gwen and Pix. There were the towers, the broken walls; and there, perched high above everything else, was the palace. Zech's eyes were glued to it.

"There," she whispered, "take us *there*," and before Saffron could ask why, the whole scene warped about them like rippling water, swirling and reconfiguring. The roas vanished as silently as they'd come, though the cloaks remained, and with a jolt they found themselves inside a palatial chamber. White stone columns stretched overhead, while the floor was patterned with gold and crimson tiles. A metal canal filled with burning oil ran along the walls, illuminating the room. To the left, a pair of double doors stood shut, their polished handles gleaming in the firelight, and to the right was a square stone altar topped with a flat, gold bowl.

The doors swung open, and in came the Vex'Mara Kadeja.

Saffron froze. For a single heart-stopping moment, she forgot that this was a dream. Her missing fingers tingled unpleasantly, and beside her Zech's breathing was rapid and shallow, her pale gaze fixed on Kadeja.

Forcing herself to stay calm, Saffron watched as the Vex'Mara approached the altar. In contrast to the finery she'd worn in the Square of Gods, she was now both barefoot and unjewelleried, dressed in a strange wraparound garment that only vaguely resembled a taal. Made of faded pink cloth, it looked at first like a loose, belted dress, except that the belt and dress were actually all of a piece, the knotted ends hanging neatly from the small of Kadeja's back. In one hand, she held a lit candle; the other bore a knife.

Reaching the altar, Kadeja set the candle down. Extending her free hand, she nicked the tip of her index finger with the blade, wincing only a little as her blood dripped into the bowl. When the bleeding slowed to a trickle, she reached up and unbound her marriage-braids, slicing off a small hank of hair and dropping that, too, into the bowl. Only then did she put down the knife and reclaim the candle, murmuring words in Vekshi as she dipped the flame over her offering.

The bowl contained more than blood and hair: the surface came alight with flames, and Kadeja knelt before them.

"Ashasa, guide me," she whispered in Kenan, touching her head to the floor – and then she switched to Vekshi again, her prayer rendered unintelligible.

"What's she saying?" Saffron murmured.

For a moment, Zech said nothing. Her eyes were wide and

distant, her features calm as a sleeping child's; which, Saffron supposed, was technically appropriate, but nonetheless disquieting. She was on the verge of repeating the question when Zech began to speak, her words delivered in a soft, dreamy monotone made all the eerier by their contrast with Kadeja's impassioned tone. Saffron's scalp prickled.

"Mother Sun, why won't you lift my guilt? I live only to serve you; I heed your truth. Your will has been put before my own. I work for the unity of your children; the unity of your word. With Leoden, I will remake this world in your image, the heathen gods revealed as sparks struck from your fire. And yet. And yet. This grieving guilt still eats at me. I know it was your will, your omen, your blessing; I know I acted only as you wished. But still you withhold your greatest gift from me. My penance continues. You will not give me a rightful child. Is this a test? Have I failed you somehow? Mother Sun, shine on me. Mother Sun, warm me. Mother Sun, light my path. Please, send me the child I'm meant to mother. Send me absolution. Send me peace."

Kadeja fell silent first, so that Zech's final words were spoken into a vacuum. Saffron stared at the Vex'Mara, trembling with an emotion she couldn't name. She hadn't understood half of what Kadeja was talking about, and yet, somehow, she felt... not pity exactly, but perhaps a sort of empathy for a woman praying in private, battling some secret sense of loss. All too well, she understood uncertainty. But that fleeting connection frightened her too; she didn't want to sympathise with the woman who'd cut her fingers, whose actions ultimately threatened her life and the lives of those around her. Zech, too, looked perturbed: some of the dreaminess had left her face, replaced with confusion. The two girls looked at each other.

"I don't understand," said Zech.

"Me neither," said Saffron. "I–"

The double doors opened again.

All three of them – Kadeja included – jumped, watching as a handsome man in his thirties entered. He too was barefoot, dressed in loose trousers beneath a plain red tunic whose short sleeves served to emphasise the sun-darkened skin of his forearms and face. His black hair was short, tousled and threaded sparsely with silver; his lips were expressive and mobile, and his dark eyes were full of secrets. Kadeja rose to meet him, smiling as he stepped forward and wrapped his arms around her.

"I didn't mean to disturb you, my love," said Leoden, dropping a kiss on her forehead. "But we've had a change of plan regarding Iviyat. I thought you'd want to know."

"Of course," said Kadeja, tilting her head to meet his gaze. "She's been recovered?"

"The opposite. We're letting her go."

For a moment, Kadeja looked shocked, then a gleam of understanding crept into her eyes. "She's running to Veksh," she said.

"As best we can tell, yes. Her only other option is the traitors' camp, but whether she's been kidnapped by Vekshi radicals or tricked into treason by rebels, dear Iviyat is the perfect excuse for moving our soldiers further north."

"Wonderful," said Kadeja, and then they were kissing, deep and slow in a way that made Saffron profoundly uncomfortable. Not wanting to watch, she turned to Zech and murmured, "We need to remember this. We need to tell Gwen and Yasha what they're planning, only last time I woke up from here, I'd forgotten everything. Have you done this before?"

"Remember," Zech said dreamily. She was staring into space. "I think... I think..."

"I think," said another voice, "you've trespassed long enough."

Saffron yelped and whirled around. Instead of a wall, she found herself staring once more at Luy and his endless field of flowers, the palace, Kadeja and Leoden all gone. Luy rolled his eyes, as though he didn't know whether to be amused or exasperated at her obvious confusion.

"I didn't expect to find you here again so soon, let alone with a friend," he said. "And who is this?"

Moving slowly, Zech turned to face him. "Zechalia," she said. "I came to find something important. A lost thing."

"Oh?" Luy quirked an eyebrow at her. "And did you succeed?"

"I'm not sure," Zech said. "I'll have to think about it."

"Why did you take us away from the palace?" Saffron asked. "I mean, I know they were kissing and everything, but we were learning something important."

Luy raised a finger. "A better question is, how did the two of you get there in the first place? True-dreaming might not be magic in the conventional sense – not always, anyway – but that doesn't mean the palace isn't warded against it. And yet there you were, eavesdropping on the Vex and Vex'Mara as easily as falling from horseback. You, I can almost understand," he said, pointing at Saffron. "You're not from this world, which lays parts of its dreaming open to you that might otherwise be closed. But as for your friend..." Abruptly, he fell silent, staring at Zech with a look on his face that somehow contrived to be horrified, elated and revelatory all at once. "No," he said, disbelievingly.

Zech paled. Reaching out, she grabbed Saffron's arm, hard enough to hurt. "I'll remember," she whispered fiercely – and then, with a strange, small smile, she vanished.

Saffron blinked at the empty space beside her. "What just happened?"

"She woke up," said Luy. "And by design rather than accident, I suspect, despite appearing to be an unpractised dreamer. Interesting."

"Why did she leave?"

"I'm not sure," Luy said slowly. "Whatever I might've

thought, I can't confirm it now, and without confirmation such words are worthless. You'll have to ask her yourself, if either of you remembers this on waking."

Saffron hesitated. On the one hand, Luy's answer was deeply unsatisfactory – he was clearly hiding something, and she wanted to know what it was. But on the other, dreams were his domain: she had no power to compel him, and in any case, a more pressing question had wriggled its way to the forefront of her thoughts.

"This dream, whatever it is," she said, weighing her words carefully, "is it magic? You said true-dreaming sometimes is, but not always, and I was wondering, if it *is* magic, is it yours or mine, or does it just exist on its own?"

Luy grinned. "Why can't it be all three at once?"

At Saffron's expression, he laughed. "Every sentient creature dreams, and whether they know it or not, every sentient race in the Many – that's the multiverse to you – has the power to walk the dreamscape. On your world, your Earth, that gift was sometimes called oneiromancy; here, the Kenans call it the *ilumet*, and say its usage is the province of the priests and priestesses of Hime, the sky-goddess. But dreaming is a sideways sort of talent, Saffron-girl. Some people have it strongly, and for them it really is magic, wielded consciously through will and thought with unmatched skill. Others who lack an inborn gift can learn it through hard practice, but even then it's a matter of luck; no matter how hard they try, not everyone can learn the trick of it.

"But even so, everyone dreams – every sentient soul on every world, all pouring their thoughts into a great subconscious web we call the dreamscape. Well, I say *we*; not everyone believes it. The Shavaktiin, though, we know the truth: that the dreamscape connects all minds across the Many, heedless of time and distance, because the Many doesn't care about clocks and seasons, decay and ageing, relative positions in time and space. There is only one moment in all of existence – one eternal beat in which every universe is born and breathes and dies, the way milliseconds and femtoseconds inhabit what we commonly think of as the smallest unit of time – and that moment is always *now*. And so it is with the dreamscape: the dreams of the past don't die because the past is past. Why should they, when neither past nor future truly exists?

"And when you dream – when anyone in creation dreams – they're connected to the dreamscape; a realm created solely by its visitors, by the very act of visiting. But sentient minds, and particularly human ones, are limited: the dreamscape is far too vast for any one soul to traverse, and there's a kind of topography to it, a sort of enforced proximity, so that the dreams you visit most easily are the dreams of those nearest to you – the dreams of others of your world, whether forwards or backwards in time. Unconscious dreams, where the daylight mind sleeps, everyone has those, and their substance lends deception to the dreamscape, which doesn't distinguish between beauty and nightmare, history and lies. But conscious dreams, like this one? Well, then your daylight mind is alive to that deception; it helps you parse true from false. But unless you remember it on waking, you might as well have dreamed nothing at all.

"And so, to answer your question, Saffron Isla Coulter – is this magic? Only if consciousness is, or if brains are. Wherever magic occurs in the Many, in whatever manifestation, it's always a disturbance: a specific usurpation of the norms of its world, or of similar worlds, whose ultimate origins and logic not even the Shavaktiin know. But everyone dreams, and everyone feeds the dreamscape – which makes it normal, and *that* means it isn't magic. Not really."

For the longest moment, Saffron simply stared. Part of her had drunk in every word, but the rest of her was dumbstruck, unable to comprehend the scope of Luy's response. Falling into another world was one thing, but the sudden possibility of endless new realms all interconnected even while stretching into infinity… It was too big to believe – and Luy must have known that. He was looking at her with suppressed humour, eyes gleaming as though, by answering her question, he'd also laid a challenge before her. Which, Saffron realised, he had: not just to accept it, but to remember.

Softening slightly, Luy reached out and tapped the side of her cheek with a finger. "You're no oneiromancer, worldwalker girl. But you might learn something yet."

Around her, the dreamscape began to fade, the field of flowers whitening into mist.

"How…" she began, but before she could form the rest of the words, both Luy and his world had fallen away, leaving only muzzy dreamlessness in their wake.

In the cold dawn light, Zech lay still and watched as Safi began to stir – she'd been lying awake for hours, thoughts churning with all the revelations of their shared dream. She'd already thought of a way to tell Yasha what she'd learned about the soldiers without mentioning that they'd seen inside the palace, but first she had to see if Safi remembered too – and if so, how much. The wait was agonising enough that even the pain in her leg couldn't wholly distract her. And what if Jeiden or Yena woke too? Though neither had so much as twitched in the time that Zech had been watching, Jeiden was a light sleeper and Yena was still curled against Safi, making it difficult for one of them to rise without disturbing the other.

Finally, Safi's eyes slid open. Zech held her breath, willing her to look over. For one heart-stopping moment, the older girl almost went straight back to sleep, but at last she met Zech's gaze, blinking slowly.

Speak now, privately, Zech mimed at her. *Please?*

Safi nodded agreement. Gently disentangling herself from Yena (the other girl only sighed and rolled over) she stood away from the others, waiting politely while Zech, still unsure how much strain her leg could bear, came slowly to her feet. Pain shot through her thigh, but it was a marked improvement on yesterday. The realisation made her overconfident – no sooner had she taken a step than she was stumbling, toppling forward. Only Safi kept her upright: the other girl lunged forward and caught her, lending support while Zech, red-faced, looped an arm around her shoulders.

Clearly, walking anywhere was out of the question until she'd seen the healers again. At Safi's tacit suggestion, Zech let herself be lowered back down, the pain easing as soon as she took the weight off her feet. Casting a wary eye at Jeiden, she opted instead for a different sort of secrecy.

"Safi," she asked in English, "what did you dream last night?"

Beside her, the older girl stiffened. "I think... ugh, I feel like it was something important, but I can't remember. Maybe you were there? I don't know, it's all sort of vague, like the more I try to hang onto it, the more it slips away. Maybe it'll come to me later." She paused, looking quizzically at Zech. "Why? Did you dream something too?"

The hope in her tone made Zech wince with guilt, but if Safi noticed the expression, she must have attributed it to yet more pain as she said nothing. *Maybe I should tell her. We could work together. Maybe we could be allies.* But the risk was too great, she knew that now; she wanted to trust Safi, but first she had to find out more on her own – had to figure out who knew what, and how badly she'd been lied to.

Instead, she shook her head. "It was nothing," Zech murmured. "Just a nightmare."

PART 3
The Counsel of Queens

15

Neither the Right Thing Nor Its Opposite

Three hours north of the riverside camp, when Pix and Viya were due to turn for Avekou, Zech suddenly announced, "I had a true dream of Leoden last night."

The hairs on Saffron's arms stood up, though she didn't know why. She stared at Zech, trepidation coiling through her stomach as Gwen and Yasha, Pix and Halaya all demanded details of the dream.

"He's called off the search for Iviyat," Zech said, her gaze lighting on everyone but Saffron. "He ordered his commanders to turn around. He doesn't want to find us anymore."

A whirlwind of discussion followed. Pix alone was sceptical, not of Zech's claim, but of the idea that the dream could be trusted in isolation, while Yasha was almost feral with pride at this newly-manifested talent. All agreed, however, that the news should change the distribution of the Shavaktiin between the two parties – if Leoden was no longer hunting Viya, then there was potentially less need to protect her, and all four women began to haggle the details out in earnest.

"Is that a kind of magic here?" Saffron asked Matu, who was the closest adult not involved in the conversation. "Dreaming true dreams?"

"We call it the ilumet," he said, and Saffron shivered with déjà vu. "Some people are more gifted with it than others, but everyone dreams, and having another type of magic often makes you more sensitive to the dreamscape." He paused, then added, "Zechalia wouldn't lie about something like this."

"I know," said Saffron – too quickly, because even though she trusted Zech, she had a nagging feeling that she was missing something. But then she'd felt that way about most things since coming to Kena; that was just her being out of her depth, not a sign of something important. The thought sent a pang through her chest, and she hunched in on herself, remembering Kadeja's blade at the fountain, the blood of the Envas road.

"Here now," said Matu, giving her shoulder a gentle nudge. "You look like you've swallowed the moon."

"Like I've *what*?"

Matu laughed. "Forgive me; it's a tale we tell children. Once, they say, there was a third moon in the sky, and she knew all the stories in the world, but she was too shy to share them. So her elder sisters wove a spell in moonlight, that if anyone drank the youngest moon's reflection from a pool, one of her stories would pass to their keeping until they died. And people drank, and the younger moon, once fat and round, grew thinner and thinner, only waxing full again when those who knew her stories passed into death.

"But as the legend grew, we began to drink the moon's stories faster than our dying could replenish her, until one night a lonely child saw the moon's reflection and drank until she was gone forever. His belly was full of stories, but he grieved her loss, knowing then that he'd taken her duty on himself, but fearing it was beyond him. And from then on, there were only two moons in Kena's sky, and our stories stayed with us even after death. And that's why, even now, the tales we tell to children are called moon-tales."

He looked at her, his dark eyes kind. "I say you've swallowed the moon because you look burdened with stories. As if you've taken more weight on yourself than you rightly know how to carry."

"Oh," said Saffron quietly. Hot tears pricked her eyes. "Oh."

Ahead of them, the women had sorted out the dispersal of the Shavaktiin. Pix and Viya broke away from the main party, accompanied by fewer riders than initially planned, but still enough that their absence left Saffron feeling strangely exposed. She raised a hand to wave them off, as did Matu – she'd already said her proper goodbyes to Viya that morning – then watched them ride away, the smaller party taking a curving path through the trees until they were out of sight. When her own mount started moving again, it was almost a shock; she jolted in the saddle, fingers clutching at the reins, and stared at a fixed point in the distance, unfamiliar earth beneath a too-white sun.

"We'll start your lessons in Vekshi tomorrow," Matu said, into the not-quite-silence of hoofbeats and creaking leather.

"Mm," said Saffron. She didn't look up.

"I could teach you other things, too, if you wanted."

There was a pause as the offer sank in. "Like what?"

"How to defend yourself," said Matu. His voice was calm and even, as though they were discussing the weather, but Saffron felt her cheeks burn, ashamed to be so transparent. "Not how to fight with a Vekshi staff – there's not enough time, and I'm hardly proficient – and Pix is the one to ask for lessons in knives. But there are... tricks, I suppose you'd say, that are helpful for defence. Ways to use your size to your advantage, your speed. Nothing complicated. Just enough to keep yourself safe, disable an opponent or get away clean. If you wanted."

Saffron thought of how helpless she'd felt when Kadeja had cut her fingers; how frightened she'd been in the battle;

how vulnerable she still felt now. It wasn't that she wanted more violence – she just didn't want other people to hurt her again.

"I'd like that," she said softly. "Please."

"All right, then," said Matu. "I'll talk you through the forms as we ride, and this evening, I'll show you in practice. How does that sound?"

Saffron took a deep breath, and for the first time that morning, it didn't feel tight in her chest. "Good. It sounds… good."

In the days that followed, Matu was better than his word. Though he never probed openly about Saffron's fears, he was quick to intuit their parameters, adapting his conversation to suit her level of comfort. Their second morning out, when talk of self-defence became too much for her, he segued effortlessly into a description of Yeveshasa, a stone-carved city set atop a massive mesa, punching up out of a plateau like the earth god's fist. The zuymet flowed between them, Vekshi words and Kenan twisting in her head, and when she tried to speak aloud, he never once mocked her accent. Gwen joined in for some of these lessons, muttering about agile young brains whenever she stumbled over a word, but Matu didn't tease her either; just rode between them, reins tied to the saddle as he grazed his fingertips against their skin, the touch both chaste and comforting.

Sometimes, during these moments, Yena would catch Saffron's eye and wink at her, leaving her flushed and smiling. Though Matu undoubtedly noticed, he politely refrained from comment. And whenever they stopped – whenever Saffron could bear it – he taught her his tricks of self-defence in earnest.

On the evening of the third day, as they sat beside the campfire, Matu explained about the nine branches of Kenan magic, each discipline tied and attributed to a particular god, though their limitations were, in his view, a product as much of custom as natural law.

"We use our magics like tools, the way we've been taught," he said. "The shape of a tool defines its use, but the substance of a tool – the how and why of its making – is a human choice."

"You're saying all magic is the same?" asked Saffron.

"I'm saying," said Matu, "that Veksh and Kena are different lands, but where their magic is different to ours, it's not because of blood."

She dreamed of the Envas road that night, a paralysing melee of blood and screams, the woman she'd killed looking up at her from under the dying horse. Saffron woke with tears on her cheeks, but not alone: she was cuddled between Zech and Yena, with Jeiden's small hand sneaking over Zech's flank to curl around her wrist.

"It's all right," Yena murmured sleepily, nuzzling into Saffron's shoulder. "We've got you."

Zech made a sleepy noise of assent, and Jeiden squeezed her wrist, and when she fell asleep again, she didn't dream at all.

Not that night, at least. But in the days that followed, more unsettling than her periodic nightmares were the dreams she didn't remember, their absence niggling at her like a half-completed chore.

Just as she'd done for the last ten days since setting out for Avekou, Viya woke to the ungentle nudging of Pix's boot. She'd protested at first, angry at having her status so thoroughly disregarded, but Pixeva only smiled and said that the dignity of rank while travelling was like a three-legged roa: both mythical and conceptually pointless. Thus far, Viya had endured the indignity of riding through rainsqualls, pissing and shitting behind innumerable bushes, and nightmares of the Envas road that unfailingly woke her from sleep. Though her complaints were only ever about the first two problems, in her secret heart she knew the latter was truly responsible for her upset. Like all women of her class, Viya had been raised to fight and defend herself, taught from childhood that there was no dishonour in taking the lives of others if it were done to save one's own. And yet the battle weighed on her – not the loss of the dead themselves, but the fear and fury of it, and the sharp uncertainty she'd felt as to whether or not she'd live.

Her nightmares were always the same: an endless, looping replay of when she'd fallen. Only seconds had passed between Mara's demise and her hitting the ground, but both at the time and in memory, it felt much longer. Viya had been paralysed, so terrified that she'd wet herself; so dislocated from her living flesh that, for the smallest increment of time, she felt as if she were floating outside her body, leaving her with an incongruous, impossible memory of staring in disbelief at the back of her own head. And then she'd slammed back into the moment, spurred by an overwhelming desire to fight, to win, to *live*. She'd slashed the hocks of the horse above and rolled away, fast enough not to be crushed by its body but too slow to avoid the sword of its rider. Her face burned as the blade came down, and after that there was nothing but blood and darkness, interspersed with flashes of light and the far-off sound of screaming.

That was when she invariably woke, sweat-drenched and trembling in the night air, the whole world silent except for the whir of insects and the breathing of her companions. Sleep never came easily after that, but eventually her body's exhaustion overruled her brain's alarm, and she'd drift back into a shallow, dreamless oblivion. She said nothing of this to Pix, of course – pride forbade her – but sometimes as they rode, she'd caught the courtier watching her with speculative sympathy, as though she were waiting for Viya to admit to it. Had the two of them been alone, it was possible Viya might have given in, but their five Shavaktiin companions

– three archers, a dreamseer and Dom the healer – were always nearby, and so Viya held her tongue.

Her scar, though still painful, was healing cleanly. She'd seen so herself on the second day out, when they'd passed a loop of the river where the water was still enough to serve as a mirror. The scar was only slightly thinner than a finger's width, taut and ridged and shiny-sallow, extending diagonally from just inside her left eyebrow to the top right of her forehead, at which point the blade had jagged back again and torn a wedge of scalp away from her hairline. Thanks to Dom, the flesh had been reattached, albeit at the expense of a small hank of hair – the skin there was weird and bald, only now beginning to prickle with new growth.

Magic could only speed up her body's natural healing, not replace it altogether: the scar, though neater and more fully developed than it would otherwise be, was still permanent. Viya had stared at it for a long moment, wondering how she felt. A small part of her was sad, but as for the rest... She was still Cuivexa; still Iviyat ore Leoden ki Hawy; still herself. And besides, bloodfather Iavan had a scarred face too, and everyone loved and respected him. Why should Viya be any different?

Now, though, in the chill dawn air, she probed the scar and winced. It hurt more when the air was cold, and after yet another night spent on hard ground, her whole body was stiff and sore into the bargain. Biting back curses, she blinked angrily up at Pix: in a break from her usual nudge-and-move-on routine, the courtier still stood over her, one hand resting lazily on a hip.

"What now?" Viya grumbled, yawning as she stretched. "More demotions? Do you want me to cook you breakfast? Shine your boots?"

Pix quirked her lips. "Either would be lovely, did you feel so inclined, but no. I've spoken with Oyako–" the dreamseer, robed in white, "–and she says we ought to reach Avekou today. I thought you'd like to know."

Instantly, Viya sat up. "So soon? I thought we were another day distant at least."

Pix shrugged. "Even with the rain, we've made good time. I'd thought we might have more of Leoden's honoured swords to contend with, but Zechalia must have dreamed it true, after all. If he's still looking for us, he's doing it in the wrong place."

"Hmm," said Viya, coming to her feet. Because of Zech's dream, Halaya had downsized their Shavaktiin escort in accordance with the reduced threat; originally, she'd planned to send swordsmen with them as well as archers, but as the journey to Veksh was deemed to be the more perilous, she'd opted to keep the bulk of her people together. Viya wasn't surprised the girl had dreamed it true – though Zech was Vekshi by birth, Ke and Na had already acted through her once, so why not again? But she'd learned from her earlier mistakes not to antagonise others if she could help it, and so she kept her opinions to herself.

Instead, she asked, "Did Oyako say when we'd arrive? Did she dream inside the rebel camp?"

Pix shook her head. "The place is warded, apparently – Amenet must have someone with the ilumet on her side, or else she's working with Hime's Kin. As for time, the afternoon is most likely. We've still a way to ride."

At this casual mention of Amenet ore Amenet ki Rahei, Viya shivered. It wasn't until the third day out from the others that Pix had finally admitted that not only was Amenet still alive, but they were on their way to meet her. Up until that point – ever since she'd first heard mention of Avekou – Viya had assumed that the allies Yasha had sent them to find were, in fact, Rixevet, Iavan and Kadu. Certainly, nobody had tried to disabuse her of the notion, and given Yasha's previous refusal to let her leave the group, it had made sense that wanting Rixevet as an ally might have caused her to change her mind. Knowing the truth, she still hadn't given up hope of meeting her parents in Avekou, but it was a small hope, one she'd done her best to keep buried lest reality prove a disappointment. Avekou was a large territory populated almost exclusively by the farms and estates of nobles. Only Pix knew to whose lands they were actually heading, and so far, she was keeping it close to her heart.

"Fine, then," said Viya. "This afternoon it is."

Satisfied, Pix nodded and turned to go, but hesitated mid-stride. "Oh," she murmured. "So *that's* what she meant."

"What?" Still rubbing sleep from her eyes, Viya peered past Pix to the rest of their camp – and promptly blinked in astonishment. Every one of the Shavaktiin was suddenly bare-armed, bare-faced, bare-headed, their veils removed and robes re-wrapped to function like taals. They looked almost normal, and yet totally, utterly alien, their strange faces attached to individuals Viya had come to know only by voice and the colours they wore.

"Why are they doing that?" she asked.

Pix answered slowly. "Dom said that today, we all become part of the story."

Viya frowned, causing her scar to twinge. "I don't understand."

"It means," said Oyako, walking up from the left, "that once we reach Avekou, we all become true participants in this tale – we must act as ourselves, as named individuals rather than anonymous, interchangeable Shavaktiin. And so we remove our robes, to acknowledge we are no longer shaping events from the outside, but from within."

Viya stared at the dreamseer. She'd recognised Oyako's voice, but the face and form that accompanied it weren't what she'd expected. Oyako was petite and brown, with wide hazel eyes and a tawny frizz of hair that circled her head like a halo – like Gwen's hair, but more tightly curled. She looked to be about Pix's age, and though the lines of her face were sharp, the bridge of freckles that spanned her nose softened the effect, while her bright smile – only those with ready access to healers had such perfect teeth – was both joyful and mischievous. She was, in fact, utterly beautiful, and the suddenness of the realisation took Viya's breath away.

"Ah," she said, uncomfortably aware that a blush was creeping its way up her neck. "I... suppose that makes sense."

Pix gave an amused snort. "Staring's rude, girl. Didn't your parents tell you? Pick up your jaw before you trip and break it."

Furious, Viya went to respond, but found that the combination of Pix's teasing and Oyako's curiously raised eyebrows had rendered her speechless. Mercifully, Oyako broke the tension by giving them both a pat on the arm and heading off to help ready the horses.

Pix ran a hand down her face. "It's going to be a long day," she said.

Viya didn't contradict her.

By the time they were up and riding, however, some of the shock at the Shavaktiin's transformation had worn off. Two of the archers were revealed to be unremarkably Kenan, while the third was from Uyu. Dom was a different matter: with her straight brown hair, pale blue eyes and skin the colour of bruised fruit, Viya thought she might be from Kamne, a tiny nation wedged between the Bright Mountains and Kena's southeast border, but she couldn't tell for sure, and Pix's expression when she brought it up suggested that asking wouldn't be a good idea. Even so, it was strange to realise the Shavaktiin didn't draw their numbers purely from her own people. Not so long ago, she never would have believed that the gods would choose to act through foreigners, but now she supposed it made perfect sense: after all, if Ke and Na had made the whole world, then surely that meant they'd made all its peoples too?

By noon, the woods through which they'd been riding

for the past two days were beginning to thin – not naturally, but as a consequence of active cultivation. Overhanging limbs had been pruned, dead wood cleared away, and the placement of new saplings ordered to ensure a passable space between trees.

"Whose land is this?" she asked, not bothering to look around. She'd thought Pix was closest, but much to her surprise, it was Oyako who answered.

"The land belongs to itself and the gods. We only pretend to own it."

Viya wrinkled her nose, reining her mare in line with Oyako's. "That's not an answer."

"It is to me."

Pix chose that moment to enter the conversation. "In law, this place belongs to Kisavet ore Kisavet ki Oreva, a shrewd old snake with an eye for beautiful husbands. Apparently, she's not given up on the possibility of adding Matu to her collection, even now that we're all disgraced, and if not for Amenet, he might well have taken her up on it. Her lusts aren't subtle, but her politics are: she's calculating and canny – not the sort to back the wrong player, but always careful to keep on pleasant terms with everyone. Which is why she's happy enough to let we rebels and rapscallions jaunt through her woods, provided we don't assume that means she's a wholehearted ally. She's still judging whether or not we're likely to succeed."

"Charming," said Oyako.

They rode on in silence.

The further they went through the woods, the thinner they became. They stopped to eat within sight of the treeline, but it was a quick meal: they were close now, and nervous anticipation spread through the group like fever. When they finally emerged onto a slim but well-maintained trail that ran parallel to the forest edge, Pix took the lead, setting a faster pace while the others followed single file.

Soon the trees fell away altogether, so that the scenery was dominated by the rolling orchards and fresh-tilled fields of Avekou. Viya had come here once before, but at such a young age that her only real memories were of the inside of her family's holdings – flashes of stairs and doorways, the view of trees from her bedroom window. Now, as estates began appearing on either side of the road, she found herself desperately searching for signs of familiarity, some memory-trigger to affirm that she knew this place, or had known it once.

Instead, she found only strangeness. Tilting her head back, her view of the sky was briefly obscured by a flash of black pain as her scar made its presence felt. Unbidden, the words of her favourite prayer to Ke and Na ran through her mind:

You are the star and the darkness,
you are the light and the loss.
Guide me like your stars in wheeling;
guide me like your dark at dawn.
Your cupped hands form the firmament – hold me
as those hands hold the world.
Beside you, I am as bright as spilled salt.
Beside you, I am as dark as smudged ash.
I am unspooled cloth awaiting direction:
weave me into your pattern.

Viya mouthed the words to the sky, and steadily the pain in her head receded. When she looked forwards again – her mare was evidently content to follow the horse in front – it was to find that Pix had turned up a tree-lined avenue leading to a sprawling estate house. A contingent of honoured swords patrolled the grounds, with several stationed on either side of the main door, and those were only the ones that Viya could see. That wasn't unusual in and of itself – many nobles in residence placed a premium on security, especially since Leoden's siege of Karavos – but the barefooted figure running out to greet them was.

It was a man: tall, slender and bald, dressed in a sumptuous red taal that contrasted perfectly with his skin, which was unusually dark for one of Kenan blood. He was shouting something – inaudibly at first, due to the length of the avenue, but as he came closer, Viya's heart almost faltered under the weight of recognition.

"Ivi! Ivi! Ivi!"

"Kadu!" she screamed. "Kadu!"

The name ripped from her without conscious volition. In that single moment, everything she'd refused herself permission to feel rushed up and overwhelmed her, a maelstrom of loss and confusion. Heedless of propriety, she leapt from her mare and bolted forwards, tears breaking free as she ran. Dimly, she was aware of Pix shouting something, but none of that mattered; Kadu's arms were spread wide, and when Viya reached him, he wrapped them around her and scooped her up as though she were still a child of five, and not the Cuivexa of Kena. Viya clung to her fourthfather, sobbing freely into his shoulder, while he hugged her fiercely and stroked her hair.

"Oh, Iviyat. Ivi. Viya. I thought you were lost."

"I was," she whispered, so softly that only he could hear it. "But not anymore."

Kadu laughed, the sound shaky with shock and relief, and began to ease away from her. Only then did Viya remember that Pix was still watching, that she had her dignity to uphold. Taking a long, deep breath, she wiped her eyes on the back of her hand – the motion caused her scar to pull – and forced herself to step back from Kadu, until they were face to face, not touching. It startled her to find that he looked shorter than usual; once, he'd towered over her, but she'd grown since then, and the gap between their heights was closing. His kind, aesthetic face was more lined than formerly: there were dark circles under his eyes, and they carried a haunted look that had nothing to do with Viya. A terrible fear took root in her chest.

"Something's happened," she said. "Kadu, what's happened? Is everyone all right?"

His lips parted, trembled, twitched as though attempting to smile, then collapsed into closure; he couldn't speak. He shook his head.

Viya felt frozen. "Who?" she managed. *Not Rixevet. Please, gods, not Rixevet.*

Tears stood in her fourthfather's eyes. "Hawy," he said. "It's Hawy. She was coming to us. When Leoden announced you were missing, she knew it wasn't right. She moved against him – finally, she saw the truth! – but it was too soon, too obvious. He'd been watching the house. He knew."

"Hawy," Viya echoed. A weight settled into her stomach. "No, you're wrong. He trusted Hawy. She dealt with him, she supported him, she–" *She gave me to him,* she wanted to say, but the words lodged in her throat.

"He only sent a few soldiers; but then, he didn't need more. When the three of us left, we took most of the honoured swords with us. We thought she'd be safe." This last came out as a whisper.

"No," said Viya. Numb. She was numb. "No, Kadu–"

"Hawy bought time for the others to escape. She fought them alone. And she fell, Ivi. Sava saw it herself."

"No."

"The palace announced it yesterday. Hawy's dead."

"*No.*"

Viya dropped to her knees – just dropped, as though her strings were cut. A low moan started to build in her throat, the sound emerging as a wordless, furious keen, building in volume until the whole world shook at the frequency of her rage, her grief.

My husband killed my bloodmother.

"Cuivexa."

The voice came from far away. *Pix*, said part of Viya's brain. A small recognition, but enough that the noise she'd been making died away. *I am the Cuivexa of Kena, Iviyat ore Leoden ki Hawy* – but no, not *ki Hawy* anymore; *ki Rixevet*, after the next most prominent member of her family. Rixevet led the mahu'kedet, now.

"Yes, Pixeva?"

"Your grief must wait. We need to go inside. Please, Highness."

"As you wish." She pressed her palms into the road, clenched briefly, then pushed herself up. This time, she met Kadu's gaze, not as a daughter, but as a monarch. Reaching out, she touched him gently on the arm.

"I'm sorry for all our sakes," she said tightly. "Leoden will pay for this, I swear by Ke and Na and the Holy Child."

Kadu nodded, his posture rigid with grief. "Oh, yes."

Viya turned to Pix. "Thank you," she murmured.

And for once, there was nothing but sincerity on Pix's face. "Lead on, Highness. We've business to attend to."

"So we do," said Viya. "Oh, we do."

The scenery didn't change when they crossed into Veksh. There were no soldiers, no fences, no signposts: nothing to indicate their passage from one realm into another, and yet Yasha claimed to know the second they made the transition. Inwardly, Gwen felt sceptical of the claim, but as there was nothing to be gained by pressing the point, she kept her doubts to herself. Despite having lived in Kena for a significant portion of her life, she'd never made the trip north to Veksh. Perhaps if Trishka had wanted to go things might've been different, but as Yasha's previous tight-lipped refusal to return had extended to her daughter, there'd never been much point.

Now, though, necessity had superseded curiosity and, in so doing, provoked it anew. They were still days away from Yevekshasa – possibly even as much as a week, depending on whether they met with assistance or opposition at the hands of the native Vekshi – but even so, Gwen felt a pleasant rush of anticipation. Thanks to Trishka and Yasha, she'd picked up some of the Vekshi language over the years, but not nearly enough to help her deal with the Council of Queens. To make up for lost time, she'd had Matu teach her through the zuymet alongside Saffron, the new words settling into her head like fine sand weighted with water. Even so, she was still a slow learner – magic or no magic, older brains required more time and effort to teach than young ones, and even the strength of Matu's gift couldn't wholly compensate for the strain of teaching two people at once.

As a result, her Vekshi was no more than adequate – which, much to her surprise, placed her on roughly the same linguistic footing as Yena and Trishka. It made sense, once she thought about it: both women had effectively learned the language in exile, and while Yasha and the other expatriate members of the compound had spoken it often among themselves, Kenan had still been the default language. Which meant, rather oddly, that of the five fluent speakers in their party, only two were Vekshi: Yasha and Zech, the other three being Matu, Jeiden – who, it turned out, Matu had long since taught on his own initiative – and Saffron, whose youthful brain absorbed new tongues with enviable ease.

By contrast, none of the Shavaktiin spoke more than a few cursory words of Vekshi; Halaya spoke the most, but even her repertoire was restricted to a few key phrases. When Gwen expressed her surprise at the fact, Halaya shrugged.

"None of us has the zuymet. It's a valuable skill, one the temples guard jealously when they have it, and which pays well even without them."

"The same could be said of the sevikmet," Gwen countered, "and yet you have two healers."

Halaya laughed. "Perhaps. Yet there's a greater inherent altruism to healing, I think – not everyone needs a translator, but everyone gets sick. Those with the gift are encouraged to use it freely, even within the temples. Other talents, though... I'm amazed your flock boasts even one with the zuymet, let alone two."

Gwen snorted at that. "My *flock*? They're hardly birds, and they're certainly not mine."

The Shavaktiin tilted her head, her green veil fluttering coyly. "Are they Yasha's then?"

"Why wouldn't they be?"

"Why not indeed?" Halaya murmured.

Gwen rolled her eyes. "Very cryptic. Consider me suitably puzzled."

"Noted," Halaya said, and though her face was hidden, Gwen could have sworn the other woman was smiling.

That had been yesterday; now their company rode two by two while the remaining Shavaktiin, Halaya included, took turns as vanguards and scouts, protecting the column at a distance. Yasha and Yena led, with Zech and Trishka close behind. Then came Matu and Saffron, clearly engaged in their daily lesson. That should have left Gwen paired with Jeiden, except that she'd fallen behind, the boy more than a horse's length ahead of her. Nudging her own mount to a faster walk – and wincing, as she did so, at the stiffness nearly a fortnight's riding and sleeping rough had forced into her joints – she pulled alongside and found him staring fixedly at Zech.

"She's hiding something," he muttered, not moving his head.

Gwen blinked, caught off guard. "What?"

"She's hiding something," Jeiden repeated. Then he sighed, running a hand through his feathery hair. "Ever since Pix and Viya left, she's been acting odd. Secretive, you know? Asking questions when Yasha's not around."

"I hadn't noticed," Gwen said, and mentally cursed herself for being unobservant. Part of her had noticed Zech's change in behaviour, her sudden avoidance of Yasha, but she'd put it down to a combination of post-battle trauma and resentment at the matriarch for making her fight in the first place. The possibility of a third explanation had never even occurred to her. "What's she been asking?"

Jeiden shook his head, frustrated. "I don't know. That's just it. She's been asking the Shavaktiin, not me – sometimes Trishka, too, but mostly Halaya and the others."

"And you're worried about her?"

"Yes. No. I don't know." He finally turned to look at her, his entire posture despondent. "I just wish she'd let me in on it."

Gwen chose her words carefully. "Maybe she's being secretive for a reason. For now, it's best just to trust her. She'll let us know when she's ready."

Jeiden nodded dutifully, but it was clear he didn't believe her – and why should he, when Gwen wasn't sure she believed herself? It wasn't like Zech to be secretive, let alone to go behind Yasha's back. Or at least, not seriously: pushing at rules and boundaries, sneaking out of the compound and eavesdropping on her elders was all behaviour understood to be tacitly endorsed by Yasha, so long as Zech didn't get caught. But this smacked of something different, and the more she thought about it, the clearer it became that, even if Gwen had spotted it earlier, she still wouldn't have had a clue what it was about.

A shout from up ahead broke her thoughts. It was one of the Shavaktiin outriders, arm raised as he pointed at the road ahead. At first, Gwen couldn't see the reason for his alarm – but then, like so much else, her long distance vision wasn't what it used to be. Squinting at the horizon, she ground her teeth in frustration as Jeiden, too, let out a cry of shock.

And then she saw it: successive showers of golden sparks, each one greater than the last, appearing suddenly in the naked air less than a hundred metres from the head of the column. As she watched, small lightnings followed, spiderwebbing outwards like fractures through stone, until a crackling web of energy arched across the body of the road. The brightness built, intensifying steadily. Then, with a whiplash-roar, a gleaming, gold-edged portal appeared before them. The column ground to a halt, formation forgotten as their snorting, wide-eyed mounts bunched tightly together, until everyone but the Shavaktiin were within two metres of everyone else.

"Arsegullet!" Yasha swore. And then, with only the slightest betraying shake to her voice: "Everyone be still. I know what this is."

"I should bloody well hope so," Gwen muttered in English, eyes glued ahead as the blinding portal, now apparently stable, disgorged three riders mounted on matching white mares. All three were women of Gwen's age or older, their hair respectfully shaved to stubble and crowned by simple circlets of braided copper, gold and platinum. Each one wore the dou and kettha – the traditional Vekshi tunic and trousers – in matching white cloth embroidered with red and gold thread. One, the middle rider, bore facial scars that were no less prominent for being old: even at a distance, Gwen could see she was blind in one eye from where some triple-clawed blade had raked down the left-hand side of her face. All carried staves that were more like ceremonial scythes, their ends fitted with curving blades, and as they approached, Gwen saw that none of them was smiling.

"Are they..." Jeiden gulped.

Gwen nodded grimly. "Representatives from the Council of Queens."

16
Ashasa's Knives

Saffron stared at the riders, wide-eyed and frightened. The last time they'd met strangers on the road, things hadn't ended well, and now her fight-or-flight reflex was screaming at her to turn around and run. Only the gentle pressure of Matu's hand on her wrist kept her steady, and even then, she could feel her pulse thumping against his fingertips.

"It's all right," Matu murmured quietly. "Trust me. It's all right."

It's not, Saffron wanted to say, but somehow she forced herself to nod. Ahead of them, Yasha kicked her horse forwards: far enough to set her indisputably at the head of their party, but close enough that everything she said was plainly audible. Despite all her lessons in Vekshi, Saffron still found it strange both to hear and to understand the language. She forced herself to listen. Now more than ever, she needed to know what was happening.

"In Ashasa's name, greetings," Yasha said. "To what do I owe the honour of your presence?"

The riders – the queens, for surely they couldn't be anything else, not crowned as they were – came to a halt, close enough for their mounts to touch noses with Yasha's. The eldest queen, distinguished as much by her scars as her age, narrowed her eyes.

"You dare to greet me in Ashasa's name? You, Yasha a Yasara, who turned your back on everything our Mother Sun stands for – who abandoned clan and duty both to live among Kenan savages as little more than a thorn in the flank of righteous Veksh? You dare call *my* presence an honour? Tcha! You lie as you breathe, traitor, and yet you have crossed the border. Why here? Why now? Speak!"

Though Yasha's face was hidden, Saffron saw her tense. When she spoke, her voice was fury-soft, the strength of her answer building like a storm.

"You of all people, Ruyun a Ketra, ought to know why I left. Tell me, where is your daughter? Where is Tavma now? You speak of Ashasa as though she was never a mother; as though she doesn't hold sacred a mother's rights. You would've seen my child broken and dead before she was old enough to cut her hair or share her sheets, and all through jealous grief that I had the strength to refuse what you could not. Shame on you, and shame on the Council, now as then! Ashasa's Knives were once pure and clean, but now they stain themselves red with the blood of children." Yasha spat to one side, contempt in her every gesture. "I am no traitor. But you, Ruyun, your whole existence betrays our Mother Sun. You chose power over a daughter's life. That can never be forgiven."

"Thorns and godshit," Matu whispered. His grip on Saffron's wrist tightened. Saffron felt sick to her stomach. What had Yasha done? All three queens looked furious. And yet – and yet! – she saw that Ruyun had visibly paled; that the other two looked shamed as well as angry. Ruyun opened her mouth, but another queen spoke instead.

"Save your rage, Yasha," she said flatly. "You didn't answer the question. Why are you here?"

"Goddess above, does it matter?" This from the third queen – the youngest of all to Saffron's eyes, though still more than old enough to have been her mother. "Would you have the portal wait all day and prove her point eight times over? You must come with us now, to Yevekshasa. All of you."

"A happy coincidence," Yasha said, "as we desire to be there."

She frowned. "Your return has raised questions among the queens. You would do well not to treat their interest lightly."

If her words held a warning, Yasha plainly chose to ignore it. "My thanks for your courtesy, Mesthani a Vekte. My people will come gladly." And then, in Kenan, loudly enough for even the farthest Shavaktiin to hear, "We ride through the portal to Yevekshasa! The queens will be our escort. Ride close, and do nothing without my say-so."

For a miracle, no one argued – not even Halaya, who had the greatest cause to dissent. Instead, she signalled her Shavaktiin to ride in, so that they once more flanked the party in a protective ring. Ruyun reined her horse to the side of the road, watching as the other two queens led on through the portal.

Saffron looked at Matu. "What just happened?"

"I have no idea." Belatedly, he dropped her wrist. "Or at least, I have some idea. But as to the rest, I don't know enough of the Council's current state to say."

By this time, Saffron was starting to get a feel for politics. She glared at him. "You mean, you know exactly what that was about, but you don't want to tell me in case I go around repeating it."

"Sometimes," Matu said sourly, "it wouldn't hurt you to be a less insightful student." Then he sighed to take the sting from his words. "You're right. I do know. But it's not my place to say – not yet, at least. Doubtless it'll all come out eventually, but until then I wouldn't dare risk Ashasa's wrath by presuming to speak above my station."

"Fair enough," said Saffron.

They fell silent then: the portal was only feet away, an

impossible white-gold mouth. Saffron gawked at it in unabashed awe. Unlike the unstable tears she'd seen Trishka produce, this one was massive, so tall and broad that their party could comfortably ride through three abreast. As they passed through the eye of it, Saffron shivered, her shorn hair standing on end. They passed into yet another strange new world.

Into Yevekshasa.

Though the little she'd seen of Karavos had looked, if not actually familiar, then like an interesting patchwork of familiar elements – markets, murals, fountains, stalls – Yevekshasa felt wholly alien. They'd emerged into a grassy space about the same size as a small football field, but that was where the comparison ended: the silky grass was knee-high to the horses, the stems milk-white and veined with orange. The whole place was enclosed on three sides by rampart-topped walls that easily stood three stories high and whose inner sides were faced with bright red tile, smooth and seamless except for the inclusion of regularly spaced, perfectly circular alcoves, each of which housed a burning flame in a small copper bowl. This last detail gave Saffron the oddest sense of déjà vu, as though she'd somehow seen the design before, but she didn't dwell on it; there was too much else to hold her attention.

Directly ahead, where the fourth wall should have been, was a two-storey building built from creamy stone and roofed in the same red tile as the walls. Broad, shallow steps led up to a pair of imposing, red-lacquered doors, while to the right was a small archway perfectly sized to admit a single mount and rider. The doors were guarded by two tall women in red armour, both of whom – Saffron looked twice, to be sure – wore their blonde hair long and braided. When the leading queens dismounted at the base of the steps, the rightmost guard came forward to take the reins of their horses, inclining her head in deference as she did so.

A sudden electric *crack!* from behind caused Saffron to whirl in the saddle, watching open-mouthed as the portal, having safely disgorged their entire party, collapsed in on itself. Only then were its origins revealed: eight red-robed, long-haired women standing against the rear wall, hidden until now by the portal they'd created through combined use of the jahudemet.

Frowning, she recalled the words of Mesthani, the youngest queen: *would you have the portal wait all day and prove her point eight times over?* She could see now that eight referred to the number of mages, but what point of Yasha's would their prolonged use of the magic had proved? Once again, the words came back to her: *you would've seen my child broken and dead.* With that realisation, something clicked into place – not the whole story, not by a long shot, but enough that when she looked at Matu, he saw that she understood, and sighed in aggrieved confirmation.

"Like I said, little worldwalker, you could try to be less insightful. Or at least try to keep your knowledge from showing so plainly. Your face is open as a beggar's palm."

"Sorry," said Saffron. She wasn't though, and when Matu winked at her, she grinned back. Her fear had gone, quieted both by Matu's reassuring presence and her newly reawakened sense of curiosity. She would've said more, but then Yasha was yelling for everyone to dismount and leave the horses, and what else could they do but obey?

Just as it had done every day since their rapid flight from Karavos, her body groaned in protest as she swung her leg over the saddle. Though not as sore as she'd been that first day on the road – *the day of the battle*, she thought, then promptly shied away from the reminder – she was still profoundly stiff from hours spent on horseback. Her thighs and lower back ached, and even though Yasha was calling again to leave the horses and walk to her, she still took a moment to rest her head on her mount's neck, uncaring of the sweaty hairs that ended up stuck to her forehead. It suddenly felt strange that she'd neither learned the animal's name nor given it one herself. He'd served her well, though, and on impulse she stretched her arms around his thick, bay neck and hugged, and was rewarded in turn with a rumbling, friendly whicker.

"Goodbye," she told the horse, and then moved to stand with the others, who were grouped behind Yasha at the base of the steps. In the time it had taken the portal to close, Ruyun had joined the other queens on foot, passing the reins of her mare to a guard who led all the queens' mounts away through the arch. An eerie stillness settled over the square (or whatever it was – doubtless it possessed some grander-sounding name), broken only by the snuffling of horses.

"Well," said Yasha, when their hosts remained silent. "Things certainly have changed. Tell me, when did the queens of Veksh become so beholden to Ashasa's Knives that petitioners were brought to temple, not court?"

Ruyun smiled icily. "Since the queens of Veksh remembered to whom they owe their first allegiance."

"Power?"

"Ashasa," Ruyun shot back. "And as for your being petitioners – well. Your presence may have been *requested*–" her emphasis made clear that refusal had not been an option, "–but that doesn't mean the queens wish to sully their eyes with the sight of you. By what right do you claim audience with the Council?"

"By right of blood!" said Yasha indignantly.

Ruyun smirked. "Traitors have no blood-rights. You are denied."

"You cannot…" Yasha began, but Saffron missed the rest of the sentence, distracted by the sudden appearance of Zech at her elbow.

"I need your help," the girl whispered urgently. "Safi, I

wouldn't ask, but there's no one else – I wanted to explain in waking first, but we don't have time. I need to know if you'll stand with me."

"Of course," said Saffron, puzzled by the request. "Why wouldn't I?"

Zech bit her lip. "Because you don't know what I'm asking."

"Still..." She broke off again, disrupted by the sudden opening of the red-lacquered doors. A stream of figures emerged: all women and all long-haired, dressed alternately in flowing robes or the red-plated armour of guards. All were armed – the priestesses with belt-knives, and the guards with short, bladed staffs. Flowing down the steps, they spread onto the weird, white grass. One by one, the priestesses began to lead their party's horses away through that single arch, leaving behind the guards, who formed a generous yet menacing perimeter around their group.

"I don't like this," Matu muttered, oblivious to Zech's arrival.

"Please, Safi," Zech asked again. "Promise you'll forgive me?"

"I promise," Saffron said, bewildered. "And of course I'll stand with you."

Zech exhaled, visibly shaky with relief – and something else too.

Fear.

Fuck, thought Saffron. *What the hell did I just agree to?*

Minnow-quiet, Zech gave her arm a final squeeze and slipped ahead of them. Uneasiness and anticipation stirred in Saffron's gut.

I guess we're about to find out.

She turned her attention back to where Yasha was still arguing with the queens. For all her passion, it was clear her words were falling on deaf ears; Mesthani interrupted her mid-sentence, one hand raised in irritated apology.

"Your need is immaterial; the Council declared you a traitor the day you left Veksh. Right or wrong–"

"Right," Ruyun interjected.

Mesthani glared at her. "Right or wrong," she repeated, "you cannot dispute that verdict now – not without a lawful petitioner to plead your case to the Council or the support of at least one queen, neither of which you currently possess."

Yasha's clenched fists visibly shook with fury. "My daughter then," she snapped. "Trishka a Yasha. Or my granddaughter, Yena a Trishka. Both will plead my case. I might be branded traitor, but that doesn't change their rights."

"They have no more rights than you do!" Ruyun hissed. "You took your daughter from Veksh, but that didn't change her duty to return once she came of age. For that failure alone, the Council can and will hold her in contempt; and as for your granddaughter, our intelligence is not so poor that a traitor's child being given a gift of the soul-skin escaped our notice. We know she bears the mark of Kara – and even if she did not, her uncut hair is blasphemy enough to deny her audience. Or have you forgotten so much of our ways as that? Well, old woman?" Ruyun's tone turned mocking. "Who else would you have petition us? Who else here claims the right to speak?"

And into the terrible silence where Yasha faltered, Zechalia said, "I do."

Everyone stared at her – even Yasha, who spun on her heel to watch, open-mouthed, as Zech stepped forward onto the stairs. She was visibly trembling, and yet every line of her skinny girl's body was taut with defiance, shoulders pushed back and chin raised.

"*You*?" Mesthani asked, her tone both incredulous and intrigued. "You're not even of age. On what grounds do you claim a petitioner's rights?"

"To say nothing of being one on whom the sun smiles and frowns," the nameless queen muttered.

The Vekshi word echoed in Saffron's head: shasuyakesani. A lifetime ago in the compound in Kena, Zech had told her what it meant: that Ashasa had either marked her as agent or traitor – that in Veksh, she could represent either good luck, or bad. A sacred confusion. A thing to tip the balance. But there was another word, too, that stood out here – *alikrevaya*, gift of the soul-skin. The zuymet had taught her the literal translation, but not what it truly *meant* – why did it matter that Yena had been given it? What was Kara's mark? She filed the questions away for later, watching instead as Zech sucked in breath and answered.

"By Ashasa's will, a priestess's child of any age may freely petition for the right to undergo either the Trial of Knives or the Trial of Queens: in body if deemed of age, or by spirit and proxy if not." She paused. "I would sit the Trial of Queens."

A shocked murmur rippled through the guards. All three queens looked taken aback, but it was Yasha's reaction that caused Saffron's heart to speed up: a mixture of fear and confusion so palpable it almost coloured the air – and yet her eyes betrayed a chilling, greedy glimmer of hope.

"The Trial of Queens." Ruyun stared at her, utterly off-balance. "You wish to join the Council?"

"I do," said Zech.

Matu went dead pale at that. "Sweet gods save me," he whispered. "*No.*"

Ruyun's lip curled with malicious ease. "A priestess's daughter, are you? Certainly, you're bold enough for it. To whose blood shall the temple compare your own, then? What name shall we call you?"

Zech's answer was clear and calm. "Zechalia a Kadeja."

Everyone froze. Everyone stared. For three full seconds, absolute silence reigned.

Kadeja's daughter.

"She is... she was cast out," Ruyun finally croaked. "A priestess no longer."

"But her exile cannot be retroactive," Mesthani said faintly. "Recall, she was with child – the girl is the right age–"

"It was stillborn, a boy. She said it died–"

"She lied," said Zech quietly. "She sent me away. Presenting the temple with a child on whom the sun smiles and frowns would have lowered her standing forever, and that she couldn't bear. Kadeja may be gone, but Ashasa's Knives will remember her blood. Test mine against it." Her voice shook. "I'm her daughter."

"A proxy!" Ruyun almost shouted the word, only barely containing herself. "Even if all is as you say, you still need a willing proxy – and who in all of Veksh would stand proxy for such as you?"

"Remember, child," Mesthani said gently, "not Yasha nor Trishka nor Yena may stand your stead. They lack the right."

Zech squared her narrow frame. "Yet one here still can. Not Vekshi-born, but four times marked by Ashasa's law, and therefore subject to it."

"How so marked?"

"By penance, magic, battle and blood. In Ashasa's name, I witness it."

"If that be so," said the nameless queen, "then let her step forth. Who stands for Zechalia a Kadeja?"

And somehow, Saffron managed to say, "I do."

Before she could change her mind, she forced herself away from Matu, coming to stand beside Zech. Her stomach quivered, but she forced herself to keep calm. *If Zech can do this, so can I.*

"How has our Mother Sun marked you?" Ruyun demanded.

Penance. Magic. Battle. Blood. Saffron knew nothing of Vekshi law, yet when she spoke, the question answered itself – as though, impossibly, she already knew the answer, born of those half-forgotten dreams whose lingering itch she'd never quite dismissed. Heart thumping, she held up her three-fingered hand.

"Kadeja cut me. The sun-tongue bound me." Sun-tongue, *shariktai*, was Vekshi for zuymet: a word she'd learned by that selfsame magic, and whose Vekshi implications Matu had mentioned offhand as they rode. Though Saffron didn't possess it herself, the fact that Zech had taught her that had special significance in Veksh: it made them sisters of sorts, and that in turn gave her kinship-rights.

As did the battle of the Envas road. Almost, she faltered, but it was like the words came from somewhere else. "I took a life in Ashasa's sight." The thumbprint Yasha had daubed on her brow was a mark of Vekshi womanhood. "And my blood is Zechalia's blood." The transfusion performed by the Shavaktiin.

Mesthani nodded. "And what do we call you?"

"Safi a Ellen." Her voice broke on her mother's name. For a moment, she stood on the brink of tears, but then Zech reached out and gripped her good hand, squeezing in thanks and strength. It saved her. "I stand as proxy."

"She could be lying," Ruyun said, but even she didn't sound convinced.

The nameless queen snorted. "They're children," she said. "What child would lie for this? If Kadeja's blood proves true, I have no objections."

"Agreed," said Mesthani.

Ruyun scowled. "Agreed," she said at last. "They sit the Trial of Queens."

The house belonged to Rixevet, but Viya couldn't remember it, and nor did she have the strength to try. The news of Hawy's death had drained her, sapping the resistance without which she would never have left the palace, let alone endured nearly twelve days on the road. Once Pix and Kadu led her inside, the

Shavaktiin following at a respectful distance, Viya was hit by a powerful wave of exhaustion. At Kadu's instruction, servants appeared to take her upstairs to the room she'd used as a child, but even that slim promise of familiarity wasn't enough to restore her. Instead, she took one look at the clean, soft bed and headed straight for it, pausing to shuck off her boots but otherwise uncaring of her road-filthy clothes. No sooner had her head hit the pillow than she was asleep, falling blissfully into some dark, dreamless void for time enough that, when she finally woke again, it was well into the evening. The world outside her window was dark, the room lit only by a single, guttering candle.

"Hawy," Viya whispered, but though her throat tightened, no tears would come.

Eventually, she forced herself up in search of the others, bewildered by the strangeness of a house she should have known. The upstairs level was vast enough that she couldn't even find the stairs; instead, she ended up in a corner library, and with nothing else to do, she let herself slide down the wall and sit.

She'd been there no more than ten minutes when the sound of approaching footsteps echoed through the hall. Her prideful half insisted she stand in case it was a servant, but despite her fears, she couldn't will her stubborn legs into movement.

The footsteps halted behind her. Someone sighed.

"There you are. When your room was empty, I wasn't sure where to look."

It was Pix, of course. Being seen by the courtier in such a state was arguably worse than if it'd been a servant, but even then, Viya still couldn't bring herself to turn around, let alone stand.

"I've spoken to Kadu," Pix went on, as though nothing was wrong. "Your bloodfather and secondmother aren't in residence, and nor are your siblings – they've gone to gather allies, and aren't expected back for a couple of days. Amenet, though, has agreed to see us tomorrow."

"Tomorrow?" The word slipped out of its own accord. "Why not tonight?"

"Oyako suggested, and I agreed, that it would be better to wait until she's spoken tonight with her opposite number in Yasha's party; the resident priest of Hime has agreed to lift his ilumet wards to let them speak through the dreamscape. At this point, the more information we can provide about the situation in Veksh, the better. And besides–" Pix placed a hand on her shoulder, "–all of us are filthy and exhausted. It would be a discourtesy to go in looking like ruffians."

"I'd murder the gods for a hot bath," Viya blasphemed.

Pix chuckled. "No need for that; I've already had one drawn for you. Come. You'll feel better once you're clean."

As though she'd never hesitated, Viya stood and followed Pix back through the twisting corridors, downstairs, through another hall and into the first room she did recognise from childhood – a sumptuous bathing parlour tiled in the blue and green of Nihun and Lomo, gods of water and earth. The bath itself was sunken into the floor: an oval depression long enough for an adult to stretch out comfortably at full length and deep enough for the water to lap at their collarbone, were it fully filled. Most extravagantly of all, it was served by water heated in a boiler and piped through taps, rather than having to be constantly filled and emptied by hand. Dimly, Viya remembered being fascinated by the taps as a child, unable to understand the repeated explanations of various parents and siblings as to how the water got there. In truth, she still didn't know why it worked, but just at that moment, she didn't care; inviting steam rose off the surface, scented with muskrake and jinsi, and it was all she could do not to fling herself into it, clothes and all.

"Here," said Pix. "Let me help you."

Shutting the door, the courtier approached and began to

undress her, deft as any servant. The clothes she'd chosen so proudly back at the palace were tattered and bloodstained, utterly unrecognisable. Her scarves were now more brown than green, the knotted silk vest frayed and filthy. The skirt had fared somewhat better, having been darkly coloured and made for use, but the blouse – the once-creamy blouse that Hawy had sewn – was a ruin of smears and tears and blood, so wretched-looking that Viya could scarcely understand how it had stayed on, let alone in one piece. That left her underthings and the bag of jewels she'd kept tucked between her breasts, which Viya removed herself. If Pix thought there was anything odd in this latter item, she said nothing, instead extending a hand to help Viya into the bath.

She was similarly silent when it came to the scars Kadeja's star-nettle whipping had left on Viya's back. The only sign that she'd noticed was a slightly indrawn breath, but though Viya braced for further comment, Pix's lips remained blessedly sealed.

The heat was scalding at first, but Viya grit her teeth and persevered, sliding down until the water lapped at her chest. Soon enough, the sting eased; the warmth was delicious, and with a sigh of relief, she submerged completely, weathering the hurt to her scar with equanimity. When she broke surface, it was to find Pix kneeling beside the bath, ready to wash her hair. Any other time, she might have questioned this uncharacteristic subservience, but it was like the usual rules no longer applied. Instead, she tipped her head forward and closed her eyes while Pix massaged scented oils into her long, unbraided hair. When prompted, she rinsed, then accepted a block of scouring soap. While Pix demurely looked away, Viya stood up and scrubbed so vigorously that when she sat back down again, it felt as though she'd removed at least two layers of skin. By then, the water was filthy, but Viya didn't care; she luxuriated in cleanliness, sitting back as the warmth soaked into her bones.

"Thank you," she said.

By way of answer, Pix dipped her hands in the water and dried them on the edge of her skirt – a clean skirt, Viya noticed belatedly, not the one she'd been wearing since the compound. "My pleasure."

Silence wreathed pleasantly between them, broken only by a steady drip of water falling from one of the taps. Viya watched as Pix shifted from kneeling to resting her weight on hip and palm, legs curled comfortably sideways.

"I'm sorry," she said. "For your mother."

"So am I," said Viya. Something in her twisted. "What can the gods mean by any of this? What purpose did it serve to let Leoden rule for even this long, when all it brings is pain?"

"The gods' mysteries are their own," said Pix. "I don't pretend to understand it; I just have faith when I can, and the rest of the time, I do what's right. Or at least," she added softly, "I try to. More than anyone else, it's Gwen and I who should bear the blame for Leoden. He tricked us both."

"He tricked more than you," said Viya, thinking of Hawy. She paused, a sudden question surfacing in her thoughts. "How did Gwen get involved? With you, I mean, not Yasha." She'd already heard the latter story on the long ride to Avekou.

Pix smiled. "It was Matu," she said. "Or Zech, rather. When her gift with the zuymet manifested, Yasha had Gwen looking for a tutor – kemeta for preference, as she didn't want to lose Zech to the oh-so-heretical temple of Sahu. Gwen was known in noble circles, though not everyone knew where she came from. Most just assumed she was Uyun; calling her a worldwalker felt needlessly exotic, even though she never hid the truth. Anyway, she heard about Matu, arranged a meeting, and convinced him to take on Zech as a student. The transgressive thrill of keeping a Vekshi girl out of the temples appealed to him, I believe." But she smiled as she said it. "Naturally, I was horrified at how badly he'd been led astray, and tracked Gwen down myself to let her know the extent of my disapproval."

"And what happened?" Viya asked.

Pix rolled her eyes. "To this day, I'm still not sure. Something in the perversity of it intrigued me enough to stay. A worldwalker living with Vekshi expatriates, yet moving in noble circles? It was like something out of a moon-tale. And here we all are."

"Here we are," echoed Viya. A strange sort of courage filled her. She'd come this far in defiance of law and custom; how could she falter now?

"When we meet with Amenet," she said slowly, "I'll need to be the Cuivexa again. Would you bind my braids for the meeting?"

Pix frowned. "Are you sure?"

"If I'm still married – and by rights, I am – then I haven't left the royal mahu'kedet; and if I never left, then I can speak on its behalf. Leoden kept me locked away, but there's no law against a Cuivexa riding freely through Kena. The only treason I've committed is against his will. Amenet needs to remember my legitimacy." *As do I.*

"It would be my honour then."

"My thanks." Impishly, Viya nodded towards the end of the bath, where an ornate pitcher sat beside the taps: the idea was for a servant to pour a final, clean bucket of water over the bather, rinsing away any lingering residue of oil and soap. "Do you mind?"

"I've done this much," Pix said wryly, moving to fill the pitcher. "Why stop now?"

Viya smiled. "Exactly."

"That's it," said Zech slowly. "That's... that's what happened."

As she finished, she kept her eyes on Safi. The older girl sat cross-legged at the opposite end of the bed, unconsciously

mimicking Zech's storytelling posture, so that her open palms
rested face up on her knees. They were alone, and had been
for some time – as soon as she'd accepted their petition,
Mesthani herself had taken them into her custody, away
from the jurisdiction of Ashasa's Knives and into the temple
proper. Zech could only assume the others were being housed
elsewhere as guests; in the aftermath of her bravery, she'd
been too shaken to think of asking after their welfare, as had
Safi. Only once they'd been brought to their current location,
an underground priestess's cell cut into the honeycombed
heart of Yevekshasa's mesa-stone, had she thought to raise the
question, but Mesthani had been disinclined to answer, saying
only that the preparations for the Trial would begin as soon as
the core Council had been informed, and that in the meantime,
they would wait where they were, under guard. Should they
need anything – food, water, bloodmoss – they need only ask;
but otherwise, it was better they saved their strength.

And so they waited: sitting apart at first, as each one
surrendered to the enormity of what they'd chosen, and
then in a kindred silence, as they remembered they weren't
alone. Eventually, Zech had spoken, words of explanation
and apology welling up from her heart like water: the story
– forgotten by Safi, but remembered by her – of how they'd
first met in the dreamscape, witnessing Kadeja's prayers and
plans; of Luy's interruption, and her realisation, guided by
her knowledge of the ilumet, that only a blood-connection
with either the Vex or Vex'Mara could have accounted for the
ease with which she'd slipped through the palace wards. The
shock had been enough to force her into the waking world,
where she'd remembered everything. From then on, she'd
gone about proving her suspicions, but delicately, neither able
to confide in Safi nor wanting the adults to know her plans.
Instead, she'd asked the Shavaktiin, and been rewarded with
more information about both her own history and Yasha's
than the matriarch had ever so much as hinted at.

Her search had continued in the dreamscape too, aided and
abetted by the mysterious Luy, who'd spoken to her more
than once, and who, most recently, had brokered a sleeping
conference between Zech and Safi. Though her composure
had remained steady throughout these revelations, Safi's
eyes had widened – she'd even gaped a bit – on being told
that she'd already agreed in dreaming to participate in the
Trial of Queens, and yet had no memory of it. The plan
had been for Zech, following Luy's instructions, to help
Safi remember her dreams in waking before they reached
Yevekshasa, but the unexpected arrival of Mesthani and the
other queens, to say nothing of their acceleration through
the portal, had forced her hand. What ought to have been
the end result of a steady, well-planned revelation, at least
for Safi, had become a sudden, unknown risk to be taken
on faith. So here they were, on the precipice of it; and Zech
was sorry, so sorry to have done it this way, but she'd had
no other choice.

Only then did she fall silent; and now it was her turn to
wait in ignorance, heart juddering fiercely, to see what Safi's
response would be.

For several long moments, the older girl simply stared.
She looked so wholly Vekshi now – on the surface, at least
– that Zech was sometimes hard-pressed to remember her
first appearance: the blasphemous hair and strange clothes,
those first few crossed conversations before the zuymet had
properly taken hold, when they'd been forced to speak in
the fragments of two different languages. Now, though,
Zech had delivered her explanation in Vekshi, and neither
of them had thought it strange – or perhaps, she supposed,
so much was now strange to Safi that it no longer registered.

As though sensing her thoughts, Safi chose that moment
to respond. "All right," she said, in careful Vekshi. "I...
All right." She paused – cheeks hollowed, eyes feverish,
lips trembling with doubt – and spoke again. "I just don't

understand how we're able to do this," she said. "I don't know much about Veksh, but the Council is essentially a parliament. It should take time and study and effort to join, not just a single trial – I'm not saying it was easy to get the queens to let us stand, but it still feels like it should've been harder, or impossible. Otherwise, everyone would be doing it. Wouldn't they?"

"It's because I'm Kadeja's daughter," Zech said quietly. "Not hers specifically, but because of what she used to be. The daughters of queens and priestesses are meant to be temple-taught, educated, bred to politics – it's assumed we already know the proper rites and rituals necessary for queenship, that we understand the risks and wouldn't dare shame our motherlines by standing on a whim, or against the advice of those to whom we owed our first loyalty. What we're doing is rare to begin with, but I don't think anyone's stood by proxy for a hundred years or more."

"And proxies don't have to be temple-taught?"

"Why would they?" Zech said, surprised. "If we succeed, you're not the one who'll be queen. You're a body in this, that's all." At the look on Safi's face, she winced. "Sorry, that wasn't fair or right. Your mind matters too. What I meant to say is, who you are and what you know beforehand isn't important, so long as you've been claimed by Ashasa's law. According to the Mother Sun's word, our inner selves – our spirits, our hearts, whatever you want to call it – are divine sparks, perfect and inviolate; but our physical flesh is mortal, prone to weakness and decay. We may alter that flesh however we choose, but we may not knowingly risk its death until we've reached the age of majority; to do otherwise is an affront to Ashasa's will."

Zech flushed. She'd never felt embarrassed by her youth before; now, the ignominy of it burned her. What she'd done – what she'd dragged Safi into – was dangerous, and though she'd agreed to help of her own volition, the promise had been given in ignorance, which meant that the consequences were wholly on Zech's head. Swallowing, she forced herself to continue.

"That's why I need a proxy; until I've either reached sixteen years or had my first bleeding, whichever comes first, my body is counted as a child's body, and the law won't let me risk dying. But my inner self is as strong as Ashasa made it, and so can stand the trial through a physical proxy."

And there, her courage failed her. She couldn't bring herself to speak the full truth: that though the trial still posed physical risks to both of them, only Safi risked death, and did so on Zech's behalf. She held her breath, waiting for the other girl to realise the implications; but to her shame and relief, Safi simply nodded, gulped and asked another question.

"Why me, though?" she asked. "Why not Trishka, or Yasha, or Yena? I know you all had reasons; I just don't really understand them."

Zech nodded, shifting her weight from hip to hip as she strove to sit more comfortably. The mattress was softer than she was used to, putting an unaccustomed strain on her joints as she sat cross-legged.

"It had to be you," she said – in English this time, as much in case the guards were listening as to be sure Safi understood. "Obedience to Ashasa defines Vekshi rights and kinship more than anything; more than blood, more than birth – but those things still matter, too. It's complicated. When Yasha left, they declared her a traitor and never revoked it, which stands against Trishka's status. If she'd ever come back of her own accord and sat the proper rites, it would be different, but she didn't, and so it clouds her too. And as for Yena... well, for one thing, her hair's uncut, and though it might be a small thing to you, it matters. I mean, you know it does." She winced at her own clumsiness, her gaze falling on Safi's missing fingers. Forcibly, she looked away. "That's not everything, though."

She hesitated. What came next wasn't hers to tell; it was Yena's truth, and Zech felt deeply uncomfortable discussing such a thing without her consent or presence. The fact that Ruyun had done so openly was an almost incomprehensible rudeness, bordering on taboo – not because of any stigma associated with being alikrevaya, but because it was impolite to speak so personally about another without invitation. And yet how could Zech do otherwise if Safi was to understand why she, and not Yena, was chosen to stand as proxy?

"Yena is alikrevaya," Zech said, finally. "It means she was born with her body and spirit in conflict, so the priests of Kara used the sevikmet to reshape her. The Kenans call it *Kara na kore*, the trickster-god's choice. In English, you'd call it–" she hesitated, sorting through the various terms she'd gleaned from Safi's vocabulary, "–sex affirmation surgery? Or sex affirmation magic, here."

Safi looked surprised, then thoughtful. "Back at the compound, I asked Gwen about magic – about whether or not there was some way to regrow my fingers. She said there was always a price for doing more than what a body could manage alone, and that there was only one transformation the temples performed regularly. She didn't tell me about Yena, though."

"Because it wasn't her place," Zech said firmly, switching back to Kenan. "Ruyun shouldn't have done it either – nor me, really. But you need to know what's going on."

Safi hesitated. "But it's not... I mean, if nobody thinks it's bad to be alikrevaya, then why couldn't Yena petition the Council?"

"Because she's been marked by blasphemy," said Zech. "Not literally, she doesn't have a scar or a tattoo or anything. But the transformation she underwent – it's holy, powerful. It ought to have been done in Ashasa's sight. But instead she went to Kara's Kin, sat rites and ceremonies in honour of a different god – a false god, by Vekshi reckoning. Even then, if she'd come to Veksh and been cleansed, offered penance and contrition for the blasphemy, it wouldn't have mattered. Instead, she arrived still tainted, with her hair uncut, in the company of traitors. And so her rights under Vekshi law are forfeit."

"All right," said Safi, after a moment. "I can understand that, I suppose. And... and why they accepted me instead."

Penance. Magic. Battle. Blood. The four words hung unspoken between them. In dreaming, Zech had explained their significance to Safi, laying out the ways in which she'd been bound by Ashasa's law – and when it had counted, despite not knowing how she knew, Safi had remembered.

The older girl ran a hand over her head. "But what does a proxy actually *do*?"

You might die, Zech thought, but still couldn't bring herself to say the words aloud. Instead, she chose to interpret the question literally.

"As proxy, you'll be bound to me. What you experience, I experience. You'll walk where I can't, but I'll be guiding your steps."

Safi frowned. "How?"

And there was the crux of it. Zech steeled herself. "I... I don't really know," she admitted. "Believe me, Safi, I asked the Shavaktiin everything they could tell me, but the rules of the trial – what actually happens, how the proxy magic works – it's sacred, and Ashasa likes her secrets kept. Yasha might've told me, if she'd wanted to, if she'd approved of what I was doing, but I knew she wouldn't, and so I couldn't ask."

A blank look stole over Safi's face. "You mean..." she began, then stopped when her voice trembled. After a moment, she went on more calmly, "You mean we're doing this blind?"

"We are." It took all Zech's courage to meet her gaze and hold it. "All I know is, we'll be judged by Ashasa's scions and marked according to whether we succeed or fail."

"Marked? How marked?" The trace of fear in Safi's voice, like the twitching of her three-fingered hand, was unmistakable.

"I don't know," Zech said helplessly. "Safi, I'm sorry. I–"

The door to their cell clicked open, cutting off whatever she'd been about to say. Mesthani stepped in, her lined face grave and calm.

"The Mother Sun wanes. From sunset to sunrise, you'll sit the Trial of Queens; unless, of course, you've changed your mind?" Mesthani paused hopefully, but when neither Zech nor Safi answered, she sighed and shook her head. "I thought not. Come, then." She held out a hand. "The preparations are begun."

17
Heart of Blood & Stone

Gwen breathed steadily, head tipped back to the wall of the cell, her crossed arms resting on her stomach. After Zech and Saffron's departure and despite Yasha's furious protestations, they'd been led out of the courtyard and into a sprawling temple complex separated from the city proper by a pair of towering white gates. Passing by stables, gardens and myriad smaller structures, they'd finally reached a single-storey building whose nominal purpose, their guards informed them, was as temporary housing for supplicants, would-be acolytes and the visiting relatives of priestesses. Made of blocky gold stone, it consisted of two common rooms separated by a hallway lined with single bedroom cells, all of which had been given over to their use. Crucially, they were no longer in the care of Ashasa's Knives, for which Gwen was duly grateful. Though most of their seventeen-strong party had long since retired – as Halaya rightly pointed out, sleep was a far more effective use of their time than worry – three of them still remained in the larger common room: Yasha, Matu and Gwen herself.

Their surrounds were sparsely furnished and austerely beautiful. Three walls boasted tapestries, woven knottily into a series of colourful, abstract designs. Two circular rugs covered the floor, while a stone ledge ran the whole way round the room, broken only by the door and, on the one tapestry-free wall, a window. Square, unclassed and unshuttered, it was this latter feature that drew Gwen's attention; despite the fact that they were clearly on the ground floor, the view it showed was nothing but sky. Yevekshasa was situated on a soaring, flat-topped mesa, with this particular building pushed right up against the cliff edge. Had they not been brought into the city by magic, Trishka had informed her, they would have been forced to ride up a perilous switchback trail that crisscrossed the mesa's sloping south face. Though the height and size of the window dizzied Gwen – falling out would've been the work of a moment – she'd nonetheless positioned herself beside it, watching as the sky slowly faded from afternoon blue to salmon-streaked dusk and now, finally, into the inky blue-black of night.

With the sunlight faded, several glass globes in the ceiling lit up of their own volition, casting a warm, gold light over everything. At any other time, Gwen would have been fascinated, pressing Yasha with questions as to the blend of magic that powered them and the manner of their creation, but even had she been inclined to ask, the matriarch wouldn't have answered. Ever since their internment, Yasha had alternated angry muttering at Zech's presumption with furious silence, and after Gwen lost patience and snapped at her over the former, she'd been blessedly mired in the latter. Matu, for his part, was wrapped in a much more thoughtful quiet, an expression that was half smile, half frown etched on his handsome features. Except for his occasional sighs, he might have been a statue.

And so Gwen made her own third silence, closed her eyes, and thought. In the preceding days, Jeiden alone had noticed Zech's change in mood, and Gwen cursed herself for having ignored his warning. But how could any of them have predicted Zech's actions, the revelation of her parentage? And how had Yasha not known of the link to Kadeja? Gwen had seen her face when Zech declared herself the Vex'Mara's daughter: not even the matriarch was that good an actress. In the hours since then, more than one person, Gwen included, had asked her about Zech's origins, how the girl had come to be in her care from such a young age, and whether she'd suspected anything, but Yasha had resolutely refused to provide anything that even vaguely resembled a satisfactory answer, which Gwen took as confirmation of the fact that she didn't have one.

She inhaled deeply, savouring the crisp, chill taste of Yevekshasa's high air. That was another thing, she thought, opening her eyes; given the height of the mesa, the open window should have left them all shivering, and yet the room was barely cool enough to raise goosebumps. *More new magic,* Gwen decided, and for the first time wondered whether she'd been right to shun Veksh all these years. With difficulty she suppressed a sigh. Not that it would've made a difference now, of course – and what had Saffron been thinking, to go along with it! Did she even understand what she'd got herself into? *Godshit, thorns and arsegullet all, preserve me from the impetuousness of children!*

But despite herself – despite every frustration and inconvenience of the last few hours, up to and including being stuck in a confined space with Yasha – she was grudgingly impressed by the pair of them. Unwillingly, she recalled her fight with the matriarch by the side of the Envas road, and the hard words Yasha had flung at her: *Those* children *saved all our lives, and ensured we were free to fulfil our purpose. You demean them; you belittle their competence.* And maybe she did; but if so, it was only because she feared for them.

Abruptly, Matu spoke, his voice eerily conversational given the silence that preceded it. "I know what it means to sit the trial. The question is, do they?"

Yasha snorted angrily; the sound was not quite laughter.

"Are you any less ignorant, Matuhasa idi Naha? Belonging to no one, beloved of no one – what do you know of the Council of Queens?"

"I know why the Shavaktiin call you the Queen Who Walked," he said softly.

For an instant, Yasha tensed. Then her lips twisted – a small smile, bitter with resignation – and some of the rage went out of her. "You know nothing," she repeated. As though in unconscious mimicry of Gwen, she tipped her head back to the wall. "Let me tell you a story, Matu, as you esteem them so. Over star and under ocean, far away yet not so far – that's how you Kenans begin your moon-tales, isn't it?"

"Yes," said Matu, when it became clear that she really did want an answer. "That's how a story ought to begin."

"Consider it begun, then," said Yasha, and closed her piercing eyes. "Over star and under ocean, far away yet not so far, in the sparse, unpeopled plains of Veksh, a girl was born who longed to sit the Council of Queens. Her life, she felt, was simple and dull, with no promise or prospect in it to compare with the glory of power wielded in Ashasa's name, and no city within a two-day walk whose sights could equal her dreams of Yevekshasa. Of course, older and wiser women told her that the Council was beyond her means. As her mother's only child, they said, she ought to learn a useful trade instead – which politics was not – and take over the family finances, raising her daughters in turn to serve Ashasa with humility and strength. But the girl was determined, and where others said no, her own mother said yes.

"*Child*, she counselled, *the strength of the mother is known by the strength of her daughter. Do not stint your ambitions for the sake of my heart, but embrace them, so that your strength might become our strength.*

"And so the girl listened, and so she grew. And in due season, she came to Yevekshasa, sought audience with the

Council, and undertook the necessary tests and rituals for one who was not a priestess's daughter to sit the Trial of Queens – which, eventually, she did. By then, of course, the girl fancied herself a woman, and so set about proving it through her queenship."

"Yasha–" Matu attempted.

"Bored already?" Yasha shot back. "And here I thought moon-tales were meant to soothe fractious children. But then you claim to already know the ending. The truth of my life is no surprise to you."

"Yasha–"

"They would've seen Trishka dead, her magic spent in Ashasa's service no matter the cost to her body. I refused to let them take her. My strength was her strength, I said, and there is no strength in death. But Ashasa's Knives were pressuring the Council; they wanted it bound in law that any child with magic was theirs to claim. The queens were split, with only a few key votes undecided. Then Tavma a Ruyun showed the gift too. But the jahudemet is dangerous. In courting the Knives, Ruyun pushed her daughter to excel, to garner the power that comes with acclaim – and in so doing, Tavma's reach exceeded her grasp. She lost control of a portal, taking others with her as she died.

"She was twelve years old; Trishka was only eight. And still the Knives claimed I owed them my child on the Council's behalf, in penance for my pride. Had Tavma had an agemate with which to train, they said, she never would have been lost. Ashasa had clearly intended their magic to work in tandem – why else would two queens have been blessed with such gifted daughters? Bad enough I'd let a Kenan man father my child; I'd refused Ashasa's will, and ought to be ashamed of myself. The Council sided with Ruyun and the Knives – in sympathy for the former's grief, in fear of the latter's strength – and I was given a choice: my daughter or my status.

"I chose Trishka and exile. In retaliation, the Council confiscated all my lands and chattels, including my horses. They thought that if we couldn't ride, we couldn't leave at all, because of Trishka's frailties; that the ignominy would shame me into surrender. Instead, I took my girl from Veksh on foot; I carried her from Yevekshasa right to the heart of Karavos. And the Shavaktiin called me the Queen Who Walked."

For a long moment, Yasha fell silent. In the strange glow of the Vekshi lights, the matriarch looked as nakedly human as Gwen had ever seen her. Her shaved, bowed head, the age-mottled white of her skin, the flaccid line of her jaw all made her look soft, as though the iron in her spine had melted. And then she straightened, her hawk's stare fixed on Matu, and she was Yasha once more: irascible, canny and wholly impervious.

"Suppose you were telling the truth, Matuhasa. Suppose I've told you nothing you hadn't already learned elsewhere. Repeat any part of the tale while I yet live, and I swear by the Mother Sun's blood, there will be consequences. Do we have an understanding?"

Slowly, Matu nodded. "We do."

"Good," she replied, and as though a switch had been flipped, she turned fiercely to Gwen. "And you, Gwen Vere – will you swear to me you knew nothing of Zechalia's plans?"

Gwen bristled. "If I had done, I'd have stopped her."

Yasha snorted. "You'd have tried. The girl is stubborn as a fox, and near as wily, but the Trial of Queens would be beyond her even with the aid of a competent proxy, which hers is not. Your Safi might walk and talk like a Vekshi woman, but underneath she's an alien. She knows nothing of what she's about to face. They need help."

"And what do you want me to do about it? Unless you've conjured up some brilliant plan for sprouting wings and escaping out that window, there's precious little we can do to help from here."

The matriarch stared flatly at her. "All these years spent among us, and still you've barely more sense than the girl. Have you forgotten the strength of the ilumet?"

"If I thought for a minute you'd trust Kikra–" the Shavaktiin dreamseer, "–with your secrets, then maybe–"

"Not *these* Shavaktiin, no. But you and I both know there's a more trustworthy option available." Yasha raised a brow in pointed invitation.

Gwen's mouth went dry. *Surely not.* "I... I don't know what you mean."

Yasha's expression softened, albeit while retaining her trademark exasperation. "Motherhood changes more of us than our bodies, Gwen. After so many years, did you honestly think me oblivious?"

Now it was Matu's turn to stare. "You have children?"

"Child," Gwen rasped. "Just the one. My son." She forced herself to swallow. "Louis. He's a Shavaktiin, a dreamseer." She turned her disbelieving gaze back to Yasha. "Though how you knew that..." She broke off, belatedly realising the absurdity of asking such a question of a woman she knew to be a spy.

With a certain slow dignity, Yasha said, "Matuhasa is not the only one of us with a knack for discovering hidden things. You clearly wished it kept a secret, and so I said nothing. But given our current circumstances–" and here her eyes flashed, sharp and hard, "–I judged our immediate needs to outweigh your privacy. Do you disagree?"

Almost, Gwen did so on principle. It rankled to think that Yasha knew of Louis at all – and did that mean she likewise knew of Jhesa and Naku? Gwen was afraid to ask, lest the question itself tell Yasha what she didn't already know, but that was a problem for another time. Right now, she squared herself to helping Zech and Saffron and said, "No. I do not."

Yasha gave a short, pleased nod. "Just so. Here, then, is my suggestion: sleep. Walk the dreamscape. Your Luy has a gift for the ilumet: call him to me, and I'll use him to reach Zechalia."

"And if I can't?" Gwen asked, her mouth abruptly dry. "If my... If I can't find Louis, or if he can't find you?"

Yasha's eyes glittered. "Then Safi a Ellen will surely be dead by morning."

Though Mesthani led Saffron and Zech from their cell, she didn't stay with them long. Barely a minute later, she handed them over to a trio of priestesses and disappeared without a word, leaving the nameless women to lead them further into the mesa, down and down through endless stone-hewn halls. Before long, Zech began to slow; her injured leg was clearly causing her pain, but even when Saffron took her arm, concerned, she shook her head and carried on, determined.

Abruptly, they emerged into a natural cavern, its round shape made maw-like by a profusion of stalactites and stalagmites. The only illumination came from a type of iridescent slime that covered the stone in places, letting off an electric blue light that mimicked the burning core of a fire. At the cavern's heart was a pool of water, almost perfectly circular and overhung by two immense, parallel stalactites that resembled nothing so much as fangs. From time to time, their tips wept droplets of fluid into the water – *like venom*, Saffron thought – and their tiny splashes were magnified as eerie, discordant echoes.

In this strange, sunless place, the priestesses stripped them both naked – not ungently, but with a calm, detached reverence that was wholly unsettling – blessed them in Ashasa's name, and told them to enter the water. Real fear blossomed in Saffron then. Being undressed by strangers was one thing, but after everything that had happened,

standing bare before a trio of matriarchal women felt
vastly less threatening than submerging herself in water
whose uniform darkness betrayed its depth, and which
might contain any number of dangerous things. Almost,
she baulked – but then she looked across at Zech, her eyes
drawn of their own accord to the terrible scar on her leg,
and somehow managed to find her courage.

The water was ice cold, the pool so devoid of shallows
that they couldn't walk in, but had to sit down and slip in
like seals, with nothing to hold them up. Zech shivered and
clung to the edge, unable to kick her legs to support herself.
Saffron trod water, gasping with cold – and then, at the
implacable command of the Vekshi women to *go under, go
under, deep as you can*, she sucked in air, shut her eyes, and
dove.

The water closed over her; pressure pounded her head
and lungs, while icy ghost-fingers stabbed at the flesh of
her wounded hand, and still she forced herself downwards,
denying her fear, compelled by a stubbornness she hadn't
known was in her. At the furthest limits of air and strength,
she opened her eyes to absolute blackness. She saw nothing,
felt nothing, knew nothing but cold that froze her flesh and
burned her lungs, and in that instant she knew that if she
spun around, she wouldn't be able to orient herself; that she
could die swimming down instead of up, and be lost to two
worlds forever.

And then she exhaled, and the bubbles of her breath shone
silver in her vision, trailing upwards like a string of guiding
stars; and Saffron kicked and followed them, swimming up
and up and up, compelled by the sudden, desperate fear that
she'd swum too deep, that she couldn't see the surface – and
then she burst free of it, gasping for air and splashing in the
silence of the cavern.

"I'm alive," she whispered – in English, in Kenan, in
Vekshi, the triple incantation hissing from her lips like a

prayer, while beside her, Zech's mottled skin shone like quicksilver as the priestesses pulled her from the pool. *Alive, alive, alive.* There were four of them now – the last had arrived while Saffron was underwater – and two piles of clothes lay folded on the stone.

They dressed in silence; or were dressed, rather, the priestesses reclothing them as deftly as they'd stripped them. Though her skin prickled with goosebumps, Saffron no longer felt the cold. It was as if she'd passed into some altered state, and as a triple-braided cord of yellow, red and white was bound around the waist of her undyed cotton shift, her shoulders inexplicably straightened. Whatever came next, she could handle it.

Soon they were being led down again, through endless paths that honeycombed the mesa's core. Saffron and Zech exchanged occasional glances, but didn't speak. The paths themselves differed wildly in type and texture, some little more than tunnels in the raw, rough stone, while others were paved and squared away, their walls adorned with tiled mosaics or stuccoed paint. Only their descent remained constant; where the floors were sloped, they sloped downwards, and the stairs they took went down as well. The last such flight consisted of broad, steep steps that took two paces each to cross, descending without deviation. The roof overhead was curved and smooth, the way lit by globes of light set in the walls.

Without any warning, the world opened up again, revealing a cavernous, oblong hall lined with massive columns. Way at the end was a pair of giant doors, each one flanked by a pedestal topped with blue-white flames. Three strange queens stood there, distinguished as such by their crowns and robes. At the foot of the stairs, their escorting priestesses halted, and without being told Saffron knew they were meant to walk the rest of the way themselves.

The queens greeted them each in turn, cupping their

hands to Zech's cheeks, kissing her forehead, then doing the same to Saffron. The first queen was so old that her stubbled hair was as milky as her eyes, but though she was blind, her movements were sure and quick as a bird's. The second queen was middle-aged, round-faced and curvy, but when she gripped Saffron's cheeks, the strength of her hands was undeniable. The third queen, the youngest, looked to be in her late twenties; the right side of her face was smooth-skinned, but the left was shiny with burn scars that extended well past her ear.

"Who sits the Trial of Queens?" the eldest asked.

"Zechalia a Kadeja," Zech answered.

"And who serves as proxy?"

"Safi a Ellen," said Saffron, swallowing nervously.

"Come, then," said the middle-aged queen, "and be tested."

"In Ashasa's name," said the youngest.

"In Ashasa's name," Zech echoed, and a heartbeat later, sensing it was requisite, Saffron copied her. *In Ashasa's name.*

Beyond the doors was another cavern, but one that completely dwarfed the room with the pool. The space was so big that it might have gone on forever, the rocky walls studded with glowing crystals, red and gold and white. It took Saffron a moment longer to realise that the phenomenon was a natural one: unlike the globes illuminating the higher levels, these crystals were a native part of the stone. Some few were as large as the stalactites had been, while others were small as fingernails, but all of them emitted light, and all of them were beautiful, the pale rock shining like gold.

"Kneel," said the eldest queen, and Saffron knelt.

Beside her, also kneeling, Zech shone with a mixture of determination and courage, unflinching as the second queen tied a blindfold over her eyes. It was made of plain linen, totally unremarkable except for its length, unspooling like a ribbon as she moved to Saffron's side and bound her eyes in turn with the opposite end. Saffron's pulse ticked up at that, though she didn't move. How could either of them perform the trial while blind and tied to another person? Wasn't the whole point of her presence that Zech didn't have to do anything?

"Here is the tale of the Trial of Queens," said the youngest queen, her soft voice echoing through the cavern. "Long ago, before Veksh was Veksh, the clan-chiefs of the twenty great motherlines were estranged from one another, riven by feuds and disagreements. War loomed, inevitable; and yet it would have destroyed us, for our heathen neighbours, sensing the disunity of Veksh, planned conquest while our eyes were turned inwards. In this time of blood and blindness, a conclave was called – one last attempt to sue for peace. But even then, so great was the enmity between the motherlines that not even the wisest clan-chiefs could enforce order. When the time came for discussion, none could be heard, for none would be silent – every voice rang out at once, and the whole conclave was in uproar.

"Until a girl-child, little more than eight years old, stepped up to the floor. None there knew who her mother was, and yet she came with Ashasa's blessing, her body aglow with holy fire. Her appearance forced silence on all those present, and when the child spoke, her words were Ashasa's words.

"This is what she said:

"*Deep in the heart of the southern mesa, the Mother Sun's scions wait. Whosoever would claim the right to speak for Veksh in Ashasa's name must venture there by dusk and test their mettle. Those who return alive at dawn and bearing the scion's mark will be counted Queens in Ashasa's sight, and given leave to speak, not only for their motherline, but for all the clans of Veksh.*

"And the clan-chiefs listened; all save one, who refused to acknowledge the child as Ashasa's voice, and whose motherline thereafter fell into decay, and was lost to the world forever. But all others heeded her words, recognising only then the dangers of the precipice on which they stood; and so it was that the conclave travelled to the mesa, which is now called Yevekshasa, and down into the stone went not only the clan-chiefs, but all who thought themselves worthy of the honour – easily a hundred souls or more. From dusk until dawn, the would-be queens sought Ashasa's blessing, but when the sun rose again, less than half remained alive, and of their number, only half again were held to have attained both mark and sign.

"These were the first queens of Veksh, in whose footsteps you now tread. Remember them, and remember in whose sight you walk. Ashasa bless you both, and fire light your way."

"Fire light your way," the other queens echoed, and in the pause that followed, a shadow loomed in Saffron's blindfolded vision; one of the three stood over her, and daubed what must have been blood on her forehead, just as Yasha had done on the Envas road. She shivered, her body recalling the cold of the underground pool, and then the shadow stepped back, and a new voice – Saffron didn't know where the owner had come from, but guessed they were either a queen or a priestess – began to speak.

"Ashasa, witness these your supplicants: Zechalia a Kadeja and her proxy, Safi a Ellen, whose worthiness to sit your trial has been won by right of law. Hand-of-dreams bind them both in spirit; blood-bond bind them body to body; sun-tongue bind their wills together. Blessed daughters, hear me now. The risen sun is sharp as steel. Can you endure her touch?"

A strange feeling overtook Saffron then, as though she were suddenly tipsy. Warmth spread through her, pins and needles pricking her hands and feet. Colours wheeled in her blindfolded vision; her head felt muzzy and numb. Abruptly, she lost all sense of balance; she tried to steady herself, but her arms were deadweight, and with a faint, embarrassed croak she keeled over sideways, thumping down hard on the cavern floor. Though vaguely aware that Zech, too, had fallen, she found she couldn't call out to her. Instead, she lay parched and panting like a sunstruck dog, unable to move and struggling to keep her eyes open.

How sharp the risen sun, she thought, and then there was only darkness.

When Gwen opened her eyes in the dreamscape, her son was waiting for her.

"Hello, Mother," said Louis.

He smiled at her, and even though they weren't really together – or at least, not bodily so; she'd long since learned that the dreamscape, whatever else could be said of it, was still a real place – she felt her heart swell with pride and amazement, that she had borne and successfully raised this man as a child of two worlds.

"Dear Louis," she said, embracing him. "Dear boy, my dearest Shavaktiin – you are, as always, a charmed nomad. What in the Many have you been doing? No, don't answer that," she continued, forestalling his half-open mouth. "Or at least, don't answer it yet; there isn't time. I suppose you've some idea of what's going on?"

His lips twisted. "You could say that, yes. Your younglings are sitting the Trial of Queens."

Gwen stared at him, not liking the trace of guilt she caught in his expression. A chill wind whipped through the dreamscape, reflecting her suspicions. "Tell me you didn't encourage them."

He shifted uncomfortably. "In my defence, it was Zechalia's idea–"

Gwen groaned. "Louis!"

"She was very persuasive!"

Gwen fixed him with a look so icy that the nearby dreamscape started snowing. Abashed (if not strictly repentant), Louis said, "I take it you want to contact them?"

"I don't. Yasha does."

Louis grimaced. "You want me to try to link you all? That's... difficult. I'm not some magical phone exchange, and besides, the trial doesn't easily lend itself to outside influence. That's sort of the whole point."

Gwen raised an eloquent eyebrow.

He sighed. "I'll try. Wait here," he said, and stomped off into the snowfall, presumably in search of both Zech and Yasha.

She watched him go, and wondered for neither the first nor last time what sort of mother she was, and whether she'd have been a worse or better parent had she never come to Karavos; if she would always have wanted both a Jhesa and a Naku, or a relationship like the one they had, or if she'd only thought to entertain the notion once she knew it was possible. They were unanswerable questions, of course, but knowing so didn't stop her from wondering anyway.

"Snow? Tcha! You know I despise the cold."

Gwen swore, startled almost back into wakefulness by Yasha's abrupt appearance. The matriarch had quite literally materialised out of nowhere. She stood imperiously with both hands resting atop her staff, her dream-self clad in the distinctive garb of queens.

"That boy of yours is skilled, I'll give him that," she said begrudgingly. "He's truly committed to the Shavaktiin, then?"

"He is," said Gwen warily.

Yasha snorted. "Of course. And what else would the son of a worldwalker be?" And then, on the brink of a full harangue, she unexpectedly pulled back. "Why did you try to hide him, Gwen? Did you think I'd try to steal him?"

"I thought," said Gwen, with as much quiet dignity as she could muster, "that I wanted at least some part of my life to be mine alone, without reference to your judgement."

"Had you admitted your motherhood, I'd have offered you more respect."

"Oh? And how much more would that have been, exactly?"

Gravely, Yasha said, "We may never know."

Gwen couldn't help herself; she laughed, and the snow stopped falling – just in time for Louis to reappear, a worried look on his face.

"I've found Zechalia," he said, "but I don't think you're going to be able to talk to her."

"Why not? What did you do wrong?" snapped Yasha. *Fighter jets would envy your temper its turning circle*, Gwen thought, but wisely did not say.

"What I did *wrong*," Louis retorted, "was try to use the ilumet to contact a mind that was already disembodied. If I'd known what to look for–"

Yasha let loose a string of Vekshi expletives, culminating in a furious, "Arsegullet! Show me!"

Jaw clenched, Louis led them on through the dreamscape, which currently resembled a vast, snowy plain beneath an indigo sky. Breaking the monotony, a shape emerged on the horizon, and though they were still too far away to see what it was, a terrible sense of premonition set Gwen's pulse racing. The closer they came, the more her anxiety increased. The shape resembled a figure – a small figure – lying on the earth; she wanted to be wrong, but when they finally drew to a halt, her worst suspicions were realised.

It was Zech; or at least, the dreaming representation of her. She was naked and curled in the fetal position, her mottled skin almost garish against the snow. Spiny, batlike wings protruded from her shoulder blades, the translucent webbing pulsing pink in time with her heartbeat. It was an eerie sight, but Gwen was much less concerned by the wings than with the fact that Zech's eyes were closed, her exhaled breath steaming slightly as it hit the air.

"She shouldn't be sleeping," she said, shocked. "I didn't know anyone *could* sleep, in this place."

"Fool of a Shavaktiin," Yasha whispered, "and more fool I, for trying to interfere with Ashasa's own judgement."

Gwen shot her an astonished look. "You're accepting blame? Voluntarily?"

Yasha clicked her teeth in anger. "Save your knives for better blood; I'm not above admitting fault. Of course your boy doesn't know the trial; of course he doesn't know the proxy magic. I ought to have remembered. I ought to have known better." This last was muttered to herself.

"Care to enlighten us?" Louis asked darkly.

By way of answer, she prodded Zech's sleeping form with the butt of her staff. The girl didn't so much as stir. Yasha shook her head. "She ought to have borrowed Safi's body, flesh and spirit linked, with the elder girl to ride as guide. Instead, you've brought her halfway here. Until the trial is done, she can't return to her own body, but neither can she fully enter Safi's. Their roles are reversed."

It took Gwen a moment to fully comprehend the implication. Once she did, she stared at Yasha, aghast. "You mean that Saffron will sit the trial, not Zech? That she'll do it *alone*?"

The matriarch sighed. "Most likely, yes. Though it's possible she can still hear Zechalia's thoughts – and maybe," she added, her tone turning thoughtful, "Zech, in turn, can still hear us. After all, a part of her is with us now." Abruptly, she knelt beside the girl, her movements more fluid than age permitted in waking. "I'll stay with her until it's done. Alone," she added, when neither Gwen nor Louis made to leave. "I've been accused of many things, but betraying Vekshi secrets isn't one of them."

Louis looked at her long and hard before nodding. "As you will." He put a hand on Gwen's arm, and only then did she see the faint lines of exhaustion marking his face. "Come on. There's nothing left for you to do."

He was right; and yet Gwen hesitated, suddenly unable to

look away from Zech's weird, translucent wings. "What are they?" she asked. "What do they mean?"

But Yasha didn't answer.

Cold and disoriented, Saffron woke on the cavern floor. Her blindfold was gone, and the Vekshi queens and priestess were nowhere in sight. Except for Zech, who still lay prone a few feet away, she was utterly alone. She didn't know long she'd been unconscious, but some internal mechanism suggested it wasn't much longer than twenty minutes. An unpleasant, metallic taste in the back of her throat prompted her to sit up, casting around to see if they'd been left any food or drink, but there was nothing. Groggily, she slouched to her knees and shuffled over to Zech. What was supposed to happen next? Up until now, she'd thought that some magic or other was meant to bind them together – she had no idea what the end result ought to feel like, but she'd assumed, not unreasonably, that it ought to be obvious somehow; that she'd be able to tell it had worked. Instead, she just felt... ordinary.

And cold, of course. Between the residual chill from the water and the natural underground cool, her teeth were starting to chatter. Goosebumps pimpled her arms and legs. Hugging her torso with one hand, she nudged Zech with the other.

"Zech. Zech. Come on, wake up. What happens now?" She paused, suddenly uneasy. "Zech?"

No response.

Very slowly, Saffron rocked back on her heels. *Try not to panic,* she told herself. It didn't work. She shook Zech's unconscious form, helplessly repeating her name, but she didn't so much as stir. *I'm panicking,* she thought, and with an effort of will forced herself to stand, taking several deep, soothing breaths. *Calm down. Maybe this is all part of the test. Zech said she didn't know everything a proxy was meant to do. Perhaps the bond comes later. I should just... get on with it, whatever that means.* And besides, it wasn't like there was anything else she could do.

Not true, a part of her whispered, her gaze drawn to the doors. *This isn't your world, and it sure as hell isn't your trial. Why risk your life for something you barely understand? You could walk out of here right now, and in a few days, once Trishka's strong enough to send you home again, none of this will matter.*

It was a treacherously attractive prospect; and yet she couldn't make herself leave. Slowly, she turned back into the cavern. Of course her actions here mattered, not just to Zech and Yasha and everyone else she'd travelled with, but to her too. If she gave up now, she'd have to live with the knowledge that she'd betrayed a friend.

And so, after looking Zech over one last time – though still unmoving, her steady pulse and even breath suggested she was in no physical danger – Saffron headed deeper into the cavern.

As she walked, the silence was oppressive. Her bare feet made no sound in passing, her passage lit by the luminescent, cat's-eye glow of the crystals. After several minutes, however, her surroundings began to change: the roof loomed inwards, the walls closed in, the crystals appeared less frequently. Before too long the massive cavern had diminished into a narrow, increasingly dim tunnel through the earth. With the walls so much closer, the sound of her breathing was abruptly magnified, its hissing echo filling her ears. The ground began to slope forward, too, as though she were walking down some monstrous throat.

Without quite meaning to, Saffron started singing. It was something she often did while walking alone, albeit quietly. There was no particular pattern to the songs she chose; she simply sang whatever popped into her head, from classic rock and pop ballads to advertising jingles and Christmas carols. Usually it cheered her up, but all too soon her voice tailed away into nothing, defeated by the cool, surrounding dark.

She continued, more weighed down than ever by the silence. The footing became softer, hard stone giving way to a layer of moss so thick it felt like walking on carpet, while the previously straight tunnel began to curve and corner like the bunched coils of a snake. The dry air turned moist. Droplets of condensation beaded the more prominent crystals; the walls were wet to the touch. Almost imperceptibly at first, but soon unmistakably, the silence ebbed away, broken by the distant chuckle of running water. Saffron halted, turning her head in an effort to tell where the sound was coming from, but though it grew louder with each passing minute, the source remained a mystery.

Turning a corner, she came to an abrupt halt. The tunnel ahead split into three different paths, but all were devoid of crystals: whichever way she went, there was no option but darkness. For the first time since leaving the main cavern, she let herself remember that the trial was meant to be dangerous – and that Zech was meant to be in charge. She'd been waiting for her perception to drop away somehow, but it hadn't happened. Surely the binding ought to have taken effect by now?

"You have to choose, Zech," she murmured. "Please. Are you there? You have to choose which way to go."

She waited, but no answer was forthcoming. Breathing deeply, Saffron examined each of the paths in turn, walking as far down the respective tunnels as the dim light extended, then hurrying back out again. She'd hoped there might be an obvious choice, but as far as she could tell, the three were identical; the moss, the wet walls and the darkness were all the same, and yet she knew, with absolute certainty, that there was only one right answer.

As much to rest her legs as to calm herself, she sat down cross-legged before the junction, rested her wrists on her knees, and closed her eyes. *Come on, Zech. You have to be there somewhere. Please. Please. Please.*

<guide you>

Saffron jerked as though scalded. Heart racing, she stared wildly over her shoulder, half expecting to find that Zech had crept up behind her through the tunnel. But she was alone; the voice had sounded inside her head, a whisper-that-wasn't, made faint by impossible distance and yet clearly determined. Saffron shut her eyes again. *Zech. I can't hear you. Which way do we go?*

One breath. Two.

<crystal is your>

<key>

<Yasha says>

<tunnels change>

<follow the>

<dark to where>

<the light>

<the burning>

<skin of the>

<egg>

<the world-egg>

<cracks>

<pass through>

<the key>

<the crystal>

<go>

The answer came in disjointed fragments, overlapping and echoing as though blown apart by the interference of some psychic breeze. Saffron shivered, trying to make sense of it. *But I don't understand*, she thought desperately. *Zech? How do I choose which way to go?*

This time, the pause stretched out interminably, until she feared no further advice would come. But just as Saffron was about to give up, Zech's voice returned, a short burst of words whose wavering cohesion betrayed the effort expended in their sending.

    <pull a crystal tooth throw down three throats follow the>

    <dark to the egg-wall into the heart of>

    <scions pull living scale and>

    <swallow trade blood for>

    <sunlight water in>

    <holy fire>

    <go>

And with that last command came a flurry of images, blizzarding Saffron's inner sight: a long, sharp crystal held in hand; a burning stone; a sun-dazzled waterfall; a pair of glowing, inhuman eyes. She sat back gasping, her lungs as empty as if she'd been running uphill, and for several minutes all she could do was lie slumped against the tunnel wall, trying to make sense of the message and breathe at the same time.

Dazedly, she stood. A strange calm overtook her, just as it had in the darkness of the pool. One hand trailing the wall, Saffron wandered back the way she'd come, casting about for a suitable crystal. This far down, the pickings were slim, and with no way to mark the passage of time, she didn't want to retrace her steps and risk invalidating the trial by failing to complete it before dawn. Her eyes lit suddenly on a nub of white-gold crystal protruding from the stone. It was hexagonal beneath the pointed tip, and nearly two fingerwidths wide, but only about a centimetre of the whole length was visible. Tentatively, she scratched at the surrounding rock, and was surprised to feel it give under her fingers, as gritty as hard-packed sand, though far less yielding. Clenching her teeth, she started digging the crystal free, grunting in satisfaction each time a chip or fragment of rock broke away from the wall. Though part of her quailed to imagine the entire tunnel structure disintegrating so easily, her rational mind considered it impossible: Yevekshasa's mesa-stone had clearly been built upon for hundreds, if not thousands of years, and if this particular patch of wall was soft enough to be permeable when all else was solid, it must have been a geological quirk.

Whatever the case, the crystal didn't loosen all that easily; her fingernails were bloody and sore before it popped free of the wall, and even then, she'd been tugging on it fiercely. A cry of triumph escaped her. The whole thing was the length of a good-sized knife, if not nearly as sharp. Thus armed, she headed back to the junction, winged a prayer to the universe that she'd understood Zech's cryptic instructions, and threw the crystal down the first tunnel. It landed soundlessly on the soft moss, casting a white glow over everything. Saffron retrieved it, wiped it clean, and threw it down the middle path. Once again, nothing happened, except that the crystal continued to glow. Unable to decide whether she felt more foolish or frightened, she picked it up and cast it down the final tunnel, which was the leftmost of the three.

It stopped glowing.

Heart in mouth, she proceeded forward, half convinced she'd simply lost sight of the thing around a corner. But after several metres spent shuffling into darkness, one hand on the wall for balance, one foot questing tentatively forward, she felt the cool length of crystal clink against her toes, and bent down to retrieve it. Briefly, she considered trying to wear it shoved through her belt, but she didn't trust herself not to let it fall by accident, unheard on the mossy ground. Instead, she gripped it firmly in her free right hand and continued onwards, into the unseen.

True darkness swallowed her whole. Saffron had known the dark of the pool, and before then had wandered outside at night without the aid of fire or torch; she'd even been in an unlit bomb shelter once, as part of a school excursion in a world that felt lifetimes away. But none of that even came close to the black she moved through now. It was almost tangible, a velvet shroud tossed over her face; she couldn't see her fingers wriggling, let alone anything else. She was trapped under stone – perhaps even under the earth; for all she knew, she'd travelled so far down through the mesa's core that she was actually below ground level – and with nothing to do but press onwards.

How long she travelled through darkness, she couldn't say. It might have been hours, and it might have been minutes; she lost all sense of herself, nerves strung out to breaking point with the fear of ending up lost, of getting caught in a cave-in, of having the ground give way beneath her feet, of any one of a hundred other terrors that could befall her in the dark. The sound of running water had grown fainter now, and played on the edge of her hearing like a half-imagined melody. She cried silently, salt tears trickling down her cheeks, the bloody nails of her left hand tearing even further as she clung to the wall, her other hand gripping the crystal so tightly it hurt.

I'll die down here, she thought. *I'll die in stone a world away from everyone I love, and they'll never know what happened.*

Her muscles ached. Thirst clawed at her throat, the sound of water a torment; her skin felt hot and tight. She wanted to give up. The weight of darkness was terrifying – and what if she'd chosen the wrong path after all? What if she was stuck travelling in an endless loop, with no way back to the surface? She was only touching one side of the tunnel – what if she'd taken another fork without even realising? She'd starve to death before anyone found her, assuming anyone looked. She slumped to the ground, shaking with fear, and began to sob in earnest.

<Safi>

"No." This time, she spoke aloud. "I can't, Zech. I'm sorry. I can't. I'm lost. I'm so lost."

<live>

"Please." She was almost delirious now. Her voice was hoarse and cracked. *"Please."*

<zejhasa>

The braided path. She remembered Trishka's words to her, back in the compound in Karavos, and tried to summon some of the courage and inner strength the concept had lent her then, but even the memory felt weak.

<get up>

"I want to," Saffron whispered, but keeled over even as she spoke, until her cheek was pressed to the mossy floor. She shut her eyes, inhaled – and instantly felt a fresh wave of terror swamp her.

<get up>

"Can't." She choked out the word, paralysed even beyond speech. *I'll die down here.* And yet some distant thought refused to stop niggling at her, itching at the back of her brain. *I'm not afraid of the dark.*

Slowly, Saffron opened her eyes, pulse racing as though she'd run a marathon. It wasn't a boast, but a statement of fact. Even as a child, she'd never found darkness frightening, though Ruby once had. The thought of her sister hit her like a dose of cold water, and in the clarity that followed, she found the strength to push herself to her knees.

Her terror ebbed slightly, and only then did she understand.

<get up>

"The moss," she said, staggering to her feet. She spoke English, the familiar words a shield against the darkness. "It's a hallucinogen, a poison – something like that. I've been breathing it in. It's making me afraid. But *I'm not afraid*!"

And with that, she began to run, stumbling blindly on, still clutching her lightless crystal, free hand outstretched as a guide. More than once, she fell, and each time it was a struggle to stand again, the toxin increasing in potency the closer she came to the source. Within minutes, she was covered in cuts and scrapes from banging into the surrounding rock, tripping at every turn. It was a nightmare run, and if the tunnel had appeared endless before, that was nothing to how it felt now. Trying to breathe shallowly left her on the brink of hyperventilation, gasping for air she knew was poisoned – how long before it took her over completely, or did some permanent damage? She tried to push the thoughts away, knowing rationally that increased fear could only make things worse, but it was impossible.

And then, with a suddenness that made her eyes sting, her crystal suddenly flared into life, a white-gold glow that literally stopped her in her tracks. Hardly daring to believe it, Saffron blinked the afterimages out of her eyes and held the thing up in front of her, convinced it would wink back out again. Trembling, she took a shaky step forward.

The light remained.

She burst out laughing, the sound high-edged and tinged with hysteria born of relief. After so long in darkness, even such a limited glow felt bright as the sun, and when, a few metres on, she felt the moss give way to hard stone, she wept a few tears of relief. With each passing minute, she felt her thoughts grow clearer and calmer; the toxic influence was fading, and with it, her fear had gone. Soon, though, she had a new reason to be grateful for the crystal's light: the footing had grown treacherous. Small stones and chunks of rock strewed the path ahead, while the ground itself was pitted and rough – exactly the sort of place where an unwary soul could turn an ankle. Picking her way forwards with care, Saffron licked her cracked, dry lips and tried to remember Zech's instructions.

What came next? It was something about an–

She rounded a corner, stopped, and stared.

"–egg," she whispered, disbelieving. "No way."

The tunnel had ended, after a fashion. She stood in a space no bigger than the average classroom lit by a smatter of crystals, and yet whose roof was so far overhead as to be almost invisible. Turning, she was confronted by a sheer, flat rock face, its only blemish the gaping crack through which she'd emerged. To both left and right, the ground dropped away into endless nothing, bordered by identical walls that sheered up into the darkness, leaving her on a slim stone bridge at the bottom of some massive, natural liftwell. She gulped, fighting the urge to peer down into the chasms, and wondered, with faint horror, how many would-be queens before her had come bolting out of the dark, only to trip and fall to that other, lightless death.

Shaking at the thought, she forced herself to look straight ahead – and baulked, dry-mouthed, at what she saw, the sight of it so alien that without Zech's warning, she might well have doubted the evidence of her own eyes.

Taking up the space where, by rights, a fourth stone wall ought to have been, was another substance entirely. It was convex as a spoon-back, absurdly smooth, and so massive that she couldn't see where it ended, except to note that it continued behind and beneath the surrounding stone rather than simply stopping – the visible flank of a larger, hidden object, rather than a disconnected panel. Absurdly, it was periwinkle blue, speckled all over with luminous gold and silver streaks.

It was part of an egg.

A massive, impossible egg.

"No *way*," Saffron said again, and flinched as the words echoed back at her. The stone bridge to the egg was narrow, but not so much that she felt the need to get down on her hands and knees. Swallowing her vertigo, she edged across as quickly as she dared, not yet convinced the egg-wall wasn't some sort of optical illusion. Reaching safety, she laid her palm on the surface and pressed – and pulled back, surprised to feel it give a little. She eyed the egg-wall critically. It wasn't so much a shell as a thick, tough membranous substance, which raised the disconcerting possibility that it was somehow alive. More reticent now, she forced herself to touch it again – for longer, this time.

The egg pulsed under her fingers.

An absurd thought came to her: *this is the true border.* The notion rang oddly within her, though she didn't know why. It was, in any case, a consideration for later. She set it aside, blinking at the egg. It pulsed again, and Saffron shuddered.

Very slowly, she pulled her hand back, fighting the urge to wipe it clean on her tunic.

<cut through>

<key-tooth>

<hurry>

"I know, Zech," she murmured. "I know. I just really, *really* don't want to."

But at this point she had no other option – not unless she wanted to recross the chasm and run back through the toxic tunnel.

That did it: the prospect was unbearable. Quickly, before she could psych herself out, Saffron hefted her crystal, screwed her eyes shut, and stabbed it into the egg.

There was a liquid tearing sound, like ripping a piece of steak in half. She didn't want to look, but as she hadn't been drenched by a gush of yolky, amniotic fluid, she found the courage to look again. Her crystal had perforated the egg with surprising ease, and as she began to saw away, a jagged gash appeared. It was almost as hard a job as removing the crystal itself had been, and by the time she'd ripped a tear in the membrane big enough to climb through, her arms were aching.

"If this is the weirdest thing I ever do in my life," she muttered, "I can die a happy woman. At home. Of old age. Very, very far from here."

Wincing only a little, she pushed her hands through the split and forced the membrane apart. The inside edges were gelatinous to the touch, but not unbearably so, provided she didn't think too much about it. Eyes shut and breath held, she shoved her head through the gap, wriggled her shoulders, splayed her arms against the inner egg-wall and alternately pushed and pulled herself out, tugging one leg through at a time.

I'm inside an egg, she thought, as her left foot cleared the hole. *How much weirder can things get?*

The wall made a popping sound. She spun around, eyes opening just in time to see the gap heal over, knitting back up into a seamless, smooth whole between one blink and the next. On this side, the egg-wall was creamy white and dimpled like a golf ball, and when she looked down, she found she was standing on, of all things, purple grass, the soft blades slim and ankle-high. It was warmer here, too – much warmer. Steamy, in fact; already, the surface of her crystal had fogged up, moisture beading on her arms and neck. The sound of rushing water was back, louder than she'd yet heard it, and there was a steady, whooshing sound behind her – almost growly, like air rushing in and out of a vent.

Or like heavy breathing.

Slowly, Saffron turned.

And came face to face with a dragon.

18
How Sharp the Risen Sun

Saffron froze.

<scion> came Zech's awed whisper.

Ashasa's scions are dragons.

The creature was as tall as a Shire horse, its scales the liquid, luminous gold of owl-eyes. Three wicked claws extended from each of its forefeet, while its muscular, serpentine neck supported a head whose long, slim jaws were studded with gleaming teeth. Its folded wings twitched with a sound like umbrellas jostling together. In lieu of visible ears, a five-tined fan of webbed spines swept back from either side of its head; each one was twice the size of a human hand, and as Saffron watched, these weird appendages flattened and raised like a cockatoo's crest, telegraphing some unfathomable, animal code. Its eyes were round – the pupils too; not slit like a cat's, as she might have imagined – and a bright electric blue.

"Oh, *shit*," she whispered, and in that moment the only thing that kept her from pissing herself was her empty bladder.

The dragon exhaled, its hot breath ripe with the scent of old blood, and flicked its ear-fans forward. Saffron swallowed a whimper of fear. She had nowhere to run, and the massive creature in front of her was all too clearly a predator. And yet it didn't attack. Though seconds ticked by, the dragon did nothing but stare at her, its wide eyes bright with the disconcerting intensity of a hunting cat's. Gulping, Saffron gripped her crystal, which was a pitiful excuse for a weapon but still the only one she had, and told herself sternly that she wasn't about to be eaten. *Be logical. If it were hungry, I'd be dead by now. It's part of the trial. It wants something from me. Think!*

Out loud, she murmured, "Any advice, Zech?"

With a rumbling breath, the dragon shifted its head sideways, breaking eye contact. Instinctively, Saffron followed its gaze, and found herself gaping a little at her surroundings.

Inside the egg – or at least, on this side of the egg-wall; whatever this place was, it sure as hell wasn't ovoid – was a luminous, alien jungle. Stretching away in front of her was an uneven, tiered expanse of translucent stone, like a series of natural stairs and platforms cut from milky quartz. Impossible patches of purple grass clung to the surface, while giant, half-furled ferns sprouted in clusters from cracks in the rock, their thick stems glittering with thorns. The whole place was lit by massive crystals that sprouted like stalagmites and stalactites from floor and ceiling, their surfaces fogged by a layer of misty steam. Combined with the sound of running water, a sharp mineral scent explained the heat; there was a hot spring somewhere nearby, which must also have fed the plant life.

And populating this bizarre, beautiful landscape were dragons; aside from the one in front of her, she counted at least three more – two bronze, one the fiery red of hot iron, all lying belly-down on the rocks – and didn't doubt there were others she couldn't see. The sight of them pierced her in a way she'd thought that only powerful music could, shooting right through her heart like rhythm and pain and joy. She could die here, yes – die horribly at the whim of creatures she'd thought were myth – and yet, abruptly, a strange calm sank into her bones. She had no energy left for fear; the tunnel had exhausted her capacity for it. *It's all the will of Ashasa*, she thought dreamily, and before her conscious mind quite knew what it was doing, she reached out and laid a hand on the dragon's muzzle.

Despite the humidity, its scales were cool and smooth as snakeskin. Saffron stared at the dragon, and the dragon stared into her. Distantly, she felt a tug on the thread of magic that bound her to Zech, conveying, not words, but a sense of trust and unity of purpose. It should have been impossible, but somehow she knew exactly what to do next; they both did.

Saffron slid her palm further along the dragon's jaw, up to where the larger scales joined its throat. There was a grain to them; the minute she rubbed the wrong way, each one snagged on her skin, turning the uniform whole into an expanse of sharp edges. The dragon rumbled low in its throat and tipped its head to one side, granting her better access to its throat scales. Questing gingerly, Saffron felt for a suitable grip, wincing as each failure left her already bloody fingers covered in tiny, stinging cuts. The dragon snorted angrily, clearly growing impatient. Saffron bit her lip, clamped thumb and forefinger to the upraised edge of the largest scale she could find, and *pulled*.

With a sudden pop, the scale came free. It was roughly the size and shape of a small guitar pick, the underside pearly and opalescent in contrast to the furious gold of the surface. The outer edge was razor sharp and smeared with blood.

Suddenly, the nearby iron-red dragon came to its feet and roared a challenge, revealing the scintillant copper-rose folds of its wings. In response, the gold dragon hissed and spun on its haunches, its barbed tail almost knocking Saffron clean off her feet. Staggering back, she slumped against the egg-wall and held the scale to her lips. She hesitated, stuck by the sight of the dragons circling each other, ear-fans flaring as their serpentine necks stretched and swayed.

<hurry!>

"Please," Saffron whispered, a helpless prayer to the universe, and then, more characteristically, "Oh, fuck it."

And before she could change her mind, she tossed the scale into her mouth and dry-swallowed.

Fiery pain burned her throat. She was choking; the scale was cutting her trachea, wounding her on its way down. She gagged and spat blood on the grass, her vision spinning like a Sunday drunk's. She slid down the egg-wall, gasping for breath, arms clutched to her stomach as the scale cleared her esophagus. A kaleidoscope exploded behind her eyes.

She fell.

She is (they are) (I am) dragon

   scale-sister (scale-sisters)

   the red circles, her scent on the air like water-smoke, fire extinguished by rain; she snarls her want for the land-fish, the leggy flesh housing my (our) (her) soul, slumped by the stone-that-is-not-stone; but she shall not have it, the claim is ours (mine) (hers) – the flesh has swallowed our flesh, a little scale-sister, the right and the blood is

   flowing as claws swipe flank, we roar

   we retaliate

   our jaws on the red-scales, red on red as the blood like fire paints our teeth, we bite, we hold at the junction of neck and shoulder, go for the kill-spot

   but the red twists, rises; she digs her claws in the root of our headspines, digs and grips and rakes sharp down; and then the pain

   our eye, there is anger in pain; but our head is open

   we lunge (I lunge) (she lunges) (together)

   wrestle and claws in belly, we hook and bite; the red screams like a hawk, a mercy-plea; we deny it; we

   ascend, lift the red by her belly; she bites our throat but still we

throw her hard to the stone; we land on her flank (her flesh is our
territory, we are her sovereigns) and wing-snap for balance; we pin
her, she struggles but cannot

  rise up, we rise and scream
  no mercy
  (we) (I) (you)

our kin sit judgement, they watch, they wait (the ritual is old
beyond the hatching of ten times ten times a hundred eggs; the-
ones-who-have-lore and scale-sisters both have told it so) and still
the red fights, she scores our scales, her claws trail wakes of pain
like fish-fins cutting through water, one headspine is all but ripped
away, the blood from it blinds an eye half-closed by the risen scales
split beside it; and still we

  fight;
  she rolls and rears
  we falter
  the red climbs over us, we
  fall
  down, down, down the stone planes (I fell) (she fell)

fern-thorns dig in our flanks, we scream – the red is insolent, she
will not, cannot – a wingbone snaps beneath our weight, the red's
teeth tear at our belly, we are overrun

  (and where is dawn?)
  (Zech–)
  (Safi–)
  (I can't, the pain but must–)
  fight
  fight
  FIGHT

our hindclaws scrabble her flank, our jaws to throat to head to
neck; the red persists, our blood in her mouth, our flesh

  (the flesh)
  our wing hangs limp, yet still we rise
  we bite
  the crack of bone, the hot blood

the red shrieks, her water-smoke scent gone oily with fear; she
reeks of death, and as our jaws tighten, her soulfire slips; her eyes
wink out like stars at dawn, and we scream
   (I scream)
   (she screams)
   the victory is ours (mine) (hers)
   and the blood
   and the pain
   is
   (mine)
   alone

Her body was screaming even before she slammed back into it,
a shipwrecked consciousness dashed on rocks of flesh. This was
worse, a hundred times worse, than Kadeja cutting her fingers
off. She couldn't see for blood – it was everywhere, sheeting
across her face and arms like warm, red rain, the red dragon's
death like ashes on her tongue. Her scream guttered out into
hard, choked sobs. Nerves spasming with pain, Saffron tried
to run a hand over her body, to tell where her injuries were,
but everything hurt and her right eye was gummed shut, too –
she'd sprawled sideways on an ever-reddening patch of grass,
and ten feet away the golden dragon was drinking blood from
the throat of her now-dead rival.
   <I'm sorry>
   <so sorry>
   <you have to get up>
   <we have to>
   <please>
There was pain in Zech's voice too – wherever the other
girl was, she'd ridden the gold alongside Saffron, ridden and
been torn in turn as their bodies echoed and replicated the
dragon's terrible injuries. Saffron moaned, an animal sound
over which she had no control, and somehow managed

to come to her knees. Blinking blood from her eyes, she
watched as the gold dragon limped away from the corpse
and turned to stare at her, its face transformed by something
like recognition. Terrible cuts raked its arms and stomach,
clustered bite-wounds distorting the scales of its neck and
flanks. One wing, the left, hung at an awkward angle,
leaving its lower edge to trail on the floor like a fallen hem.

But the worst injury by far was the one to its head. The
red dragon's claws had struck so deeply on the righthand
side that the entire ear-fan – spines, webbing and all – had
been almost torn free, the ruined appendage left hanging
by only a thread of scale and sinew. In its place were three
parallel gashes stretching from high on the back of its skull
to just above its right eye, which was swollen shut.

As the dragon approached, Saffron lurched to her feet,
crying out again as her legs nearly gave out from under her.
Yet somehow she managed to stay upright until it came
alongside, proffering its least injured shoulder for her to
lean on. No longer afraid of the creature, Saffron threw an
arm over its back and rested as much of her weight on it as
possible.

"Please," she whispered, beyond caring if her actions
made sense. Her voice was cracked beyond all recognition.
"Show me the way out."

The dragon rumbled – it sounded almost friendly now, like
a big cat purring – and started to amble forwards. Though
it led her slowly, Saffron was not only badly hurt, but dizzy
from blood loss; black spots swam before her vision, and her
breathing was ragged and sore. Her shift hung in tatters,
shredded by whatever force had dealt her the dragon's
injuries, and despite the heat of the cavern-egg, she began
to shiver violently.

Soon it became impossible to rest her full weight on her
right foot; she stumbled and would have fallen, except that
she grabbed at the dragon's wing and hung on for dear life,

knowing in some distant part of herself that if she lay down now, she wouldn't be able to rise again.

Then the dragon stopped, lowering itself to the ground and sweeping its good wing aside in such a way as to indicate that Saffron could climb on its back. Weeping openly, she practically fell on the creature, whimpering with gratitude as she wrapped her arms around its neck. It was hardly comfortable, but the wings helped keep her in place, and as the dragon continued on, she began to drift in and out of consciousness, the purple grass, crystals and spiral ferns of the cavern bleeding together like colours in a psychotropic vision.

<hang on>

Flashes of sound and colour; a glimpse of a running stream below. *So thirsty*. They ought to stop and drink. She tried to reach out, but her arms wouldn't answer, and soon she drifted into the black again.

<Safi>

Dried blood crusted her body, though her wounds still wept; the dragon's sharp scales abraded her skin, so that myriad tiny injuries – *like papercuts*, a part of her thought – were inflicted with every step. Abruptly, her thirst turned into nausea, and before she could even turn her head, she vomited blood and bile onto the dragon's neck, where it stuck, forcing her to carry on with her face in the mess.

Her pulse was weak and thready. The world of the cavern slipped away, replaced by a glimpse of Zech, her limbs and head bound with bandages, being borne on a stretcher down a steep rock stairwell. The women who carried her were dressed in the garb of priestesses, their faces grave in the predawn light. The vision flickered and changed: a naked Zech lay curled on the ground in a blank white space, with Yasha crouched beside her. Sensing an intrusion, the matriarch whipped her head around, eyes narrowing as she lit on Saffron; yet when she spoke, her voice was uncharacteristically gentle.

"Go back, girl," she said. "You're nearly there."

Her lips trembled. "But it hurts. Everything hurts."

Yasha smiled. "That's how you know it's real."

Unable to answer, Saffron closed her eyes. The blackness took her again, but unlike the black of the tunnel, this was a friendly darkness, warm and safe. She swam within it, just as she'd swum in the underground pool, and lost all sense of time and space. *I could stay here,* she thought, and for the longest moment, it felt as though the choice had been taken from her. But then the stars came out – a trail of gold and silver lights winding their way overhead – and she thought, *not yet,* and followed them.

With a sudden crash, Saffron came back to herself, coughing to regain the breath the fall had knocked from her lungs. *Fall?* She blinked, trying to make sense of what had happened, and rolled onto her back. The dragon stared down at her, its ruined head tilted to one side, as though it were surprised to see that she was still alive. Snorting softly, it lent down and nudged her chest with the tip of its muzzle, blinking with evident satisfaction when she groaned at the contact. And then it turned and walked away, leaving Saffron to watch dazedly as it approached the unmistakable blue exterior of the egg-wall and shouldered its way through a dragon-sized gash, which promptly healed shut behind it.

At first, Saffron didn't understand. Was she back beneath the mesa then? Surely not: the ceiling overhead was visible, a soft-coloured stone barely visible in the pale grey light. The sound of rushing water thundered in her ears, and when she looked to the side, she saw a stream gushing forth from the rock beside the egg-wall, flowing out into... what?

<hurry>

Wincing, she rose to her feet and lurched forward, propelled by a nameless urgency. Somewhere deep within herself, she knew she was well beyond the edge of her endurance; that whatever propelled her now was borrowed

strength and wouldn't last much longer. Staggering beside
the stream, her bad foot dragging at the ankle, she didn't
immediately notice when the stone overhead gave way to
naked sky, nor did she fully register that the ambient light
was no longer cast by crystals. Instead she followed the
water, desperately wanting to drink yet fearing to stop.

And then she rounded a corner, and everything came into
focus.

To her right, the stream became a waterfall, thundering
down the mesa's flank with reckless abandon. Ahead of her
was open air, the sky alight with the promise of daybreak, yet
still sunless. And to her left was a platform of rock beneath the
mesa's flank, where nine torch-bearing women – six queens,
three priestesses – stood facing her in a semicircle. At their feet
was a stretcher, and on the stretcher was Zech, unconscious.

"Mother Sun, have mercy," one queen whispered. "She's
still alive."

But Saffron barely heard her. Stumbling forwards – she
could hardly support herself now – she fell to her knees at
Zech's side, staring transfixed at the bandages which covered
the other girl's wounds. And only then, as she reached out
to Zech, did she remember that she'd never dropped her
crystal – it was still clutched in her right hand, smeared with
blood and muck. She'd been holding it for so long that it
took a conscious effort to let go, and as her hand spasmed
open, the crystal fell onto Zech's narrow chest. Shuddering,
Saffron braced her palms on the stretcher's edge and slowly
keeled forwards, until her forehead was pressed to Zech's.

"We made it," she rasped. "We're done."

And as she spoke, the sun rose above the horizon, its bright
rays turning the waterfall into a crashing river of light.

"The Trial of Queens is complete," intoned the priestesses.
"Zechalia a Kadeja is here declared a Queen of Veksh, and
Safi a Ellen, her proxy, is made a Queen's Equal. Let the
dawn bear witness. Ashasa wills it so."

"Ashasa wills it so," the waiting queens echoed.

"Oh, thank fuck," Saffron whispered.

Then she passed out.

When Saffron woke again, it was to the sound of distant arguing. Though unable to make out more than a handful of words, the general tenor was unmistakable – as were the voices involved. *Mesthani and Yasha*. She opened her eyes to look.

She was lying in bed opposite an open, glassless window; the view beyond was nothing but sky, while the warm light streaming through it was suggestive of late afternoon. Every cell of her body ached. Sluggishly, she turned her head, and was just in time to see Mesthani shooing an aggravated Yasha away from the room, an encounter which culminated in the former firmly shutting the door in the latter's face. Not quite smiling at the sight, Saffron looked the other way and found she wasn't alone. Zech was beside her, fast asleep in a different bed. Her bandages were gone, her injuries healed. Her new scars, though, were a sight to behold: the one arm Saffron could see was ribboned with cuts, but as it had been with the dragon, the worst injury was to her face, a triple clawmark that stopped just short of her eye.

Yet something was off about it. Frowning, Saffron sat up a little, trying to put her finger on the dissonance.

"They're inverted," Mesthani said, startling her.

Saffron jumped, then instantly regretted it – the sudden motion set her head spinning. Frowning, Mesthani poured some liquid from a glass pitcher into a fat ceramic mug, which she handed to Saffron.

"Drink this. It's mixed with herbs, to replenish what the healing cost."

Her thirst returned with a vengeance. Saffron downed the lot in seconds. The taste was sweetly astringent, like wasabi blended with orange peel. The first cup gone, she let

Mesthani pour her a second, third and fourth serving, all of which she gulped down with indecent speed. Only with a fifth and final cup safely in hand did she feel sufficiently capable of speech.

"What do you mean, inverted?"

Mesthani nodded at Zech. "Her scars are the inverse of yours. Where you are marked on the left, Zechalia is marked on the right, and vice versa. A consequence of the proxy magic."

Unconsciously, Saffron raised a hand to her face, probing the right side. Sure enough, three raised scars stood out against the stubble of her hair, each one only slightly thinner than a finger's width.

"Show me," she ordered.

Her face expressionless, Mesthani handed Saffron a small bronze mirror. Though slightly blurred, her reflection was still clear enough to make out the extent of the damage: not only did the scars extend from eye to skull-base, but the top of her right ear was missing, a good thumbswidth of cartilage sheared raggedly away. She touched what remained of it, and wondered, with a certain bleak humour, why she wasn't more outraged. *Perhaps it's hard to miss an ear when you've already lost two fingers.* Or then again, it might have been sheer relief that the dragon-battle had spared her eye, which would have been a far more grievous hurt. As it was, the pointed scar-tips had missed it only by millimetres: the first bisected her eyebrow, the second clipped its outer edge, and the third ran right alongside the eye itself.

She reached inwards, trying to find the shock and anxiety she surely ought to be feeling. After all, her injuries were signs of yet more trauma she'd somehow have to explain back home, and a permanent disfigurement into the bargain. If her vanity had been troubled by her missing fingers, then how much more alarming was a ruined ear and a trio of facial scars, to say nothing of the numerous ugly cuts to the rest of her body? But despite her probing, all she found was a sense of relief that she'd lived to be scarred at all, coupled with surprise when she remembered that Viya, too, had taken a similar injury back on the Envas road.

Was that merely a coincidence, or something altogether more magical? It felt presumptuous to doubt the existence of fate at this point, but by the same token, it also felt unbearably egotistical to imagine that she mattered on such a grand scale. As if in answer to this dilemma, she suddenly recalled a word she'd learned in last year's English course – *syzygy*, which meant a kind of poetic repetition – and felt absurdly pleased that such an obscure term now had personal relevance. *Maybe the universe has a sense of humour, after all.*

Slowly, she set the mirror down, and belatedly noticed that someone had taken the liberty of tattooing her left wrist while she slept. Saffron blinked. The design was simple enough: two entwined snakes biting each other's tails, one red, one gold, and both delineated by a sharp black outline. Together, they made a continuous loop that encircled her wrist like a bracelet, their sinuous forms wrapped in a way that reminded her simultaneously of Celtic knotwork and Aztec glyphs. The ink was vibrant and unmissable: bloodred crimson, sunbright gold, seal's-eye black. The snakeheads faced in opposite directions on the top of her wrist; she stared at them, then turned her hand around and showed the design to Mesthani.

"What is this?"

"It marks you as a successful proxy," she said. "Your rights in Veksh are now effectively equal to that of a queen, and as you bear a queen's marks visibly, there was a need to distinguish your status. So." She tapped the tattoo. "This means you may sit on and speak to the Council, though you cannot vote; you have a senior priestess's right to wear your hair long, though should you choose to do so, you must offer weekly blood-penance to Ashasa's fire; all

Ashasa's temples save the House of Knives and the Great Temple's inner sanctum are open to you; you may carry a bladed staff freely; and, should the need arise, you may call on any trueborn daughter of Veksh for aid, and expect it to be granted." She paused. "It was more expedient to bestow the mark while you slept, so that the healing might void your pain."

"Oh," said Saffron. What else could she possibly say?

Mesthani smiled gently. "It's a lot to take in, I'm sure. But for now, you ought to rest. The trial is a draining ordeal."

Saffron licked her lips. "What happened down there, with the scale and the, the *scions*..." she fought the urge to use the English word, *dragons*, instead, "...All the queens do that?"

By way of answer, Mesthani pulled aside the collar of her robe, revealing a massive scar that plunged across her clavicle to disappear under her left armpit. "We do not speak of the trial," she said softly. "And especially not of the scions. Ashasa's secrets are hers to keep. But yes. We have all fought, as you did. As both of you did," she amended, glancing at Zech.

"And what happens next?" Saffron asked.

"Next?" Mesthani smoothed her robe, the scar once more concealed. "Next, I'd imagine the pair of you will address the Council on Yasha's behalf, and after that, who knows? But for now, Safi a Ellen–" and here she brushed a thumb to Saffron's cheek, "–you should rest. The healers have done well, but flesh still has its limits, and you exceeded yours hours ago."

Saffron opened her mouth to protest – she needed to know what was happening; wanted to ask if Trishka was fully recovered yet, where Gwen and Matu and the Shavaktiin were, what the Council thought of Zech joining their ranks – but all that came out was a yawn. Of their own accord, her eyelids fluttered closed again, and after that, there was nothing but peace and silence.

19
Queen's Gambit

Viya woke suddenly, jolted out of yet more dreams of the Envas road. She remembered that Hawy was dead; that secondmother Rixevet now led her family mahu'kadet; that Kadu was here, a member of the rebellion. For a moment, grief threatened to swamp her, but Viya refused it. The promised meeting with Amenet was still to come; she couldn't afford distractions. *Today, I am the Cuivexa, and the Cuivexa must show no weakness before her enemies.* Not that she was among enemies here; but it wasn't lost on Viya that if Amenet ore Amenet ki Rahei were to become her ally in truth, then sooner or later the question of marriage would have to be raised – specifically, the question of who would succeed Vex Leoden once his reign was overthrown.

A glance at the window told her that dawn had long since passed, and yet she'd been left to slugabed. She frowned. Why hadn't Pix woken her?

She sat up with a lurch. The courtier's absence could mean only one of two things: either Pix had never intended to let Viya meet with Amenet – which would imply that Kadu had somehow been duped into complicity – or else the meeting had been unaccountably postponed. Ignoring the fullness of her bladder, Viya considered the latter option. The only reason they hadn't met the previous night was the need to wait for news from Veksh. But what if no news had come? Perhaps Oyako hadn't been able to reach the other Shavaktiin. Or maybe it was the opposite case, that the dreamseer's news of Yasha had thrown their plans in turmoil.

Either way, she had some catching up to do. Pix and Kadu might not go so far as to purposefully keep her ignorant, but letting her sleep while events unfolded without her input was a different thing entirely, especially with Hawy gone. Of all her parents, Viya had always considered Kadu to be the gentlest and most considerate – noble attributes, to be sure, but she'd been away from him for long enough and under such dangerous circumstances that his concern for her was perilously close to manifesting as protectiveness, or worse still, pity. At dinner the previous evening, his manner more than his words had betrayed his desire to keep Viya safe – not only for her own sake, but because she alone of all the mahu'kedet's children had called Hawy bloodmother. That made her special in his eyes, but if that specialness came at the expense of the respect she was owed as Cuivexa – and at a time when she badly needed her rank to show – then she would have no choice but to refuse it. Her heart twisted. *For the time being, at least.*

Rising quickly, she made her ablutions, straightened her clothes, checked that the braids Pix had bound for her the previous night were still intact (they were), and hurried downstairs, hunting for the others. After several fruitless minutes, she finally thought to check outside, and was surprised to find not only Pix, but Kadu, Dom and Oyako standing aimlessly on the front drive. All four looked up as she approached, but it was Pix that Viya addressed, and Pix who answered.

"Well? Have we heard from Veksh? What's happened?"

"Something rather unexpected." The courtier pursed her lips. "Zechalia has undertaken the Trial of Queens with Safi as her proxy. I'm not quite clear on the details, but evidently it was the only way to gain audience with the

Council. And..." She hesitated. "It appears that Zechalia is... is Kadeja's daughter."

Viya's mouth hung open. "*What?*"

Oyako cut in. "At dawn, I spoke to Kikra–" the other Shavaktiin dreamseer "–and all he could say was that both girls had lived, though whether their attempt had succeeded or failed, he didn't yet know. Since then, I've contacted him every hour for details, but each time, he only says the same thing: that the girls are healing, that Zechalia is acknowledged as a child of the Vex'Mara's blood, and that not even Yasha has been permitted to see them."

Kadeja's daughter. The revelation boiled in her bones. It was Ke and Na at work, it had to be – what else could explain how Viya had been taken in hand by the child of one she fled? The gods themselves had offered Zech as apology for Kadeja's actions – and if that were true, then it was Viya, not Leoden, whose plans and alliances were supported by heaven. *There shall be a pact with Veksh. We are two different peoples. We always were. But now, perhaps, we can be allies.*

And if Zech had sat the Trial of Queens... thanks to Kadeja's angry lectures, Viya had some idea of the significance of the test, but not what it entailed. Given the Vex'Mara's taste for violence, she could all too easily imagine that Zech and Safi had been subjected to some suitably bloody barbarian ritual. Even so, and as much as she disliked the spittle-skinned old bat, Yasha's exclusion from the matter could hardly bode well for their plans. *But if Zech is made a queen, then Yasha doesn't matter. She's been circumvented.*

Too many thoughts. Her pulse quickened, as did her breathing. Realising she'd been silent for too long, Viya spoke.

"What does it mean?"

Kadu glanced worriedly at Pix. "We were just discussing that very matter," he said.

And you didn't think to wake me? Viya thought angrily, masking her irritation with some considerable effort. "And?"

"At best guess, it could be one of two things," said Pix. "Either they passed, and the Council is stalling for time because they didn't expect it and don't want to deal with Yasha, or they failed, and for some reason the Council is split on what should happen next. If I were a betting woman," she added darkly, "I'd lay coin on the latter. Trying to understand Vekshi politics is like wrestling an armful of oiled snakes – grab all you want, but either the truth will slither away, or you'll end up thoroughly bitten." She snorted for good measure.

"Don't be too sure," countered Dom. "Not about the snake part, I mean, but about their having failed."

"Why?" asked Viya.

Dom smiled sharply. "If they'd failed, they'd be dead."

Viya shivered. *Zech, a queen.* "Whatever the case," she said, "we still need to meet with Amenet, and we still need something to tell her."

"We're due for an audience in just over an hour," Pix said. "I've held out as long as I could, but the longer we wait, the weaker our position looks. I was about to come and wake you," she added, almost sheepishly, "but after yesterday, I thought you could use the rest."

Kadu's expression softened. "And if you don't feel up to it–"

"Father, please!" Viya cut him off. Kadu was visibly taken aback: the words had come out more forcefully than she'd intended. Viya gritted her teeth and tried again, more calmly this time. "Please understand, as Cuivexa, I need your confidence and wisdom. Concern can wait."

Inhaling, Kadu smiled gently. "I... Forgive me." Reaching out, he briefly touched a hand to her cheek, then let it fall again. "It's a father's prerogative to see his children as children even when they're grown. And you have grown, Cuivexa Iviyat, since last we met."

An unexpected lump rose in Viya's throat. "My thanks," she said, and surprised even herself by leaning in and giving him a peck on the cheek.

Pix raised an eyebrow. "If you're quite done?"

Viya's answering look could have curdled cream. She went to offer a retort, but found herself forestalled by a shout from the end of the drive. A quartet of riders was approaching: a handsome older woman, two honoured swords – one male, one female – and a fourth whose identity was concealed beneath a voluminous cloak, despite the sun's warmth.

A shiver of premonition ran through her; instinctively, she knew the cloaked figure was Amenet, which meant that the older, unarmed woman was Kisavet ore Kisavet. The style in which she wore her marriage-braids was distinctive: two thin plaits looped back on either side of her head until they joined a third, with the rest of her iron-grey hair worn loose. Viya thought it suited her; the observation was strangely steadying.

Beside her, Pix stiffened and muttered a curse. "They're early," she said. "They wanted to catch us off guard. Leave the talking to me."

There were times when anger brought Viya clarity, a terrible bright mood that quickened speech and motions both, her thoughts turned river-swift. This was one such time. She'd had enough of feeling slighted and powerless, at the mercy of her elders, and now, in a single moment, all her thoughts and fears and hopes crystallised into a single driving ambition.

"No," she told Pix, too electrified by her own intentions to enjoy the courtier's shock at being gainsaid. "Let me."

And before anyone could contradict her, she walked forward to greet the riders. Viya bowed as they halted – not so deeply as to indicate obeisance, nor so shallowly as to betray pride. It was a gesture perfectly calibrated to establish them all as equals, and the significance of it clearly wasn't lost on Kisavet, who raised a brow and smiled.

"Iviyat ore Leoden ki Rixevet," she said, dismounting. "I met you as a child, you know, though you've doubtless forgotten the occasion."

"Not at all," lied Viya, racking her brains to recall the encounter even as she accepted the noblewoman's proffered hand. "Kisavet ore Kisavet ki Oreva, be welcome here – you, and your... associates." Her gaze flicked pointedly to the cloaked figure, who, like the honoured swords, remained silent and mounted.

Kisavet frowned slightly. "Might I suggest we repair inside–" she began, but was cut off by a rasping chuckle.

"Gods in a bottle, Kisa, don't be so coy. I'm sick to death of playing dead." The cloaked figure pushed back her hood. "Amenet ore Amenet ki Rahei, alive and..." She cocked her head, lips twisted bitterly. "I want to say *well*, but that wouldn't be strictly accurate, would it? Still. I'm alive, and I'm here."

Mercifully, she chose that moment to dismount, giving Viya space to control her surprise. Pix had said only that Amenet had struggled to regain the use of her limbs after Leoden had poisoned her, not that she'd suffered facial paralysis, too. Yet the whole left side of her face was flaccid: the eyelid drooped, her mouth turned down at the corner, the skin visibly sagging. Only when Amenet began to limp forwards did Viya understand; it wasn't just her face, but the whole left side of her body that had suffered. Her left arm hung limp, her left foot dragged, and while the rest of her hadn't been spared either – her right hand shook with palsy, though she wasn't yet thirty years old, and her black hair, worn back in a lose singleton's tail, was brittle and thin – the left side damage was clearly the most severe.

Yet for all that, her presence still commanded respect. She was tall and dignified with a determined gleam in her dark eyes. Her features were strong and broad; more handsome than beautiful, but nonetheless arresting, and though recovery had taken its toll on her famed voluptuousness, she was by no means skeletal. Her dress was simply cut, made of rich crimson cloth and tied with a broad belt of gold-bossed leather beneath the unassuming brown of her cloak.

Powerfully, Viya was reminded of the fact that Amenet was meant to have been Cuivexa, not her. Leoden had promised them each a future, then stolen it back with violence and lies and Kadeja's aid. Now they were exiled queens together, both broken, both older, and both with an equal claim to the crown; and just for a moment, the enormity of it all forced Viya to acknowledge, as she'd refused to do since the first day she bound her marriage-braids, that although there was no fair measure by which she could rightly be called a child, she wasn't quite a woman yet either. Amenet was older, wiser, and cannier – but if Viya were to successfully determine her own future, then only she, and she alone, could negotiate her position.

Behind her, she was aware of Pix's impatience: the courtier was clearly itching to regain control of the situation. Viya inhaled deeply. *Ke and Na guide me.*

"Amenet," she said. "I think the two of us should speak. Alone," she added, before anyone else could interject.

"Ivi!" Kadu said, shocked. Inwardly, Viya winced to be called by her childhood name at such a time, but managed to keep her expression still.

Amenet's gaze flicked to Pix, to Kadu, to Kisavet before finally landing on Viya. A small, sharp smile turned up the good side of her mouth.

"I would like that, Iviyat. Very much." She said this firmly, forestalling Kisavet's obvious wish to comment. She and Viya exchanged a knowing look, the two of them united in their desire to be free from well-meaning interference. "Please, lead on."

Viya did.

Gwen stared at her hands, remembering how young she'd been the first time she'd noticed that the skin of her fingers was no longer perfectly smooth. When, as a baby, Louis had curled his whole hand around her thumb, she'd been overwhelmed, not only by the thought that his hands would one day be bigger than hers, but the fact that the years of her life were written on her skin, while his was still sweet and unblemished. Since then, whenever she was stressed but unable to act, she'd fallen into the habit of examining her palms, fingers, knuckles; imagining when each crease and line and callous had first formed, recalling the origins of scars, wondering if she'd live long enough to see their changes ten, twenty, thirty years in the future.

Saffron and Zech had been gone for more than half a day now. Though more than one person had reassured her that both girls were still alive and safe, that was as far as it went. The few queens they'd spotted had all refused to yield to Yasha's furious questioning, and since then they'd been kept in limbo – waiting, as the queens were surely waiting, to see what happened next.

Yasha had gone quiet some time ago: a bad sign, if Gwen was any judge. They were back in the rooms Mesthani had originally provided them, and with the exception of Jeiden, Trishka and a handful of Shavaktiin, who were asleep, everyone was out in the main room, basking in the sun streaming through the glassless window and trying, with varying degrees of success, to keep calm.

Gwen, however, had long since sought the relative peace and quiet of Trishka's room, where she'd settled herself in a sparse wicker chair by her friend's bedside. Though Trishka's burns were all but healed, distinguishable as recent injuries only by the lighter shade and pinched shininess of the new skin, the consequences of ripping open an unplanned portal were yet to diminish. She'd woken briefly since they'd arrived, enough to be updated on the progress of Zech and Saffron, but not since; and Gwen, despite herself, was beginning to worry. In all the long years that they'd known each other, she'd never stopped feeling guilty at the fact that

Trishka routinely risked pain and exhaustion to send Gwen back and forth between Earth and Kena (and sometimes, without Yasha's knowledge, to other worlds entirely). Over and over, Trishka had tried to reassure her: it wasn't the distance that caused the difficulty, but how familiar she was with the end location. By now, she'd visioned so much of Earth and opened so many portals there that it had long since become second nature. But when they'd fled the compound, she'd been flying blind, groping desperately for safety with no time to prepare. The strength it must have taken – of mind, of magic, of body – was incredible.

Gwen's fingers clenched. It had all gone so horribly wrong, and it all came back to her and Pix. If they'd only known–

"Stop torturing yourself. I know that look."

Startled, Gwen jerked her head up. It was Matu, leaning insouciantly against the doorframe. His long hair, usually sleek, was a dishevelled mess; not unattractively so, because he was still Matu, but enough to mark him out as preoccupied.

"I didn't even hear the door open," Gwen grumbled, by way of greeting.

Matu grinned. "My stealth is legendary." Glancing at Trishka, he came inside and shut the door. "How is she?"

Gwen sighed. "As well as can be expected." She rose, not liking to sit while he stood. Though Matu was taller than her, they were almost of a height. Without volition, her fingers began to twitch against her thigh. She badly wanted a cigarette, but Matu's supply of cahlu had run out days ago, thanks in no small part to his consistent generosity in sharing it with her.

Matu grimaced. "I don't think I can bear the waiting much longer. It's too much. Waiting for Zech and Safi... I still can't believe I didn't catch what she was planning. If something's happened to her..." He shook his head, visibly pained, and forced himself to continue. "Waiting for Trishka. Waiting for Leoden to make his next move. Waiting to hear from

Pix again. Waiting for… waiting for Amenet." He laughed bleakly. "But then, I've always been waiting for Amenet, one way or another. And it never gets any easier."

He fell silent then, and his silence matched hers, each sliding towards the other like oildrops in water. Gwen's fingers twitched again, refusing to be still. Without even thinking, she reached up and brushed a lock of Matu's hair back from his cheek, smoothing the long, soft strands behind his ear – and then she paused, cheeks burning like a teenager's, when she realised what she was doing.

Yet she didn't drop her hand.

Matu looked at her, handsome and calm, a strange smile tugging the edge of his lips.

"Gwen–"

"I'm a foolish old woman," she said.

"Not as old as all that, surely?"

"Matu, I–"

He leaned in and kissed her. Softly at first, and she was so surprised that she almost pulled away, thinking it must be charity, he was doing her a kindness, there was no other explanation (*stars in the Many, let there be another explanation*), but then he moved his own hand to cup the back of her head and she knew, she *knew* it was more than that (*I'm not so old, there's blood in me yet*), and she kissed him back as she hadn't kissed anyone in years, not even her marriage-mates, pulse thundering like a waterfall.

Matu sunk his fingers deep into her hair. When he finally pulled away, he withdrew the hand slowly, letting his fingertips graze her softly from cheek to chin. He was smiling.

"Do you know," he said, "I've been wanting to do that for quite some time."

"I… me too," said Gwen, still somewhat dazed. "But I… We… That is, I mean–"

"Gwen." He took her hands in his. "You're already

married. I know that–" *well, Gwen thought, that answers that question*, "–just as you know that whatever else I might say or do, I've never stopped loving Amenet. But that doesn't mean you aren't beautiful to me, or that you're duty-bound to ignore such wily charms as I have to offer."

His self-deprecating smile as he said it prompted a snort of laughter from Gwen. "Such wily charms indeed." She raised an eyebrow. "So this was...?"

"A kiss between friends," said Matu seriously, with only the barest twinkle in his eye, "exchanged in the spirit of mutual respect, attraction and affection, and also because we're out of cigarettes." So saying, he raised her hands, dropped a kiss on her knuckles, and let them go again. "Fair, my lady?"

"Fair," said Gwen. Her lips and knuckles tingled from his touch, and deep in her core, she felt as though part of a burden had been lifted. Jhesa and Naku would tease her shamelessly for it, when she told them. She allowed herself a moment to look forward to that conversation, then paused, breathed deeply, and changed the subject. "How's Jeiden?"

"Guilt-ridden and desperate to see Zech. I can sympathise," Matu sighed. "In fact, I should get back to him. Yasha isn't exactly known for her sympathy, and the Shavaktiin have their own problems."

Gwen crossed her arms. "Matuhasa idi Naha. Did you, or did you not, come in here with the sole purpose of kissing me once and then leaving again?"

Matu's answering grin lacked even the barest flicker of contrition. "Not the *sole* purpose. I also wanted to see how Trishka was doing. And now I have, and will take my leave."

And before Gwen could answer, he gave a cheeky half-bow and ducked out of the room again.

For a long moment, Gwen was silent. *Did that just happen? Did I really just–*

"Now *that*," said a weak voice from the bed, "was interesting."

"Trishka!" Gwen whirled, rushing to kneel by the bedside – a little too enthusiastically, as the sudden motion sent a pang of pain through her knees. Cursing, Gwen resettled herself, and found that her friend was looking up at her with the exact same expression she'd once worn while watching a much younger and boisterously drunk Gwen fall down an incline seconds after uttering the immortal phrase, "Nothing can stop me now!"

"Don't," she warned. "Don't even say it."

"You *vixen!*" Trishka exclaimed – in English, not Kenan. It was an old joke between them, dating back to when Gwen had first been dragged through the Many. There was no equivalent expression in Kenan that conveyed the same sense of scandalous female behaviour, because there was no cultural sense in which female sexuality was considered particularly scandalous in Kena, and they used it – now as ever – to express their wicked delight at each other's actions.

Gwen could have wept with relief. "Vixen yourself," she murmured, squeezing Trishka's hand. And then, switching to Kenan, "How are you?"

With visible effort, Trishka squirmed upwards in bed, until she was half-sitting against the wall. "I've been better. But more importantly, I've been watching the queens. As much as I can do, anyway. Most of the citadel is warded against crying through the jahudemet and ilumet, but the rooms where they're keeping Zech and Safi are clear."

Gwen's heart seized. She wanted to say, *you shouldn't have pushed yourself, you need to heal,* but instead she asked, "Did you hear anything, or was it just images?"

"Here and there," Trishka replied. "You know how it is; everything comes and goes, especially when I'm tired. And don't look at me like that," she added, as Gwen opened her mouth. "You know perfectly well that a little tiredness on my part doesn't matter against war and queenships."

"It matters to me," Gwen said softly.

Trishka smiled wearily. "I know." She closed her eyes in a long, slow blink, then opened them again. "The queens are divided. That's why they've kept Yasha from seeing Zech and Safi. The fact that they passed the trial... when Zech invoked the law the way she did, some of the queens said they ought to have set a precedent and forbidden her to even attempt it, on the grounds of Kadeja's expulsion from the temple. They'd never had to deal with a retroactive case before, and in the end, they only agreed to let her try because the dissidents believed she'd die in the process. But both girls lived, and now there's uproar. They can't invalidate her trial, they can't deny Safi's new rights under Vekshi law, but they want to, Gwen, and badly. Ashasa's Knives have too much power now. That's why they're stalling. But I think..." She trailed off, eyes going glassy as she dipped back into her magic. Gwen waited, holding her breath.

"I think," said Trishka, after a minute or so, "that things are starting to settle. Either that, or they're unravelling in a way that's to our advantage. The girls need to see someone friendly, and as much as I love her—"

"—it shouldn't be Yasha," Gwen said, rising. "I'll go, then. Gods be willing, Yasha won't notice."

"Good." Trishka folded her hands on her lap, then added innocently, "Matu will still be here when you get back."

"You're enjoying this far too much," Gwen muttered darkly. "What are we, still green girls?"

Trishka smiled. "Forever and always, in our hearts. It's only flesh that ages."

Viya sat on one side of the table, Amenet on the other. In truth, it was less a table than it was a writing desk, but after finally managing to exercise some control over events, Viya hadn't been in a position to stop and casually ask which of the house's many rooms would be best suited as a venue for her negotiations. Instead, she'd made a snap decision and headed straight for the library, on the not unreasonable basis that she was at least familiar with it. Once there, she bled off some of her nervous energy by dragging Kadu's desk away from the far wall, clearing the surface, and setting a second chair before it.

If Amenet was at all perturbed by these makeshift surrounds, she didn't show it. Instead, she sat gracefully in the nearest chair (the mismatched one, Viya noticed – was she making a statement, or simply opting for convenience?) while Viya shut the door.

Now that they were alone, the silence felt thunderous. Viya's thoughts whirled. All her calculated braggadocio, every claim she'd ever laid to power and respect by virtue of her status as Cuivexa suddenly felt hollow. Leoden had married her, but she'd been Cuivexa in name only, and for so brief a time, under such exceptional circumstances, that it scarcely mattered. All this time, she'd been looking for the deference she felt was her rightful due, but what if it wasn't owed her at all? *Power should be earned,* she thought suddenly. *I cannot be Cuivexa for myself; only to serve others – to serve Kena. But what if that means stepping aside? What if I really should defer to Amenet?* She bit her lip, struggling to hear the will of Ke and Na. Their answer struck her like a blow. *If my only true act as Cuivexa is to give up my power to one who deserves it more, then in that moment, I will still have been a better ruler than Leoden ever was.*

"You look thoughtful," Amenet said, breaking her reverie.

"I am," said Viya, gulping. "And I think... I think that we should be honest."

"Honest?" Amenet raised her right eyebrow, so that her face looked even more lopsided than it already was. "A dangerous proposition, where politics are concerned. How do you know you can trust me to do likewise?"

Viya met her gaze. "I don't," she said, simply. "But after what Leoden did – what he's done to both of us – I expect we're both tired of lies."

To her credit, Amenet didn't flinch. "Speak honestly then."

It was a challenge – even now, Amenet was too much the politician to take an offer of peace at face value. *But then,* Viya's rational self reminded her, *if you had been poisoned and left for dead by the last person to propose such a peace, how trusting would you be?*

The moment weighed on her shoulders like a giant's hands. Everything she'd done since leaving the palace – everything that had happened since Hawy, gods keep her memory, had sent her off to be married, and Rixevet, Iavan and Kadu had left her family mahu'kadet – all boiled down to this.

"I can't rule," Viya said. "I haven't earned the right. When Leoden and Kadeja are overthrown, I will support you as Vexa."

Amenet stared at her. "And what do you ask in return? To be retained as Cuivexa?"

Viya inhaled deeply. "I ask nothing in return. I want only to serve Kena – to do what is right in the eyes of Ke and Na, and the people we serve. If that means stepping aside, then I will step aside." She pressed her palms flat to the tabletop. "After fleeing the palace, I found myself in the company of Vekshi women, among others. Leoden lied about their involvement in the death of the Uyun ambassador to justify chasing them all from Karavos. There will be consequences for that, once the truth is discovered. I know nothing of Uyu, but if we're going to avoid enmity with them once all this is done–"

"Once all this is done?" Amenet said. There was a strange note to her voice.

"Of course!"

There was a moment of silence. Then Amenet began to laugh, a dry, throaty chuckle that set her shoulders shaking. "You are," she said, "exactly the opposite of what I expected."

Viya didn't know what to say to that, and so remained silent. Amenet shook her head and spoke again. "The first time I came back to myself after dying – and I did die, for a time – I couldn't move. Not my arms, not my legs, not my head. I was trapped, helpless. I couldn't even speak. Being awake was bad enough, but falling asleep was worse, because I'd never know if I was going to wake up again, or what would've changed if I did. One night, I woke up in the dark. I was completely alone – there were no sounds, no lights, nothing. I didn't know if I'd gone blind, if I'd been abandoned, or if I really was dead after all. I couldn't cry or scream. I just stayed like that, trapped in the dark for hours." She laughed softly. "Or at least, it felt like hours. I'll never really know how long it was. But eventually, someone came back, and I knew I was still alive.

"As you can see, I did get my movement back in the end. But it took a lot of work and a lot of time, and all the while… in the middle of everything, when I was at my weakest, that's when I heard that Leoden had married you. That his Cuivexa was little more than a child, the daughter of one of his followers, practically given to him by her mother, and thereafter never seen in public. I heard you were spoilt, reclusive and stupid. I heard you were a pawn, a hostage to ensure your secondmother's good behaviour. I heard you were Kadeja's plaything."

"I was all of that," Viya said softly. "Once." *And not so long ago. Far away, yet not so far. Like a moon-tale.*

"And I hated you. I hated you because you were young and whole and alive, and because as much as you didn't deserve what was being done to you, you didn't deserve the slender chance at power it gave you either. I was… very bitter. I still am. But not towards you, now." She reached across the table, her fingers ghosting above, but not touching, the scar on Viya's face. "We have both been marked by this." She let her hand hover a moment longer, then pulled it back.

"I came here thinking we'd argue. I came here thinking you would demand the crown despite being ill-suited to wear it, and wondering whether I'd have the strength to tell you no when in my heart, I'd gladly give it up."

"Your heart..." Viya stared, unable to comprehend what Amenet was saying. "You don't want to rule?"

"I want to rule. But I fear, despite all I've done, despite everything... I am not what I was." Abruptly, Amenet looked away. "I have seen the dark, and the dark has seen me. Once all this is done, as you put it, Kena will need strength – strength, and will, and courage. But mine has been spent. I have fits now. Seizures that strike me when I'm stressed, when I'm cold, when I'm tired. I have nightmares–" her voice broke on the word, wavering awfully, but somehow she gathered herself and continued, "–and waking dreams, sometimes, when it feels as though the paralysis has returned and I'm trapped again. Some of this will fade in time, the healers tell me. Some of it will not. But worst of everything is the self-doubt, this feeling as though I've missed my moment. I was *there*, Iviyat, at the start of Leoden's scheming. As much as he fooled Pixeva ore Piexeva and Gwen Vere, he fooled me too. I might have prevented all of this. I didn't."

"Maybe it wasn't for you to prevent," said Viya. "Maybe Ke and Na planned all of this." But though she said it, she couldn't make it feel true. For the first time in a long time, reaching for her faith felt like worrying the socket left behind by an empty tooth. She believed in the gods, she did – *you have taught me so much; I have so much to learn* – but just at that moment, with Amenet ore Amenet ki Rahei sitting opposite, her dark eyes reddened and her left side slack, the will of Ke and Na felt alien and unfathomable, as far distant from this moment as the faintest stars were from Karavos.

Amenet didn't answer; she only smiled, and said, "So where does this leave us then? If neither of us can rule..."

Her voice trailed off, and for a moment, Viya felt utterly defeated. But something in Amenet's phrasing niggled at her. "Alone," she said, slowly.

"I'm sorry?"

"You said that neither of us can rule, but that's not right.

It's that neither of us can or wants to rule *alone*, or with some other stranger as Cuivex or Cuivexa. So what if we rule together?" The rightness of it sang through her, a rush of joyful purpose. "Not as Vexa and Cuivexa, I mean, but as equals: *Vexa i Vexa*, side by side. Like Irivet and Alixat, in the Year of Broken Moons."

"That's ancient history!" said Amenet, startled.

"But still a precedent," Viya said, leaning forwards. "And it solves our problem. Alone, I wouldn't be taken seriously; I'm too young, too much an unknown quantity, and tainted by marriage to Leoden. And I... I'm spoilt, as you said. I have a temper about it. Sometimes I speak when I ought to think, attack when I ought to retreat. I'm learning, but it takes time, and right now that's something we don't have." It hurt her to admit as much, and even as the words left her mouth, she tensed up, her anger preempting the condescending agreement that was sure to come from Amenet. But the other woman did no such thing, and in an instant, Viya deflated. Her reaction had only proved her own point, and while part of her struggled to deal with that, the rest of her kept talking.

"And you – you're healing. You said it yourself: the problem isn't what's been done to your body, it's learning to cope with it afterwards. You need time too, and support, and if you were Vexa alone, you wouldn't get it; not in the same way, not like you need. You'd have to show everyone a strong front, pretend you'd taken no hurt. It doesn't matter how poor Leoden's rule has been, how many nobles he's alienated by his marriage to Kadeja. Once he's overthrown, whoever takes his place will still have enemies. The first few months will be crucial–" she remembered that Kadu had said as much, once, "–and if you show any hint of weakness, they'll use it against you."

Amenet frowned, and for a brief moment, her whole face went blank. And then she said slowly, "You may be right. If I were Vexa and you Cuivexa – or if those roles were reversed, even – there'd be those at court who would cleave to one of us over the other, looking for a way in, some disparity to exploit. And whichever one of us took the secondary role, they'd take it as a sign of inferiority; they'd say that either I'd lost my nerve, or you were still only a figurehead, a remnant of Leoden's reign. But as co-regents – as Vexas together – we would be strong. Just by announcing it, we'd be forcing people to recognise that we'd negotiated the match on an equal footing."

Viya heard the warming enthusiasm in Amenet's voice and seized on it. "It's unexpected too," she said. "It'll throw people off balance, and we'll need that among the courtiers. As for the people, well – the ballad of Irivet and Alixat is classic. Everyone hears it in childhood; stop anyone on the street, and I'll bet they could sing at least part of the chorus."

At that, Amenet cracked a smile and obliged, her voice true despite a slight lisp:

> *"The younger held the elder's arm;*
> *they bore each other's weight –*
> *two heads to a crown, two hearts, two minds*
> *within the wheel of fate."*

Unable to help herself, Viya joined in:

> *"And tongue by tongue, they swore their vows*
> *beneath the palace stair,*
> *and the gods, who are three in one, looked down*
> *and saw one ruler there."*

They sang the last verse together, voices rising in fragile, strengthening unison:

> *"And from that day, when one soul spoke*

she used the other's voice —
they lived and died at each other's side
and ruled as one by choice."

They fell silent, smiling at each other. Viya extended a hand across the table. "By the grace of Ke and Na, and at their will, I will rule with you, Amenet idi Kena ki Rahei."

Amenet clasped her palm. "And I with you, Iviyat idi Kena ki Rixevet."

Viya shivered in anticipation. "Well," she said, "there's only three things left to do now."

"Oh?" asked Amenet lightly. "And what are they?"

"First, regain contact with our allies in Veksh. Second, defeat Leoden. And third, and most importantly, decide which of us has the honour of telling Pixeva and Kisavet that they've been outmaneuvered."

Amenet laughed – the first truly happy sound that Viya had yet heard from her. "Why, Iviyat! Is it really so hard a decision to make? I say, begin as we intend to go on."

"Together, then?"

Amenet's eyes shone. "Together."

Rising, Viya was halfway to the library door when a distant sound stopped her. A sudden chill coiled in her stomach.

"What is it?" Amenet asked.

"Did you hear that? It sounded like–"

A thin wail clawed the air.

"Screaming." Amenet paled. "Someone's screaming." She forced herself to her feet. "We're under attack."

20
Rites of Passage

Saffron woke from the deepest, most restful sleep she'd had in months to find herself looking up at Gwen. As the events of the trial came back to her, she flinched back into the mattress, fully expecting the older woman to start lecturing her – to say she wasn't *angry* that neither Zech nor Saffron had trusted her with their plans, just *disappointed*; to say they should never have done something so foolhardy and dangerous in the first place; to point out, with weary resignation, how her new scars and tattoo would make everything back on Earth so much more difficult to explain.

But Gwen did none of those things. Instead, she fondly touched two knuckles to Saffron's cheek, a slow smile spreading across her face.

"You're alive," she said. "You impossible, wonderful girl! You're still alive, and near enough a queen."

Saffron's mouth went dry. "You're not... you're not cross with me?"

"I was cross, yes. But not at you or Zech."

"Zech." Saffron forced herself to sit up, looking around for the other girl. "Where is she?"

"She's safe. She's fine." Gwen laid a gentling hand on Saffron's shoulder. "Mesthani had her moved to another room. She's sleeping, but you can see her soon. The Council is meeting in session from dawn tomorrow, and the two of you will be expected to be there. That's when you'll make our plea, so it's best that you and Zechalia sit down beforehand and figure out what you're going to say. As much as I'd love to be there with you, it's not permitted. Anyway." She pulled her hand back to her lap. "That isn't why I came to see you now."

"It's not?"

"No." She hesitated. "I've been thinking about what happens when you go home again. When we go back to Earth."

Saffron tensed. *Here it comes.* "And?"

"I told you, when we first arrived, how I came to be a worldwalker?"

"You did," said Saffron, remembering the story. "Trishka's magic broke loose and opened a portal to Earth; you fell through it, you had some adventures, and then you ended up liking it here."

"More or less," said Gwen. She took a deep breath. "I also said that going home raised questions."

Saffron tensed. They'd had a variant of this conversation too, the morning when she'd awoken without her fingers. Ever since then, she'd been doing her best not to think of it, but in the wake of the Trial of Queens, she could put it off no longer.

"When I finally went home again," Gwen said, "the hardest part wasn't keeping the truth secret – it was making up lies to replace it, and remembering them, and telling them over and over until eventually people believed me."

"What... what lies did you tell?"

"Poor ones," Gwen said, with a quirk of her lips that was half a wince and half self-deprecation. "What does matter, though, are the lies we'll tell together."

"Together?" Saffron blinked at her. "But I mean, haven't you been doing this for a while now? Why do you need to lie?"

Gwen gave a sad smile. "Because I accosted that boy at your school and made myself conspicuous. Maybe the police know I was there, and maybe they don't, but I'd rather err on the side of caution, and either way, you'll need an excuse for why you wanted to talk to me. We need to explain my presence in your story first, or else they'll assume that what happened to you was me. And they'd be right, in a sense – just not the way they think."

It took a moment for the full implication to sink in. "They'll think you're a suspect?" Saffron said, not wanting to believe it.

"We vanished off the face of the Earth. Literally. There's no other evidence to suggest I didn't do it, because we didn't leave any behind. I twisted that boy's arm; we were seen together. There's a link between us."

Abruptly, Saffron remembered something. "Oh god, Gwen. I went looking for you, too – my sister said her friend had seen you behind the chem labs, and I ran straight off. She'll have told them about you for sure."

Gwen blinked, surprised. "You said you wanted to talk to me when we first arrived, but I don't think we ever reached the point of you telling me why. What was so important that you followed me through a portal?"

Saffron let out a strangled laugh. "I don't even really remember." The words came from far away, too calm and flat for comfort. "Isn't that strange? It feels like it ought to have mattered more. I think I just wanted to talk to you, but I don't know what about. Just talking in general, maybe." She looked up at Gwen, her throat too tight. "Why do I feel like this is going to haunt me, if I can't remember?"

"Because it might," said Gwen. "If you don't. Or even if you do, depending on what it was. So before you start racking your brains, take a moment to think about which would be the worst option."

Saffron forced a smile. "I'll do that."

"In any case," said Gwen, after a pause, "it works in our favour, that you went looking for me. It's not exactly an alibi, but it puts a hole in the theory that my abduction of you was premeditated, and that's nothing to sneeze at. Which brings me back to my original point: once Trishka sends us back, we need to know what to tell everyone. We need to have our stories straight."

Saffron nodded. "How much time do we have? I mean, when do you think Trishka will be ready?"

Gwen looked at her. "Well, that depends, doesn't it?"

"On what?"

"On you. You've come this far, girl – you've been branded a heretic, dabbled in politics, fought at the side of queens and damn near become one yourself. Which isn't to say I'd blame you or think less of you if you wanted to head on homewards the very second Trishka was able to manage it. But right here, right now, you need to make a choice. Do you want to see things through to the end?"

"Do I have a choice?" Saffron held up her left hand, three-fingered at the end of her tattooed wrist. "This world has sunk its teeth into me. I'm bound to it, now. I never asked for any of this, but going back will be hard enough without spending the rest of my life wondering what might've happened if I'd stayed a little longer, if I'd been there to help. I mean, I don't know that I'll ever get to come back again."

"You could," said Gwen, carefully. "If you wanted to."

"But I don't know that yet, do I? Right now, it's all just hypothetical – get home, explain why I was gone, and then what? Years of therapy? Years of alcoholism? Both? I'm already having nightmares, Gwen, and sometimes I think the only reason they're not worse is because I haven't really processed everything yet. Since I've been here, we've never really stopped – so many people have been hurt, and I fucking *killed* someone, Gwen. I took an axe and I killed her and that horse–" her breathing became rapid as she spoke; she could smell the blood as though it were still happening, and it took all her energy just to fight the memories off, "–but it's all been *normal*, somehow. I mean, I don't mean *normal* normal, just that everyone else has kept on going too, because we've had to; because there hasn't been a choice. And so I keep waiting for someone to come along and say to me, *You're traumatised, you need help*, only nobody does, and so I can keep pretending I'm not and that I don't, but that's the point, isn't it? As soon as we get home again, that's all anyone will ever say to me, all they'll ever see in me. Because–"

"Because," Gwen finished softly, "there's no lie you can tell to explain all this that won't leave people thinking you're a victim of something horrific."

For a moment, the world fell away from her. "Am I, then?" Saffron asked hoarsely. "Is that what all this has made me? Just a victim? Nothing else? Because I still can't decide whether coming here was the best or worst thing that's ever happened to me, or if it can somehow be both and neither at the same time."

"I've spent thirty-three years trying to puzzle out that question," said Gwen, "and the closest I've come to an answer is, maybe. It depends."

And in that pinpoint moment, when the terrible weight of everything came crashing down – the air gone glassy and thick, her stomach clenched like a boxer's fist at the thought of going home – Saffron burst out laughing, because it was laugh or cry, and there were tears enough in her past and her future that just this once, she could set them aside. And then Gwen was laughing too, the pair of them holding their sides and roaring as the tears leaked out of their eyes; and only after they'd finally stopped, when the last wrenching chuckle fled her lungs and healthy silence reigned again, did Saffron look back to Gwen and say softly, "I know what the lie should be."

Viya and Amenet stared at each other. The screams grew louder and louder. *Outside*, Viya thought numbly. *It's coming from outside, not downstairs.*

Which means there's still time to defend ourselves.

The spell broke. Wheeling, Viya strode across the library, looking for anything she could use as a weapon. There was a small, ornate hand axe mounted on the far wall, which was certainly an option, but apart from being too high up for easy access and too securely fastened to remove without difficulty, it was clearly made for display: the blade was heavily decorated with gold and other soft metals, and with every second potentially vital, Viya disliked expending precious energy to obtain a weapon in whose usage she wasn't schooled and which might well break or buckle under the strain of actual fighting. That left a wicked-looking letter knife she'd pushed to the side of the desk when she first came in; it was small, but undeniably sharp, and made from a strong enough metal that even if she couldn't use it to turn a blow, it could still acquit itself by landing one. Decision made, Viya reached for it – but Amenet got there first, closing her fist over the handle and drawing it slowly into her lap.

They looked at each other again.

"They're here for me," Amenet said calmly. "You know that. I can't fight, and I won't be taken by them. Not again. The best I can hope for, if they make it up here, is to ensure there's nothing left to take."

Viya's mouth went dry. She fumbled for words, but couldn't find any, and all the time the screams were growing louder. Instead, she stood by and watched as Amenet pulled aside the folds of her clothes, revealing a leather belt hung with two proper Kenan throwing knives. "I carry them out of habit," she said, using her shaky left hand to unbuckle the belt, which she handed over. "You take them."

Quickly, Viya donned the belt, drawing one blade and making sure the other was loose in the scabbard. "They won't make it this far. I promise."

Amenet's smile was equal parts cold determination and kindness. "My Alixat. Make no promises you can't keep."

"I never do," said Viya, and left before fear could stop her.

As she hurried downstairs, she could hear shouts coming from the front drive, intermingled with those same screams as before. But who was it? The loss of Hawy suddenly struck her afresh, and she almost doubled over at the sudden fear that the screams could be coming from Kadu or Pix. *I can't lose any more family.*

I can't do this again.

And then she was shaking in earnest, Amenet's blade dropping from her hand with a clatter – she was right back at the battle of the Envas road, rolling beneath a horse's hooves and feeling her head explode in lines of fire as the skewed blow raked her face. She dropped to her knees at the foot of the stairs, unable to move, unable to do anything except think, distantly, that if she died now and nobody saw, then at least she wouldn't be remembered as a coward.

The screaming cut out, though the distant shouting continued. Viya barely noticed. Her awareness of the world had shrunk into tunnel-vision, her pulse erratic, her breath too quick, and yet she was frozen in place, unable to move despite an absolute, bone-deep conviction that staying still meant dying. *I'm going to die. I should be dead already.*

Suddenly Pix appeared, crouching before her. "Iviyat," she said softly. "Viya. Can you hear me?"

After a moment, Viya managed to nod.

Pix exhaled. "A group of soldiers attacked the house. Not many; only seven or so. They weren't after you or Amenet, though; they didn't even know we were here. We took them by surprise, and now they've all been taken care of. It was one of them who was screaming. Everyone else is fine."

Very slowly, Viya came back to herself. "The soldiers," she said, her voice as thick as if she'd been woken from a deep sleep, "what were they after?"

"Apparently, they've been dogging Rixevet for days. She kept beating them back, so they thought they'd try a different tactic – riding hard to beat her here, and taking Kadu hostage. Instead, they found us."

"Rixevet?" Hope swelled in Viya's heart. "Is she here?"

Pix shook her head. "She won't arrive for another day; that was the point of the ambush, apparently. But the soldiers are all gone now, either dead or fled or captured. You don't have to fight. It's over." She hesitated. "Viya? I'm going to hug you now, if that's all right."

"It's all right," Viya whispered, and as Pix put her arms around her, she collapsed against the courtier, not even sobbing, but *howling*, a raw, ungainly sound that felt strong enough to be shredding her lungs as she made it. Her whole body shook, but Pix just stroked her braids and held her close, her voice a sad yet comforting murmur in Viya's ear.

"You've been so strong, little fox. You've done so much, I let myself forget that there's always a cost. I let myself believe we weren't making you choose between grief and respect, but we were, we were, and it's pushed you too far. I'm sorry. I'm still a mother. I should've known better. I'm sorry."

Still crying, but more quietly now, Viya leaned back from Pix, the other woman's palms braced warmly against her shoulders. She looked at the courtier, really *looked*, and something in the action calmed her as even the long-overdue apology hadn't. Pixeva's eyes were wide, her braided hair dishevelled. Three stray drops of blood sat high on one cheekbone, and her left eye was bloodshot.

"I'm a coward," Viya said, voice trembling. "I came to fight, but I couldn't."

Pix's gaze flicked sideways, taking in the dropped knife, then fixed on Viya again. "Listen to me. *Listen*. When Zechalia first brought you to us, I thought... I don't know what I thought. But it wasn't charitable, and I didn't give you even a quarter of the credit you deserved. Yet all you've ever done – all you've ever tried to do – is live up to the honour of being Cuivexa. And after the Envas road, as we travelled here, I always woke you from nightmares. Every morning I woke you, and I never said anything, because you didn't. You talked in your sleep. Sometimes you even cried out. But because you didn't say anything, I told myself you were coping; I let myself believe that you didn't remember them. But of course you did. That doesn't mean you were any less a Cuivexa; but being Cuivexa doesn't mean you're any less wounded either. You're allowed to be both. You're allowed to ask for help."

Viya trembled. "I am?"

"You are," said Pix, "but I still need to apologise, because Cuivexa or not, you've been a young woman under my care, and you shouldn't have *had* to ask, or to steel yourself into not-asking, just because I was too busy with politics to see you as a person. But, Iviyat – to walk down here alone, willing to fight, after everything you've been through, for no better reason than that you thought it was the right thing to do, even though you were frightened? That takes more strength, more bravery, than fighting ever could. You are not a coward. You are *magnificent*, and whatever comes of all of this, you have my loyalty."

And she lifted Viya's fingertips to her lips, and kissed them to show her fealty.

"Pixeva ore Pixeva ki Tahun," Viya said, too overwhelmed to manage anything else. Which, as it turned out, was fortuitous; at just that moment, Oyako came running up. Viya jerked to her feet, self-consciously wiping the tears from her eyes, but if the dreamseer noticed her disarray, she gave no sign of it. Her face was alight with purpose.

"Word from Yevekshasa!" she panted, coming to a halt. "Kikra reached me just as the last of them fled."

"What news?" said Pix, standing.

"Zechalia and Safi both live, with the former now counted as a queen of Veksh. The Council meets at tomorrow's dawn, and when they do, not only Zech's ascension to their ranks, but Gwen and Yasha's plea for aid, will be heard and judged."

Pix's brows shot up. "So soon? We've not much time for planning then."

"No," said Oyako, then hesitated, her gaze flicking to Viya. "Which is why we think a conference might be in order."

"*We*?" said Pix, sharply. "And who, pray tell, is *we* in this situation?"

"The Shavaktiin," said Oyako, her eyes still fixed on Viya. "Please, Cuivexa. Whether you've always known it or not, the Shavaktiin have been your champions even before we found you by the Envas road. In fact, it was one of our number who helped you escape the palace."

Viya opened her mouth, then closed it again. *Luy.* In all this time, she'd barely thought of him, let alone truly contemplated the relevance of his being a Shavaktiin – and nor, she realised belatedly, had she ever disclosed his aid to anyone.

"How do you know that?" she asked, more sharply than she'd intended.

Pix stared at her. "You never mentioned any Shavaktiin when we took you in."

"I didn't trust you then," said Viya stiffly, not liking to admit it, "and afterwards, it didn't seem important. His name was Luy, and he was Leoden's advisor. In any case, he gave the impression that other Shavaktiin thought badly of him. That he needed to redeem himself. And given that he otherwise stood at my husband's side, I didn't see any reason to doubt it."

"Luy." Pix looked thoughtful. "I feel like I've heard the name before, though I can't quite remember..." Her voice trailed off as she stared dreamily into the distance; several seconds passed before she shook her head, abandoning the attempt at recollection. "It doesn't matter."

"Actually, it does," said Oyako. "Not that you've heard his name before, I mean, but Luy himself. It's true, what the Cuivexa said – there are some among the Shavaktiin who believe him to be a traitor, that his interpretation of the Great Story is flawed and his role in steering it a form of sacrilege. But not everyone in our order thinks likewise. The members of our coterie are numbered among his supporters." She hesitated. "Halaya and he are lovers."

"Truly?" said Pix. "And here I'd been thinking you were an order of celibates."

Oyako laughed at that. "Though we wear robes, they yet conceal flesh and blood. The fact remains, however," and here she turned serious again, "that Luy's actions have become integral to the story. Which is why – assuming you agree to a conference of minds, Cuivexa – Luy will be one of those present."

"A conference of minds?" asked Viya.

"A meeting in the dreamscape," Oyako said. "Facilitated by Luy, Kikra and myself, enabling a conversation between yourself, Zechalia a Kadeja, and Safi a Ellen."

"But not me," said Pix, "nor Gwen, nor Yasha, nor any other soul? Why?"

"Because the story is theirs," said Oyako, simply. "We participate in order to guide them, not to be guided by other interests."

Pix hesitated, then glanced at Viya. "The Cuivexa has my loyalty. I trust her to make the right decision."

Oyako inclined her head. "As you should."

"My thanks," said Viya, finally finding the strength to speak, "but the decision isn't mine alone to make." And she told them about the pact she'd made with Amenet.

Both women fell silent. Viya became acutely aware of the sweat dripping down her neck.

"A wise decision," Oyako said eventually – and despite the delay, it sounded as though she meant it. "But even so, she cannot join in the conference; it would drain us too much to include another mind for such a length of time."

"I understand," said Viya – and then remembered, with a horrible, guilty lurch, that Amenet was still in the library, waiting for an attack that would never come. "But even so, I should go to her. Now."

"Of course," said Pix. "In fact, we all should. If only you are able to attend the conference on this end–" and here she shot Oyako a calculating look, "–then we should at least discuss what might be said, or not said, beforehand."

"Agreed," said Viya. Breathing deeply, she forced herself to be calm. "The library is as good a place as any for such a discussion. While I confer with Amenet, Pix, you can gather Kadu and Kisavet, and Oyako, you may bring any other Shavaktiin whose input you feel will be of use during such a discussion. But only one, mind. There's still a need to maintain some privacy." And she held her breath, hoping neither order would be questioned.

"Of course, Cuivexa," said Oyako, bowing. "We will meet you there."

"As will we," said Pix. "Is there anything else you require?"

The relief that flooded Viya was so powerful, she almost swayed. *Pix was right. I can grieve* and *lead. The one doesn't contradict the other.*

"No," she said, feeling stronger and more herself than she had in weeks. "That will be all. For now."

A stillness crept over Saffron once Gwen left. Up until now, the biggest lie she'd ever told her parents – told anyone, in fact – had involved a fictitious sleepover at a friend's house to cover up their sneaking out to a local music festival, and even then, she'd still slept over there afterwards. But this, what they were planning now... it was so much bigger, so inescapably *permanent*, that even the thought of telling it left her numb.

Once this lie was told, she'd be living in its aftermath forever. There could be no going back.

She swung her legs over the edge of the mattress. She'd risen only once since waking after the trial, just long enough to piss in a bronze pot, but now she stepped away from the bed, testing her legs. Though her muscles burned from her run through Yevekshasa's tunnels – though her new scars pinched and stung as the fresh skin stretched with motion – she was able to keep upright. She was also naked, something she'd noticed earlier without feeling bothered about, though someone had left a kettha and dou folded neatly on a side table. Both were made of soft red cloth, the hems edged in thick bands of a stiffer gold fabric marked with blocky white-and-black patterns. Doubtless, there was some significance to it, but as Saffron put them on, she found she didn't much care what. She just needed to get out, before the smallness of the room and the largeness of the lie smothered her.

Even so, it could be dangerous. Her proxy status was no guarantee of protection against the violence of Vekshi politics, but Saffron had fought a dragon – had *been* a dragon, even – and what about this unknown, unseen city could frighten her after that? She smiled at the thought, her lips a twisted sickle of black humour, and just for a moment, she fancied she felt the scale she'd swallowed burning in her chest.

She opened the door and would've stepped through, if not for the fact that Yena was on the other side of it, hand raised for a knock that never came. Eyes widening, she lowered her hand, and Saffron's mouth went dry.

"I was going to ask if I could come in," said Yena, "but I'm not sure that's the right question anymore."

"No," said Saffron. "It's not. I mean, I was going for a walk, but... you could come with me? If you wanted, that is. If that's, um, if it's allowed." She ran a rueful hand over her head. "I'm not really sure how things work here."

"Nor am I," said Yena, smiling. "But however much you've irked the queens, you're still a proxy, and that means you have power, of a sort. No one will challenge you outside – no one you can't afford to ignore, anyway – and if I'm with you, then no one can send me away either. Except perhaps you, if you tire of me."

The lilt in her voice, though utterly lacking in affectation, produced in Saffron the same bodily effect as if Yena had whispered the words in her ear while trailing a finger down her spine. She shivered pleasantly, remembering in a sudden flash the way the other girl had touched her cheek on the Envas road, and felt her heart speed up.

"That's... unlikely," she managed. "Do you know the way out?"

Yena looked surprised. "Don't you?"

"I wasn't exactly conscious when they brought me here," Saffron said, dryly.

"Oh. Right." Yena blushed, but didn't lose her self-possession for long. Stepping back from the door, she waved Saffron forward. "This way, then. Where do you want to go?"

"Somewhere I can see the sky," said Saffron, thinking of the place where she'd emerged from the caves. "Not just overhead, but from a distance. Is that all right?"

Yena laughed. "This is Yevekshasa. I think we can manage it."

As Yena led on down the hall, Saffron felt a momentary twinge of uncertainty. Should she be looking for Zech instead, or Yasha or Halaya? She didn't have so much time left before the Council met that she could afford to squander it; but when Yena, sensing her hesitation, beckoned her onwards, Saffron had a feeling that, when she looked back on their excursion, *squandered* would be the very last thing she'd think.

As they walked, they passed priestesses robed in Ashasan red and a handful of brown-clad women Saffron assumed were servants, but not a single queen. If her own appearance raised some pale Vekshi brows, none of their owners so much as spoke to her, let alone told her to stop.

And then, just like that, she was outside again, the sudden drench of afternoon sunlight flooding her body with warmth. Some of the tension she'd been carrying left her. She came to a halt, savouring the sensation, and noticed that though the exit had been unguarded on the inside, the exterior wall was patrolled by no fewer than six armed women, and – Saffron blinked – two men. This last intrigued her, and she turned to Yena for answers.

"Can men serve Ashasa, then?"

"That depends on two things," Yena said. "Namely, what you mean by *men*, and how you define service. Bodies are bodies, and hearts are hearts. The priesshood admits women only, though flesh plays no role in such determinations; but those we just passed were guards, not acolytes, which means they could be anyone." She paused, glancing sideways at Saffron, and when she spoke again, her voice was ever-so-subtly softer. "After everything you've learned – after Ruyun a Ketra denied me, on the steps of Ashasa's Knives – am I right in thinking that alikrevaya has meaning for you?"

"It does," Saffron said, pulse fluttering in her wrists. "Zech explained it to me. After what Ruyun said, she had to."

Yena laughed. "You're blushing, Safi a Ellen," she teased, and quick as a darting fish, she brushed a kiss on Saffron's neck. The touch was electrifying. Saffron gasped and came to a halt, hand flying up of its own accord to graze where Yena's lips had been. "It's really very sweet," Yena continued, putting herself in front of Saffron, arms crossed and smiling. They were in a stone courtyard, Saffron noted distantly, with a slice of sky in the background, but her eyes were all for Yena. "Now, tell me truthfully: what has you walking on eggshells? You must remember, I've known Gwen Vere since childhood, and she's told me many things about your world, including some of its... uglier aspects." Her smile vanished, then reappeared just as quickly, a sun briefly hidden by scudding clouds. "Not to scare me, you understand, but in answer to my very persistent questions. And so, I ask: does my nature, if I can call it that, disquiet you?"

"No," said Saffron, dizzied into unhesitating honesty by the power of the kiss, which had perhaps been the point of it in the first place. "You are who you are."

"Well, then. Are you going to ask me whether I chose my name, or if it was given to me, or if it never changed at all?"

"No."

"And why not?"

"Because it's not my business. Not unless you want to tell me, that is, and there's no worldly reason why you should do, just because I might or might not be curious."

"Rightly so," said Yena. She took her by the hand and pulled her onwards, over to the wide, pale sky that hung beyond a fat stone railing. They stood there, hands joined and smiling at each other, and just that moment all by itself did more to knit up Saffron's hurt than any amount of magic or medicine ever could, and then they were kissing, they were kissing and time stopped, they were kissing and the sun poured through them, knuckle to throat to hip to thigh, and they were seamless, they were light, and it was beautiful. Yena's hand splayed on the curving space above Saffron's right hip and below her ribs, and when they finally broke apart, Saffron leaned in and rested her head in the hollow where Yena's neck met her collarbone. They stood like that, silent and close, until a cool wind whipped so playfully past that they each stepped back a bit, laughing at it.

All at once, Saffron stopped smiling, chest tightening sharply at the realisation that she wanted more of this, whatever it was – but how was that meant to happen if she went home again? The question must have shown in her face before it ever reached her lips, or else Yena was thinking the exact same thing, because she reached across and brushed her fingertips gently against the scars on Saffron's head.

"This isn't fealty," she said softly. "It doesn't exclude, doesn't obligate, doesn't demand or censor. This is what it is, and when you come back to me – yes, I say when, not if; I have that much faith in our turning worlds – then I'll be here, and you'll be here, and so this will be too."

This time, it was Saffron who kissed Yena, slow and deep. "I'll hold you to that," she said finally, and would have said more, if not for the sudden interjection of a firm, polite cough.

Turning in time with Yena, Saffron found herself staring at two Shavaktiin: Halaya, distinguished by her green veil and dark hands, and another robed in pale yellow.

"Forgive the interruption," said Halaya, her voice coloured with genuine apology, "but Safi, you're needed for a conference."

"Conference?" asked Saffron. "You mean, about the Council?"

"Among other things." Halaya gestured at her companion, who bowed. "This is Kikra, our remaining dreamseer. He can link you and Zechalia to Oyako, and through her, to Iviyat." She held out a hand. "Come with us."

"What about Yena?" Saffron asked. "Can't she–"

Kikra shook his head. "There are limits to the ilumet. Just the little queen, and you. Yes?"

"But Yena may come for company," Halaya added.

"My thanks," said Yena wryly.

The moment was broken, but while it lasted, it had somehow been enough. Sighing, Saffron stepped away from the sky and back into Vekshi politics. "Whatever you say," she said to Halaya.

The veil made it hard to tell, but from the tone of her voice, she thought the Shavaktiin leader was smiling.

"Perhaps," she answered cryptically. "One day. In a manner of speaking."

Zech stared at the ceiling, waiting for the inevitable fourth knock at the door. She didn't know who was coming, only that someone would. Since waking in her new room, she'd had a total of three separate visitations, each of which had burdened her with a new set of troubles. But four was a sacred number in Ashasa's lore, and after everything that had happened, Zech would have been a fool to discount its significance. *Three knocks brought problems,* she told herself, *but the fourth will see them solved.*

Or so she hoped.

Her first visitor had been Gwen. The worldwalker had just been in with Safi – "I tried you first, but you were asleep," she'd explained – and told her what nobody, not even Mesthani, had remembered or bothered to say earlier: that the Council of Queens was due to meet at dawn, and that she and Safi had best be prepared for it. Zech had schooled her expression into one of dutiful calm, all the while panicking internally. She'd undergone the trial in full knowledge that success would make her a queen, but even though she'd gambled Safi's life on the idea that they could pass, she still hadn't allowed herself to think about the consequences of doing so. All she'd wanted – all she'd really been thinking – was of a way to ensure they'd be able to speak their piece before the Council, and she'd somehow managed to say as much to Gwen.

But once the worldwalker had gone from the room, she'd admitted to herself that the truth wasn't nearly so simple or altruistic. It hadn't been about helping. It had been about proving herself worthy.

Zech had no memory of her life before she'd come to live in the compound. Right from the first, Yasha and Trishka had instilled in her the appropriate sense of pride and connection to her heritage, but despite their best efforts, Veksh had always been a distant idea, and they hadn't been her only teachers. Matu had given her more than just mastery over her magic: through his lessons, she'd come to feel a connection with Kena, a sense of belonging that her interactions with Pix and even Jeiden had only helped to cement. But living in Karavos wasn't the same as truly inhabiting it, and the walls of Yasha's compound were made of more than stone. Zech had prayed to Sahu at least as often as she did to Ashasa, but quietly, not knowing how to reconcile the one faith with the other. Did the gods exist, and did she truly believe in them? Sometimes it felt like they did, though admitting as much in Yasha's hearing would have earned her a smack and a scowl for blasphemy at the very least.

When, soon after her marriage to Vex Leoden, Kadeja had started saying that all the Kenan gods were really nothing more than Ashasa's shadows – divine aspects of a single goddess refracted into different beings by Kenan ignorance – Zech had been angry, but she'd also been uneasy too. Though the Vex'Mara's actions were horrible, like cutting off Safi's fingers, deep down part of Zech had wondered if maybe, despite her awfulness, there could be some truth to what she said. She'd repressed the idea violently, disliking the idea that she and the hated Vex'Mara could have anything in common.

And then she'd been revealed as Kadeja's daughter.

All her life, she'd been taught that knowing and honouring one's mother was key to her Vekshi identity. The fact that her own birth mother remained unknown – that she'd cast her off as a baby – had bothered her at times, but under those same laws, she'd come to see that Trishka was her real mother, Yena and Sashi her real sisters, Yasha the real matriarch to whom she owed ultimate obedience. That was right and proper. But if she was born a child of Kadeja's blood, then what did that make her, really? Was she a traitor too – was that why she'd prayed to Ashasa and Sahu both before she'd ever heard the Vex'Mara say they were one and the same? Once people knew who she really was, being judged for it – or worse, used as a tool because of it – felt inevitable, if not by Yasha, then surely by someone else. And the man from the dreamscape, Luy, he'd seen the truth at the same time Zech did; he'd *known*, and even though he'd helped to formulate her plan – even though, somehow, impossibly, he'd been there with her during the trial, relaying advice and lending her strength, which she'd lent to Safi in turn – she hadn't been able to trust that a stranger, a man she'd never met in the flesh, would keep her secret long.

And so she'd undergone the trial: a way to prove she was nobody's implement, least of all Kadeja's, but a queen in charge of her own life. All this she'd admitted to herself as Gwen closed the door of her sickroom, and the realisation had been paralysing.

What would happen next? With Safi's help, Luy's guidance and no small amount of luck, she'd done something that by rights ought to have been impossible. She wasn't just a queen of Veksh, but one of the youngest women in history ever to hold the title. Once they'd petitioned the Council for aid in removing Kadeja from Kena, there was a new life waiting for her here, a life lived free of Yasha's dominion and the compound's walls; a life of power and prestige and politics; a life lived in service to Ashasa, but not Sahu.

A life she didn't want.

Such had been her state of mind, overwhelmed by the implications of her actions and unable to see a way out of them, when her second visitor had arrived. It was Yasha, of course, and even though Zech had known she'd have to face the matriarch sooner or later, the prospect had still filled her with dread.

Without waiting for an invitation, Yasha took a seat on the single chair set at the side of the bed. Zech had been prepared for anger, resentment, accusation – even for hostile silence.

She hadn't expected praise.

"You brilliant girl!" Yasha crowed, gripping her hand so tightly it was a wonder the cuts on her knuckles didn't reopen. "I've always known Ashasa, in her infinite wisdom, had sent you to me for a reason, but I never suspected it was anything near this grand!"

Somehow, Zech managed to speak. "You never knew? All this time, and you never knew I was Kadeja's daughter?"

Yasha snorted. "Of course I didn't know! If I had, I'd never have agreed to take you in, which is doubtless why Ashasa saw fit to keep the truth from me all these years. No, girl, no. I heard about you from a friend of a friend – a little shasuyakesani girl, her mother dead in childbirth with only an unwilling, undaughtered uncle to claim her. And I thought to myself, well, I could always use an extra pair of hands, and of course it didn't hurt any that Jeskia a Keta owed me a favour for it. Hah! More fool her!"

Zech endured this gloating speech in silence, though the effort cost her six new cuts, three on each palm, from clenching her fists so tightly that her fingernails broke skin.

"I knew Ashasa wouldn't deny me forever," Yasha said, with a fervency that was downright alarming. "I gave up my queenship to save Trishka's life, but the cost, the cost! Living in exile, forced to sweat and toil and bleed in the shadow of heathen gods, to ally myself with the disreputable, the dissolute, the deranged – making myself a spider, a skulking creature, kept from prestige and power until my youth and strength were spent, and all that was left was this–" she plucked angrily at the wrinkled, hanging skin of her arms, "–this decrepit flesh. All these years a mockery of myself, of my goddess. But you have redeemed all that, my Zechalia.

"Here is what we must do."

For the next twenty minutes, Zech sat, miserable and helpless to offer a contradiction, as Yasha laid out her plans for how she thought Zech ought to deal with the Council of

Queens. Kadeja was still to be taken and held accountable before Ashasa's Knives – "We've done this much, it would be a waste not to see it through," she said – and a Vekshi force still sent to help pacify Leoden's troops, but afterwards, she was determined that Zech would persuade Iviyat to cede certain disputed northern territories back to Vekshi control as payment for their aid. She wanted Vekshi women at court; she wanted herself installed as the Vekshi ambassador to Kena.

"That might take some doing," she admitted, "but if you are able to reclaim even so small an area as the Bharajin Forest for Veksh, it will give you enough clout with the other queens to make the bargaining easier."

In addition to these and other plans, she also delivered a monologue on the ins and outs of Council politics as Yasha remembered them, her theories about what had changed, and her impressions on which of the queens she'd known during her own tenure who were trustworthy (Cehala, Mesthani, Jairin) and those who weren't (Ruyun, Taksha, Vosi). Her words washed through and over Zech like a river, and rather than fight the current, she let that river carry her, nodding when it was appropriate and praying fiercely in her heart – to Ashasa, to Sahu, to any god that was listening – that the ordeal would end before she reached her breaking point.

Finally, mercifully, her prayers were answered. Having scarcely drawn breath for her entire visit, Yasha fell silent, her hawkish face turned thoughtful.

"Forgive me," she murmured. "I had not... I have been in exile from Veksh a good many years, Zechalia a Kadeja, years in which I have dreamed of return more often than... *tcha*!" She broke off, dismissing her words with a single cutting gesture, and stood. "Doubtless, I have given you much to think on. Heed my advice or don't. Our Mother Sun has ever held my heart to her coals and let the flesh blacken. You know where I'll be."

Zech opened her mouth to reply, but Yasha had gone before she could find the words. Heart hammering in her chest, she was left alone again – but not for long. Just as she was beginning to wonder whether she might go in search of Safi, or failing that some food, there was another knock at the door. By then she was resigned to receiving unwanted visitors, and so was pleasantly surprised to find that her new guests – two of them, this time – were both people she actually wanted to talk to: Matu and Jeiden.

"Come i–" she began, but didn't get out the rest of the sentence; Jeiden ran across the room and flung himself at her, wrapping her in a hug so tight it squeezed the air from her lungs. Much to her surprise and delight, Zech found herself hugging him back, his head pressed to the crook of her neck as his feathery hair tickled her face.

"The next time you're planning something like this," he whispered fiercely, "you tell me, all right? You *tell* me. I wouldn't have stopped you." He leaned back, his dark eyes black with intensity. "I would only have wished you luck, or helped, if you wanted help."

An unexpected lump rose in Zech's throat. "I promise," she managed. Jeiden nodded, evidently satisfied, and then, in the space of two seconds, appeared to realise that not only had he been hugging her, but that he'd leapt on the bed to do so. Colouring prettily, he scuttled backwards along the blankets and stumbled to his feet, scratching pointedly at his neck while hiding his face in his elbow. Matu entered more sedately, ignoring the chair in favour of resting on his haunches by the bedside. A quiet smile lit his face, and though he restricted his display of affection to briefly squeezing her hand, the effect was somehow more touching than if he'd gathered her up in his arms.

"If you're going to tell me how stupid I was, get it over with," Zech said, forcing a smile so fragile that it trembled at the corners. Until that moment, she hadn't known how frightened she was that Matu would disapprove of what she'd done.

"You weren't stupid," he replied softly. "What you did was extraordinary. I have no wish to demean or diminish you for it, and as frightened as I was of losing you, I'm a hundred – no, a thousand times more impressed with you for having succeeded. But..."

He paused, and Zech's heart froze in her chest.

"You risked Safi's life instead of yours. That wasn't fair, Zechalia, and it wasn't right. She had no idea what you were getting her into; not that you did either, but that hardly makes it acceptable, does it?"

Don't cry, Zech told herself. *Whatever you do, don't cry.*

"I didn't have a choice," she said, struggling to keep her voice even. "We'd been meeting in the dreamscape – I'd explained everything, she *agreed* – but she didn't remember in waking, and then there wasn't any time. I had to act quickly–"

"But you didn't." Matu's eyes were sad. "If the queens had turned us away, even if they'd imprisoned us, we would have found another way. Thanks to the portal, we arrived in Yevekshasa days ahead of schedule; we still had time for Yasha to reach out to her old contacts, for Kikra and the Shavaktiin to speak with Pix; we had time to make plans, Zech. Different plans. Safer plans. You chose this." His voice was so gentle, and yet his words cut deep. *"You chose this. And maybe one day, you'll tell me why. But until then..."* He shook his head and laughed. "Listen to me. There's no right way to do this, so I'm doing it all wrong."

"A right way to do what?" Zech asked, proud that her voice didn't tremble.

"A right way to say you did something dangerous. You risked someone else's life in service of your plans, and you should feel the weight of that choice, so that you understand exactly what it meant – what it still means. But even so, Safi might have refused you; she didn't. You might have backed down; you didn't. She might have died, and you might have failed. *But you didn't.* And together, what you've done is extraordinary. I don't know what's going to happen next, what this means for you or any of us. But I'm proud, Zech. I'm proud of you. And I'm glad beyond the telling of it that you lived."

And with that, he lent forward and dropped a kiss on her forehead, the way a fond older brother might.

He and Jeiden stayed for a little while after that, talking of inconsequential things, or trying to; there wasn't much to be said just then that didn't have some sort of ulterior meaning, and eventually their collective attempt to pretend otherwise faltered. Though Jeiden clearly wanted to stay longer, Matu recognised Zech's exhaustion and gently led his other charge away, leaving her in silence.

And so she sat, waiting for the fourth and final knock that stubbornly refused to come.

There were many sacred fours in Ashasa's lore, but the one currently foremost in Zechalia's thoughts was the four of elements, all of which she and Safi had faced as part of the Trial of Queens. First had been water, that numbing plunge into the unknown; second was stone, exemplified both by the heart of the mesa itself and the crystal-knife they'd pulled from it; third was darkness, the long nightmare of the lightless tunnel; and fourth and last had been fire, the bloody scion-battle. She shivered at the memory, her new scars tingling sharply as though raked by ghostly claws, and she wondered, as she had wondered several times since waking, how she would ever find the strength to sleep again, and whether it could possibly be without nightmares if she did.

The silence was oppressive, weighing on her like walls of rock. Unbidden, an old Vekshi childsong sprang to mind, a tune she'd not heard since Sashi and Yena were younger than she was now. They used to sing it while playing catch-as-catch-can in the compound yard. Recalling them both, Zech whispered it under her breath:

"One for silence, two for strength;
three for grief and four for wrath,
five for sound and six for weakness,
seven for joy and eight for peace;
hold you close and hold you under
only fire brings release."

She finished and looked to the door again, half-convinced her recitation would summon the final knock. But the room remained stubbornly silent, and all Zech had the strength to do was lie back and stare at the ceiling, waiting for a solution that refused to come.

There was a knock.

Blinking slowly, Zech sat up. "Come in?"

The door opened, revealing Safi, Yena, Halaya and a yellow-robed Shavaktiin whose name, she dimly remembered, was Kikra.

Her heart began to pound. *Ashasa heard me.* "Yes? What is it?"

"We're needed in the dreamscape," Safi said.

21
Dreams of Power

"How do you know I'll remember this in waking?" Viya asked nervously.

"Walking unguided in the dreamscape is one thing," Oyako said, her voice as soothing as a cold cloth laid on fevered skin. "But entering with the direct aid of a skilled dreamseer is quite another." Pulling a chair up to the bedside, she sat down and gently took Viya's hand. "Close your eyes and count backwards from twenty."

"Out loud or in my head?"

"It doesn't matter, so long as you space the numbers between breaths."

Until that moment, Viya had forgotten the young acolyte of Teket's Kin who'd mended her childhood scrapes. Not every healer asked their patients to count, but theirs always had – it helped to distract her patients, she said – and doing so now made Viya feel as safe and comforted as if she were once more five years old, snug beneath her three-coloured quilt while winter rain drummed on the roof. Her grip on Oyako's hand relaxed as her breathing slowly deepened.

Three. Two. One.

She opened her eyes in the dreamscape.

Beneath a dome of silver-streaked night, she and Oyako stood amidst an endless stretch of soft black grass, its long stems shifting and whispering in the breath of some unfelt breeze. The grass grew from the vast dark of an underfoot sky: instead of flowers, the velvet field was dotted with the pinprick lights of stars. They ought to have fallen through, tumbling forever into that impossible firmament, but the ground felt real enough beneath her bare feet, as springy and soft as moss, and when Oyako led her forward, she didn't stumble.

"Is this... Does it always look like this?" she whispered, awed. The place was so beautiful, it almost felt worthy of Ke and Na themselves.

Oyako looked at her strangely. "You didn't dream this on purpose?"

"Me?" Viya blinked. "You mean this isn't yours?"

"My dreamscape is all frozen waterfalls and red snow," said Oyako. "I've never seen any of this before. You've brought it with you. This *is* you."

For a moment, they both just stared. The silver lights overhead changed colour, flickering through shades of gold, red, blue and green, like the streaky tails of comets. Then, with an audible exhalation, Oyako shook her head.

"Come on. We need to find the others."

"How?"

By way of answer, Oyako reached down and plucked the nearest star-flower from the grass. It glimmered brightly, hovering just above the surface of her palm, before she enclosed it in her fist. When she opened her hand again, the star was gone, replaced by a small white bird.

"Find Kikra," she told it, and the bird shot off, leaving a trail of tiny white feather-stars floating in its wake. Delightedly, Viya touched one; it popped against her fingers like a soap-bubble.

"Do we follow?" she asked.

"We do," said Oyako. "Better not to keep the others waiting."

The feather-stars led them to a gentle slope above a curving valley. Four figures stood below them: Safi, Zech, and the

Shavaktiin dreamseers, Kikra and Luy. Like Oyako, the men wore no veils, their bare faces unfamiliar, yet even from a distance, Viya felt absurdly certain that the taller, darker man, with his row-braided hair and subtle smile, was Luy. As they came closer, the mirrored scars on Zech and Safi's faces drew her attention. Without quite meaning to, she broke away from Oyako and ran to them, stumbling down the slope, and when they ran to meet her too, it felt entirely natural. Zech and Safi opened their arms, and with the perfect logic of dreams, they wrapped each other in a tight, three-way hug, inhaling together, scars touching scars, before pulling away again.

There was a silence, neither awkward nor exactly comfortable; it fitted them like a shirt they were yet to grow into. Viya smiled at Safi, raised a brow at Zech.

"I hear we are queens together, of a sort."

Zech grimaced. Her grey hair was streaked with white around her scars, which were themselves particoloured against her calico skin. Once, Viya would have found the combination perturbing; now, it arrested her. "You could say that."

"I helped," said Safi wryly. "They gave me a tattoo."

"I've allied with Amenet," Viya said, seeing no reason to dissemble. "We'll rule together, Vexa i Vexa."

"How very... Vekshi," said Zech. Her tone was innocent enough, but a certain sly gleam in her eyes betrayed her awareness of the pun. "We're due to meet the Council soon. But I'm not sure what to say to them. What I've done... What we've done–" she glanced at Safi, who straightened, "–has thrown things into turmoil. I have no allies, no power, and nothing to bargain with."

"What about Yasha?" Safi asked.

"She wants to make me her proxy," Zech replied, with unexpected bitterness. "A tool for her pride, her ambitions. Which is fair, really. After all, it's what I did to you."

Gently, Safi laid a hand on the other girl's shoulder. "You didn't force me to do anything, Zech. I wanted to help."

"But you didn't understand what it meant! Not really."

"Neither did you, and what's done is done," said Safi firmly. "And anyway, this isn't the place. We shouldn't waste time."

"You're right," Zech said, and turned to Viya. "How stand your forces?"

"As ready as they can be," she replied, "though truly, it's not me they follow. They obey Rixevet and cleave to Amenet – I haven't even addressed them. But my name still has weight, as does the confusion surrounding my disappearance. Leoden's mistreatment of me, I'm told, has become a rallying point; dissenters have been moving their forces north, to Avekou and the surrounding territories. In open battle, my husband would still overwhelm us, but that's the whole point of striking at him through Kadeja, is it not? To avoid open battle. You say you've little power, Zech, but setting Ashasa's Knives on the Vex'Mara – have you sway enough to achieve that much?"

"Possibly," said Zech, after a moment. "The Knives are strong at the moment – too strong, Yasha says, and I agree with her. Maybe we can use it to our advantage, maybe not. But either way..." she faltered, looking Viya straight in the eye. "Either way, I don't want Vekshi forces inside Kena. Not if I can help it. Yasha wants me to make our aid a toehold in your government; she wants court positions and trade concessions and a dozen other things, but she forgets I was raised in Kena, that my love of Karavos exceeds her own; she doesn't imagine I pray to Ashasa and Sahu together. I might be a queen of Veksh, but if she knew my heart..."

"What do you want then?" asked Viya. Her head was spinning. "That day in the Square of Gods, you pulled me from the mob and took me to Yasha. I thought your allegiance was to her above all else. Yet here you are, betraying her."

"To your advantage," Zech said sharply.

"So you say. I find it hard to believe." But though she

spoke the words, it didn't feel true, and from the look on Zech's face, it was plain the other girl knew she knew it too. There was just something about the dreamscape that made lying harder – even (or perhaps especially) to herself.

"I want stability," said Zech softly. "Stability and peace. Leoden's coup fractured Kena at a time of strength, and that's bad for everyone. Kadeja claims her version of Ashasa, the goddess-as-all-gods, is meant to bring unity, but unity is what we lost when she and Leoden came to power. If she only wanted people to choose for themselves, that would be one thing, but instead she's pushing her change by force, like... like pulling out people's hearts and telling them to bleed a different colour."

"Decapitate a snake, and the body dies," Safi said suddenly.

Zech and Viya both stared at her. "What?"

Safi blinked. "It's a saying where I'm from. I just mean that armies aren't the problem here, not really: it's Leoden and Kadeja. Take them away, and everything else falls into place. If your forces aren't strong enough to fight theirs, and if Zech doesn't want to put Vekshi troops in Kena, then don't. Go straight to the source."

"You make it sound easy, worldwalker," said Viya. "The palace is guarded by protective magic, the doors and gates by thousands of soldiers and arakoi. How?"

Safi opened her mouth. Closed it again. A strange look came over her face.

"Magic is new to me," she said slowly. "I mean, until I came to Kena, I never even knew it existed. But I've been around a lot of it the past few weeks, and I think I'm starting to get a feel for how it works. There are limitations, sure, but the rules aren't fixed; they can bend, if you work it properly. That's what Matu thinks anyway, and I believe him. And if that's right, then maybe... maybe I have an idea."

"Go on," said Viya and Zech together.

And Safi did just that.

Viya listened quietly, a growing hope in her chest. What Safi proposed wasn't like anything she'd heard of before, not even in a moon-tale, but perhaps that was the point: that only a worldwalker – someone who hadn't been raised on temple-lore, on the many crucial differences between ilumet and jahudemet, sevikmet and maramet – could dream up something so radical. It ought to have been impossible, but when she probed the logic of it, testing for flaws, to her utter astonishment, she found none. Not that it wasn't risky, of course – there was a real chance, if things went wrong, that the whole thing would backfire spectacularly. *And yet...*

"It could work," she said, glancing at Zech. "For my part, it could definitely work. But what about yours? You still need something to trade, some leverage with the Council."

Zech chewed her lip, clearly frustrated. "I know! But there's really only one thing they want from me, and that's..." She broke off, eyes widening. "The look on Yasha's *face*," she whispered. "Oh, I have leverage, all right. It'll work."

"We're agreed then," said Viya. "Ke and Na willing, there'll be no mishaps, but if there are, send word through the Shavaktiin."

While they'd been speaking, Oyako, Luy and Kikra had encircled them, standing far enough away to give them privacy (or the illusion of it, Viya noted sharply; after all, this wasn't a real space, which meant the usual rules of eavesdropping didn't apply) but close enough now to make their presence felt.

"All right," said Zech, grinning wickedly. "Safi? Does that suit you?"

"Why wouldn't it? Besides, you're the queens – well, queen and Vexa. I'm just a spare."

Viya looked at her. "That's a strange way of putting it. What makes you say so?"

Safi shrugged, visibly discomforted for the first time in the entire conversation. "I just... I was never meant to be here, that's all. In this world. It was an accident, and now… if everything goes to plan, I'll go back home again."

"And why should that be relevant? You still matter; your actions still matter. How and why you came here isn't the same as how and why you'll leave – it's what you do in the middle that's important."

"I suppose it is," said Safi slowly. "My thanks, Iviyat."

"Don't thank me," said Viya, loftily. "*I* had nothing to do with it." Not waiting for an answer, she exchanged a courteous bow with Zech, then turned away to Oyako, who was smiling.

"I take it that was productive?" the dreamseer asked, not quite innocently.

Viya lifted her chin. "I take it that's a rhetorical question, as you doubtless overheard everything?"

"Something like that." Oyako hesitated. "It's very beautiful here. We could stay awhile. We don't have to go straight back to the waking world."

It was a tempting offer, so much so that Viya almost accepted it without question. *Frozen waterfalls and red snow,* the Shavaktiin had said. But she had sworn herself to Amenet, just as wholly – and perhaps unexpectedly – as Pix had pledged to her, and if Safi's plan were to have any chance of working, then they'd need to begin preparations as soon as possible.

"No," she said, regretfully. "Another time, maybe. When Leoden is gone, and Amenet and I have come into our power."

"Another time, then," said Oyako, and each of them smiled as if it wasn't a lie.

Waking from the dreamscape, the first thing Saffron saw was Kikra's yellow robe, some subtle draft making the hem flutter like a butterfly's wing. As her gaze panned slowly upwards, she experienced a moment of disorientation: only moments earlier, she'd seen the dreamseer barefaced, and it was jarring to find that his quiet smile was once more obscured behind a latticed veil.

"Thank you," she said, awkwardly.

He bowed his head. "My pleasure."

On the other side of the bed, Zech groaned, her pale eyes fixed on Saffron.

"We're here again," she said. "And you know what? I am *hungry*."

As soon as she said it, Saffron's stomach growled. "Me too." She turned to Halaya and Yena, the room's only other occupants, both of whom had brought in chairs from elsewhere. "How long were we out?"

"Hours," Halaya said. "It's after dark now."

"If you like, I can get you some dinner," Yena offered. "Well, a late dinner."

"That would be–" she wanted to say *awesome*, but the idiom didn't quite translate into Kenan, "–very much appreciated. Thank you."

"My pleasure," said Yena, rising. Her expression turned sly. "You always look so sweet when you're sleeping."

Saffron went bright red.

"Has anything happened?" Zech asked Halaya, as Yena slipped out the door.

"Nothing important," Halaya replied. "Or nothing we know about, anyway. The fact that we've been allowed out of our rooms is a positive sign, but anyone who's tried to go much further than the courtyard has been politely but firmly encouraged to turn back. The last I saw of her, Yasha was bribing the younger acolytes to take messages through to the queens, evidently with some success – she's had a few visitors, hooded and cloaked, of whom the guards asked no questions." She hesitated. "Zechalia, you also had visitors while you slept, though of course we had to turn them away – Mesthani a Vekte and Cehala a Dahun."

The second name wasn't one that Saffron recognised, but judging by the way her brows shot up in surprise, it clearly meant something to Zech. "Can you call them back?" she asked. "Preferably without Yasha knowing?"

"I've no magic beyond dreaming," said Halaya, "but I'll see what I can do. The Shavaktiin have some currency here, and right now we have little to do but spend it." She hesitated, hands stirring in her lap. "Whatever you said in the dreamscape, Kikra, Luy and Oyako know to keep their silence. But we have only a few hours left before the Council meets. If I knew what you intended, I might be better equipped to help you achieve it."

When Zech remained silent, Saffron answered cautiously. "That depends."

"On what?"

"On whether your *currency*, as you have it, carries weight with Ashasa's Knives."

Halaya inhaled sharply. "I see." For a long, tenuous moment, she remained silent, the clean lines of her arms and shoulders silhouetted beneath her green robes. "It might," she said, finally. "It just might – provided, of course, that the blade in question isn't yet blunted."

The odd turn of phrase made Saffron blink. Inquiringly, she looked to Zech for an explanation, but to her surprise it was Kikra who answered.

"Individuals belonging to Ashasa's Knives are known as *yshra*, blades. When they die or retire from service, they become *tak* – blunted."

Saffron took a moment to process this. Thanks to the zuymet, she already knew the Vekshi words; she just hadn't heard them used in context. The magic worked on the basis of practice, repetition and familiarity, each new conversation calling forth knowledge so concrete yet ephemeral it felt like something she'd learned in a dream. Or not, she wryly supposed; the ilumet was something else entirely.

"You know an old blade?"

"I might," Halaya said. "But if I do this for you – if I can find and bring her here, and if she has the influence you need – I will ask three things in return."

"Name them," said Zech, without hesitation.

"First, that I be present when you talk to her. Second, that if your plan succeeds – and I have every confidence that it will – you will let me, and by extension the Shavaktiin, tell your story in full. And third, a favour from each of you, to be redeemed in the future at my discretion."

Neither of them had to even think about it. "Done," they said together – just as Yena returned, laden with food.

Halaya stood. It was difficult to tell from stance alone, but Saffron though she was pleased. "Well, then. It seems we have work to do. Kikra?"

The dreamseer rose, bowing a polite, wordless farewell to the room at large, and made his exit. Halaya moved to follow him, then paused in the doorway. "Who would you prefer to see first – queen or blade?"

"Blade," said Zech.

"Very good." Halaya inclined her head. "I will do my best."

And then she was gone, the door swinging shut behind her.

Gwen stared up at the ceiling. She'd given up hope of sleep hours ago, but that didn't stop her from wishing for it. Her whole body was tense in anticipation of dawn and the meeting of the Council of Queens – which, she freely acknowledged, was pointless. Though Yasha had continued her machinations long into the evening, there was little else Gwen could do to help. Whatever happened next was out of her control, and even though she didn't like it, by this point in her life, she ought to have been pragmatic enough for acceptance. Instead, she was restless, every muscle as rigidly tense as a hypocrite's moral outrage.

"Gwen? Are you awake?"

She jerked upright, swearing under her breath. It was Trishka, hovering beside her half-open door.

"I am. Come in."

Soft-footed and silent, her friend came and sat on the edge of the bed. "I'm feeling better," she said – redundantly, as she was up and about. Gwen made no answer, waiting for Trishka to come to the point.

"I was watching today, Gwen. When you met with Safi – and with Zech, for that matter – but I know you. Against all reason, it's the Earth-girl you're more worried about."

"It's not against all reason," Gwen grumbled, then realised she'd just admitted the very point she meant to refute. Even in the darkness, Trishka's smugness at having procured the confession was as radiant as sunburn, and stung just as much. "Oh, don't look at me like that – you know it's not. Not now, anyway. Zech was never risking death, and I doubt even Ruyun a Ketra would stoop to assassinating an unblooded girl just to spite Yasha, queen or no queen."

"But in service of her own interests, with spiting Yasha as a pleasant side effect? Never underestimate the venom of Veksh, Gwen." She laid a warm hand on her knee. "But, here. I'm not trying to shame you over Zech; I only meant that you're taking Safi personally, because she reminds you of you."

"Perhaps," Gwen said begrudgingly. "You saw our meeting?"

"I did," said Trishka. "I even heard it too."

"Oh."

"Yes, oh."

"And?"

"Just keep the braided path in mind."

"I'm not her mother, Trishka. Her mother is the woman back on Earth, worried sick about a child who'll come home changed in ways she'll never be able to understand. How does your zejhasa apply to her?"

"The braided path applies to all parents, whether they believe in it or not. That's the whole point. But you're missing mine."

"Which is?"

"That when you first came to Kena, it was alone, and when you returned home, you were lonelier still. But Safi has you. And in one way, that's a good thing. You can be there for her; you can give her someone to talk to, someone to lean on. But it also infuriates and, yes, frightens you – don't glare so, you know I'm right."

I don't know anything of the sort, Gwen wanted to say, but the lie proved far too heavy for her tongue to lift, and she set it aside with a sigh that was one part resentment, three parts relief.

"I'm terrified," she admitted. "Those early years were a nightmare. So much went wrong so badly; there was so much I couldn't say. Even with help, it still would've been difficult, and that's the point – no matter what I do, the consequences won't go away. Her scars alone will change everything. She'll need me enough that I don't have the option of walking away, but what if I get it all wrong, Trishka? What if I make things worse?" She laughed. "Godshit, listen to me. I haven't been worked up like this since the week before Louis was born."

"Guardianship comes in many forms," said Trishka, "very few of which have anything to do with blood. You've lived in Kena long enough to know that."

"I do know that. And yet."

Mercifully, Trishka fell silent. Gwen closed her eyes, letting her friend's comforting presence relax her knotted muscles. Against all expectation, she even drifted off to sleep.

A voice from the doorway – Yasha's – startled her back into wakefulness.

"What is it?" Gwen muttered, stirring against Trishka. She hadn't heard the first time, and her eyes were still bleary.

"It has begun," said Yasha again. A chill that had nothing to do with the temperature raised goosebumps on Gwen's arms. "The Council is meeting now."

Entering the amphitheatre, the rumbling murmur of the queens made Zech feel as though she were standing at the heart of a swarm of wasps. Which, in effect, she was: she could feel their eyes on her, a hundred odd women staring down at the child-queen they viewed as enemy, interloper, pretender, problem, and it was all she could do to keep from turning to Safi, who stood behind her, for support. There were several senior priestesses present too, their bloodred robes like beacons amidst the white and gold of the queens. The top tier of seats was ringed with armed, masked yshra, their presence silently menacing. Ostensibly, they were there to serve as guards, but according to Mesthani, their inclusion was a recent tradition that many (she had whispered) took amiss.

Overhead, threads of sunlight streaked the dark like corruption marbling an old wound. Once the sun was fully risen, the Council would commence. As was traditional, the oldest living queen and the seniormost priestess of Ashasa would officiate. Mesthani had pointed out each one in turn while they'd waited outside – the former was Hekve a Rin, a tiny, fierce-looking woman with bird-bright eyes and a missing right hand, and Sahma a Sani, whose iron-grey hair was long enough that, even confined in a single thick braid, it brushed the backs of her knees. Now, Hekve and Sahma stood side by side on the raised speakers' platform. As though aware of Zech's scrutiny, they chose that moment to turn her way, their expressions hard and unreadable. A sharp, cold pain stabbed through the sword wound on Zech's thigh, making her wince. Despite everything both Shavaktiin and Vekshi healers had done for her, she still walked with a slight limp, the scar itself a deep, ugly fissure in the flesh of her leg.

"Keep walking," Safi hissed, though Zech hadn't meant to stop. Cursing inwardly, she hurried over and sat down in the very front tier of seats, which Mesthani had indicated they should use, and laced her hands tightly together to keep from fidgeting. Her new kettha and dou itched, and the red paint daubed on her face, which marked her as the newest member of the Council of Queens, left her skin feeling taut and strange. Beside her, Safi was nervous but hiding it well; if Zech hadn't known what to look for (finger flicking, a slight twitch in her right knee), she'd never have seen it at all. Not for the last time, she wished she'd spoken to Trishka before the Council met, but after seeing both queens and Halaya's yshra – a quiet, calculating woman named Kari a Tavi – there hadn't been enough time. What happened now was an all-or-nothing gambit.

Silence fell as the sun rose over the amphitheatre.

"In Ashasa's name, in the first light of our Mother Sun, we meet!" called Sahma.

"The Council of Queens is open," echoed Hekve. "My sisters, you know why we gather today. The trial has been sat. A new queen sits among us – the youngest in over a century – as does her proxy, now granted the rights of a Queen's Equal. Zechalia a Kadeja. Safi a Ellen. Step forwards, that we may know you."

The words and phrasing were ritual. They ought to have been deserving of her deepest respect, yet Zech still struggled to keep from laughing. The queens already knew her, or thought they did. But she kept her composure, walking slowly back to the speakers' platform – why had they even bothered to sit down, she wondered? – and stood to one side with Safi just behind her. Mesthani had warned her about what would likely happen next. Zech braced herself accordingly.

Up close, Hekve was more intimidating than when seen from a distance. Though more wrinkled even than Yasha's, her face still held a commanding strength, and when she spoke, her deep voice didn't quaver. "Zechalia a Kadeja. Your courage in sitting the Trial of Queens is undisputed, as is your success in having done so. None may gainsay your right to sit this Council."

Her sharp gaze flicked to the audience, daring contradiction. The queens remained silent as stone.

"However. There are many – myself among them – who question your motives for doing so. The Council of Queens is a sacred institution, and the heart of Ashasa's realm. Yet though you know enough of her laws to have claimed the trial, you have never lived in Veksh. Your only allies, if allies they may be called, are the exiled Yasha a Yasara and her family, an Uyun woman, two Kenan men and an unruly flock of Shavaktiin. Heathens, every one of them; not a single soul who may rightly claim to shine in Ashasa's light. Even your proxy, Safi a Ellen, was not born a woman of Veksh, but is – you claim – a worldwalker."

A ripple of sound ran through the amphitheatre. Hekve acknowledged it with a wave of her hand, and continued, impassioned. "It is unprecedented! More than that, it is *suspect*. How are we to take you into our trust – you, a girl on whom the sun smiles and frowns – with so many questions raised against your character?"

Zech was proud of her steady voice. "Precisely because, honoured Hekve – and as you yourself have said – the sun both smiles and frowns on me. I was marked by Ashasa; marked to do her will. If our Mother Sun had abandoned me, do you think she would have sent me a sister to stand as the proxy I otherwise lacked? Would she have guided me through the trial? Would I be standing before you now? My mother, Kadeja a Ksa–" the queens hissed at the name, and not just out of loathing for Kadeja: naming the living mother of an exile was taboo, and it had taken all Halaya's Shavaktiin cunning to learn who Zech's grandmother was,

"–gave me up because she feared my markings would lose her status within the priestesshood; because she feared her peers would judge her as you judge me now. My loss put a hole in her that never healed. Because of that, her actions now threaten not only Ashasa's law, but the peace of five nations."

Outrage from the assembled queens; but not all of it was directed at Zech. Sensing chaos, Sahma raised a well-muscled arm and summoned fire. Holy flames licked along her arm, curling in her hand. With a sharp cry, she threw the fireball into the air, where it exploded in a crack of light and a shower of sparks.

"Order!" she barked. "We will have order!" Staring into the crowd, she lowered her arm and pointed at a queen whose shaved head was pink with burn scars. "The Council recognises the right of Lekma a Tari to speak."

Lekma stood, eyes narrowing as she addressed Zech. "Zechalia a Kadeja, do you really expect us to believe that your mother's heretical views can be blamed on her fear of censure? That everything she did – against Veksh, against Ashasa, against herself and yes, even against you – can be ultimately blamed on the priestesshood?"

"Not at all," said Zech. "My mother's actions are indefensible. I only mean that she feared what I might be, and that her fear ultimately drove her to do terrible things. It would be... ironic, I feel, for the Council to do likewise."

"Careful," Lekma snapped. "Your words tread perilously close to insolence. A queen you may be, but you still owe respect to your betters."

"My *betters*?" Zech said icily. She turned to Hekve. "Has there been a misunderstanding, Hekve a Rin? Am I not the equal of any on this Council?"

"You are," said the old queen slowly, staring hard at Lekma, who realised belatedly that she'd overstepped her bounds.

"Elders, honoured Hekve," Lekma gulped. "I meant that Zechalia should respect her *elders*."

"Perhaps. But you did not say so, and the slip is telling," Hekve said coldly.

"What do you want, Zechalia?" someone called out suddenly. All eyes turned to the speaker, who came to her feet just as Lekma sat. It was Ruyun, of course, and she visibly bristled with anger. "Let us have no more posturing, no dancing about the issue like farmboys at a festival – tell us why you're here."

"The Council recognises Ruyun a Ketra," said Sahma, after a moment.

"Well?" said Ruyun, when Zech hesitated. She spread her arms. "Have you no clever answer for us, girl? You pledged to sit the Trial of Queens only when your exiled companion, Yasha a Yasara, was denied an audience with us. Hekve a Rin has already asked why you joined this Council – a question you've avoided answering. Are you only here to speak on an exile's behalf, with an exile's voice, in the interest of heathen Kenans?"

Deadly silence. *This is it,* Zech thought, and gathered her courage.

"Yes," she said simply. "But ask yourself this: would I need to be here at all – would Ashasa have let me pass the trial – if she didn't hold my words, my presence, my *point*, to be necessary?"

Ruyun stiffened. "*What do you want?*"

"I want my mother removed from Kena and brought to Veksh, to be held accountable for her crimes against Ashasa."

"And why," said Ruyun, after a moment of stunned silence, "should the Council indulge you in this matter? Kadeja the *Motherless*–" she snarled the title, a deliberate rebuke of Zech's refusal to use it, "–is now the Vex'Mara of Kena, powerful and protected in her heresy, cowering in a palace where our magic cannot reach. Would you have us go to war with Kena for the sake of a single woman? What do you have to offer us as compensation for such a risk? What can you bargain, with allies such as yours?"

Zech lifted her chin. "The heresy of one woman might be a small thing, were that woman not the joint ruler of a country and her heresy not a direct threat to the sovereignty of both Veksh and Ashasa. As for what I can offer... Well. There are three things, actually."

"Really?" Ruyun laughed. "I very much doubt it."

"You don't want me here," Zech said flatly. "That much is plain. You know Yasha a Yasara as the Queen Who Walked. Remove Kadeja, and I will, firstly, offer you my absence from this Council – and from Yevekshasa itself, if need be – for five full years and a day. I will become the Queen Who Waited, and you, Ruyun a Ketra, will be free of me for all that time."

The queens began to murmur again. Ruyun, however, was unimpressed. "Is that all? You–"

"Secondly," said Zech, cutting her off, "I will enable you to reclaim Vex'Mara Kadeja directly from the palace in Karavos without the need to send Vekshi troops into Kena. And thirdly, in return for your cooperation in this, the Cuivexa of Kena, Iviyat ore Leoden ki Rixevet, soon to rule Vexa i Vexa alongside Amenet ore Amenet ki Rahei, will return control of the Bharajin Forest to Veksh. Or is that worth nothing to the Council?"

Ruyun looked gobsmacked. Queens and priestesses alike began to shout their reactions, and in the confusion before Sahma once more raised her arm and chose a speaker, Zech allowed herself a quick glance in Mesthani's direction.

"The Council recognises Ksa a Kaje!" Sahma bellowed, but at her choice of name, the noise in the amphitheatre only intensified. Zech felt her knees go weak.

"Silence! Silence!" Hekve called, thumping her staff on the platform, but Zech was close enough to hear the hoarse emotion in her voice, and to feel it echoed in the sudden, frantic twitching of her fingers.

Grandmother.

The woman who stood was a priestess, her brown hair silvered with salt-and-pepper streaks and bound in a braid. She was tall, regal-looking, and missing her left eye, the empty socket scarred and lidless. Against all protocol, she stepped out from her sixth-tier seat and began to walk down the amphitheatre's centre aisle, her stately passage silencing all those she passed.

With quiet more deafening than the aftermath of thunder, she stepped into the main circle.

Zech alighted the speakers' platform without any conscious volition, ignoring Safi's frantic tug on her hem. Her eyes were fixed on Ksa, whose single eye was fixed on her, and in full silent sight of the Council of Queens, they came within arm's reach of each other, the moment tense with the poignancy of a lineage lost and rediscovered.

Slowly, so slowly, Ksa reached out and cupped Zech's chin with her cool, thin fingers. "I thought that all of her was lost to me," she said softly. "I thought *you* were lost to me."

Zech's throat was tight with tears. "I was lost," she whispered. "But I came back."

Ksa dropped her hand to Zech's shoulder. Without turning her head, she spoke again, loudly enough that the whole amphitheatre heard her. "For too long, I've endured my grief in silence. Kadeja broke my heart and Ashasa's law both, and we let her go because it was easier to have her be someone else's problem than to claim responsibility. But no more! If she poisons Kena against us – or worse, succeeds in spreading her false truth – then sooner or later, Veksh will wear the consequences. If my granddaughter has found a way to stop that now, without the need for any military action, then I stand with her."

And then, with a quick squeeze of her hand, Ksa a Kaje

turned and walked slowly back to her seat, while the Council of Queens sat stunned and silent.

Ruyun was still on her feet, her face distorted with fury. "How is this miraculous rescue to be effected then?" she asked. "How can a child do what Ashasa's Knives cannot, and reach safely into the very heart of Karavos?"

The question hit Zech like a slap, startling her out of her reverie. Voice still thick with emotion, she forced herself to answer. "Because," she said, "Kadeja is my mother. In the dreamscape, I was able to see what ought to have been concealed from me, because I share the Vex'Mara's blood. Better still, I did so undetected. We have a Shavaktiin ally in Vex Leoden's court, and with his aid and the aid of Ashasa's Knives, my blood can be used to make a portal into the palace. My alliance with Iviyat ore Leoden ki Rixevet will see two women – two queens, in truth, with no hostility to Veksh – installed on the Kenan throne. We remove Kadeja to the care of Ashasa's Knives, and leave behind our allies in her place."

Ruyun scoffed, but her face was pinched. "And what of Leoden?"

Zech's voice was flat. "We kill him."

"That's all very well," she said, triumph creeping back into her tone, "but who among the Knives will stand with you? Why should Ashasa's finest sully themselves with your heathen scheming?"

"Because, Ruyun a Ketra," said a new voice, snapping across the amphitheatre like a whipcrack, "Kadeja the Motherless is our responsibility. Because Ashasa's Knives are not so much your creatures that we've forgotten our duty to Veksh, or to common decency. Because war with Kena – and there will be war, if things continue this way – serves none of our interests. Not yet, at any rate, and not like this."

Several queens gasped. Even Samha looked shocked. "The Council recognises Kiri a Tavi," she said faintly.

The priestess of Ashasa's Knives didn't bother to stand; she didn't need to. She was withered and sharp as fractured bone, a woman of angles and edges. Her hair was brittle and white as the sun, and her robes were the red of dried blood. She laughed at Sahma – a rattling sound, like broken stones starting an avalanche.

"Recognise me? You're half afraid to name me; it's a wonder you even remembered the words. This Council is rotten as stonefruit left in the sun, and half the reason, Ruyun a Ketra, is women like you who'd rather hoard power than use it. Ashasa's Knives were never meant to be the military arm of the Council, and yet that is what we've become. Yasha a Yasara was right, all those years ago, and before she leaves again I plan to tell her so, and a great many other things besides!" She made a sharp cutting gesture. "Enough regrets! Let the queens vote now, before more lies can pollute the verdict. You know where Ruyun a Ketra, Lekma a Tari and their cabal stand; you know that Ksa a Kaje, Kiri a Tavi and Zechalia a Kadeja stand against her. Shall we bring home Kadeja the Motherless? Hekve!"

At this last, Zech turned, only then remembering that Hekve a Rin was meant to be running proceedings, a fact that even Hekve, as startled as anyone at Kiri's entry into the debate, had momentarily forgotten. Still, as one would expect from an elder queen, she recovered quickly, banging her staff on the ground and calling for the vote.

"All those in favour of Zechalia a Kadeja's motion to recall the Vex'Mara Kadeja, stand now."

Zech held her breath. If they'd failed now – if even Kiri's support proved inadequate – there was nothing to be done. For a hideous moment, the amphitheatre remained still.

And then, one by one, the queens began to rise.

Ksa was first, then Kiri, heaving herself up with visible effort. Mesthani and Cehala followed suit, as did a woman Zech recognised as Jairin a Jaisi, whom Yasha had also named as a likely ally. But it wasn't just them: other queens, and even some of the priestesses – who technically held no voting rights, but whose actions nonetheless held the power to influence others – were rising like a spring tide, coming to their feet, and all the while Ruyun's face grew whiter and whiter, as though pure rage had drained the blood straight from her body. Within moments, the vote had a clear majority; behind her, Zech heard Safi stifle a shout of joy, and though Samha was frowning, the slightest of smiles was evident at the corner of Hekve's mouth.

"*No!*" screamed Ruyun. She leapt to her feet, heedless of the fact that the action counted as a formal vote, and before anyone could move to stop her, there was a knife in her hand. Zech stood, dumbstruck, as Ruyun threw the blade at her. Time slowed, and she knew, with absolute certainty, that the queen's aim was true – that the point would hit her square between the eyes.

A blinding flash of light; a sound like iron exploding. Zech yelped in fright, her ears ringing with the outraged shouts of her sister queens, and as the starbursts left her vision, she saw the knife lay shattered at her feet.

"Now *that*," said Kiri a Tavi, in the pause that followed, "was a very poor move indeed. Seize her!"

Ruyun screamed again, a wail of inarticulate rage, and tried to run; she made it little more than three steps before the yshra were on her, tying her hands behind her back and marching her out of the amphitheatre with all the speed and precision for which they were famed.

"The motion passes," Hekve said, silencing the queens once more, "and on that note, I think it wise to adjourn the Council. Unless, of course, there's any other business to discuss?"

If there had been, no one was fool enough to raise it after Ruyun's performance.

"Ashasa guide us," Samha intoned. "Let her wisdom

follow us from this place as surely as our Mother Sun tracks across the sky."

Hekve thumped her staff a final time. "The Council of Queens is adjourned."

Dazed, Zech swayed on her feet, unable to take her eyes from the broken remnants of Ruyun's blade. She didn't know which of the priestesses had acted to break it, or whether some older magic laid over the amphitheatre had saved her; only that she'd survived. Forcing herself to look up, she saw that Ksa was glancing her way, and felt a rush of commingled guilt and joy at the prospect of reuniting with her grandmother.

Like an encroaching shadow, Safi stepped up behind her. "The Bharajin Forest," she said quietly. "You said that Yasha had mentioned it, but you never asked Viya to cede it back to Veksh."

"I lied," said Zech, without turning. "Just my leaving wasn't enough. I had to offer something more; it was the only way to get Kiri a Tavi on side."

"You lied," Safi echoed. It wasn't quite an accusation. "Why?"

"Politics."

"Politics? That's it?"

"I wanted to win," she said, thinking it was what Safi wanted to hear, but realised as she said it that it was also true.

Safi sighed. "You'll still have to explain it to Viya, you know. She won't be pleased."

"She won't," Zech said, "but in return for stopping a war and putting her on the throne, I think she'll understand the loss."

"I thought you wanted out of all this," said Safi, frustration creeping into her tone. "I thought you wanted something else."

"So did I," said Zech, feeling her heart lift as Ksa approached. "I still do. But maybe I can want this too."

"Can you still have it, though? You said it yourself – you'll be the Queen Who Waited."

"For now," said Zech. New strength surged through her, potent as blood. "But one day, not too far from now, I'll be the Queen Who Returned."

PART 4
Home Again

22
Reality Break

"You're sure we can trust them?" Amenet murmured.

Viya squeezed her hand, watching in resentful awe as a gold-edged portal opened before them. "Not in the slightest," she said, "but what choice do we have?"

A day ago, her reply might have been more trusting, but that was before Kikra had spoken to Oyako through the dreamscape and blithely reported that Zech had laid claim to the Bharajin Forest. Viya had been furious – not at the loss of territory, which she could well afford to cede, Kena's monarchs having kept it largely to spite Veksh rather than out of any real need or practical use for it – but at the presumption of claiming the deal had already been made. She had *trusted* Zech, and to find herself so betrayed in return – there being no way for Viya to dispute the claim without appearing weak – was unbearable. *I will have vengeance for this*, she thought. *In Ke and Na's name, I promise you that, Zechalia a Kadeja.*

Such were her thoughts as the portal widened, revealing their purported allies: Zechalia, Safi and everyone else she'd travelled with from Karavos, the various Shavaktiin, and a quartet of stern-looking Vekshi women, their faces as pale as undercooked bread. Beside her, Amenet tensed, and Viya couldn't blame her. The only reason she'd agreed to Safi's plan in the dreamscape – or at least to the part of it that involved her portalling through to Veksh – was her faith in Zech to keep them safe. At the time, it had been a calculated risk, but now… now, Viya was angry.

"Matu," Amenet whispered, her grip on Viya's hand tightening.

Inwardly, Viya cursed. She'd been so consumed with the matter of Zech's betrayal that she'd forgotten all about the other bargain she'd struck with Amenet – her promise that Matuhasa idi Naha could become their Vexa'Halat. Just for a moment, she let herself forget her own schemes, and watched as Matu stepped through the portal and bowed to both of them.

"Cuivexa. My lady Amenet," he said softly.

He was, as he always managed to be regardless of the circumstances, beautiful. His unbound hair gleamed warmly in the sunlight, his face transformed by a soft, shy smile that Viya had never seen before. Beside him, Jeiden bobbed nervously in place, his courtly manners forgotten – assuming he had any to begin within, that is; Viya still wasn't clear on that point – in the face of his master's reunion.

"Rise," said Amenet, and Matu obliged. He stood like a statue, and when Amenet pulled towards him, Viya didn't protest. She suddenly felt like an interloper, or worse, a voyeur, caught up in some sacred exchange she had no business witnessing. As Amenet put a hand on Matu's arm – as the two of them leaned in close, pressing their foreheads together and murmuring words too quietly even for Viya to catch – she found herself desperately searching for something safe to focus on. She found Jeiden, who was similarly embarrassed; the two of them shared a look, and when he grinned and rolled his eyes, she found herself having to repress a very un-regal giggle. A Cuivexa she might have been, but despite the admiration she felt for Oyako, there were still some few ways in which Viya both enjoyed and acknowledged her youth.

"It seems," said Matu, when he and Amenet finally pulled apart, "that I'll be staying here for the moment."

"And me?" asked Jeiden anxiously. "Can I stay here too?"

Amenet smiled at him. "I don't see why not."

Pix, who until that moment had remained quietly in the background, strode forwards and favoured Matu with a sisterly kick to the ankle, which he endured with only minor complaint.

"Hey!"

"That's quite enough of that," said Pix. "As happy as I am for you – for both of you–" she added, nodding respectfully at Amenet, "–the portal can't wait all day. There's still Leoden to contend with, and unless you plan on dethroning him through the power of love alone, I suggest you let us get on with it."

"Far be it from me to stop you," said Matu. He and Amenet moved to one side, and after a moment, Jeiden followed them. "Be careful," he added, his tone turned suddenly serious. "Both of you."

"Of course," said Viya, and just like that her focus came flooding back.

"Together?" asked Pix.

Almost, Viya was tempted to refuse; to stand her ground and keep clear of Veksh forever. But at her back were Kisavet's hand-picked fighters: the small, elite squad whose job it would be to defend Viya from the likely predations of Leoden's guards, men and women who looked to her for strength. She'd come too far to back out now, whatever the justification.

"Together," she agreed.

The portal sent shivers through her skin, as though she'd been doused with ice water. Emerging on the other side, she found herself in a suitably alien-looking courtyard, full of white grass and whiter women. As the portal slid closed behind them, Zech opened her mouth to speak, presumably in greeting, but Viya found she had no taste for pleasantries.

"Let's get on with it, shall we?" she said, masking her hostility with false cheer. "The Vex'Mara has control of my country. I'd rather like it back."

And Leoden killed my bloodmother, she thought, but didn't say.

Though Zech looked slightly thrown by this, she recovered well – an adaptation that Viya admired even as it irked her – and turned towards one of the Vekshi women, speaking to her in their terrible, jawbreaking language. *It sounds like they're swallowing stones,* she thought acidly, but took care to keep the observation from showing on her face.

"Good to see you again, Pixeva," said Gwen, paying no attention to Zech's conversation.

"And you, Gwen," said Pix wryly. "You always find a way, don't you?"

"More or less. But I didn't do this. They did." She nodded to indicate Safi, Zech and Viya in turn – an inclusion which, of all the absurd reactions, made Viya blush. She might have interjected then, but the Vekshi woman had fallen silent.

"Not long ago," said Zech, switching back to Kenan, "Luy and I checked the palace through the dreamscape. Kadeja, we think, is in her suite; Vex Leoden is in the main audience hall."

"That could be tricky," said Viya, after a moment. "He has guards there, lots of them." Turning, she addressed her captain, a quick, clever-looking man by the name of Rahos. "While I've no doubt that you and your honoured swords would defend me fiercely against any number of assailants, I would prefer to kill as few of the palace guards as possible – they're only following orders. Leoden's arakoi, however, you may consider fair game." She paused, thinking. "The main audience hall has only two doors. Both would be guarded from the outside, but with fewer troops than are likely to be stationed inside, and both are accessible from the silver foyer."

"Should we barricade them in, Cuivexa?" Rahos asked.

"I think that would be best," said Viya. "At least initially. Then we can deal with them later at our leisure. Agreed?" She turned back to Zech, one brow raised as she waited for an answer.

"Sounds sensible to me," said Safi, when Zech hesitated.

One of the Vekshi women – a queen, Viya assumed – looked her way and started talking. When she'd finished, Zech translated.

"Mesthani a Vekte wishes to know if you require additional Vekshi forces beyond the single jahudemet-user already agreed upon. While she has no desire to see Kenan civilians harmed at Vekshi hands, she suggests it might be more expedient for everyone if the Vex'Mara Kadeja were ousted by Ashasa's Knives alone."

This time, Viya turned to Pix, gauging the courtier's reaction. Just at that moment, she didn't trust her own feelings towards Veksh to be either rational or impartial. "Pixeva?"

"It might be for the best," she said, slowly. "That way, her removal won't seem so much a coup as a consequence of her own actions. Of course, there'll be those at court who won't care to make the distinction, but on balance–"

"Of course," said Viya, gritting her teeth. She'd hoped to avoid more Vekshi involvement than was strictly necessary, but she could see the wisdom in the suggestion, and forced herself to swallow her pride. "Please tell Mesthani a Vekte that Kena is grateful for the aid of both the Council of Queens and Ashasa's Knives. As I understand it, four is a sacred number in Ashasan lore–" Kadeja had whipped her in sets of four and claimed this as the reason, "–so three additional priestesses might be best suited for Kadeja's recapture."

Turning to Mesthani, Zech relayed this message in Vekshi; a look of surprise crossed the queen's face midway through – presumably, Viya thought, at the idea that a heathen

Kenan might know anything of Ashasa – that culminated in a satisfied smile. Raising a hand, she called out something indecipherable and beckoned to several of the red-robed women who'd been lurking ominously in the background. Viya didn't need to be told that these were her priestesses, all of whom were armed with bladed staffs.

Only then, as the priestesses formed up alongside her squad of honoured swords, did Viya realise that the one voice she'd most expected to hear had been absent from the conversation: Yasha hadn't said a word. Finding the silence suspicious, she looked at the matriarch. Yasha's arms were crossed, her sharp gaze fixed on Zech. Though her face was just as inscrutable as ever, there was something both disappointed and calculating in the set of her shoulders, as though she'd been dealt a setback and was still in the process of planning her response. Viya felt an unexpected stab of solidarity; clearly, she wasn't the only one to have been wrongfooted and betrayed by Zech's actions, and for all she'd once disdained the woman, it was oddly comforting to know that Yasha, too, had been fooled.

"We should go," said Gwen, breaking the silence. "Let's get it over with."

"Agreed," said Viya, and raised a brow at Zech. "Shall we?"

Zech lifted her chin – she was always doing that, trying to compensate for her lack of age and height – and just for a moment, the fact of her youth was blinding enough that Viya felt some of her anger melt away. Whatever else she'd done and regardless of who she was, Zechalia a Kadeja, though no longer a child by any reasonable measure, was younger even than Viya. But she was also extraordinary, possessed of a wit and strength that belied her skinny frame, her mottled skin, and made her into something – someone – bigger. She was a queen of Veksh, and, for better or worse, Viya and Amenet had allied themselves with her.

Still looking at Viya, Zech said something to Mesthani, who relayed it in turn to the remaining priestesses. There was a rumbling sound, like thunder in the distance, and as one the queens and priestesses began to step back from the group, distancing themselves from what would happen next. Zech, however, moved forwards, standing alone at the centre of the courtyard. Pulling a blade from her belt, she extended her arm and cut herself in the crook of her elbow. Blood welled up, bright as hope, and dripped into the air. Instead of hitting the grass, it hung suspended in space, coagulating into an eerie bead of white light. Zech gasped, as though the breath had been pulled from her lungs, and stumbled into Safi's arms. The light intensified, ripping wider and wider – a burning, gyrating hole in the world – until the portal was wide enough, though barely, for a grown adult to walk through.

Someone screamed; it was one of the jahudemet-wielding priestesses, overwhelmed by the strain of keeping the portal open. She was doubled over, clutching the courtyard wall for support, and suddenly everyone was moving at once.

"Now! Go now!" Yasha bellowed. "They can't hold it for long!"

As if to prove her point, the edge of the portal roped out wildly, a whip of pure magic more lethal than a swordstrike. Viya grit her teeth, refusing to give in to fear. *It's just a door. It's just a door.* But her feet stayed firmly rooted to the earth, and the roar of magic swelled and grew like a thunderstorm.

"Let me go!" yelled Zech, fighting against Safi's hold of her. "It's *burning*, Safi, I need to go! Please!"

But Safi refused. "You know what Kiri said!" she shouted, straining to be heard. "You have to go last – the portal will shut as soon as you pass through it!"

"*Please!*" Zech screamed. "Safi... I can't... I can't hold it–" There were tears streaming down her cheeks, and just like that, Viya found she could move again.

"With me! With me!" she said, and in a single, stubborn rush, she darted through the portal and into Karavos.

Gwen watched, horrified, as Iviyat vanished from sight. The portal was unstable, its outer edges seething like the coils of an angry snake, and as Pix darted through, the structure wavered dangerously, threatening to take off her head. But Pix, as always, proved stubbornly hard to kill; she dodged the portal-edge with all the grace of a courtier performing a formal dance. Not to be outdone, Viya's guards dashed through in quick succession, followed in turn by the Vekshi priestesses, and all the while Zechalia was wailing in Saffron's arms, begging to be let go.

"Arsegullet!" Yasha swore. "Trishka, go! Yena stays here; I'll not risk you both."

Yena wavered, torn between fear of Yasha and fright at Zech's agony. Almost imperceptibly, her gaze drifted to Saffron. "But–"

Trishka shook her head, cutting her off. "I'll see you soon," she said, touching two fingers to Yena's cheek. "Stay."

Obedient, Yena nodded, stepping back to Yasha's side. Then it was Trishka's turn to brave the portal, and Gwen experienced a moment of heart-seizing panic, remembering all too well her friend's previous hurts. But her worry was for nothing: Trishka crossed with incongruous calm, as spry as a child.

Zech screamed again, bucking fiercely against the arms that held her.

"Gwen!" shrieked Saffron. "Hurry!"

The portal spasmed, shrinking and billowing, a pulsating hoop.

Yasha blanched. "Gwen, you go. See it through."

"The Shavaktiin will stay, too," said Halaya, pulling back to Yasha's side. "The story moves regardless."

Gwen opened her mouth to argue, but there wasn't time. Swallowing her fear, she approached the portal, all while looking straight at Saffron.

"You'll have to follow after me," she said in English, doing her best to keep her voice steady. "Just make sure she comes through last, OK? Don't let her get through the portal ahead of you."

Saffron nodded; there were tears in her eyes as Zech let out a sound that was half nails on chalkboard, half deathrattle. Sucking in breath, Gwen turned back to the portal. It was vibrating now, almost painful to look at. She watched it undulate, shrinking and growing, waiting for the right opportunity.

Three. Two. One.

She jumped.

And found herself in the middle of a melee. All around her, Iviyat's honoured swords and the Vekshi priestesses were fighting back to back against twelve, no, *thirteen* of Leoden's guards, trying desperately to keep them away from the portal and their respective charges both. The hallway – they were in a hallway, she noted dimly – rang with shouts and the hissing clatter of blade on blade. Dodging the backswing of a nearby fighter, she dashed across to the far wall, where Viya, Pix and Trishka were arguing furiously. Pix was armed, a throwing knife in each hand, and as Gwen approached Trishka darted over to one of the fallen guards and claimed his sword.

"I thought there weren't meant to be guards here!" she yelled, straining to be heard over the din. "At this rate, the whole palace will know we're here in minutes!"

"Sheer bad luck!" Pix shot back. "A damned troop was going past when the portal opened. So far, they've no reinforcements, but if we don't move fast–"

A sound like a sonic boom cut her off, followed by a pulsing wave of energy that nearly knocked Gwen over.

The palace floor shook, a sullen rumble purring through the stone, and everyone still upright either fell or staggered, swearing in their confusion.

"Zech!" Pix shouted, in the same breath that Trishka said, "It's gone!"

Even without looking, Gwen knew that something was wrong. A sick feeling clawed at the pit of her stomach.

She turned.

Saffron was on her knees, Zech cradled bonelessly in her arms. The Vekshi girl coughed wetly.

"Made it," she croaked.

She spasmed and went limp.

I was too slow.

Oh. Help. Help me.

Zech?

Saffron was frozen. The world was a roaring void, full of cold noise and hard, bright surfaces that she could neither bring into focus nor identify. Zech was ash-pale, her scars so white and ridged, they looked like bone. She was barely breathing, the deadweight of her numbing Saffron's legs. Someone – Gwen – was asking her questions, full of *how, why, what,* and she answered them in English, mechanically, her voice sounding distant and strange.

"She just kept screaming. It was hurting her, the portal. I had to keep on holding her, or she would've run through and left me on the other side. I *had* to. So I grabbed her wrists, and I turned my back – I came through backwards, I mean, so that I could pull her after me – but as soon as she stepped through it, there was this moment where we were stuck between *there* and *here*, in this floating place that wasn't a place, and there was some *force*, some energy, that was trying to pull her away from me. And I looked at her, and she said something – I couldn't hear her, even though it was silent – and then we came through…" She stopped, the knot in her throat so hard and sharp, it was like she'd swallowed a diamond. "Will she be all right? What happened?"

"I don't know," said Gwen, helplessly. "I hope so."

A thump and clatter broke through Saffron's shock. For the first time, she noticed what was going on around them – or rather, what *had* been going on. The sound she'd heard was a guard's body falling to the floor, the last survivor of a brief and bloody battle. The hallway was a killing field: not only the palace guards, but several of Viya's honoured swords lay dead on the ground, their blood pooling on the hard stone. Saffron fought the urge to vomit.

"We can't stay here," Gwen said, turning to the others. "Iviyat, which way?"

"It's–" Viya began, but Trishka cut her off.

"It's gone, Gwen," she said, urgently. "Not the portal – the palace protections. Every scrap of magic that was defending this place vanished when Safi and Zech came through."

"So?" said Pix. "What does that matter?"

"It *matters*," Trishka snapped, "because every magic-user in the palace will know something's wrong, and doubtless a good many others within a nearby radius. Thorns and godshit, *I* felt it go, and I wasn't even connected to it! You don't just rip down a working that big without anyone noticing, let alone without consequences. Who knows what else was damaged? But more importantly," and here she looked straight at Viya, "it means you have a choice. The original plan was for Kadeja to be returned to Veksh outside the palace; but if you wished it, your jahudemet-priestess, Jesha–" her gaze darted sideways, indicating the tallest of the red-robed women, who was busy wiping the blood from her staff-blade, "–could portal her straight there. But if you do that, you must admit to the Vekshi that the heart of Karavos lies bare and vulnerable. It would be expedient, to be sure, but even if Zech were in a position to speak for us, would you trust them not to invade?"

Viya opened her mouth, then closed it again. "Jesha already knows the protections are gone?"

"She'll know something's changed. It's possible she doesn't know what, but I doubt it."

As if to underscore this point, the palace rumbled around them. Trishka swore, and Viya licked her lips.

"How long will it take to restore them?"

"A day. Maybe two, depending on what else is happening."

"Enough!" hissed Pix. "Talk and move! *We can't stay here.*"

Not waiting for a reply, she marched over to the honoured swords and started issuing orders. Their leader still looked to Viya for confirmation, but at her nod, he saluted Pix and led his troop further into the palace – presumably, Saffron remembered, to take care of Vex Leoden. That left the yshra, none of whom spoke Kenan, a fact that Pix only remembered at the last minute: she strode over to Jesha, stopped, then turned on her heel and hurried back to the others.

"You," she said to Saffron, her voice wavering only slightly as her gaze skated Zech's ashen face, "you tell them to come with us. You're the most fluent in Vekshi now."

"But Zech–"

"–needs you to help us!" Her tone was harsh, but the look Pix shot her was fear and pity commingled. "Please. We need to go."

"Here," said Gwen. "I'll take her."

Zech coughed again, sputtering back into consciousness. One eye rolled open, bloodshot and pleading. The veins stood out in her throat. "Go," she rasped. "Got us here. Do the rest."

Swallowing, Saffron eased her friend into Gwen's arms, flinching at Zech's pained whimpers. The girl wasn't burned or bleeding, and yet she was somehow broken. But when Gwen went to hoist her up, Zech shook her head.

"Can walk," she said. "Can stand. Just... help." And then, with a flash of her old imperiousness, she glared at Saffron, her words an echo of Yasha's. "Don't wait. Go!"

Not daring to disobey, Saffron nodded and hurried over to the remaining priestesses, all of whom were staring at Zech.

"What ails Zechalia a Kadeja?" Jesha asked.

Saffron swallowed. "The portal drained her. She'll be fine."

Jesha touched her forehead reverently. "Ashasa's will be done."

"That's all fine and fair, but we still have to hurry. We need to find the Vex'Mara."

"Kadeja," Jesha growled, and said alone, the name was a curse. "Her heresy is a blight upon the world. We are ready."

Viya was tense as a bowstring as they hurried through the palace. Bad enough that they'd had the misfortune to run into some of Leoden's guards, but with the wards gone and the ground periodically shaking – and whether that was their fault or due to some other danger, she didn't dare speculate – they had even less time than planned to find Kadeja. And what of the soldiers she'd sent to barricade Leoden? For all she knew, they were dead already, her husband at large in the palace, and though their own brief battle hadn't drawn any extra attention thus far, that was due to geography more than luck. Kadeja had a sharp temper and keen ears, and not only the palace servants, but everyone from minor functionaries to senior courtiers had taken to avoiding her chambers, opting to walk the longer route through the upper gallery. Only the guards ever did otherwise, and then sparingly.

But if the Vex'Mara was in her chambers – and they'd gambled that she was – she'd surely heard the furore, and *that* meant she'd likely fled. Heart pounding, Viya tried to think where Kadeja would go. She hadn't passed them in this direction, which left two other options: east, towards the gardens, or north and down, into the palace heart. She didn't want to divide their meagre forces, but it might prove necessary. She suppressed a snort at the strangeness of her allies. Four fearsome yshra, a Vekshi exile, two meddling worldwalkers, a Kenan ex-courtier and whatever Zech was hardly made for a fearsome arsenal, but she'd use them as best she could.

Rounding a corner, Viya sighted the double doors of Kadeja's rooms and halted.

"There," she said.

"I recognise it," Safi said softly. "I think – that first time, in the dreamscape – I think we saw it."

Viya looked to Zech for confirmation. The Vekshi girl was mottled and pale, staggering along with one arm looped around Gwen, who was practically carrying her, and yet she kept on stubbornly moving. Viya was still angry at Zech, only now she didn't know what to do with it. She choked on her outrage like gristle, the feeling gone cold and sour with guilt; she hadn't anticipated how much the portal would take from her, how dangerous it was. "Is she right?"

"She is." Coughing, Zech disentangled herself from Gwen and straightened. "Let me go first."

Viya stared at her. "You can barely stand. She's my marriage-mate; she's my responsibility."

"She's *my* bloodmother," Zech said flatly. "Or did you forget?"

Viya flushed; she had indeed forgotten, albeit briefly. And no matter how dearly she wanted to make Kadeja pay for every stripe of skin she'd ever taken out of her back – despite how angry she was – she couldn't deny Zech her right to a confrontation.

"Go, then," she said.

Just for a moment, Zech hesitated. Her lips twitched, as though she had something else to say.

But she didn't. She walked silently on, a conquering queen, and flung open the doors.

And stopped, staring.

There stood Kadeja: barefoot, dressed simply in a Kenan gown of pale blue belted with silver. Her face was puffy and tear-streaked, her head so newly shaved that shorn wisps still clung to her neck and temple.

She was holding a knife to Luy's throat.

His veils were ripped, the tattered fabric fluttering against his chest and shoulders, leaving him barefaced and breathing hard. One arm was twisted savagely up behind his back, his free hand clutching Kadeja's corded forearm. Shivering, Zech recognised the knife as the same one which, an age ago, had severed Safi's fingers in the Square of Gods.

This is my bloodmother. This is the woman who bore me.

Beside her, Jesha stiffened in anger. "We can reach her–" she began, but Zech shook her head.

"He's an ally. I won't risk his life."

Kadeja smiled as the priestesses lowered their staffs.

"Such obedient things you are," she sneered in Kenan. "The yshra of Ashasa's Knives – let all Yevekshasa tremble before them, who obey a child!"

"Not a child," said Zech. "A queen."

Kadeja's gaze narrowed as she took in Zech's telltale scars, her mottled skin – then widened again in sudden recognition.

"The girl from the fountain," she said, startled. "You claimed my omen."

"She claimed *me*," said Safi, stepping forwards. She held up her maimed hand, displaying her missing fingers, her tattoo clearly visible. "And in return, I stood proxy for her."

A strange look crossed Kadeja's face. "A shasuyakesani child-queen, aided by a proxy?" she said. Her voice was oddly quiet, though her grip on Luy was no less fierce. "Ashasa's will is strange indeed."

Something in Zech broke, some fragile hope she hadn't known was there until suddenly, brutally, it wasn't. "You truly don't know me, do you?" She laughed, the ugliness of it twisting her heart. "I don't know why I'm surprised. You must have hardly looked at me before you passed me on."

"Who *are* you?" Kadeja hissed.

"Zechalia a Kadeja, a queen of Veksh and your unrightful child," she said, trembling. "Let him go, *mother*. Ashasa wants you home."

A piercing silence fell, broken only by the raggedness of Luy's breathing as the blade at his throat drew a few beads of blood. Kadeja stood still as a hunting cat. Slow and predatory, she flicked her gaze from Zech to Viya.

"And what say you, little marriage-mate? Does the Cuivexa of Kena stand alongside a queen of Veksh?"

Zech almost jumped when Viya replied; she'd all but forgotten the other girl was there.

"I do," said Viya, steadily. She moved up to Zech's right side, so that she and Safi were flanking her. Zech shivered, as though the air were suddenly full of lightning. "You never owned me, Kadeja. And once I rule with Amenet ore Amenet ki Rahei, you and Leoden both will be forgotten."

Another rumble from the palace; the floor beneath them shuddered like a stretching cat, and for the first time it occurred to Zech to wonder if the vibrations were caused by something other than the removal of the wards. *Not that I can do anything about it.*

"Stand down," said Safi. "There's nowhere left to run."

Emboldened by Kadeja's silence, Zech stepped forwards, and then again, until she was within arm's reach of Luy.

"It's almost funny," she said in Vekshi, forcing herself to ignore the blood trickling down Luy's throat. "I was Ashasa's gift to you: a daughter on whom the sun both smiles and frowns. Together, we might have done anything, but you refused me. You left me to be raised by women who've since become your enemies – and all these years later, Ashasa gave you a second chance. She put me right in your path, but you were so busy maiming a worldwalker–" Kadeja's eyes widened, her gaze skewing fractionally to Safi before once more fixing on Zech, "–that you didn't even recognise your own daughter. You let me go a second time, and how did Ashasa respond then? By making me a queen of Veksh; by smiling on my alliance with Kena, with the Shavaktiin, with worldwalkers – by giving me the chance to make the unity you've dreamed of real, but founded on peace, not war. And here you stand, defying her still, because you're too afraid to admit the truth."

"Truth?" Kadeja's laughter was high and wild. In Kenan, she said, "What truth is that?"

Zech took another step closer. "That I was your only true omen, and *you gave me away*. Since you came to Kena, Ashasa has never once smiled on you, and now she never will."

"*Liar!*" Kadeja screamed.

The world and its motions slowed to an infinite pause. Kadeja shoved Luy away, hard, and for a terrible instant as he fell Zech met his gaze; saw his mouth widen in shock as Kadeja kept going, her knife-arm arcing up towards Zech – the blade red-limned and silver-bright, like an evil star – and then there was pain, a screaming knot of sunbursts as the knife punched through her throat – numb, she was numb, and her mouth was full of blood, and *this wasn't supposed to happen, oh gods, no, not this, not like this* – she was on her knees, the world tilting violently – a fog came down, and through it she saw panicked faces, Safi and Viya and Luy, and she wanted to tell them it was all right, *it's really all right, because it can't end like this, I didn't survive queens and dragons to die here, I've got so much to do* – but the words wouldn't come, there was just blood bubbling from her mouth, blood and air and a sudden, seizing pain in her chest like her ribs were turning inside out–

And then there was darkness, and then there was nothing at all.

23
End Game

Zech fell, and the whole world stopped.

Or at least, it did for Saffron. She was frozen in shock, her eyes fixed on the knife in Zech's throat, on the spreading pool of redblack blood in which she lay. Around her, the yshra were moving, a flurry of blades and outraged shouts as they captured Kadeja, and even then the Vex'Mara wouldn't stop raging, struggling against her bonds as Trishka surged across, too late, and pulled Zech into her lap.

"Liars!" Kadeja screamed at them. "Liars, heretics, false daughters, false—"

The butt of Jesha's staff hit her solidly in the face; Kadeja gave an abortive cry and slumped, supported by two swearing priestesses.

"Get her out of here!" Gwen snapped, and though she spoke in Kenan, the meaning was clear to all. Kadeja was gone within moments, Jesha's portal to Yevekshasa opening and closing like an angry, golden eye. The palace shook again, harder than before, but Saffron didn't care; had barely even registered Jesha's farewell. As though it were a looped video, she kept reliving the awful, juddering moment when Zech's back had arched, eyes widening into stillness as the last pink bubble popped on her lips. She realised she was screaming, fighting to get free of the arms that wrapped her close, and when had that happened? She didn't remember dropping to her knees, didn't know who held her; only that Zech was out of reach, and shouldn't be.

"It's too late," someone whispered, "leave it, leave it alone, she's gone, she's *gone*, you can't bring her back–" but it was all just noise, and Saffron shook her head wildly, unable to comprehend it.

"Zech!" she shouted. "Zech Zech Zech *Zech*!"

Her voice cracked, deserting her with the suddenness of gunfire. She started weeping, collapsing into those cursed arms – into *Pix's* arms, she realised dimly; Pix, who'd been holding her steady.

"She's gone, Safi," Pix said again, voice rough with tears. "She's gone, but we need to go, we need you here, all right? Come back to me. Come back to me, please, we can't lose you both."

It was like a dream; like piloting a video game version of herself. Saffron heaved a breath and pulled away, her skin gone cold and alien. She tried to look at Zech again – at her body, at the thing that had been Zech, gaze skating over Trishka – but her eyes refused to focus.

Instead, she looked at Gwen. The worldwalker was hugging Luy, hard. Their eyes met over his shoulder. And in that moment, Saffron knew she was done. Kadeja was captured, the Vekshi gone, and her own utility, such as it was, had expired. Since coming to Kena, she'd learned she was a lot of things, but strong enough to keep fighting when her friend was dead wasn't one of them.

"Send me home," she croaked.

"*Now?*" said Viya, all outrage belied by her visible shellshock. "But we have to go, before the whole palace knows what's happened!"

"The whole palace *already* knows! The *whole palace*," Saffron said, voice stiff with tears, "is *shaking*, and I don't... Thorns and godshit, Viya, but if I stay, you're going to have to run from here – you're going to leave this room, you'll leave her here, and I can't–" her voice cracked, slipping into English, "–Jesus, I can't do it, OK? I can portal right the fuck out while you're all still here, but I can't, I can't walk off with you and leave her *alone*, like she's just, just – and I'm useless right now, the Vekshi are gone, you don't need me, *you never needed me*, and Trishka can do it now, right? She can send me home?"

This last to Gwen, who suddenly looked more exhausted than Saffron had ever seen her. "Ask her yourself," she said tiredly, in Kenan.

Trishka.

If Kadeja had been Zech's mother in blood, it was Trishka who'd raised her in truth. It was easy to forget that sometimes.

Not now, though. Not ever again.

Trishka knelt with Zech's head in her lap, her face so tremulously calm, she looked like a wave on the cusp of breaking. Her eyes – *soft, soft* – were fixed on Zech, her fingers carding gently through that scraggle of grey hair. Without looking up, she said, "If it's what you want, I can send you home. Perhaps it's best." Her gaze flicked to Saffron, raw and sad. "You'd be safer there."

Saffron nodded, throat tight with tears. She was shaking in every limb, and part of her whispered *coward, Zech would want you here*, but Zech was dead and she just wanted everything to stop, and if she stayed, it couldn't.

Wordlessly, she tugged away from Pix – not standing, but crawling, crossing those last few feet to her friend. Trishka, she noted distantly, was sitting in blood, which Saffron couldn't afford to touch, though at that moment she'd quite forgotten why.

The knife was still in Zech's throat.

It stuck out obscenely, like an oversized thorn, and yet the thought of removing it made Saffron want to vomit. The floor shook again, more lightly than before, as though in gentle chastisement of their delay. Her gaze flew to Trishka's: she was crying too.

"She would want you safe, I think," said Trishka softly.

Nodding, Saffron choked on a sob.

She reached out and closed Zech's eyes. *I'm sorry. I'm sorry. I'm sorry.*

"All braids tie off," Trishka murmured – a reference to the braided path, for all the good it did them now – and in her mouth, the phrase was curse and benediction both. To Gwen, Trishka added bitterly, "I assume you're staying here?"

It wasn't like Saffron had expected Gwen to come with her now, but even so she flinched at her answering nod.

"But you'll find me, though?" Saffron blurted. "Later?"

"I will," said Gwen. She stood beside Luy now, one hand gripping his shoulder, and as Saffron saw the clear resemblance between them – the shape of chin and cheek and nose – she realised, with that strange little lurch which betokened the return of dreamscape-knowledge, that Luy was Gwen's son.

"And so will I," said Luy, unexpectedly. "The ilumet links all worlds, Saffron Isla Coulter. However long it is before we meet in waking–" the palace gave another ominous rumble, and Pix swore softly under her breath, "–I'll find you in the dreamscape before then."

Saffron nodded, a hot lump in her throat. She staggered upright, stepping back from Zech and Trishka, unable to look away. A part of her screamed frantically that she ought to stay, but she was too afraid, too weak, and there were no regret-free options left.

The glow of Trishka's magic was pink and raw, an electric wound in the world. The portal spun itself open like an exploding Catherine wheel, and when Saffron looked around the room – at Gwen, Luy, Trishka, Pix and Viya – their faces were all bathed in its eerie glow. She didn't say goodbye, just squared herself and moved, because part of her didn't want to go, and part of her was numb beyond choosing, and part of her couldn't get away fast enough.

At the very last moment, she turned on the threshold, an over-the-shoulder glance as she passed between worlds. She wanted to say something, anything, but as she opened her mouth, the doors to Kadeja's room swung open, and in stormed Leoden, flanked by guards. Unable to check her momentum, Saffron kept going, an abortive cry on her lips as she stumbled home.

The last thing she saw as the portal snapped shut was the look on Leoden's face.

He was furious.

Gwen's hackles rose, fists clenching of their own accord. Their party was only five-strong now, and Leoden had brought nearly twice as many guards–

"The prisoner," said a hard-faced woman, "demanded to speak to you."

It was such an impossible statement, it took Gwen almost three full seconds to process it, during which interval the floor shook yet again, rattling the bowl in Kadeja's altar.

Prisoner. Leoden is the prisoner.

"Demanded to speak to all of us?" Viya asked, into the sudden silence. "Or to one of us in particular?"

"To the worldwalker, my Iviyat," Leoden said, smiling thinly. "Your presence here is irrelevant."

Viya stiffened, and before anyone could stop her, she closed the gap between them and slapped her husband hard across the face. He clearly hadn't expected it; he growled, arm moving to return the blow, but the nearest guard hooked his elbow and stopped him.

"You killed my bloodmother," Viya said, cold and uncowed. "You killed Hawy. She was loyal to you, and the minute she realised what you were, you had her cut down like a stand of rotten reeds. So don't you call me *my Iviyat*. I was never yours. But I *am* the Cuivexa of Kena."

With that, Viya turned away from him. Leoden snorted, but without heat, and all at once he was as discomposed as Gwen had ever seen him. It wasn't just that his hair was wild, or that his clothes were dishevelled, though such details were incongruous enough. It was the fact that his mask was gone: that perfect, polite control that had so comprehensively hidden his true nature from her and Pix. Gwen didn't know if its absence was deliberate or calculated, but either way it was something she hadn't expected to see. It threw her off balance – as, indeed, did Leoden's apparent capitulation – and *that* made her wary.

"What do you want?" she asked.

Tugging his arm free of the guard who held him, Leoden took a step forward. His eyes darted around the room, widening slightly as he noticed Zech's body. In a quieter tone than Gwen had expected, he asked, "Where is my Vex'Mara?"

"Gone," said Gwen, as much to try and gauge his reaction as for the satisfaction of provoking it. Leoden clenched his jaw but didn't speak, and after a moment, she added, "Taken to stand trial in Veksh, for crimes against Ashasa."

Leoden's fingers clenched and straightened. "I hear that Amenet still lives."

"She does, no thanks to you."

"A pity," he said, then added, in a faster, sharper tone, "I won't ask how you brought down the palace wards. What you need to know, Gwen Vere, is that they aren't the only thing your recklessness has broken. Or has it completely escaped your notice that the palace is coming apart?"

"Coming apart?" Pix gave an incredulous snort. "Don't exaggerate, Leoden."

"I'm *not*," he shot back, and as if to emphasise the point, the building rumbled again, longer and louder than before. The hairs on the back of Gwen's neck stood up. She'd thought the shaking was a consequence of the broken wards, but if it was something else–

"Explain," she said. "Fast."

Leoden shot her a withering look. "Very well. The wards were tied to a magical artefact in one of the lower chambers – it's believed to be a weapon of sorts, though Sahu's Kin are still arguing about its exact function. Breaking the wards has evidently caused it to activate, and as it is currently housed in a room to which only I have access... Well." He smiled thinly. "You can see the problem."

Pix scoffed. "How convenient."

"Funny," said Leoden. "I was thinking just the opposite. Whatever you might think of me, Pixeva ore Pixeva, I have no desire to see this palace brought to the ground. If that were the case, I'd have fled it already rather than let myself be captured by these–" he waved an unimpressed hand at the guards, "–*nobodies*. Or did you honestly think I'd come to you easily, willingly, without a good reason?"

"I think you always have reasons," Pix said, "but seldom the ones you profess."

"Easy enough to find the truth," said Louis suddenly. "Find one of Nihun's Kin, someone gifted with the ahunemet, and have them see if he's lying."

It was the first time he'd spoken since Saffron's departure, and Leoden did a double-take at the sound of his voice. Gwen briefly wondered why, until she recalled that Leoden had never seen her son's bare face before, only his veils. (And soon enough, she'd sit down with Louis and ask what the hell he'd been playing at, pretending to give Leoden aid. She'd nearly had a heart attack to see him in Kadeja's arms; it had taken all her willpower not to cry out and betray exactly how valuable a hostage he made. But then, she supposed, it explained a great deal about his involvement in things.)

"Well," said Leoden lightly, for all that the betrayal had clearly startled him. "And why I am even surprised? Never trust a Shavaktiin, the saying goes. I ought to have heeded it."

"And a great many other adages besides," said Louis. "Such as, for instance, not blaming the murder of visiting dignitaries on unlikely culprits. The Uyun ambassador's entourage were very interested to learn of your penchant for poisoning, and consequently rather keen to take revenge. Right about now, I expect their guards are helping to incapacitate yours – the ones who aren't already drunk, drugged or turned against you, that is."

Gwen's heart filled with pride. *That's my boy!*

Leoden cupped his hands and proffered them in a gesture of mock-respect. "Well played!" he said, a hint of snarl in the words. "And here I'd been wondering how this rabble of dunces had managed such an effective strike. I hadn't considered that they had *inside help*." He tilted his head, mouth twisting cruelly. "Have you betrayed your vows for this, Shavaktiin? You told me you were outcast within your order – what does the Great Story say about this?"

Louis didn't flinch, and Gwen was proud of him for that, but she had a mother's knowledge of his tells, and the subtle tremor in his throat said that Leoden had struck a nerve.

"The story doesn't care for you, Leoden," Louis said. "That's all you need to know."

"Hurry." The single word dropped into the conversation like a stone. All eyes turned to Trishka, who was breathing heavily, still cradling Zech's body. "I can feel it in my magic. There's something in the palace, something... wrong." She lifted her chin and looked at Gwen. "Whatever it is, you need to shut it down. Fast."

"There!" said Leoden, exasperated. "*Now* do you believe me?"

"I believe *her*," said Gwen. Another tremor shook the palace, violent enough to unsettle her footing, but any triumph in Leoden's gaze was quickly supplanted by a flash of real fear, and if Trishka's words alone hadn't been enough to spur her to action, the combination certainly would've done it.

"Take us there," said Gwen, to the guards, as well as Leoden. "Now."

The lead guard flicked her gaze to Viya. "Highness?"

To her credit, Viya didn't hesitate. "As she said."

"I'll stay," said Trishka, quiet and sudden. "I'll only slow you down."

"Trishka—"

"I don't want to leave her alone."

Grief rose in Gwen's throat. Her boy was alive, and Trishka's girl was dead. If she let herself think about that now, she'd never leave the room. She looked at her friend, and in a moment of wordless communication, she felt their doubled grief like a hammerblow.

"We'll leave you guarded then," Viya said, breaking the silence. She didn't wait for Gwen to agree, but singled out two of Leoden's entourage, murmuring instructions for them to keep watch on the chambers.

"Are you quite done?" Leoden said, irritation bleeding into his tone.

"Mind your tongue!" snapped Pix.

"We'll come back for you," Gwen said to Trishka – needlessly, because of course they would, and yet she couldn't bring herself to omit saying it. "Both of you."

"We'll be here," Trishka said, and then they were leaving Kadeja's chambers, necessity reasserting itself in the face of private grief. The remaining guards formed up around Leoden, Gwen half-leading beside him. As much to anchor herself as for any more pragmatic reason, she watched the Vex side-on, wondering what he was planning. *Fool me once,* she thought bitterly. She didn't believe for a second that his intentions were purely altruistic, and on top of everything else, she was suspicious of how calmly he'd taken the news of Kadeja's disappearance and Amenet's return.

"You don't trust me," Leoden said, quietly enough that Gwen alone could hear him.

"Is there any particular reason why I should?"

"The word of your friend isn't grounds enough?"

"Honesty about one thing doesn't preclude lying about another."

"True," said Leoden, as though the admission cost him nothing. And perhaps it didn't; the man was layers on layers, and just because he was unsettled enough to let Gwen see this much of him didn't mean he had nothing still hidden.

It was a terrifying thought, and one that preoccupied her all the way through the palace. They moved quickly, quietly, the shaking ground more evident the deeper they went in the structure. More than once, they heard the sound of distant fighting echo through the halls, but they neither slowed nor stopped, and once they reached the lower levels, it ceased altogether.

Gwen had never been this deep in the palace before, and as they alighted yet another twisting stair, she began to feel uneasy. Grief and tension hung over her like a pall. As Leoden led them down narrower and narrower paths, even the guards grew anxious.

"This isn't a trap," said Leoden, suddenly enough to startle even Gwen. His voice rang in the tight space, his eyes made tawny by the spelled glow of firelights studding the walls. "I have no allies waiting."

Pix muttered something that might have been a Vekshi curse, and before Gwen could think to reply, a violent tremor startled her words away. Viya yelped, and two guards swore as they almost lost their footing, drawn swords clattering uselessly against hard stone. The very air twisted and growled, as though they were approaching the lair of some massive, snorting beast, and when Leoden said, "We're close," Gwen shuddered.

The next turn brought them to a single door set in a

dead end, dark and imposing. There was no keyhole and no handle: instead, Leoden pressed his palm flat to the surface and spoke a word Gwen didn't know. A blue ripple flashed through the metal surface, and with a sudden hiss, the door swung open, revealing a tight, dark aperture. Leoden made to enter first, but before he could cross the threshold, the guard captain held out an arm and stopped him.

"Highness," she said, head tilted back towards Viya, "I would suggest my honoured swords go first."

Leoden rolled his eyes, but Viya said, "Of course."

Gwen's neck prickled with foreboding, but as she had no reason to gainsay the suggestion, she kept quiet as a trio of soldiers took the lead, the captain just behind. She came next with Leoden, followed by Pix and Viya and, behind them, the remaining guards. The space beyond the door was so narrow that it was impossible to walk more than two abreast – and even then, it was a tight fit – and so dark that, for a moment, Gwen couldn't see anything. The passage zigged and zagged, sharp turns in the black.

"This was originally a treasure vault built by Vexa Yavin," Leoden murmured. "Or so the archivists tell me. It was sealed up and forgotten since her death." With a smile in his voice that Gwen more felt than saw, he added, "I put it to use once more."

And then the passage turned again, opening into searing brightness, and in the seconds where Gwen was blinded, several things happened at once.

The whole room shook with a furious roar, a blast of unseen power knocking them back like the leading edge of a hurricane.

The guards screamed, a visceral sound the roaring couldn't quite disguise, chilling Gwen's blood as she scrabbled for purchase.

Leoden darted forwards, evading Gwen's grasp. She swore, stumbling as her vision came back, blinking away the after-images of whatever the flash had been–

–in time to see Leoden leap through the heart of an anchored portal, its blue-black edges snapping out like angry, electric tentacles to crash at the tethering stone. Its wild, lashing magic had brought down two of the guards; the portal itself was the source of both sound and shaking. Leoden vanished from sight, and though Gwen lunged after him, the portal collapsed on itself before she could follow him, as though it had only awaited him all along.

The sudden silence was deafening, like having her ears boxed. One of the injured guards whimpered, and in a daze that was half due to Leoden's absence, half in shock at what had happened, Gwen kept moving forwards.

And found herself at a railing above the edge of a deep, round pit.

She looked down.

There were people chained down there. No, not just people – at least one prisoner clearly wasn't human at all, but something else entirely, covered all over in pale green scales with slitted eyes and too-long legs that bent the wrong way at the knee. An iron shackle circled its overlong neck, but the blood dripping from an open gash on its temple was red as her own. But the others – the others were people, but...

"Worldwalkers," Gwen whispered, appalled. "They're all worldwalkers." She gripped the rail, hard, because just at that moment, it was the only thing keeping her upright. She stared down at a frightened girl with purple hair – whether dyed or naturally so, Gwen couldn't tell – whose ragged clothes showed the bruising on her skin. Shivering in her bonds, the girl refused to meet Gwen's gaze, chains clanking as she wrapped her arms around herself. Gwen counted twenty-odd captives – five of them inhuman to her eyes – before she looked away, all of them battered and bruised in ways that spoke to endurance of torture.

"Gwen, what–? Oh. Oh, *gods*." Pix halted beside her,

staring into the pit with a look on her face of abject horror. "Are they...?"

"Yes."

"And he just...?"

"Fled," said Gwen, leadenly. "No telling where. For all we know, he's left the world completely." She bowed her head, fighting a fruitless impulse to smash her fist on the railing. "Thorns and godshit, I *knew* he was planning something!"

Pix's voice was high and tight. "But what did he *want* with them all?"

Gwen stared into that awful pit – at Leoden's bloody, battered captives – and felt her throat close over. On top of everything else, it was a complication they didn't need, the weight of her failures pressing her down like a second, malevolent gravity.

"I don't know," she said, helplessly. "Gods help me, but I've no idea at all."

24
Only Fire Brings Release

Saffron hit the ground hard, gasping as the breath was knocked from her lungs. Her thoughts were a thunder of pain and regret and grief all mingled – *no, no, no, I should've stayed, I should've* helped – but the portal was gone, the night air sharp with its absence, and nothing she could say or do would bring it back again.

Too stunned to move, she lay like a ragdoll, staring blankly ahead as her tears soaked into the dirt. It was night, but even in the darkness, she already knew that the grass beneath her was green Earth-grass, that the sky above was a black, Earth-sky populated with familiar constellations like the Southern Cross and the Big Dipper and illuminated by just the one, nameless moon, and that when the sun rose, it would be her familiar, yellow Sol, and not the whiter, too-big sun of Kena and Veksh.

She was home again, and Zech was dead.

Home, where mum and dad and Ruby would be waiting for her, out of their minds with fear and grief that she'd been abducted, abused and dumped in a ditch, or fretting that they'd somehow driven her away. Home, where her friends would still be going to Lawson High, like Saffron would be expected to do. Home, where no one would expect her to battle dragons or soldiers or involve herself in politics, and where every scrap of power she'd amassed in

Veksh and Kena from doing just that would be denied her. Home, where nobody knew to mourn the loss of a calico girl who'd made herself a queen.

Home, which would never be home again.

She closed her eyes, breathing in the familiar scent of dry earth and crushed gumleaves. Careful of her newly-bruised arms, she rolled onto her side and sat up, running her hands across her stubbled head. She was still dressed in her Vekshi clothes, a fresh kettha and dou she'd donned only that morning, made of plain white fabric which could, she supposed, pass for a homemade karate gi, if anyone asked. Which they would, invariably; of course they would.

And Saffron would have to lie.

"It's too soon," she said, hopelessly. But she was alone. There was no one left to answer her, and this had been her choice.

Hadn't it?

A bubble of thwarted rage swelled and popped in her chest. All her life, she'd grown up with stories about Alice and Dorothy and the Pevensie children, happy little worldwalkers whose travels were cathartic, preordained, complete; and even though she'd known, from her very first day in Kena, that none of those rules applied to her, she'd still assumed she'd be there for the finale. Would she still have regretted leaving, if not for that glimpse of Leoden coming through the doors? Saffron didn't know, which was somehow worse than if she had. She needed to know, with an ache that threatened to split her in half, that her friends were all right; that Leoden hadn't simply walked in and killed them all; that someone would go back for Zech's body and see her buried, not left to rot in Kadeja's chambers.

But now she was home, and it wasn't about what Saffron needed, not anymore. She was here for her family, she realised, not for herself; here to end their misery at the expense of prolonging her own. She bowed her head to the ground and imagined Gwen was there beside her, offering that particular blend of practical truth and comfort which had, in another lifetime, won Saffron's trust. She heard her thoughts in Gwen's voice, warm and rueful, a mix of things she'd said before, or that she imagined her saying.

Life isn't a story, no matter what the Shavaktiin say. There's no neat beginnings, no happy endings, because everything always keeps on going. That's just life, girl. That's all it is: life, and lives, and all of them lived overlapping. The beauty and curse of mortality is we only live once, in just one place and just one time; our lives don't stop because important things are happening to other people, but their lives don't stop for us, either. Right here and now, you're home, and you have to deal with it. You have to keep going. OK?

"OK," Saffron whispered.

Somehow, impossibly, she stood, and only then did she recognise the Lawson High grounds. She was in the same scrap of bushland where Trishka's first portal had opened.

You don't know that weeks have really passed, she suddenly thought. *Maybe Gwen was wrong, and it's still the same night.*

It was a beautiful lie, and one that Saffron dearly wished were true. But she couldn't make herself believe it, not after everything that had happened.

All at once, the night felt oppressive. The distant sound of cars driving past, once so familiar as to be wholly unremarkable, almost a non-noise, now sounded alien and out of place. Zech's death had torn a hole in her heart, and coming home had only made it worse.

She remembered her lie, the one she'd helped to build with Gwen. She'd have to change parts of her story to fit what had happened, but it still ought to work. She turned, trying to remember the quickest route to the police station, and forced herself to start walking.

Let's get this over with.

The station was further away than she remembered, but after so much time spent tramping around Kena, the extra distance didn't faze her. From outside, the electric lights looked cold and forbidding, but Saffron had faced a dragon beneath the bones of Yevekshasa, and with that thought, she made herself walk in. There was no need to hide her weariness, her fear. They would, after all, be expected.

The place was empty except for the duty sergeant, and as soon as he spotted Saffron, his eyes went wide.

"Fuckin' Christ," he said, and then remembered himself. "Shit. Sorry. Shit!" He came to his feet in a scramble, yelling out into the office, "Someone get DS Roycroft up here, now! His missing person just walked in!"

Sure enough, when Saffron glanced at a nearby corkboard, there she was: or rather, there she had been. The girl in the photo was long-haired and smiling, dressed in the white collared blouse of the Lawson High uniform – her most recent school photo, taken at the end of last year. There was no corresponding photo of Gwen.

And then the police were there: not only the startled desk sergeant, but two female officers and, eventually, the fabled DS Roycroft, who'd been running the (unsurprisingly fruitless) investigation into her disappearance. Though he did his best to hide it, he was clearly startled when Saffron assured him, as firmly as she could, that the strange woman seen loitering on school grounds the day of her disappearance hadn't been her abductor, but a fellow captive. They'd tried to escape together, but had gotten separated in the attempt.

"I don't know where she is now," she said, and then added, with a raw, unfaked honesty, "I don't even know if she's still alive."

Roycroft's suspicions abated at that, though his curiosity remained strong. Not strong enough, however, to completely forget police protocol. Rather than ask more questions, he handed Saffron over to the care of the female officers, who in turn took her to have a medical examination. Though she'd expected as much – even without her obvious scarring and missing fingers, the fresh bruises Zech had left on her arms were enough to raise questions – her heart still lurched with anxiety.

She felt awful for thinking it, but the kindness of the attending officers and the female medical examiner only made things worse. They treated her as if she was made of eggshells, voices soft, avoiding eye contact. It was like they were simultaneously afraid of her and for her, but couldn't bring themselves to say as much out loud. The worst part was when they asked if she wanted a rape kit; she shook her head, not wanting to be swabbed anywhere, let alone her genitals, and pointedly refused to let them take any other samples, either. Gently, they tried to explain that it could help catch her assailant, especially if she still had their skin under her nails, but she refused; the only DNA they'd find that way was Zech's, and possibly a residual trace of Viya or Pix, and while none of those samples would trigger anything on the police database, her recent proximity to multiple strange women would contradict her made-up story.

Finally, after what felt like an age, it was over. Her clothes were taken away as evidence (she gave in on that count only because it made her look cooperative, and because in the event that strange DNA was found on them, it would be easier to argue that she didn't know how it had got there). In place of the kettha, dou and Vekshi underwraps, she was given a plain pair of cotton undies, a bra that was a size too big, a pair of white slippers and a pale blue slip that was functionally identical to a hospital gown, with the notable exception of not gaping open at the back.

Only then was she led, quiet and somehow feeling more naked than before, to a dull-looking interview room. The floor was hard blue carpet, the chairs beige, the single table made of cheap brown chipboard. DS Roycroft was already there. As she was a minor, he said, protocol dictated that they wait to conduct her interview until either her parents or a representative from DOCS, the Department of Child Services, arrived to supervise. Then he paused, licking his lips, and said, "But if you want to get it over with, we can just go right ahead."

There were two female officers who could do the job, he added, but if Saffron didn't object, it would just be himself and PC Thomas. The latter was a round-faced white girl with a galaxy of freckles and red hair pulled back in a messy braid; under different circumstances, Saffron suspected she might have liked her. Almost, she was tempted to make Roycroft give up his spot out of spite, but she was exhausted by then, and didn't feel it was worth the effort, and she sure as hell didn't want to have to wait any longer to tell her lie, let alone give it in front of some DOCS worker or – worse still – her parents.

"OK," she said, hoarsely.

Gwen Vere – that's the other woman who vanished, the one from the school – she stopped me from being harassed by another student, Jared Blake, at lunch. She said she was thinking of applying for a job at the school and wanted to get a look at the campus. I wanted to thank her for helping me, so after school, I went looking to see if she was still there. She'd been for a walk along the cross country track, and I found her by the chemistry labs. We started talking. She was nice. We got quite close to the footpath that runs by the road, but we had our backs to it, and suddenly this guy jumped out and attacked me. He was white, somewhere in his forties; I don't remember much more than that. I think he'd seen my uniform and thought I was alone, but when he realised Ms Vere – Gwen – was there too, he went for her as well. She tried to fight him off, but he was pretty strong, and then I got knocked out. I think I was put in a car boot after that, but the next thing I remember, both of us were tied up in a basement, and the guy was wrapping a blindfold around my head.

He kept talking to people who weren't there – not invisible

*friends, but characters in a story. He wanted to play the hero,
someone he'd created, and that's why he'd taken us, to be his props.
So everything he did to me – he was really only interested in me;
he cut Gwen a bit once, when she started yelling at him to stop – it
was all just part of the story. It doesn't really make sense, I know,
but even though he was the one doing everything, he only thought
of himself as the hero, and I was the damsel he needed to save. But
before he could save me, somebody had to hurt me, so there was
something he could rescue me from.*

*No, I don't think he was mentally ill. He was lucid. Functional.
He'd just made up a story, and he wanted me to be part of it. No, I
didn't see him take any drugs or pills. Not even once.*

*He cut my fingers off on the first night, after he shaved my head.
He was acting like someone else then, but once it was done – once
he'd "saved" me from the villain – he sat me down and stitched
it all back up again. No, I don't know if he'd had any medical
training; I didn't even see what he did. He kept the blindfold on me
the whole time. But I guess I've healed pretty well. He did disinfect
my wounds, I know that much – it hurt so much when he did
my fingers, I screamed and passed out. But at least he cleaned it
up. The other scars... that was weirder. It was hard to tell, but I
think part of the story was about rescuing me from dragons, like a
captured princess in a fairy tale. So he had this sort of glove, like a
claw-glove – I mean, I guess that's what it was. It's not like he had
an actual dragon or anything, and the blindfold wasn't so dark
that I couldn't see the outline of things. It was blurry, but it just
looked like he had something weird strapped to his hand. And he
used it on me.*

He used it on me a lot.

*But it was like with the fingers, too. As soon as it was over, he
cleaned everything up. He wanted to save me, he said. It wasn't
really him, it was the villain, it was the dragons, it was always
something else. The tattoo was part of it, too; he did that when
I was knocked out, like everything else. I don't quite remember
when. And Gwen – well, I guess she was his audience. He only ever*

spoke to her if she interrupted. But most of the time, he just left us alone in the basement. He'd untie us, but keep the blindfolds on, and tell us he had a knife or a gun, and to stay where we were until he was out of the room. Then, once the door closed, we could take the blindfolds off, and he'd have left us food. There was a sink and a toilet in the corner, and a couple of old mattresses, but that was it. And when he wanted to come back in again, he'd stand outside the door and say the same thing: that he was armed, that we had to put on the blindfolds and face the wall, or else he'd kill us. Then he'd come back in, tie us up, and the story would keep going.

I didn't really know how long we were down there. It was hard to keep track of the days. There was one window, but we'd sleep during the day, and he didn't always come down to us at the same time.

No, he never touched me. Not that way. Not even once. He didn't touch Gwen like that, either. Why would I lie about something like that?

How did I escape? It was Gwen. The last time he came down, she just charged him – charged right at him and told me to run. He tried to grab me as I went past, to keep me back, but Gwen just leapt on him and kept yelling at me to go, go, go. Then I heard a weird noise – not a gunshot, I don't know what it was, but it sounded like Gwen was hurt. Then something hit me over the head – I still had my blindfold on – and he shoved a cloth to my mouth and told me the story was over. It must've been chloroform, or something like that, but whatever Gwen did, it must've rattled him enough to let us go. Or to let me go, anyway; when I woke up again, I was back at the school, and there was no sign of her. The only thing was, he'd dressed me in new clothes while I was unconscious.

I'm certain he didn't touch me then – why would he, if he hadn't before? Please, just stop asking about it. Please. Please.

I don't know if he was planning to kill himself. I don't know what he meant when he said the story had ended. All I know is, he let me go, and I really hope he let Gwen go, too.

I'm so tired. I don't want to say anymore. I just want to see

*Gwen again. I just want to go home. Have you called my family
yet?*

   I think I'm going to be sick.

Saffron barely made it to the toilet in time. She threw up
violently, knees cracking into the tiles, the taste of bile hot
in her mouth as she emptied her stomach, retching until her
sides ached. The story, and Roycroft's reaction to it, had left
her feeling physically ill – not just the utter, barefaced falsity
of it, but the awful way Roycroft's expression had lit up when
she'd talked about the characters, the story. She'd practically
heard him thinking, *it all makes sense if the guy was crazy!* And
she'd tried, she'd tried to steer him away from that conclusion
– no drugs, no pills – but it hadn't worked; she hadn't said the
right thing. But what else could she have done? Unless she'd
invented a story that involved some form of sexual assault or
sadomasochistic abuse – or worse, both – there was no other
way to plausibly explain what had happened to her. In order
to have been missing for weeks, she and Gwen had to have
been forcibly abducted; if they'd been forcibly abducted, then
the perpetrator had to have a criminal motive; given Saffron's
injuries, she had to have met with violence, which statistically
made the abductor male; and if his primary motivation
hadn't been either sexual or sadistic, then there was only one
conclusion the police could draw, no matter what Saffron tried
to say to the contrary.

   Which didn't make it any less of a terrible thing to have done.
If you were mentally ill, she knew, you were far more likely to
be a victim of violence than a perpetrator; she'd learned that
from her friend Lyssi, whose cousin was schizophrenic. But
the truth didn't matter, not when people wanted so badly to
believe the opposite; not when "crazy" made for a better and
more convincing explanation than dragons and queens and
holes in the world. Maybe, if she were braver, she could have

feigned amnesia, pretended to remember nothing, but Gwen had advised her against it, back in Yevekshasa: it would only invite extra psychological scrutiny of Saffron herself, the kind of analysis she couldn't bluff her way through, and in the meantime, her family would still be imagining the very worst sort of ordeal. But oh, god – if they ever found someone who fit her description, some innocent person, and arrested him for hurting her – if she couldn't get him set free, and he went to jail because she'd lied–

She threw up again, and again, and again, until there was nothing left.

Wiping her chin on a square of toilet paper, she flushed the vomit away, eased herself to her feet, and went to rinse her mouth at the sink. The story she'd told was pragmatic, and ostensibly victimless. The police would never find anyone to pin the abduction on, she told herself firmly, because the abduction had never taken place. But even so, it left her feeling criminal in a way she hadn't anticipated, as rotten as last month's apples. *False accusation. Liar. Liar. Liar.*

It was worse when her family arrived.

She'd only had a bare minute to prepare herself before her mother and father burst in through the door, a trembling Ruby in tow. Ever since she'd first set foot in the station, Saffron had been bracing herself to see them again. She'd promised herself she'd be calm and collected, that the most important thing was to let them all see that she was safe and well, but a single glance at how harrowed they were – at the weight both parents had clearly lost; at the dark circles under her mother's eyes, the new grey hair on her father's head; at the wobbling of Ruby's lip, and the way she fixated on Saffron's shaved head – something inside her snapped. A slow wail inched its way up her throat, as treacherous as an escaping tapeworm, and as her parents opened their arms, she flung herself at them, sobbing as though her ribs were snapped and her heart torn out.

They all collapsed together, three sets of knees hitting the station floor with a thump like a truck tipping over, and then Ruby was hugging her too, her sister's thinner arms sneaking in through the gaps to clutch at her shoulders. All of them were crying, hard and desperate, while the police officers looked on quietly with the satisfaction of a job well done. It was only when they'd regained their feet, still huddled and wiping the tears from their eyes, that Saffron realised Roycroft was gone, slipping out unnoticed like a cat through a half-open door. She pointed this out, and her parents were dismayed; they wanted to thank him, they needed to thank him for finding their baby, even though he'd done nothing of the sort, but of course they could talk to him later, in daylight.

And then there were forms to sign – the DOCS worker showed up just as they were leaving, and despite her clear shock and irritation at having missed Saffron's interview, she was either unwilling or unable to make them stay longer – and then it was time to go home.

The ensuing car ride was surreal. Without the police audience, all of them fell eerily silent, unable to ask the questions to which they so clearly wanted answers, like: *where did you go?* and *are you OK?* and *did he touch you?* The silence was so loud, it might as well have been screaming.

Then Ruby said, in her smallest voice, "I didn't think you were coming back."

A lump rose in Saffron's throat. "Ru–"

"So I stole your red skirt. The one with the pandas on it. I'm sorry. I'll give it back." She paused. "But if you don't want it anymore, then maybe I could keep it?"

"You are *not*," said Saffron, with as much sternness as she could muster, "keeping my panda skirt. But maybe – just maybe – you could borrow it."

Ruby's face lit up, and everyone started laughing – not just nervous laughter, but the deep-seated, joyful relief that can only be found on the other side of tears.

I'm whole, Saffron told herself, remembering Trishka's long ago words, *and so is my family.* And just for a moment, she let herself believe it, right down to her marrow.

But of course, it wasn't that simple, braided path or not. Nothing ever was.

GLOSSARY

KENAN

Ahunemet – Mind-magic, telepathy. This gift is associated with Nihun, god of water.

Arakoi – Soldiers whose service is sworn directly to the reigning Vex or Vexa.

Cahlu – A green-blue smoking leaf.

Cui'Halat – One of the three chosen marriage-mates of a Cuivex or Cuivexa. The Cui'Halat is traditionally chosen for their embodiment of the quality of liveliness or vitality (halat), which is usually taken to mean physical beauty.

Cui'Mara – One of the three chosen marriage-mates of a Cuivex or Cuivexa. The Cui'Mara is traditionally chosen for their embodiment of the quality of kinship or blood (mara), which is usually taken to mean that they represent a favourable political alliance. For this reason, 'mara partners within the royal mahu'kedet are generally held to be more powerful than their other marriage-mates, and can sometimes hold more political sway than a Cuivex or Cuivexa.

Cui'Sehet – One of the three chosen marriage-mates of a Cuivex or Cuivexa. The Cui'Sehet is traditionally chosen for their embodiment of the quality of soul or wisdom (sehet), which is usually taken to mean intelligence, whether scholastic, magical or strategic.

Cuivex – The primary male consort of a Vex or Vexa.

Cuivexa – The primary female consort of a Vex or Vexa.

Halat – Vitality, especially in the context of physical wellbeing and liveliness. Halat is one of the three primary attributes by which partners in the royal mahu'kedet are chosen.

Hime – Goddess of the sky, and one of the six gods of the Second Tier of the Celestial Hierarchy. Her counterpart is Lomo, her sacred colour is lilac, and her marital attribute is vitality (halat).

Ilumet – Dream-magic, oneiromancy. This gift is associated with Hime, the sky goddess.

Jahudemet – Portal-magic, worldwalking. This gift is associated with Ke, the star goddess.

Kara – The Heavenly Child of Ke and Na, and one of the three gods of the First Tier of the Celestial Hierarchy. Kara is a trickster who governs the moons, considered to be both sexless and all sexes. They have no consort, and their sacred colour is silver.

Karavos – The capital city of Kena.

Kashakumet – Telekinesis. This gift is associated with Na, the god of heaven.

Ke – Goddess of the stars, and one of the three gods of the First Tier of the Celestial Hierarchy. Her primary consort is Na, her secondary consorts are Yemaya, Sahu and Lomo, and her sacred colour is white.

Kedebmet – Plant-magic, terramancy. This gift is associated with Lomo, god of earth.

Kemeta – Magic-users who aren't bound in service to a temple.

Lomo – God of earth, and one of the six gods of the Second Tier of the Celestial Hierarchy. His counterpart is Hime, his sacred colour is green, and his marital attribute is halat (vitality).

Mahu'kedet – Literally, the "many-bond", which is the Kenan equivalent of marriage. Though the royal mahu'kedet has a specific number of partners, all representing ideal virtues and with specific relationships to one another, for most Kenans, the mahu'kedet is a polyamorous union of two or more individuals whose relationships are not always romantic or sexual, but which is constructed around a culturally specific idea of family.

Mara – Blood, particularly as relates to kinship and family. Mara is one of the three primary attributes by which partners in the royal mahu'kedet are chosen.

Maramet – Blood-magic, commonly used to determine paternity. This gift is associated with Kara, the Heavenly Child.

Na – God of heaven, and one of the three gods of the First Tier of the Celestial Hierarchy. His primary consort is Ke, his secondary consorts are Nihun, Teket and Hime, and his sacred colour is black.

Nihun – God of water, and one of the six gods of the Second Tier of the Celestial Hierarchy. His counterpart is Yemaya, his sacred colour is blue, and his marital attribute is mara (blood).

Roa – A long-haired, bipedal beast of burden. Friendly, herbivorous and native to Kena.

Sahu – Goddess of wisdom, and one of the six gods of the Second Tier of the Celestial Hierarchy. Her counterpart is Teket, her sacred colour is yellow, and her marital attribute is sehet (soul).

Sehet – Soul, intelligence, strength of character. Sehet is one of the three primary attributes by which partners in the royal mahu'kedet are chosen.

Sevikmet – Healing magic. This gift is associated with Teket, god of passion.

Shavaktiin – An order of mystics and storytellers who believe that history is shaped by human stories. They go robed and veiled when acting as agents of the Great Story, to signify their participation as interchangeable servants rather than as distinct individuals, but are known to unveil when taking up discrete roles. (Though how they distinguish between these instances is seldom clear to outsiders; and, indeed, is a continuing subject of debate among the Shavaktiin themselves.)

Taal – A traditional Kenan garment made of a single piece of cloth wrapped and knotted around the body in specific ways.

Teket – God of passion, and one of the six gods of the Second Tier of the Celestial Hierarchy. His counterpart is Sahu, his sacred colour is purple, and his marital attribute is sehet (soul).

Vekenai-asahuda – Worldwalker: literally "all-worlds pilgrim". The word *asahuda* derives from Sahu, the goddess of wisdom, indicating one who travels divine paths in search of knowledge.

Vex – A male monarch.

Vex'Halat – One of the three chosen marriage-mates of a reigning Vex. The Vex'Halat is traditionally chosen for their embodiment of the quality of liveliness or vitality (halat), which is usually taken to mean physical beauty.

Vex'Mara – One of the three chosen marriage-mates of a reigning Vex. The Vex'Mara is traditionally chosen for their embodiment of the quality of kinship or blood (mara), which is usually taken to mean that they represent a favourable political alliance. For this reason, 'mara partners within the royal mahu'kedet are generally held to be more powerful than their other marriage-mates, and can sometimes hold more political sway than a Cuivex or Cuivexa.

Vex'Sehet – One of the three chosen marriage-mates of a reigning Vex. The Vex'Sehet is traditionally chosen for their embodiment of the quality of soul or wisdom (sehet), which is usually taken to mean intelligence, whether scholastic, magical or strategic.

Vexa – A female monarch.

Vexa'Halat – One of the three chosen marriage-mates of a

reigning Vexa. The Vexa'Halat is traditionally chosen for their embodiment of the quality of liveliness or vitality (halat), which is usually taken to mean physical beauty.

Vexa'Mara – One of the three chosen marriage-mates of a reigning Vexa. The Vexa'Mara is traditionally chosen for their embodiment of the quality of kinship or blood (mara), which is usually taken to mean that they represent a favourable political alliance. For this reason, 'mara partners within the royal mahu'kedet are generally held to be more powerful than their other marriage-mates, and can sometimes hold more political sway than a Cuivex or Cuivexa.

Vexa'Sehet – One of the three chosen marriage-mates of a reigning Vexa. The Vexa'Sehet is traditionally chosen for their embodiment of the quality of soul or wisdom (sehet), which is usually taken to mean intelligence, whether scholastic, magical or strategic.

Yaramet – Fire-magic. This gift is associated with Yemaya, the fire goddess.

Yemaya – Goddess of fire, and one of the six gods of the Second Tier of the Celestial Hierarchy. Her counterpart is Nihun, her sacred colour is red, and her marital attribute is mara (blood).

Zuymet – Word-magic, language transference. This gift is associated with Sahu, goddess of wisdom.

VEKSHI

Ashasa – The Mother Sun, the fire goddess of Veksh.

Dou – A square-necked tunic.

Etmahsi – Motherless; a title of disowned women.

Kettha – Loose trousers that wrap at the waist.

Mege – A hot, sweet tea brewed from caffeinated leaves and soup stock, popular with traders.

Nekveksanayun – Literally, "neither the right thing nor its opposite". The state of being in between, uncertain or undecided.

Shariktai – Literally "sun-tongue", the Vekshi word for language-magic, equivalent to zuymet in Kenan.

Shasuyakesani – Literally, "one on whom the sun both smiles and frowns", indicating a person born with mottled skin. Shasuyakesani individuals are varyingly considered to be either very good or very bad luck, and as such are treated with a mixture of caution, contempt and respect.

Yevekshasa – The ancient capital of Veksh. The city is built on a mesa.

Yshra – Literally, "blade" or "blades" (the singular and the plural take the same form). The word refers both to an actual knife, and to warrior-priestesses in Ashasa's service.

Zejhasa – Literally, "the braided path". An important Vekshi concept describing the complicated relationship between mothers and their children, especially as those children age and begin their own lives as adults.